WHEN THE GREY BEETLES TOOK OVER BAGHDAD

WHEN THE GREY BEETLES TOOK OVER BAGHDAD

BY MONA YAHIA

GEORGE BRAZILLER, INC. / NEW YORK

First published in the United States of America in 2007 by George Braziller, Inc.

Originally published in Great Britain by Peter Halban Publishers in 2000.

© 2000 by Mona Yahia

For information, please address the publisher:
George Braziller, Inc.
171 Madison Avenue
New York, NY 10016

Library of Congress Cataloging-in-Publication Data:
Yahia, Mona, 1954—When the grey beetles took over Baghdad / Mona Yahia.
        p.   cm.
ISBN-13: 978-0-8076-1582-9
ISBN-10: 0-8076-1582-X
1. Teenage girls—Fiction. 2. Jews—Iraq—Baghdad—Fiction. 3. Baghdad
(Iraq)—Fiction. 4. Domestic fiction. 5. Jewish fiction. I. Title
PR9510.9.Y34W48 2007
823'.914—dc22
2006023779

Designed by Rita Lascaro
Printed in Singapore

To my parents,
Who gave me languages instead of roots

ACKNOWLEDGEMENTS

The Mahdawi trials (chapter 4) were depicted from descriptions in *Republican Iraq* by Majid Khadduri (London, 1969), while *All Waiting to be Hanged* by Max Sawdayee (Tel Aviv, 1974) provided me with background information for the years 1967–9.

This book took its years to be written, time during which I needed and was lucky to get sincere support from many friends. Among them, I owe a special debt to Michael Lawton and to Kirsten Lehmann, whose help cannot be overstated. Michael spent countless hours in reading my drafts and correcting language mistakes without sparing me any editorial criticism, while Kirsten discussed every stage of the book with me, following my line of thought with remarkable understanding. My thanks also go to Uta Ruge for the pictorial material, and to Joyce Sopher for her unbeatable memory. Finally, I would like to thank Martine Halban, who received a manuscript and returned a book.

CONTENTS

PART I

THE SEVENTH DAY

—When the astrologers announced to Abu Ja'afar al-Mansour, in the year 145 of the *hijrah*, that the stars were favourable to his scheme, the Abbasid Caliph laid the foundation stone for the planned city on the right bank of the Tigris. The construction work lasted three years, from A.D. 762 util 765. Can anyone tell me how it was built? Correct. It was laid out in concentric rings of walls, and pierced by four gates at the cardinal points. A few years later, al-Mansour struck coins, on which he engraved *Dar al-Salam*, the City of Peace, referring to his capital. However, Suq Baghdad, the name of an old Persian village that once stood on the site on the bank of the Tigris, somehow stuck. Now I really need not tell you about Baghdad's grandeur during the Abbasid times, how it flourished and prospered in the golden prime of al-Mansour's son, Haroun al-Rashid, the most celebrated of all caliphs, who erected palaces and mosques, archives, libraries and academies. Don't forget that it was in these very academies that the works of Aristotle and Socrates were translated into Arabic and eventually saved from destruction.

Our teacher singles out some sleepy student to elaborate on the past glory of the Islamic empire. My watch tells me: still fifteen minutes to go. You may stuff dozens of decades into one hour, yet you will never make time move faster. My neighbour taps me on the shoulder, passes the note sent forward. I unfold the scrap of paper:

Is Haqqi ill, or has he deserted us for a better world?

Though the message is unsigned, I immediately recognise Selma's large handwriting. I turn round, meet her inquiring look with disapproval. What if the note had fallen into the hands of our teacher? She should have encoded her question or simply left the sentence unfinished. I would have understood instantly; the issue is haunting me no less than her. Unable to reproach her from my desk, I just shrug my shoulders. No, I have heard nothing. Selma thrusts out four fingers, points them to the vacant desk, two rows to my right. I know, I know. It is the fourth day that Haqqi has not shown up.

—It's also in Baghdad that Madrasat al-Mustansiryah, the first Islamic university, was founded. It is one of the oldest in the world. Yet don't think that Baghdad was only a scientific centre, for it was no less a centre of trade and material affluence. Orchards and pleasure grounds sprang up, bazaars expanded and attracted merchants from all quarters of the Arab empire—an empire which extended from the Indus to the Mediterranean and from the Caspian Sea to the Arabian Gulf.

I prop up my head on my fist, longing for Hulagu to storm our history with his hordes of savages, raze the great metropolis, pillage its palaces, set its gardens on fire. The massacre was so ruthless, they say, that within hours the streets were stained red, that within days they stank from the unburied remains of the thousands of slaughtered inhabitants. The Tigris was darker than the night itself, due to the ink dissolving from the mountains of manuscripts which the Mongols had flung into the water.

The headmaster strides into the room, without knocking, without taking the trouble to shut the door either. We promptly stand up—our standard show of obedience which

our teachers mistake for respect. The history teacher interrupts his description of the trade routes used during the
Rashid's reign to greet the headmaster. Then he retreats to
the window, handing the stage over to him.

—Class, your afternoon physics lesson has been called off!

The familiar sound of the bell ringing rounds off his declaration, relieving us this time of two lessons simultaneously.
One unrestrained shriek of joy is heard from the rear of the
room. Someone's giggle escapes in response. Two manifesta-
tions too many, oblivious of the headmaster's presence. The
latter tucks his hands into his pockets, holds his head high,
staring us down until silence has prevailed.

—You may go home now, he says harshly, pointing to the
open door.

Yet his stiff, unrelenting posture detains us. Pupils from
other years saunter past, make funny grimaces or derisive
remarks. We wait for the verdict, our eyes frozen on him, the
way they freeze when posing for some group portrait, only
with smiles missing.

—What's wrong? Didn't you hear the bell? I thought you
were eager to go home?

His grin sharpens his pointed features, narrows his small
grey eyes into two vicious flickers. Our headmaster is the
only person I know who looks more menacing when he
smiles. The history teacher titters, out of sheer politeness.
We persist in our safe meekness until the headmaster has
lost interest in his taunts. The two men nod to each other.
Forty students rise to their feet. Teacher follows headmaster.
Their wooden footfalls trample on our silence with undis-
guised disdain.

Out of sight, the two no longer exist.

The students roar their hoorahs, their dirty words,
repeatedly slam the lids of their desks, pack their satchels,
run off, return to linger for last-minute jokes. While the
room gradually empties, one small group hangs round the

entrance, whispering. Whispers signify tidings, inside stories, sometimes rumours which the school janitor or the non-Jewish teachers should not overhear. I join the group of whisperers. Selma follows me. They validate our suspicions. In spite of the heavy snowfall in the north, the Shamashes reached Iran safely yesterday. Furthermore, it seems that Sami, our physics teacher, has taken off, too, presumably with Haqqi's family.

For weeks now, no family has fled. The detention of eighty Jews during their failed escape in October has discouraged the rest of us from similar undertakings. Moreover, the icy winter in the northern Kurdish provinces seems to have paralysed illegal traffic with Iran. Seeing no prospects of departure in the near future, my parents purchased two low-priced rugs for the living room, finally had the leaking tap in the toilet repaired, the fractured window pane in the kitchen replaced. Their deeds spoke for them. They had resigned themselves to the idea of spending one more winter here.

When we have parted from the last students, Selma goes over to Haqqi's desk.

—Let's see what treasures he's left behind.

She sits down, lifts up the lid.

I return to my own desk, wanting no share in her intrusion.

The news has thrown me into turmoil. Not only has it filled me with envy, it has stirred new, vain hopes—instead of letting them hibernate in peace.

—An Arabic dictionary! That's a book lucky Haqqi can now do without.

I make my selection of the schoolbooks to take home.

—No love letters, no banknotes, what a pity! she muses, as she rifles through the pages.

I pack my satchel, fetch my overcoat from the rack.

—The concise edition of al-Munjid, fine lexicon, don't you think?

Selma tears out the fly leaf on which Haqqi's name is written, scribbles her own on the inside of the dictionary.

—I think your looting should wait! Perhaps they haven't really fled. So many rumours go round nowadays.

—Last time I waited, Tina pinched David's fountain pen, Selma justifies herself while swinging the wooden lid.

David was the first to make it, early this term. Laila followed two weeks later. Now it is Haqqi's turn. David, Laila, Haqqi, our lucky prizewinners. But these are prizes they did not win for their remarkable school performances, or their good looks, or good manners, or even the good names of their families.

—The hinge doesn't creak, I'm moving! There's no better place than the one behind this mass of Farouq. Besides, it's two benches closer to you.

—Don't take me so much for granted!

Taking no notice of my remark or my wish to go home, Selma draws out her jackknife from her satchel.

—Do me a favour, will you, fetch me the bin. I've got to clear up the mess and scrape off all the stale chewing gum.

I do her the favour. She removes the pistachio shells, too, the pencil shavings, the pencil stubs, wipes the dust with tissue paper. Only then does she put in her own textbooks, grouping them in two stacks, placing Haqqi's lexicon with the hardbacks. Finally satisfied with the order, Selma runs her palm over the wooden lid to detect splinters. Finding none, she picks up her jackknife once more, this time to score her name on the sloping lid.

I watch the scene in wonder. Despite our transitory existence, Selma's intimacy with her environment has remained intact. Neither detachment nor listlessness nor withdrawal, none of the symptoms which have taken possession of me over the last three years, show in her.

I draw near, look over her shoulder. Without dots or ornamental vowel points, Selma's freshly scratched name sweeps the desk from right to left, dissecting other smaller, darker words—traces of previous occupants. To the right of Selma's name, two unnamed intertwining hearts hover frivolously near the edge. Inside the dry inkwell, Einstein's equation of relativity is noted in tiny, greyed letters. To the left of the inkwell, under the hollow for the pens, one deeply engraved sentence reads: "On the Seventh Day, God created Memory."

Pulling the splinters out of the scored wood, Selma shifts the jackknife to her left hand, scratches her name for the second time, from left to right, in majuscule Roman letters. The two Selmas, identical in sound, foreign in looks, face each other without touching.

I grumble, slipping into my overcoat:

—Have you finished marking off your territory? One would think you're staying here forever.

Selma examines her watch, refolds the jackknife.

—No, no. I'll carve it properly some other time. What are your plans for the afternoon?

—Go home, what else? Walk home, I suppose.

—I can give you a lift. Home, or elsewhere! she says, unable to hide her pride.

Taking my speechlessness for misunderstanding, Selma hastens to explain:

—The Beetle's at the gate!

Selma's father taught her to drive last summer. Since then, even though underage, she has often taken her mother's Volkswagen to go shopping in the neighbourhood. I have frequently joined her on these short trips, enjoying them no end. Still, the thought of two sixteen-year-old girls racing through the turbulent streets in the heart of town gives me the shudders.

Some other unruly voice is talking me into it.

We pick up our satchels, walk out of the room, down the stairs.

—You must have gone out of your mind! You're under-age, remember?

—Come on, Lina, we're only in Alwiyah, ten minutes away from home, perhaps fifteen. What catastrophe is likely to happen?

—What if some traffic warden stops you? What if he wants to see your licence?

—Why, for God's sake, should a warden want to stop us? I'm a born driver, you say it yourself, and I'm easily taken for eighteen. Anyway, just to calm you down, Mama's licence is in the car. I'll show you the picture. It dates back thirty years: she looks exactly like me.

Selma's face registers neither irony nor mockery. She is earnestly trying to reassure me with her recklessness. We pass through the school gate. The sight of the green Volkswagen, parked impeccably on the opposite side of the street, destroys my illusion that she was only joking. I stand still, unable to make up my mind. Selma explodes:

—Listen, it's a beautiful day, we have a car at our disposal, and we aren't expected home before three o'clock. What more could we ask? It's a unique opportunity, and who knows if it will ever repeat itself? Now take it or leave it. Either join me or be a good girl and walk straight home. I'm off.

—Not without me! Wait, Selma, wait for me.

My spirits suddenly lifted, I skip to the Sudanese vendor, puchase his two last paper horns of hot peanuts. Selma starts the engine, shows off her smooth U-turn in one try. I jump into the passenger seat while the vehicle is on the move. Having verified that my door is properly shut, Selma puts her foot down.

She works her way through sideroads to Shari'el-Nidhal, Struggle Street, then, without hesitation, signals right, the direction opposite to home. I swallow hard, trying not to imagine my parents' opinion of this exploit. In no time we make it to the Square of the Unknown Soldier, where I expect

to find hordes of traffic wardens waiting for us. The only uni-
formed man in view is the soldier on patrol, guarding the
memorial fire under the parabolic monument. The muezzin
in the nearby Martyrs' Mosque has just laid down his microphone, gathered the faithful under the gilded dome to launch
with them into the third prayer of the day.

—Let's go to Abu-Nuwas, I love the river bank, even in
winter, Selma says.

She flicks the indicator once more, drives straight to the
riverside.

In spite of the sun, winter melancholy has taken over the
promenade. The occasional strollers, the empty outdoor
restaurants, have reduced this lively, well-frequented place to
desolation. Selma seeks out one of the parking spaces overlooking the river. I roll down my window, inhale the thick
tang of silt. Though its intensity varies from one season to
the next, the odour stirs the same vague longings inside me.
Some elderly man wearing the traditional *zboun* is strolling,
rapt in the river. Selma switches the engine off, stretches herself out:

—Thank you so much for this golden afternoon, Sami,
wherever you are!

The sun strokes her profile through the window, emphasises her freckles, sets her ginger locks on fire. She undoes
her paper horn, tosses the first peanuts into her mouth.
Slowly, our moods quiet down, tune themselves to the steady
flow of water. We watch the river in silence, munching, waiting for some swollen dead dog or donkey to drift past—the
way our mothers must have entertained themselves in their
youth, prior to the invention of television. My gaze hops to
the opposite shore, to Karkh, wanders over lofty palms, dense
orange trees, old oriental houses with latticework terraces
jutting out over the water. The hue of their tall walls is so
similar to that of the muddy river that they seem to have
emerged from it.

—I wonder why they mark rivers ultramarine on maps. I've never seen the Tigris ultramarine, I remark.

—I'll miss the Tigris, Selma responds, suddenly soft, sentimental.

—The world's full of great rivers: the Thames, the Seine, the Rhine, the Danube, the Mississippi. Just pick . . .

—I'd still choose the Tigris. I'm sure no other water tastes as sweet, she replies decidedly, then shuts her eyes, warding off further discussion.

I pursue Haqqi in my mind, keen to savour the sweet safety of his exile. With what ecstasy must he have greeted his rebirth on the other side of the frontier! Dressed in some smart track suit, he is jogging in the snow, jumping up slopes, skipping over electric fences, escaping the shots of the frontier guards, running faster than their dogs. He shows no signs of fatigue, hunger, fear, or loneliness. I stay with him to witness the great moment, when he will set foot in the free world. Yet Haqqi seems permanently on the move, in no hurry to reach his destination. His spearmint gum never leaving his mouth, he sends kisses towards the horizon, to the giant lady, the Statue of Liberty, no less.

—You're living out of a suitcase, aren't you? Selma shoots, her eyes suddenly wide open, roving over my face.

—No more than the rest of us, I falter, sitting up, uncomfortable with her prying.

—Except for Baba! He's in no hurry to emigrate. He says we'll never be able to live like this again: the spacious house, the garden, the two cars, the maid, and so much leisure. I bet he'll be the last Jew in Baghdad. I wonder what he'll do with all his leisure then. Chat with the pressure cooker? Play hide-and-seek with the cars?

—Your father's one of the very few Jews whose life has remained unchanged since the war. He was neither sacked from work, nor thrown into prison, nor roughed up, nor put under surveillance . . .

Selma is not listening. She has shifted her focus to two men, dressed in modern suits, sauntering towards us, ogling us without inhibition. Security men? The older one grins, tilts his head, then turns up his palm, posing the tedious question. No, just men. I sigh in relief. Selma sighs in exasperation. We turn to each other once more, demonstrating our lack of interest in them. They stop several steps from us. I spot them motioning to us to join them in the sun.

—Let's lock the doors, Selma suggests.

I roll up my window, too. She puts her seat upright, then picks up her thread:

—It's unsafe to flee nowadays, people say. They say the border is heavily guarded.

—So what? People also say it's no problem to grease the palms of the guards. What wouldn't people say just to have something to say? The trouble is that nobody knows what the government is up to. One day they seem on the watch, the next day they pretend not to see. The only fact we have is that Haqqi has just made it.

—A fact? How interesting! An hour ago you were arguing it was just a rumour.

It is useless to discuss the subject with her. Selma is resolved to flick off every grain of hope I keep groping for, the way she used to knock out my marbles in kindergarten.

—Will you confide in me before you run off? she ventures, emptying the paper horn into her mouth.

—Out of the question! The issue's too delicate.

—You love making it sound dangerous, far more dangerous than it really is.

—That's not fair! Eighty Jews were picked up in October on their way to the frontier. Have you forgotten? They're still detained. Nobody knows what lies in store for them.

Selma puts her finger on her lips, signalling me to drop my voice.

—Are you insinuating that you'll just disappear one day, like Haqqi, Sami, Laila, David, and the rest?

—*Inshallah*! If we're lucky enough, yes! That's exactly how it will look, I snap, eager to end our exchange.

—This winter? Selma persists.

—No idea. My parents don't discuss these matters openly with us. Yet even if I knew, I wouldn't tell you. You're satisfied now?

—Not before you answer this one, please! Have you actually set your mind on this winter?

—For God's sake, stop this interrogation. I'm not even supposed to go into this with you. Father said nobody's to know of . . .

—But I'm not just anybody, and you're appallingly straight and square! You're all set to go. You gave yourself away, just an hour ago. Yes, back in the classroom, don't feign innocence. You told me not to take you for granted, right? What did you . . .

Selma starts up, looks into the rearview mirror.

—Dogs, go screw your sisters instead . . .

—What!

—The two men, they're still here, she whispers.

I spin round, spot them through the oval rear window, standing on either side of our vehicle, slightly leaning on it. Devouring me with their eyes, their hands keep shaking inside their trouser pockets, the way one grates nutmeg. Our Volkswagen is slightly rocking, or so I imagine. Drops of sweat have gathered over Selma's upper lip. She grabs the keys, tries to insert her door key into the ignition.

—Selma, that's obnoxious! What's the matter with them?

She finally turns the ignition key. The Volkswagen jolts into reverse. It fails to startle them or even spoil their pleasure. Quite the opposite: without moving, they guffaw, make wild weird gesticulations. Selma shifts into gear, speeding off. I watch them dwindle in my rearview mirror, two neat young men rearranging their trousers, readjusting their neckties, merrily waving us farewell.

—What were they doing, Selma?

—Masturbating. Green must have turned them on. The bastards! You noticed how amused they were at our panic? I swear it aroused them all the more.

—Perverts!

She raises her eyebrows,

—Since when does a good girl like you use such language? Don't tell me you've been looking through *Playboy*!

I do not reply, used to her jibes. The incident, too mundane to waste words on, yet too upsetting to forget, hangs over us. Selma is *enf nar, enf duchan*-one nostril smoky, one on fire. She hoots, swears, makes rude gestures, overtakes every vehicle in front of her. My heart is fluttering. I would give the world to reach home safely. Having failed to overtake us from the left, two young motorcyclists try now to sneak past on the right. The speedometer rises. If only Selma would keep her eyes on the road instead of picking on the taxi next to her. Yet I dare not speak up, for the last thing she is willing to hear right now is my opinion of her driving. The trees on the pavement fly past. We pass one square, two, three. Drawing near Hindiyah, our neighbourhood, Selma relaxes, reduces speed.

—I'm sorry it turned out this way. Next time we won't stop. But then we'll go really far, as far as the Luna Park.

—The Luna Park? You know your way that far? Selma, you're unique, the finest driver in town!

—I'd love to drive across the border! With such heavy snowfall, they must be using chains nowadays. That would be quite a ride. Can't you recommend me to your father?

—Selma, your father will never let you go on your own.

—Who'd ask him!

—You're underage, my father won't . . .

—I know, I know, I was just kidding. Taxi's at your door, young lady. *Yallah*, don't dream of perverts tonight, and remember, your Mama needn't hear of our afternoon adventure. See you tomorrow, provided you haven't fled by then.

—Tomorrow's Saturday.

—Till Sunday then, so long.

Selma drives off. I ring the doorbell. Mother's head peeps through the window. She opens the door, lets me in. The smell of roasting meat is wafting from the kitchen. Quite unusual for this hour of the day, for mother normally prepares our food in the morning. I drop my satchel, remove my overcoat. Mother has not greeted me yet. She is looking into my face, reading the full report of our last two hours. Hoping to take her mind off me, I quickly spill out the latest news.

—Mama, the Shamashes made it this week! Sami Nathan, too. You know who that is, our new physics teacher.

—Good for them! she replies, sincere yet unconcerned, lacking the inquisitiveness such news usually elicits.

Her look still fixed on me, she goes on,

—I've got news myself: Curry is due for his chicken!

Mother is referring to the tiger-striped red tomcat who frequents our garden. I once vowed that, prior to our departure, we would recompense our pet with this sumptuous farewell dinner.

—What! Heavens, when? Why didn't you tell me earlier?

—Tonight! We were notified this very morning, shortly after you'd left for school!

FIRST WORDS

Bellou and I are riding in an *arabana*, a carriage pulled by two black horses. She is seated beside the driver. I jump from her lap, push the two of them apart, and sit between them. The driver has a thick moustache and hairy arms. He clicks his tongue and whips the horses to a gallop. For my sake, he says. We race with the cars along Sa'adoun Street and proceed as far as Bab-el-Sherji. Then we sprint around Tahrir Square and generate wind in the windless summer afternoon. The speed and the sound of the galloping hooves dazzle me. I stand up, clap my hands, and cry with joy. Bellou snatches me back to her lap. She says something to the driver, and we slow down.

Bellou speaks Syriac with the driver. They are both Assyrians, descendants of the great ancient people, he says.

—And you? What are you?

Iraqi, I tell him.

—What else?

Iraqi, I repeat.

The two glance at each other. He winks at her.

—So am I, he says. But I'm also an Assyrian, and also a Christian. Now, what else are you beside being an Iraqi?

I could tear him to pieces. I can tell exactly what he is after, what he already knows, and what, for some reason, I am resolved not to reveal.

—I'm an Iraqi, and nothing else, I insist.

Bellou pats him on the arm.

—Leave the girl in peace, she says in Arabic.

The carriage driver obeys. I stay in Bellou's lap till the end of the ride.

The horses halt before our gate. Bellou carries me down with one arm. I kiss her and call her my little mother. She guffaws. She is taller and stouter than mother. Her squinting eyes roll in all directions.

Bellou is our live-in maid and my nanny. She washes me daily, cleans the house, and helps mother in the kitchen. She makes delicious salt cucumber and the largest *Mossul kubbas*—patties stuffed with spiced meat—in the neighbourhood. As round and large as the plates themselves, yet they never break while cooking. Bellou's daisy-patterned dress smells invariably of sweat and flour. Around her neck is a multi-coloured thread, darkened by wearing, from which hangs a wolf fang between her breasts. It is to ward off the evil eye, she says.

I am walking barefoot in the courtyard in midsummer. Soon the ground scorches my soles. I yell, run back to the shade. Bellou pours a bucket of water on my feet. Steam rises from the concrete ground.

—We are living one floor above hell, she says.

She is the strongest person in the house. When father does not manage it, he passes her the cleaver, and Bellou effortlessly chops the rock-hard hunk of Kurdish cheese. She alone can haul the Persian carpets to the courtyard in the spring, where they are to be beaten and rolled and dragged into the storeroom until next winter. Our carpets not only have beautiful designs but also exquisite names: Kashan, Kerman, Isfahan, Shiraz, Tabriz, Bidjar, Hamadan. Although she has never been to any of these towns, Bellou can give a vivid description of each one of them.

—Hamadan is the abode of mighty Hercules, a town of

harsh winters, haunted by hurricanes and hawks and *houris* who play the harp day and night. In Bidjar, waterfalls pour endlessly into bottomless jars. The sky of Tabriz, as of all Azerbaijan, the Land of Fire, is red, while the eyes and hair of its people are in permanent flames. In Shiraz reside Shirin and Scheherazade and other beautiful princesses. Isfahan is a city of saffron domes and sapphire minarets, where the sun bathes its rays in golden dust before it rises, and preserves them in silver powder after it sets.

—And Kashan? And Kerman? I demand, tagging along after her.

Bellou is squatting in the kitchen, sewing okra into a chain. I sit crosslegged beside her, scribbling in my drawing pad. She is telling mother about the Assyrian massacre in the north, one summer, a long time ago. Mother is rinsing rice. Bellou relates that Arab, Kurdish, and Yesidi tribes looted their village. Then the soldiers turned up and machine-gunned everyone. Even the women and the children. Even the dogs. Mother shuts her eyes while she is frying the rice. I sketch a woman with two black plaits. Bellou was a child then. She and her sister did not budge from their hideout for two days. Until no footfalls were heard. Until the last moans ceased. Until the village was finally silenced, except for their breathing under six mattresses and for the rustling of fig trees blown by the breeze. Mother pours boiling water into the rice pot. Bellou and her sister set off on foot. My Bellou is running, holding a small girl by the hand. Her two plaits are flying with the wind. The rice is cooking on a low fire. The okra chain is sewn. Bellou rises to her feet and hangs the chain in the courtyard.

In winter the dried okra will be cooked with lamb and fresh tomato.

Father is carrying me in his arms, showing me a nest where a brick is missing in the wall. A pair of swallows. *Sind-ou-*

hind, we call them in Arabic, which means, those from the lands of Sind and India. They will spend the winter in our garden, and then fly away in the spring. *Sind-ou-hind* keep coming and going, like guests in this world.

When I am a good girl, the swallows leave me a small present, in summer or in winter. Father and I are scouring the room for it. We look above the cupboard, under the bed, on top of the lampshade. It is father who finally finds a Kit Kat on the window sill.

—It's not the bird, it's Baba who's putting on a show for you, brother reveals.

He also claims that it is only a fabrication of father's that apples and bananas get offended when I refuse to eat them, that Wonderland is a fairy tale, just like Sindbad, Aladdin, and Ali Baba.

One afternoon, father returns home driving a car. Dusk falls and he is still struggling to park it, in spite of Zeki's directives and hand signals. Zeki is father's colleague and friend. He speaks the Muslim dialect.

The first car father ever saw was in 1914. He was a boy of six then. The Ottoman commander-in-chief sat in the back and let himself be driven through Urfa. The townspeople crowded to watch. Some trailed behind the mysterious vehicle that was propelled without an animal.

One of father's first memories is the Armenian holocaust. He witnessed Ottoman soldiers forcing families out of the Armenian Quarter in Urfa, and marching them out of town. Bathtubs stood before some houses, filled with water to quench the thirst of the condemned on their way to be shot.

Everyone seems to drag one massacre or another along in their memory.

By the time the Allies occupied the whole of the Ottoman Empire in the First World War, father's family had moved to Mossul. The British barracks stood next to their house.

Father could not take his eyes off the soldiers, playing football in their leisure time. He had never seen a ball before.

Four years later, he received a scholarship and set off for Oxford. He travelled by train from Mossul to Basra, and from Basra sailed on a cargo ship to Portsmouth. They docked for ten days in India. In Karachi, he tasted bananas for the first time.

Every year, father's old friends send him English stamps and a Christmas cake from Oxford. Recently, I received a present myself, a record, "Alice in Wonderland." Father and I listened to it together while he told me everything about Alice falling into a hole and growing very tall and very short and talking with white rabbits and quarrelling with flowers. But father does not have the patience to listen to the record as many times as I do, and he is astonished, weeks later, to find out that I have learned the songs by heart. I want us to go to Wonderland.

—Not before you have learned English properly, he says, because in Wonderland, everybody speaks English, even mice and oysters.

—Let her learn Arabic first, mother says.

I have no idea why she is saying this, because I have been speaking Arabic ever since I can remember. In fact, I understand most of what is being said, except, of course, for the stuff that does not make sense. Like shutting one's face or losing it. When I ask where can a face be lost, and if somebody else can find it and keep it, brother says my stupidity knows no limits. Mother has already explained that these expressions are metaphors and, therefore, are not to be taken literally. But I do not know what metaphors are. So I still do not understand what it means when mother asks Bellou not to pull a long face, while Bellou's face is as round as ever. Blood, too, has other qualities apart from being red. People can be hot- or cold-blooded, while Baghdadi blood can boil any moment. A tongue can be as long as a slipper, a mouth as foul as the sewers, and not because it has not been properly rinsed. Milk teeth do not smell like ice cream, and wisdom teeth do not speak. Bellou keeps telling me that my eyes are hungry, bigger than my stomach, which is rubbish, only go and explain such things to Bellou who cannot read or write anyway. The evil eye is, thank God, real, not a metaphor. That is why it is easier for me to envisage it.

May your hands live, father wishes mother, when he likes her cooking.

I refuse to eat until Bellou has fetched me a fork instead of the spoon they keep laying beside my plate, as if I were still a baby.

We are boating down the Tigris. Zeki is pulling a good oar. Father and brother dive into the water. Zeki's daughters jump after them. Only I, the youngest of all, must wait for the shore. I fidget inside my red and yellow life jacket and urge Zeki to speed up. The boat bounces up and down and tosses me from side to side.

We've reached the shore, I tell mother. She is absorbed in Dunia's account of somebody's breast being devoured by small cancers. I tap her shoulder. Not yet, she says, not bothering to check up on my words. Brother is floating on his back. The two girls are splashing and playing in the water. Move your legs, Zeki cries after them. I wish he would concentrate on rowing.

We're at the shore, I repeat. The cancers are cut out of the breast on the operating table. I pull the tail of mother's shirt. Stop nagging, she grumbles. I slip out of my life jacket and fling it into the water. Nobody takes notice. I climb up the gunwale. My legs are shivering.

—The girl! Watch the girl behind you! Zeki cries out.

Mother gives a start, turns around.

—Don't . . . she quavers.

Is she imploring or is she threatening?

I throw myself into the river, plunge headlong underwater. My legs paddle. My body recognises the prenatal element. I can hear the roar of my mother above the water. Although mother cannot swim, her voice still pursues me. I sink further to defy her fright, avenge it, punish it, drown it.

I fall on a muddy bed, the source of the river's colour. Now that I have been to the bottom of the Tigris, what I will have to see next is the edge of the Earth. My legs kick river and earth away and push me upward. I float up to the surface. Air! My head emerges at the side of the boat. I did not swim so far away after all! Everybody is looking at me as if I have popped up from the underworld. Mother's face is as wet as mine.

—Mama, I saw little cancers down there.

—We'll never take you on a boat again!

In the summer, we sleep on the roof at night. I keep turning in my crib. Sucking my thumb does not relax me. The stars hang in the sky, like streetlights without lampposts. There are as many trees in the woods as stars in the sky, they say. My eyes close. Dark, as if in the woods, where trees crowd beside each other, like people in the *suq*. The wolf has devoured Laila's granny, and is now after Laila. The farmer slashes his belly open, and out springs granny, looking quite wolfish herself. I open my eyes. The stars reassure me.

Mother is restlessly pacing about the roof, instead of going to bed. It has to do with her two sisters, I believe, who emigrated long ago to America. Sometimes they write, but mother never got over their departure.

I will leave the pogrom buried in my mother's memory for another occasion.

They say that our night is day in America, and their day is night here. Which one is the correct time? I ask. They laugh, as they always do when they are short of an answer. They tell me that while I am asleep, my aunts in New York are having lunch. Probably that is why mother is upset at night. She must be longing to join the faraway meal.

Pacing the roof will not take her to America, though.

I am sitting on my potty chair in the corridor and spinning the wooden abacus balls on the arm rest. Suddenly I spot yellow fluid streaming along the floor. Only when it reaches the end of the corridor, and is about to cascade down the stairs do I realise that the pot inside the stool has been removed. In fact, I am not supposed to use the potty any more. Mother has practised it with me several times. We would sit back to back on the wooden toilet seat, giggling, our buttocks pushed together. Then we would release our pee, in turn, and giggle again at the sound of the trickling. It was great fun, and I begged her to repeat the lesson every day. But mother stopped it as soon as she noticed that I had forgotten my fear of falling inside the bowl.

I hitch up my trousers and go and play in my room. I want to have nothing to do with the mess in the corridor. A while later, Bellou shows up and tells me off. It was brother, I retort. She knits her brows. So small and such a big liar, she bellows and goes off.

Mother soon appears and scolds me again. Bellou has told on me. The bitch. So what if it is not the first time. I burst out crying. They do not care. I hug my new teddy bear and creep under the bed, determined not to come out ever again.

It must be winter, for the scent of orange peel singeing on the stove wafts through the house. Teddy-Pasha's tummy is wet with my tears. I turn him over and bury my face in the fur of his back. From the back, Pasha still smells like a visitor. The odours of Orosdi-Back, the department store, also cling to his head and to his feet.

I pull my foot up to my nostrils. The woollen sock stinks slightly. I remove it, sniff my toes, and sniff the sock again. My nose detects a third ingredient. I pick up my bootie, and plunge my face inside. It's leather, I knew it. Leather, wool, and foot sweat have mingled their smells on the web of my socks. If only Bellou does not find out, and I can keep my feet unwashed and my socks unchanged a while longer, then the odours will grow pungent and blend into one dark heavy mass.

Again I have mixed blue and green and yellow and red. Again they have yielded a lump of grey. I knead the plasticine into a ball, then roll it into a cylinder, a fat worm, a piece of dung. Soon it lengthens into a cigar, a candle, a hose, a snake. The snake coils itself and sleeps. While it sleeps, I make a ball of it again. Did someone tell it to go to sleep? From the ball I shape an egg, then a bulb, then a bottle. The bottle falls and breaks its neck. Now it's a fat worm again.

I stretch the worm and smooth one side with my thumb. Then I fix a triangle of a head, attach a looping tail, and add four bits for the limbs. The lizard is ready. I place it on my parents' bedpost.

Mother will turn frantic at the sight of a lizard.

I call her to the bedroom, point my finger at the framed picture standing on her night table. Two girls are sitting crosslegged in a courtyard. Their faces in the picture have been smeared. A plate of watermelon segments is placed in front of them. A smaller girl stands between the two. Her features are clear. My mother. She is smiling.

—Tell me about your sisters and the watermelon, Mama, I say, and lie on her pillow.

She seats herself on the bed and relates the story I know by heart. That the elder sisters wanted to be photographed without her. That they used all kinds of threats and stratagems to keep her away from the camera. That she, nevertheless, would not budge . . . I lean on the bedpost and suck my thumb, waiting for her to detach her eyes from the photograph, scheming how to manoeuvre them to the lizard above me.

—And in the end I appear in the picture, between my two sisters. But in real life, they're gone, and all I'm left with is the watermelon.

To hell with the watermelon! How many times did I remind Mama that she was not alone, that she had me and father and brother, ten times worthier than faraway sisters. I creep towards her, hold her face in my two hands, and turn it in the direction of the bedpost. Mother jumps up, retreats a few steps, and begins to yell. A laugh escapes me. She thinks my model is real.

She stands as if trapped, staring at the reptile and shouting. If father were here, he would have chased the lizard with a broomstick. But father is at work, and the deaf creature refuses to move away. Mother now slaps her face in helplessness. The scene disturbs me. I hasten to pacify her. I even give away my secret. It's not a lizard, only a toy. Plasticine, believe me, Mama, don't be upset, please.

It is too late. My words will not deliver her from her fit.

I pick up the plaything. Look, Mama, it's not real. Seeing it in my hand, she lets out a long shriek of horror. Her voice runs through my body, and blows breath into the lizard in my hand. Repelled, I fling the reptile on the floor. Now mother and daughter yell together, bound by the same fright.

A while later, mother gains control over herself. She tramples and disfigures the animal, flattens it into inanimate matter again. I fetch a broom and sweep the lump away, down the stairs, along the courtyard, and out to the street. A hungry cat might smell the lizard hidden in the plasticine. The sheer memory of its touch between my fingers sickens me. It is mother who is now in tears of laughter. She resembles the smiling girl in the photograph.

I am flicking through a Semir comic on the balcony. Semir is an Egyptian schoolboy who keeps getting into trouble because of his stupid friend Tihtih. Mother is sewing in her room. Bellou is singing in her incomprehensible language in the kitchen. From time to time I stick my head out between the rails of the balustrade. We are waiting for father to come to lunch. For the twentieth time I ask mother where father is and when he will at last show up. And for the twentieth time I hear one and the same answer. Father is at the *suq,* he should be here any minute.

Any minute is getting as unreliable as a metaphor. I announce that I am going to fetch father from the *suq* myself. Mother hums something while cutting a thread with her teeth. It does not sound like an objection. I slip Semir under my arm and take off.

The next moment, I am at Suq al-Hamidiyah. I do not remember how I got there, only the pride I felt on reaching the neighbourhood market all by myself

Two Bedouin women, with nose rings and tattooed blue dots on their foreheads, squat at the edge of the *suq.* One is plucking dead hens. The younger is selling eggs in a basket. A snivelling toddler is tied to her back. A baby sleeps in her arms. Its mouth clings to her nipple, pulling her breast halfway to her belly.

The iceman, with the hairy chest and the stained under-shirt, is forever chopping pieces off a huge block of ice. Behind him, the pomegranate and tamarind sherbets trickle down into glass containers.

I smell the bakery. Father always lifts me up to watch the discs of bread crusting on the inner walls of the clay oven.

Father! I have forgotten about him. Where is father?

Scales clink. A bespectacled client, dressed in pyjamas, is examining the iron weights with mistrust. The grocer grumbles, and tosses a few more loquats into the pan.

Watermelons huddle together in the next store. Oval and as tall as myself, they stand in rows, supporting each other. Halves recline lengthwise outside, their red flesh glowing. My mouth waters. If only I can stimulate mother's appetite for watermelon again.

I walk by the confectioner's shop. Trays of *baklawa*, *halawa*, *malfouf*, . . . and a horde of flies hovering like a black cloud about the stand. I accelerate my pace. I do not like sweet things anyway.

Steam carries the whiff of broad beans from the cooking pot. The vendor is pushing his three-wheeler in my direction. I scrabble through my pockets for a coin in vain. Where is father?

The aroma of coffee and the click of dice call my eyes to the coffee shop slightly above ground level. Two men are playing *tawla*, backgammon, on the veranda. A third customer, with a checked black and white *kaffiyah*, is sitting at their table, holding the *nargilah* tube, the water pipe, in one hand and a fly swatter in the other. His gaze is glued to the butcher's shop across the street.

Skinned and beheaded carcasses of sheep are hung on hooks. Their heads, swarming with flies, are nailed above them, like hats above matching suits.

In the shade of the coffee shop veranda, the *hammal*, porter, prostrates himself on a prayer rug. His lips move in a soundless recital of prayers. The hubbub of the *suq* does not reach his ears. Nor will any fly dream of accosting him.

A few steps away from the butcher's I spot the shoeblack. The Kurd with the grey beard and embroidered skullcap is sitting on his stool, sipping tea from a *stikan*, tea glass. I always run to the gate when he rings our bell, and cast a heap of shoes at his feet. Then he allows me to remove his skullcap and marvel at his shining bald head.

As I cross the street towards my shoeblack, a herd of sheep sweeps along and shuts me in. They block my sight. Their wool scorches my skin. They bleat. They stink. They almost hurl me to the ground. I drop my comic book. Its pages disperse under their hooves. I cry out for father and realise that I am all on my own.

I burst into tears.

The shoeblack is advancing in my direction. The herd passes by. A woman in a black *abaya* collects the pages from the ground. I am still sobbing. The Kurd stretches his arms to me. I recoil from his touch. The black *abaya* hands me back a rumpled Semir, soiled with hoof marks. I push her hand away. They all terrify me. I want to go home. I am not certain that I remember the way back.

She's lost, I hear a man say.

I find myself at a crossroads. The sight of Bellou and mother striding from a sidestreet calms me down. They have spotted me, my two dear mothers, the real and the surrogate, the small and the tall. The one smiles, the other frowns, and then vice versa. This time, I will be spanked, I can smell it.

—Next time I'll go farther still, as far as Sind and India, as far as Wonderland . . . I grumble later, sucking my thumb in bed.

Bellou tells me the story of a little girl, who, like me, is again and again tempted by unknown faraway worlds. Yet each time she sets out, the little girl loses her way and cannot return, like a cat who has climbed up a tree and cannot climb down. Gradually, she learns that no way back is possible, that her only option is to move onward. Or upward, in the case of the cat.

And then? What happens then?

And then an angel turns up, and meets her halfway.

In autumn, a carriage pulled by two black horses halts before our gate. The horses are wearing garlands around their necks. Bellou's suitcase lies in the backseat. She presses me to her breast with a vigour that almost squashes me, and pokes something into my hand. She smells of laurel soap. The horses look foolish, I say. As if they were the ones getting married.

Bellou and the coachman wave goodbye. I open my hand and find her amulet! The wolf fang will have to wait until my breasts grow big enough, so that it can fall between them.

Mother says that Bellou will be happier with him than she used to be with us.

But why?

Because from now on, she will be washing her own children, cleaning her own house, and preparing plate-sized *Mossul kubbas* for her own family.

In her empty room, the mattress is folded in two. My drawing of her, running away with her sister is pinned on the door. Bellou did not take it with her. After tomorrow, I am going to nursery school. No maid will sleep at our place any more.

What is after tomorrow?

—After tomorrow is going to bed and waking up, then going to sleep again and waking up again, father says.

After tomorrow is an indefinite time, any time after tomorrow, brother says.

FIRST DAY AT SCHOOL

Small children are crowded in front of the nursery. The door is closed. Boys and girls are standing stiff, like pawns removed from a chessboard. It is their first day. Half of them are crying.

A long bell rings. The door unlocks. An obese woman appears. Her hair is arranged in a heavy chignon. Smiling, she leads the children inside. A young assistant makes the children sit at tables for two, lined up in five rows. The nursery teacher takes her place behind them, at the back of the room.

I sit in the first row, nearest to the door, sobbing. The girl beside me has two carrotlike plaits. Her eyes are dry. She grins at me, almost motherly, and promises to tell me a secret if I stop weeping. I quiet down, start sucking my thumb. She says her name is Selma. That's all? Her fishlike lips approach my ear and whisper. *Sit* Sarah, the obese teacher, steals the children's lunch. What? I swear it, by Baba's life! The *sit* exchanges red apples for yellow ones, big bananas for rotten ones, drinks half our Coca-Cola and dilutes the rest of the bottle with water. My eyes are wet again. Selma reassures me. *Sit* Sarah would never lay hands on hot pickles or non-kosher food.

—Pass it on to your Mama. It's the only way out.

Mariam, the assistant, distributes wooden cubes. Selma builds towers, not stopping until they collapse. With my free hand, I help her pick them up.

—You'll come tomorrow, won't you? she asks.

I nod, sucking my thumb.

Tomorrow, next year, and for many years to come, I will still be sucking it. But it is not only my thumb I do not easily relinquish. It is infancy I am clinging to, our doctor friend claims, the way I clung to mother's womb four years back. After several days of labour, the poor woman gave up, and I thought I had got my own way and would be left in peace, forever inside. But soon a blinding light assailed me. They had cut mother's tummy open, and out they dragged me, screaming and kicking at the world.

For a whole year, each morning, the same struggle recommences. I exhaust all methods of manipulation to avoid the social programme imposed on me: I cannot dress myself, I mess up the soft-boiled egg, have a stomach ache, cough, snivel, throw up. I tell stories about the witch who is starving us, about the boy who urinates on my patent leather shoes, about the dirty words they are teaching us, about cockroaches in the toilets and worms in the water. Mother is exasperated. The school bus honks. Brother rushes out. She will either yield to my pressure and let me stay at home or lose her temper and haul me into the bus. The chances are fifty-fifty. It is worth the trouble.

When I am absent, Selma watches over my bench, next to hers.

Though she was born three weeks after me, she is a head taller already. Because, unlike me, Selma drinks milk, finishes her breakfast, and goes regularly to nursery. She has barely any eyelashes, though, and is the only redheaded child in the class. King David was red-haired, she tells everybody. Her skin is freckled, translucent; her fingers are pink. Next to hers mine look yellowish, like those of a chain smoker. Her nipples are red, her buttocks square, her ear-lobes fleshy, and her nostrils large and round. Her small white teeth easily vanish from sight when she is devouring a hot pickled sandwich. Her tongue can reach the tip of her nose. Her left ear can wave hello. Her eyes are honey-coloured. With the passing years, they will deepen into brown. Her forearms are less hairy than mine, but then she has a graceful line of hair running down her back. The hairs above her lip gather beads of sweat at midday. Her navel sinks inwards while mine sticks out. Her wee-wee is surprisingly smaller than mine. Our bellies are similar, both puffed up, as if we have swallowed a basketball.

Selma and I are holding hands and bounding down the stairs into the courtyard with the drinking fountain. We count each step out loud as we jump. One. Two. Three. Four. Five. Six. Seven. Eight. Only eight steps? But we can count to ten! We leap up again, counting in English this time. It is the only courtyard where the nursery children are allowed to play. In two years, when we will be in primary school, we will be free to play everywhere.

The school premises consist of two long colonnaded galleries onto which the classrooms open. The two-storeyed galleries join at a right angle, drawing a square space between them in which is assembled a maze of courtyards and additional classrooms. Yards and building are surrounded by gardens that, in their turn, are encompassed by tall walls to shut out chaotic, unpredictable Baghdad. The solidity of the architecture gives the place a fortresslike feel. A sports club nearby is linked to our school. It has several ping-pong tables, four tennis courts, a basket- and volleyball court, and a huge lawn for the smaller children to run about in. Our club is open only during the summer holidays. Both the school and club premises belong to the Jewish community, but there is no nameplate at either entrance.

About 600 girls and boys, aged between four and eighteen, receive preschool, elementary and secondary education here.

At five, they play hide-and-seek behind the bulky columns. At six, they scour the premises for the Rat Room. At seven, they scrape their elbows against the rough plaster, playing "seven tiles." At eight, they steal flowers from the garden. At nine, they carve their names on the desks. At ten, they borrow books from the library. At eleven, they steal tubes from the chemistry lab. At twelve, they complain about the lack of mirrors in the toilets. At thirteen, secondary school begins. They move upstairs, to the first floo

At thirteen, the Six Day War breaks out.

Ten years after the war, the Jewish community will cease to be. Only some elderly individuals and a few families will stay in Baghdad. The school will be appropriated by the state. The new name will stand on a big plate, hung at the gate. To its right, a wall poster will read: "One Arab Nation, with an Eternal Message." It will be an elementary school for boys. They will pee standing, even in the girls' toilets. They will speak Arabic in the Muslim dialect. They will convert the small synagogue into a storeroom. They will dispose of the foreign books in the library. The eight steps will remain intact, but all the same, I would have lost my way in the new landscape.

We have moved on to kindergarten, which is one year above the nursery. We are no longer the youngest class in the school. You are grown-up children now, they tell us, but still inspect our nails everyday and fumble through our hair for lice once a week. We carry wooden pencil boxes, reading and exercise books in our satchels.

We are learning the alphabet.

Three women teachers are in charge of our class. All three are very fat, yet none is interested in our lunch boxes. Each demands a separate exercise book. Each teaches a different type of alphabet.

A wooden rule hangs beside the blackboard, for lazy fingers.

The Arabic *alif* is easy. It consists of a vertical, straight line. Any child of five can draw it. The *hamza* above requires some practice though. Three zig-zag lines, like a step, slightly slanting.

In English, there is one big *A* and one small *a*. The small is not the miniature of the big. In fact they do not even resemble each other. My curved lines are shabby. My straight lines curve in the middle. I am incapable of making edges touch. I would rather draw houses.

Hebrew has two *alefs*, one for writing, one for printing. I can manage none. I will never learn to write.

And why so many alphabets?

Arabic is your language, Hebrew is the language of your ancestors, and English is your future.

In five years, we will be learning French, too. More future, I guess.

The double-lined exercise books give us spatial and dimensional orientation. Yet my small *a*'s still look more like cracked eggs, and the printed *alef*, at its best, a crooked branch. I rub out the eggs and the branches, again and again, until the first page is torn. I will end up a shoeblack or a porter, the fate of the stupid and the lazy, so our teachers say. But before that, they will send me to the Rat Room.

The Rat Room is a dark and squalid cell, where the lazy, the stupid, and the disobedient are dispatched for punishment. The rats gnaw their fingernails and chew their earlobes. Everyone at school has heard of this room. Yet even those who swear they have seen it cannot indicate its exact location.

I suck my pencil, waiting for the school bell to end the lesson, dreaming: again, the Tigris has overflowed its banks and drowned Baghdad. Mud-brick houses dissolve and bridges twist and break. The flat city sinks, together with its *suqs* and *casinos,* coffeeshops, and parks and military bases and no-longer-royal palaces. Those agile among the Baghdadis clamber up minarets and palm trees. The rest use car tires as life-buoys. Thumbing their amber worry beads, they slump inside the black tires and drift in the water amid red double-deckers and khaki jeeps.

In spite of its stable foundations, our fortress of a school is instantly uprooted. Classrooms break apart and travel aimlessly in the water. Water knows no boundaries. The Tigris and the Euphrates have joined hands to inundate the land between them. We are sailing. Our exercise books are floating, like cream in a milk pot. It is fun to be on board. It looks like a journey without an end. A faraway land comes into view. Fair children are speaking English on the shore. They are a bunch of fools, their teacher says dismissively. Our teachers rush us back to the benches and assault us with *bee* and *cee* and *dee* even if we are not through with *ay* yet.

Selma is going through harder times than I. She is left-handed, but the teachers, all three, compel her to use her right. After weeks of clashes a compromise is reached: she may use her left, provided it is the right which eventually carries out the task. Left is allowed to begin. It attempts to reproduce what the eyes report. After some fairly good lines, the pencil passes to Right. Right emulates the gesture performed by Left, reruns the route which Left initiated. Selma's upper lip is sweating. Her right will always linger behind her left. Whatever the class does, Selma must do twice. It's her fate, she says, to lead a double life.

With the blue ballpoint she has found in the garden, Selma draws a circle on her right wrist. Then she adds a few dashes inside, and a thin strap around the wrist to buckle the watch. Now I'll know when the school bell will ring, she says. I borrow her ballpoint and copy her watch on my left wrist. Now I'll know when cartoons are on TV. Selma snatches back her pen and marks, with her right hand, another watch, a clumsier one, on her left wrist. When the teacher discovers our drawings, she immediately reaches for the wooden rule. Are we Bedouins to tattoo ourselves left and right? She calls us filthy girls and confiscates our ballpoint. I open my right hand to receive my punishment. Selma is hit on both hands.

We rub out our distorted letters, again and again. At the end of each day, shreds of rubber are heaped on our desks. Selma has a recipe for plasticine: add some spittle to the shreds of rubber, knead them together, and let the mixture dry in the sun. We try this for two years. The shreds do not fuse into dough. We rub away white and pink and green rubbers against the bench. Selma swears that at home the operation always succeeds. With her chewing gum, Selma can blow the largest bubbles in the class. She can coil herself like the *Melwiyah*, the spiral minaret of Samarra, and I believe every word she says.

B, *ba'a*, and *bet* are more difficult to sketch than *a*, *alif*, and *alef*. If every new letter is more complex than the preceding one, what a toilsome childhood is awaiting us!

Arabic has three *ba'as*. One is put at the beginning of the word, one in the middle, and one at the end. *Alif* and *ba'a* form words together: *ab*, father, *bab*, door, *baba*, dad. I can write! I am writing! Soon I will decipher the signs in the street, and read out those blinking neon ads. Soon I will learn to write my name, Lina, in three languages. And when all three alphabets are acquired, I will already know more than any of our three teachers.

REVOLUTIONS

A yellow balloon lands on my nose and kisses it. It is the side on which Abd al-Karim's face is printed which has touched me. I tap the balloon back into the air. Abd al-Karim, our leader, spins and somersaults in the blue sky. I chase him around our backyard, longing for his smell of warm rubber. The balloon falls again, this time into my arms. I hold Abd al-Karim by his thick head of hair, and after making sure that nobody is watching, press my lips on his dry mouth to apply a long, thirsty kiss, the way lovers do in foreign films.

His portrait hangs in every store and coffee house in Baghdad. It is printed on banknotes, exercise books, chewing gum cards, calendars. In our classroom, we have *al-Zaim*, the leader, framed above the blackboard down to the chest, in uniform, smiling, waving us hello. During the break, we play musical chairs as we sing:

> Long live *al-Zaim*, long live Abd al-Karim.
> Stand up, stand up and salute him.
> Back to your seats, all of you,
> except for the odd man out, ha, ha, ha.

It does not really work in English.
Father teaches me to arrange postage stamps in sets and to

insert them behind the transparent film in the album. I handle them with care, these delicate perforated squares and rectangles in assorted colour combinations, illustrating landscapes and animals from other countries. They introduce me to famous personalities: Queen Elizabeth II, the Shah of Iran, the Greek royal family, Madame Curie, Abraham Lincoln. I am particularly keen on those in which Abd al-Karim appears. He is saluting the new republican flag on the second anniversary of the July Revolution. He is reviewing a file of troops on Army Day. His profile watches over *Medinat al-Thawra*, Revolution City , which he built to house the squatters. He is shaking hands with farmers on a set of four stamps commemorating the Agrarian Reforms.

Every corner of Baghdad urges me to love the leader of the Revolution. He, and he alone, has put an end to the monarchy and to the corrupt *Ahd al-Ba'id*, the Old Regime that served the British rather than our people. He has wiped out feudalism and established social justice. He will bring about peace with the Kurds. Even father, who had lost his heart to the British, retains a soft spot for Abd al-Karim. He calls him the ugly duckling, the pauper who has grown into a torch-bearer, the daring brigadier who played at revolution and won—soaring very high that glorious 14th of July.

Every year in July helicopters showered Baghdad with colourful leaflets, celebrating the Revolution and its hero—that is, until the glorious 14th skipped to another month, reserved for another hero.

Ramadan has fallen in winter this year. Around nine in the morning, we are reciting classical Arabic poetry in class, when we suddenly hear shellfire. It issues from more than one direction. In no time textbooks are closed and tucked into our satchels. School buses are sent for to drive us home. Father, too, returns early from work. We switch on the radio. A shrill female voice blesses the Revolution of the 14th of

Ramadan and barks out proclamations on behalf of the National Council for the Revolutionary Command. She is accusing Abd al-Karim of having betrayed the goals of the Revolution of the 14th of July.

The station has fallen to the rebels. Explosions are heard in stereo, from the radio and live.

A curfew is imposed. We cannot go to school the next day, that is certain. Neighbours are sauntering outside, men in pyjamas, transistor radios in hand, paying informal visits to each other. Children are cycling in the middle of the street. As long as vehicles are banned, no pedestrian restricts himself to the pavement. I chalk hopscotch squares on the roadway. Wafa', our neighbour, keeps skating in and out of them. Next to us, the two boys playing Red Indians have knelt down and pressed their ears against the ground to eavesdrop on children's doings in the neighbourhood. A few miles away fierce street fights are taking place between pro-Abd al-Karim July Revolution troops and soldiers backing the Ramadan counterrevolution.

The shelling stops at sunset, the time when Muslims break their fast. The radio claims that good has conquered evil and that with the help of Allah, Abd al-Karim's resistance has collapsed.

I wake up late the next morning. Artillery fire tells me that the battles continue. My parents and brother have already breakfasted, and are listening to the radio in the livingroom. The sight of father unshaved, in his bathrobe, astonishes me. He always shaves first thing in the morning and never stays in his pyjamas once out of bed. Not even on holidays. It is his eleventh commandment. The one which only the revolution could tempt him to break.

Neighbours come in and out. The friend of somebody's brother has seen tanks and armoured cars in Rashid Street. Someone's father-in-law has heard planes strafing the Ministry of Defense, where al-Zaim's headquarters are located.

—Abd al-Karim has accumulated too much power. Such corruption could not last.

—But who are the new boys? Will they do it better?

—Their proclamations repeat the same stuff: struggle against imperialism, liberation of Palestine, Arab unity, democracy, Arab-Kurdish brotherhood . . .

—Big words! Nobody surpasses us when it comes to words.

Zeki has come all the way from Battawin to Alwiyah on foot, together with his dog. He says the Ba'ath's National Guards are patrolling every neighbourhood he has crossed, hunting for Communists—Abd al-Karim's allies. Bored by their constant talk, I go out to the garden, turn on the hose for the black mongrel. He drinks eagerly, wagging his tail, then licks my hand in gratitude. He has never done this before!

—What about us? mother wonders, after all our guests are gone.

For no ruler in Iraq, since King Faisal I in the 1920s, has granted the Jews equal rights the way al-Zaim has done.

At noon the firing stops. Abd al-Karim has surrendered. The National Council of the Revolution appoints Abd al-Salam as president. Abd al-Salam, Abd al-Karim's former protegé, his friend and collaborator in the July Revolution, has overthrown him. Worse. He has stolen the Revolution from him.

A new public holiday is added to the calendar. The Ramadan Revolution, loyal to the principles of the July Revolution, will now correct the deviations of Abd al-Karim's regime.

In the evening I am reluctant to watch TV, lest they show Abd al-Karim dishevelled, humiliated, bruised perhaps. Although nobody has told me, I know that the hero with the boyish gaze, bushy eyebrows and timid smile under the greying moustache is gone for good. I fear the worst for him. That he will be dragged through the streets like the

Crown Prince, Abd al-Ilah, at the time of the July Revolution. So I was told. When the army delivered Abd al-Ilah's corpse to the mob, they dragged it along the bridge to the west side of the capital and hanged it at the gate of the Ministry of Defense.

The body of Nuri al-Said, the Prime Minister, resented for his pro-Western policy, did not receive any better treatment. On the morning of the 14th of July, the elderly statesman scuttled along the banks of the Tigris, disguised as a woman, seeking a hiding place. But the woman soon aroused the suspicion of passersby. Her black *abaya* and black veil were ill-matched with the men's pyjama bottoms underneath, which the fleeing Prime Minister had had no time to remove. When he was recognised, General Nuri shot himself on the spot. He was buried by the army, but two days later, the masses dug up the grave and virtually swept the streets with the Prime Minister's corpse.

Abd al-Karim is neither tortured nor dragged through the streets. On the day of his surrender, a court martial sentences him to death. He is shot that same day.

The next day, the curfew is lifted and we are back at school. Above the blackboard a pale patch stands out from the white wall. A black nail protrudes on its upper margin. For five years the wall behind Abd al-Karim's portrait has not been painted. When the classroom undergoes its annual whitewash, the pale patch will vanish. But, lacking the five layers of paint from Abd al-Karim's time, its outline will still be traceable.

During the break Selma pulls me into the back garden, and indicates a window overlooking the cellar. It is the same cellar that, as smaller children, we suspected to be the Rat Room. I peep inside. Scores of framed pictures lean against the wall. In each, al-Zaim smiles behind glass, waves us goodbye.

Selma says that very late last night Abd al-Karim was shown on television. He was seated on a chair, with bullet holes all over his body. The programme was lengthy with repetitive scenes of the Ramadan Revolution and dead generals. Just as she was about to go to bed, a soldier grabbed Abd al-Karim's head by the hair and spat into his lifeless face.

Colonel Mahdawi, too, was displayed on television, his body lying next to Abd al-Karim's. The function of the People's Court was to try the enemies of the people and punish the conspirators against the country. The trials were broadcast on radio and television and were followed in every café in the country.

"*Mahkamah*," a hoarse voice cries out, announcing the opening of the session. Mahdawi enters the court. The audience greets him with enthusiastic applause. The Colonel opens with a wise maxim, followed by his opinion on matters of the day. His tone changes as he turns to the defendants and bombards them with insults and rhetorical abuse. We hear laughter from the audience. A chuckle escapes mother. Immediately she corrects herself and calls him vulgar, arrogant. Mahdawi is now reciting some poem which supposedly echoes the present case. His voice, deepened by the eloquence of its inflection, impresses me. I do not catch the moral, though. If only his achievements in military college were half as good as his distinction in Arabic poetry, our neighbour comments, cracking pumpkin seeds. Several spectators leave their seats and dance a *dabka* in the middle of the court. The audience claps hands to the rhythm of the dance. Mahdawi looks pleased with himself. Some judge! mother says. Would you be sitting there at all if you weren't Abd al-Karim's cousin? The officer next to him whispers something in the Colonel's ear. Mahdawi stops the dance with a gesture, and embarks at last on the proceedings of the court. I flit to the kitchen, fetch myself a packet of potato crisps. Mahdawi points at the man in the brown *dishdasha*, who is standing among the defendants at the dock. Those to his left are sentenced to five years in prison. The brown *dishdasha* and those to his right are to be set free.

Sometimes, the trials ended with capital punishment. But, as in a film, the convicts were not, in reality, put to death. Or only seldom. Abd al-Salam himself, for instance, had once been sentenced to death by the Mahdawi Court, charged with the attempted assassination of Abd al-Karim. He was released after three years' imprisonment.

Father, a passionate philatelist, transfers his mint sheets of Abd al-Karim stamps over to another drawer, stacked with older sheets of King Faisal I in Bedouin attire, King Faisal I in a European suit, King Ghasi in profile, King Faisal II as a child, a youth, a young man. What a shock it would have been for Abd al-Karim had he known that his revolutionary icon would be stored in royal company—a bunch of disgraced celebrities.

National anthems, flags, stamps, currencies, street names, and other state emblems do not last long in Baghdad. They do not age, wear out, or fall apart. They abruptly burst in and out of history, at a pace no individual memory can adapt to. Even now mother calls the first modern bridge in the city by its original name, Maude, after the British General who captured Baghdad in the First World War. It was the boundary her family forbade her to cross without the escort of a male relative. By the time my mother was a young girl, however, the British army had left Iraq and the bridge had been renamed after King Ghazi. When the monarchy was overthrown and the statues of both General Maude and King Faisal I were torn down by angry crowds, while the corpse of Abd al-Ilah was dragged from one side of the capital to the other over this bridge, it became the *Shuhada'*, Martyrs' Bridge, adjusting itself, like a linguistic chameleon, to the vocabulary of the latest supremacy.

Nine months later, in November, we are sent home early again. Abd al-Salam has initiated another coup. He expels the

Ba'ath, his Ramadan fellow revolutionaries, dissolves their National Guard, and forms a new government.

On the next anniversary of the Ramadan Revolution, helicopters whirr in the skies of Baghdad, dropping small nylon bags filled with sweets. Although they fall faster than paper, the little gifts still take their time, swinging and hovering, indifferent to our cries of impatience. One such bag is hanging above my head, about to land on our roof. Just when it appears within reach, the bag changes its mind and drifts away. I dart downstairs to follow it from the street. A puff of wind drives it further south, towards the river. From a sidestreet a girl in a striped *dishdasha* rushes in the same direction. The girl, smaller than me and barefoot, soon overtakes me. I try it her way—take off my shoes, and sprint along. In no time, a sharp stone grazes my sole. I stop to examine it. Only scraped, not bleeding, but my chances of winning have been crushed. I put on my shoes again and walk back, slowly recovering my breath. The sky is quiet and clear, devoid of surprises. I have been deprived of the sweets of the Revolution.

When I reach home, a bag of toffee is awaiting me in the garden! I rip it open and try the first candy. It turns out to be of the worst quality. The *serifa* girl passes by, a similar bag in her hand. *Nestala*, she says, flaunting it proudly. Nestala is the slang for chocolate, a corruption of Nestlé—a brand so expensive that I doubt the girl has ever tasted it. I smile back. She gathers the hem of her *dishdasha*, and seats herself at the threshhold of our house. I join her. We have never been so close before, although the Bedouin clan has been living for years in *serifa*, squatter huts on the bare piece of land behind our house. A blue spot is tattooed on her forehead. A golden ring pierces her nose. Her skin is ebony, dark as her own shadow. Her soles are calloused, asphalt black. Mucus is about to run out of her nostril. A sniff calls it up again. A bronze anklet adorns her left foot. I offer her my pair of shoes for the one anklet. No way. She shakes her head, slurping and sucking the sweets strewn in memory of Abd al-Karim's fall.

Three years after the Ramadan coup, we are sent home early again. It is now Abd al-Salam's turn to give his life for a day off. On its way from Qurna to Basra, his helicopter explodes. The event is reported as a tragic accident. Nobody in Baghdad believes such reports. Abd, our bus driver, a loyal fan of Abd al-Karim, is mostly enthusiastic about the news. It inspires his imagination and, by nature, Abd verbalises. At each gate where he lets a child out, his pleasure regenerates as he conveys the account to the concerned mother.

—Don't worry Sister, it's only Abd al-Salam. Al-Mushir, the Guide, has just exploded in the air. Boom, like a balloon. See the black cloud up there, that's the victor of three revolutions, July, Ramadan, and November. One was not enough, he had to grab three, and all for himself. Now they'll drop carbon paper from the sky, some mourning leaflets for our charred hero, don't you think?

The cautious mother draws her child quickly inside, before any neighbour or passer-by associates her with the big-mouthed driver.

In spite of the rigid and demanding education we are subjected to, the school authorities take no chances as far as our safety is concerned. We are sent home at the slightest unrest. Even a demonstration about domestic politics can, at any moment, be twisted into agitated support for the Palestinian cause and wind up at the gate of our Jewish school.

—The whole year, *chirri mirri*, goings and comings, Abd says one day. How can one learn anything under such conditions? Your headmaster's overdoing it with his safety precautions. There's no need to tremble whenever a firecracker explodes.

It is 10 o'clock in the morning. A restive crowd, roaring and catcalling only a few streets away, is advancing in our direction. Not even shellfire, and our tyrants of teachers are acting like guardian angels. No time to assign homework. The math problem can wait till next week. The premises are to be evacuated as soon as possible. Upon my arrival home, mother switches on the radio. The local station does not report any unrest in the capital. Not even in the evening. Only the next morning does it appear in the papers. An inflamed crowd of impassioned men was babbling and whistling, chasing after an Egyptian female singer, who made the mistake of wearing trousers and exploring, on foot, the city of The Thousand and One Nights.

BROTHER

Sultan lies stiff and motionless in my cupped hand. His eyelids are closed, his claws withdrawn, entangled in one another. My little finger caresses the canary's yellow feathers. Delicate as ever, and yet it does not feel like Sultan any more. Were those tiny breaths all that made him? I press my finger on his chest then let go, press down briefly again, hoping to revive his heart. His body remains petrified, destitute of will. I open his beak and blow my own air inside him, the way they demonstrated artificial respiration on dummies last week on television.

Nothing doing. Sultan is no more.

Brother digs a small pit in the garden. My canary is laid inside. He does not even look as if he is resting. Sultan used to doze on his feet. Unlike the multitude of dead cats I have seen sprawled on rubbish dumps, or the carcasses of dogs squashed flat on the roadway, I have never come across a dead bird before. Do wild birds simply plummet down from the sky when they are done for, the way rotten mulberries let go of their tree?

Tears wash my eyes. Sultan turns into a yolk, sinking in thick chocolate.

—Didn't I tell you that Samson would outlive Sultan? brother exclaims I knew it!

I snivel.

—Don't worry, he goes on more softly. My Samson too will eventually die. As well as the new Sultan you'll be getting very soon.

My tears stream in currents.

—You've got to face it. Every bird must die one day.

I suck my thumb.

—Everybody must die. Without exception. Even Mama and Baba, and so will you . . . and . . . so will I. Everybody.

No, I am not prepared for it—that Sultan is only the beginning, and that mother and father will follow. Father! Father is older, he will certainly have to go first. Or worse still, they might leave this world together, he and mother. In that case, brother will be in charge of me. I do hope nothing of the sort will happen, at least not before I am grown up. Otherwise, brother will demand unconditional respect and boss me around all day long, the way he does whenever our parents go out in the evening.

Brother. It is time he got a name. Time I accorded him a chapter in my life.

Let me call him Shuli, short for Shaul—after our maternal grandfather—and place him a few years ahead of me in the world.

A framed photograph of him, riding on the unfinished sculpture of the stone Lion of Babylon, hangs in our sitting room. The lion is trampling on a man. Shuli is seated on the lion's head. His legs are astride its mane, and his hands clasp what could have been the lion's ears. The ear-to-ear smile of a winner lights up Shuli's face. He is almost six.

Those were his happiest years, he tells whoever happens to be looking at the photograph. Years when his parents had made him the most valuable of all their valuables, their one and only God. When she arrived, the word "fair" was admitted to the family. Whatever it originally meant, "fair" granted her the natural right to grab half of his possessions.

Half the room, half the cupboard, half the carpet, half the bath, half his father, half his mother, and all cakes and sweets divided in half.

Smarties are sorted according to their different colours, each of which is thereafter divided into two equal shares. He swallows his share within minutes, while I store mine in the fridge. I hardly care for sweets; it is the fifty-fifty principle for which I stand. Like a watchdog, I count my Smarties twice a day to make sure he is not pilfering.

He is wearing a Robin Hood hat and practising archery. I am holding the target. His arrows whizz. My ear escapes by a hair's breadth. Father spots us and spoils the game. So he dresses up as a cowboy, with a ten-gallon hat, a red waistcoat, a lopsided cartridge belt, and a brace of pistols which he easily slips in and out of his holsters.

"*Gemaaar,*" fresh cream. The robust voice is coming from the street. We streak out to the garden and hide behind the gate to ambush the enemy. A vendor is passing. She is bearing a round tin tray as big as a bicycle wheel on her head. That's no real *um-el-gemar,* he growls, that's a spy. He shoots, bang bang, not too loud, lest she hears and curses us back. The fake vendor drops dead. We take hold of her tray and devour all the cream.

A tall Bedouin in a white *dishdasha* is passing by, selling salt from the desert. A camel is walking beside him. Bang bang, I cry, not too loud, aiming my water pistol at the spy from the desert. Wrong, Shuli grumbles and shoots down the camel, who falls on the Bedouin and kills him.

We hear a familiar tolling. The paraffin-cart has just entered our street. "*Nafet,*" sings out the driver. That's a fake *abu-el-nafet,* I growl and, bang bang, shoot down the donkey. Wrong again, Shuli groans as he fires at the green tank, throws himself on the ground, and shields his head with his hands. I do the same just before the paraffin tank explodes with driver and donkey.

We watch the Flintstones on television, then mold mud cakes and let them bake in the sun on the balcony. They will serve as ammunition for the Stone Age War we will be staging at Shuli's tenth birthday party next month.

Before my fourth birthday, I am determined to learn to piss standing. As I drench my trousers again, Shuli pokes out his cock and makes a comparative study between his penis and my wee-wee.

—You'll never make it! Not in a hundred years.

Years go by and reduce the ratio between our ages, and shift the proportion between my reverence for him and my defiance of him.

The red waistcoat, the cartridge belt, and the silver sheriff badge pass on to me. I paint, with mother's kohl, two horizontal black lines above my lips. Then I put on the ten-gallon hat, and wink at the cowboy in the mirror. I am ready for a fair fight at last.

He is lolling on the sofa in the sitting room, reading.

—Stick em up! I yell, holding the pistol in two hands, aiming at his heart.

My hands remain stable as his eyes take their time to rise from the page and sweep an empty gaze over me.

—Aren't you a bit late? The Red Indians have been exterminated, the black slaves are free, the Second World War is over, and they've just captured Eichmann.

That said, he returns to his book. A dog-eared book, bound in brown, with a cream call number on its spine: 421 KAL 238. That far I am able to read. Had I not feared for my skin, I would have snatched his *Kalila wa Dumna* and flung the animal tales out of the window. It would not have been of much use, though. Shuli has outgrown our battles, our peace treaties, our cops and robbers, even our pillow fights. When did we last hose each other down? Growing up seems, indeed, like a voyage of no return. Poor Shuli, there is nothing I can do for him. I slip the pistol back into my holster, and slam the door behind me. When I have learned reading and writing properly, I will write a book and recapture his soul. I will write hair-raising stories about Antar, the famous black slave who raided all the other Arab tribes and at whose name alone fear and wonder echoed through the desert.

But Shuli's attachment to any book ends once he has finished it. After that it will be lost amid the dusty mass of comic strips, paperbacks, and hard covers piled against the wall in the corridor, threatening to collapse on my head whenever I rush down to our room.

After we have moved into a bigger house, Shuli piles the books in his room. Father proposes to buy him a bookcase, but Shuli turns down the offer.

—But books eat dust, son, mother adds. Better you sorted them out.

—Tsk, Shuli replies.

At school they say that he has set his sights on the *Encyclopaedia Britannica*.

It is true, he can sketch the lives of Tolstoy, Trotsky, and Telemann as well as territorial behaviour or the sinking of the Titanic. He can shed light on the origins of the tango, on Tibetan dialects, the shroud of Turin, telepathy, and tandoori cooking. He is able to simplify and explain the theories of time and the basics of the Talmud, the telegraph system, thermodynamics, the structure of tragedy, and the construction of trumpets.

He must have finished with T.

Besides, no other pupil can solve problems in math, physics, and algebra with his swiftness. And he does not even wear glasses.

Teachers credit him with brilliance. Classmates maintain a distance out of respect and mistrust. He is an exception, he concludes, and behaves like one, condescending to the ordinary.

Secondary school. Shuli is still first in his class. Father is displeased. The boy is getting used to effortless success.

Mother, too, is concerned. Her boy is growing edgy, remote, impenetrable, like a closed book.

On their class excursion to Ur, Shuli took on an endless journey on the staircase of the ancient ziggurat. He climbed up and down the whole day. What did he see? Hundreds of stairs made of bricks, and thousands of bricks made into stairs, yellow dust above and yellow sand below, and then vice versa. What did he hear? His own footfalls, treading behind him, whispering who knows what promises in his ear.

He spent all his trip allowance on a chalk model of the ziggurat. It displays a three-storeyed buttressed tower with a rectangular structure at the base. Like a pyramid, the walls slope inward as they go up. Three exterior staircases of a hundred steps each, he says, converge at the shrine on the summit.

A fly lands on the summit. It rubs together its forelegs then stands still, like a black queen resting on a white throne.

—The construction of the temple tower began during the third dynasty of Ur, about the 22nd century B.C. Later, the ziggurat was also employed as an astronomical observation post. Forty-two centuries separate the original ziggurat in Ur from the model on my desk, can you imagine? More centuries B.C. than A.D.!

bc-ad? I thought the right order was a-b-c-d!

The triple stairway tempts me. Two of the flights of steps lean against the wall while the third projects straight out from the front of the building. My forefinger touches the foot of the central stairway. One by one, it climbs up the white tiny steps, smooth and cool.

Twelve, thirteen, fourteen, fifteen, sixteen . . . thwack!

His hand hits out at both finger and fly.

—Don't touch! How many times must I tell you not to touch my ziggurat. White chalk is easily stained.

A black and white drawing is pinned on the wall behind his desk. The Hanging Gardens of Babylon and the bank of a river, the Euphrates. Shuli copied it recently from an illustration in the *Britannica*.

The gardens are laid out in a series of ziggurat terraces and roofed with stone balconies supported by colonnades. Climbing plants, tropical trees, shrubs, and greenery appear on every terrace. A flight of stairs connects one storey to the other. A fountain pours at each landing. People are strolling along the gardens. A couple is leaning on the parapet at the top. They look as if lost in the clouds.

—The Hanging Gardens were built in the 6th century B.C., by Nebuchadnezzer, the great military commander who crushed the Egyptian army, invaded Syria, and attacked the Arab tribes in Arabia. The same king who occupied Judea and deported us to Babylon.

Shuli points to the river in the drawing, as if it provided the proof to his words.

—There, by the Rivers of Babylon, our ancestors sat down and wept for Jerusalem. Ironically, Nebuchadnezzer's wife, a Median princess, shed tears as well. She, too, was longing for her homeland.

It must have driven the poor king mad. Everyone about him homesick and tearful.

—So, to comfort his wife, Nebuchadnezzer worked out a replica of her native land in Babylon. He constructed gardens that hung in the air and simulated the green mountains rooted in her memory.

—Was the queen satisfied? Did she stop crying?

—History reports scarcely anything about Amytis. As to the Hanging Gardens, there is no trace of them, either in archaeological remains, or in cuneiform texts. Perhaps they were only a legendary monument preserved by dreamers through the ages.

Why is he telling me all this if it is only fiction?

—What about our ancestors? Did they weep very long? I ask, reverting to history.

—Oh no! Soon after that famous sobbing by the river, the Judean captives got up and set to work. From a people of farmers, they turned into a people of traders, replaced their beloved Temple with synagogues, and made their home in exile.

On the ceiling of his room, Shuli has pinned colourful magazine cutouts of spaceships revolving in starry nights. A huge leap through history. Yet the distance to heaven has not contracted. And the sky seems nothing but an abyss turned upwards.

My fingernails are pared and clean. The smell of soap wafts from my hand. He might relent and let my fingers run over the white ziggurat and be tickled by the edges of its stairways.

He is reading in his room. I stick my hand under his nose.

Only then do I notice. His books, which have always been piled haphazardly against the wall, are now stacked close to each other, in ascending order. They look more like bricks, built into a flight of stairs, which begins at ground level in one corner and ends at the ceiling of the opposite corner. In the sunbeams, motes of dust are dancing up and down the stairs, about to be eaten by the books.

—Mealtime? he mumbles.

—What's this?

But he has already left the room.

I get a new canary, and we call him Sultan again. Just as Shuli predicted, he, too, dies one day. Shortly afterward, Samson, Shuli's canary, also becomes a carcass and falls down from the swing. We bury Samson between the two Sultans.

To prevent our garden from turning into a bird cemetry, Shuli and I dispense with canaries altogether. Shuli piles dirt in the bottom of the empty cage and sticks in two stems of cactus.

—Anyway, birds should be buried in the clouds, he murmurs as he fastens the catch.

MILK TEETH

A girl is gazing into the camera, suppressing a smile which would have disclosed her two missing front teeth. A striped hair ribbon, tied in a bow, crowns her head for the studio portrait. A small medallion hangs around her neck, but one can barely see the relief of New York City. She is hugging a teddy bear, squeezing it against her chest. The gesture could be easily read as a sign of affection. Its purpose, however, is to conceal the animal's missing left leg.

It is a winter afternoon, mother and I have just returned from a stroll, and I suddenly realise Teddy-Pasha is no longer under my arm. Mother, still in her overcoat, walks back the way we came. Twenty minutes later she comes home with a mutilated Pasha. The guard at the Monument to the Unknown Soldier had picked up the single-legged animal from the pavement across the square. I drag mother to the Square of the Unknown Soldier again. We comb the place but fail to find the amputated leg. For the first time I step inside the monument's parabolic arch and lose myself in the transparent blue and grey tiling, which looks like a mosaic sky. Mother taps me on my shoulder. We should go, it's getting late, she says. Not before I have saluted the guard who is standing to attention by the commemorative fire.

Teddy's next mishap took place shortly after that.

In one of our frequent rows, Shuli snatches Pasha from my hand and flings him into the toilet bowl. As I scream in distress, he unzips his fly and pees on my teddy's face. The roar brings mother to the scene. Shuli's penis is dangling out, dripping, Pasha is floating inside the lavatory, and she still asks what the matter is. I scream, as loud as I can, that I want my Pasha back.

—But you're not taking him to bed again, she says.

Shuli smugly does up his fly. I start whining. Mother shouts until her voice drowns out mine. She will rescue Teddy-Pasha only when I keep quiet.

I hush and suck my thumb.

She flushes the water—to rinse him, she explains. Afraid to lose Pasha to the sewers, I fret and groan and grumble.

—Not another word, she warns between closed teeth.

The speed of my sucking increases. Four or five times, mother pulls the chain. Each time I think that's it, Teddy-Pasha will be swallowed up by the drains. And each time the water jets, he swerves and somersaults. When it ceases, he makes a headstand, his lone leg rising obliquely in the air. I bite my thumb in mute frenzy. Mother puts on a blue plastic glove and fishes him out at last, only to dunk him into a bucket of detergent. His fur immediately falls out, the canvas of his skin is bleached. Mother gives him one last extensive rinse, after which she hangs him by the ears on the clothesline on the balcony. The next morning, a bird shits on his head. Mother claims it will bring good fortune.

The straw of his innards takes a couple of days to dry. Only then is Teddy-Pasha allowed on my pillow again. He gives off an impersonal smell of purity.

A few months separate the studio photograph from the toilet incident. A year at most. A year during which I begin to lose my milk teeth. One after the other, they fall out, leave a gap, and sprout up again. Thank God they do it by turns. I waggle the wobbling tooth with my tongue for hours, waiting for the moment when pleasure shifts into pain.

—What happens when the permanent teeth fall out?

—You'll grow gold teeth, Shuli says.

Together with my milk teeth I am losing my spontaneity. My loyalty to a one-legged teddy bear will falter before the camera. I avoid thumb sucking in public. I stare longer in the mirror. My neck is too short, my ears are too large, my eyebrows too thick, my smile too wide.

I avoid speaking to father in the presence of my classmates. His speech is embarrassing me lately. Though his Arabic is impeccable, he has an elusive accent. Neither foreign nor vernacular, neither Jewish nor Muslim, a bit close to the Christian dialect, but not entirely that either.

His accent leads Laila to ask me whether my father is Jewish.

—Of course he is, I retort, feigning confidence.

—So why doesn't he speak like it then?

The question haunts me for a long time. I dare not confront father for fear of hurting his feelings. Mother, on the other hand, is unreliable. She would say anything just to reassure me. Shuli will not help out either, not with that disdainful look of his, as he considers whether the issue is worth the effort of answering.

I will find it out all by myself, I decide, and begin to size up my father. I examine his looks, study his habits, observe his bearing, and use every bit of information to gain clues about his origins.

He cannot read Hebrew. He cannot recite a prayer, either. His Sabbath is on Friday. He eats ham or luncheon meat at supper. We never celebrate the Seder. On Passover, he crunches his toast as if the Children of Israel had never crossed the Red Sea. His closest friend is a Muslim.

Is he Jewish or is he not?

He is a member of the Jewish School Council, which runs the educational programme in our school. He fasts and attends the synagogue on Yom Kippur. All his relatives have long ago emigrated to America. He is sceptical of each new revolutionary regime, but avoids a political opinion.

Is he Jewish or is he not?

He neither smokes, nor drinks anise-flavoured *arak*, and never stuffs himself to the full. He does not wear a moustache, does not play cards, and never cracks pumpkin seeds. He shaves daily, and wears pyjamas only in bed. Otherwise he is dressed in a suit and a tie. He eats with a knife and fork, even the drumstick, even when we have no guests. He steps aside to let mother pass first. He does not show off or raise his voice, not even around us children. He rarely acts on impulse, and is impossible to push over the brink. Though he hardly complains, he is actually very hard to please. He does not say much, but means every word to the letter.

Is he Iraqi or is he not?

His father comes from Damascus, his mother is a Baghdadi. He was born in Turkey. He counts in English. When he is upset, foreign words slip out in spite of himself. His eyes are grey-green, and his skin's so light that it instantly burns in the sun. His grizzled hair used to be light brown. Physically, I bear no resemblance to him whatsoever.

Is he my father or is he not?

He was educated at a public school in Oxford, or so he says. For four years he rowed, swam, played chess, football, and cricket. They showered in cold water and refrained from celebration, even when their team was winning. Oxford taught him self-discipline, but much about loneliness, too. Like the English he sticks to his principles, notwithstanding the changing map of the world. Like them he regularly attended the Sunday service in church.

Is he Jewish or is he not?

If he is not Jewish, he does not belong to us. And if he is not one of us, will I still be allowed to love him?

Mixed marriages are unheard of in our community, and when they do occur, the wrongdoers are completely shut out of Jewish life. Their families will sit *saba'a* for them, and no lips, not even their mothers', will utter their names again.

Contradictory data are confusing me. I would rather give up this investigation, accept the way father speaks, and love him the way he is.

It is Selma who asks next.

After a moment's hesitation, I open my heart and share my torment with her. Together we delve into the subject, stroll alongside the walls of the school grounds and go over the pros and cons. After six circuits, we are back to square one. Selma suggests asking her father, who is well acquainted with mine.

I anxiously wait for her call in the evening.

—Baba has just burst into laughter. It's beyond doubt. Your father's no less a Jew than mine or anyone else's. Yes, he's positive about it. Of course you can take Baba's word; it's as good as mine.

Her word dissolves my doubts and restores my peace of mind. Nevertheless, one word alone cannot tie together all the odd threads in my father's biography.

One morning I join him in the bathroom. His shaving brush taps the tip of my nose with foam. He is about to shave his armpit when I ask what made him, a Jew, attend church services in Oxford.

When father turns to me, I can see him blush under the lather.

—I wasn't keen on having the rough time the other Jewish boys had.

I nod, as if I have understood what he is talking about. What counts is that he did not deny being Jewish, and I am grateful enough for that. In fact, they are already falling into oblivion—his Sunday service, his apology, his anxiety, and the ordeal of the Jewish boys at the public school in Oxford.

LAURENCE

—*Inglis*, Khaled brakes to report as I come out to the street with my kite.

Pointing at the newly-let house on the opposite side, my next door neighbour gasps,

—I was the first to see them. Yesterday. They brought fourteen suitcases along. The place has been rented for 400 *dinars*, imagine!

I glance at the large two-storeyed house, which was recently redecorated, its front repainted in light green. No curtains are hanging at the windows yet.

—Is that a lot of money?

Khaled shrugs.

—I don't know! But they came by taxi. All three. Father, mother, and son. He's our age, eleven or twelve. He's got yellow hair. They all have yellow hair.

—Any idea what they do?

—IPC, Iraq Petrol Company. The father's the chairman of the Kirkuk pipeline, Khaled replies, breathlessly demonstrating his knowledge as if in a civics lesson.

—Phew...we've got some important people here. A French manager, a Danish diplomat, and now an English...

—So what? My father's a lawyer, too, and my grandfather was a cabinet minister during King Faisal's reign.

—I know, I know all that. Tell me about the English boy. What does he look like?

—I've said it already. English. Yellow hair and blue eyes. What else there is to tell?

—His hair? Is it golden yellow?

He shrugs his shoulders.

—Honey yellow? Lemon? Straw? Kraft cheese?

Khaled purses his lips thoughtfully until a malicious smile spreads over his face.

—Urine yellow!

—Is he good-looking? I persist.

—How should I know? Such trifles don't interest me anyway. They're girls' concerns, he snaps, and gets on his bike again.

As Khaled pedals away, I blow at the sumptuous tail of my kite to open it out. A long chain of white paper rings flies and falls like the veil of a bride. I wait for a car to pass then start off into the clear roadway. The kite takes to the air. I pay out string. It soars further up to the height of the roof, revealing to me the sky's third dimension, one that my eyes tend to overlook, reporting a flat surface—a kind of blue sheet hovering above the earth. Abruptly, and for no apparent reason, the kite dips. For lack of wind, I tell myself, and speed up. Nevertheless, the kite spins all the way down until it strikes its forehead against the asphalt.

I run back and pick it up, examine the edges, the skeleton, the tail. All intact. While I am rewinding the cord, the hinges of a door or window creak. My neck cranes in the direction of the green house. The front window on the ground floor has opened. I cross the street to their pavement, the kite wiggling in the air at shoulder level behind me. Leaning it, as though by chance, against their iron fence, I pretend to be untying some knots, before I casually raise my head and peer into their window. Tiny squares in different shades of grey obstruct my view. The wire netting! I should have known better. Suddenly it occurs to me that by standing outside, I am more liable to be seen from inside than the other way round. Embarrassed by the possibility of having been caught peeping, I hasten back to our side of the street.

I give the kite a second try. No use. To hell with it. I carry the kite back to the house, and return with a bag full of biscuits in the shape of animals. Still no trace of the new boy. I climb onto our fence, and seat myself on the iron railing, legs dangling over the climbing plants, my face to the street, as if waiting for a military parade to pass. Khaled, too, must be on the watch. Otherwise, he would not patrol up and down our road when his mother has recently extended his boundaries as far as the supermarket. I pour a mound of biscuits into my lap: cows, camels, fish, butterflies, giraffes. Enough to keep my teeth busy for the rest of the afternoon. Unless, of course, mother calls me to order with a tirade I know by heart: I am damaging the climbing plants, I am ruining my skirt, I am not a boy who climbs fences or an urchin who cracks seeds in the street.

I munch on a giraffe. Bite off the ears, chew the head, nibble the neck down to the hindquarters, and let the crumbs of the legs melt on my tongue. With the same thoroughness, I crunch the other animals, while cars pass by and Khaled shows off his mastery on his new Raleigh, pedalling with one wheel in the air as if on horseback. Making countless figures of eight without falling down or even getting dizzy.

While I am munching the head of a camel and Khaled is riding down the road with his hands off the handlebars, the front door of the green house clicks open. My heart misses a beat. This time, I will be the first to catch sight of our new neighbour. A boy steps out, shuts the door quietly behind him. My eyes follow him in disbelief. He gives the iron gate a push, and comes out into the street.

Where does he think he is to wrap his head in a *kaffiyah*? It is not the common gauzy black-and-white, worn by

Bedouins and peasants, but a cream *kaffiyah*, made of silk, like that of an emir. Imported directly from The Thousand and One Nights!

The sight reminds me of a card game in which people in different national and professional dress are drawn on cards and cut breadthwise into exchangeable parts. The goal of the game is to form as many complete pictures as possible, while the fun of the game is to make grotesque combinations: Eskimos in sandals, Africans in Scottish kilts, Bullfighters with legs of belly dancers, Bedouins in swallow-tailed coats.

The new boy straightens his *agal*—the cord keeping the *kaffiyah* in position—feels its adorning amber beads. Only now do I notice the rifle slung over his shoulder. Although it does not look particularly heavy, its barrel is uncommonly thick. The English boy is inspecting the street with a dispassionate gaze which is, beyond doubt, blue. It wanders from the cars parked on the side of the road, to the eucalyptus trees on the pavements, up to the streetlamps, and lingers on the birds on the telephone wire. While he is scanning the front wall and the balcony next door, my body freezes, as if about to be physically touched. I vacillate between a friendly smile and a more ambiguous, enigmatic expression. The English boy ducks me altogether by skipping his focus across our roof to the next house in the row.

At least I did not waste a smile on him.

He pulls down his rifle and aims at the telephone wire above me. No, at the birds lined on the wire. After several single shots, he kneels down and empties the gun at one go. Orange, green, yellow, violet, red, blue, and pink ping-pong balls pitter-patter along the street and pavement. In no time, Khaled appears. He rights his bicycle on its stand, and chases, together with our English neighbour, the hopping hollow balls.

A moment later, the rifle passes into Khaled's hands.

Tossing up a pink ping-pong ball in my hand, I approach the two boys. They are loading the rifle and discussing the

latest wonders of the toy weapon industry. One is speaking
in what must be the Queen's English, the other in Arabic
English. I try in vain to exchange conspiring glances with
Khaled, but he is so absorbed in the mechanics of the gun
that the English boy could be wearing underpants on his
head and he could not care less. Our new neighbour
stretches out his cupped hand towards me. I pass him the
ball, making sure our hands do not touch. He nods curtly,
then resumes his lecture on the muzzle of the rifle. I consider offering him some biscuits, but decide against the idea,
for I would not like to appear too eager to please him. So I
stand on tiptoe, my lips close to his *kaffiyah* where I
roughly estimate his ear to be, and whisper another offer.
Quietly, lest Khaled should hear and burst into laughter. For
the first time, the English boy looks me in the face. A violet
rim surrounds his dark blue irises and gives his eyes a glistening veneer, like that of a Cadbury wrapper. His eyebrows
are very fair, almost invisible.

—Show me!

I motion to him to follow me. He entrusts the rifle to
Khaled and lets himself be led, his hands tucked behind his
back. Khaled fires at the telephone wire although the birds
have flown away, since the onset of the ping pong game. The
skeleton of an old kite sways about the wire, wearily turning
in its grave.

In our back garden the English boy stands still, waiting for
my promise to be fulfilled. I point to the neighbours' loquat
and pomegranate trees across the wall, trying my best to find
a decent way out of my fabrication. His brows, quite visible
now, knit in silent indignation. He turns his back on me and
walks off. Easy come, easy go, I tell myself, withholding my
tears. He will never speak to me again. With a literal mind
like his, he must have taken my jest for a lie.

—Wait . . . listen . . . I can explain . . .

My words dash swifter than my thoughts. English words,

sounds which I can hardly claim as mine are emerging from my throat.

—My father was a camel driver, I hear myself say, as the borderline between joke and lie stretches like chewing gum into fiction.

The fiction I launched into the moment I slipped into the foreign language.

The English boy halts and looks back. His blue eyes pierce my heart like a can opener. His iceberg of a face looks exactly like a younger version of Peter O'Toole, a son of Paul Newman or of James Dean . . .

Apparently, I cannot tell blond people apart.

—He owned a camel company, I go on. It was the biggest in town. It did all the transport in the city centre.

He does not bat an eyelid.

—He would have brought his camel service to the suburbs, if not for the revolution.

The English boy wavers, then walks back. I take a deep breath, groping for a path between the fanciful and the credible.

—The government of the revolution arrested him and threw him into jail. For months he lived on dry bread and dirty water. All his camels were taken. But with his savings he later opened a shop in Suq-al-Ghasel and sold camel wool.

My English friend seats himself on our back door step. I sit beside him. The tail of his *kaffiyah* resting on the ground marks a delicate border between our thighs.

—On my tenth birthday, I received a baby camel as a present. The first weeks, I fed him on milk, bread, and dates. Every afternoon, we took him for a walk along the river bank. People pointed at him, gave him sweets, and . . .

Missing the word in English, I use my hand.

—Scratched him, he softly says.

—Yes, scratched him under the chin. When he was four months old, I threw sticks and he ran to fetch them. But not whole-heartedly. He was not really playful by nature.

—At the age of six months, his toilet training began.

The English boy voices no objection.

—By the age of eight months, he learnt his name. I called him Jemil, meaning beautiful. Not that he was a beauty in particular, but because beautiful and camel sound very similar in Arabic, *jemil* and *jemel*. Can you hear the difference?

He nods. I do not believe him.

—Well, Jemil had his difficulties. He responded to both words the same way. He'd shake his head and... and... how'd you say... bark?

He shrugs his shoulders.

—Yes, he barked whenever one spoke the word "camel" in his presence. It made people go crazy. They thought the camel understood Arabic!

The English boy giggles. I begin to feel uneasy. His own gullibility is far more ludicrous than the story I am inventing.

—When he was ten months old, we hung a basket around his neck and sent him to the *suq* with a list of groceries to bring back. But soon we had to stop, as Jemil started to devour all the dairy produce on the way back.

The English boy bursts out laughing.

—When his milk teeth fell out and the permanent ones came in, he began to eat whatever crossed his way. His jaws chewed the whole day, as if he were reflecting on some serious matter. Slippers, food cans, and books with hard covers suffered the most. Whenever we caught him with such stuff between his teeth, we'd shout *"khalas!"* and it was enough to drive Jemil to a frenzy. He would spit out the schoolbook, now a shapeless, shapeless... what? Lump? OK, now the schoolbook became a shapeless lump swimming in his saliva. Then he'd run down the stairs, bump himself left and right, jump over the parapet and escape through the living room to the garden, but not before he'd knocked a vase off a table, a picture off the wall, or even knocked down a whole bookshelf!

The English boy looks amused. I can see my words illustrated as comic strips above his head. I venture one step further.

—When he was one year old, I rode him to school.

His jaw drops with fascination. He must have lost his critical faculty. Otherwise how does he swallow all the rot I am stuffing him with? Suddenly, I take no pleasure in my conquest any more. There I am playing at Scheherazade, putting the English boy under the spell of the Orient. All well and good. But at whose expense the joke is, I can no longer tell.

Doesn't he see that we drive cars and not horses and camels, that we live in houses and not tents, that we cook on gas stoves and not on camp fires, that we turn the red tap for hot water, that we, too, have our paved streets and victory monuments, that in spite of the heat we use toasters and hair-dryers, that we cannot do without laxatives and sleeping pills? And yet he can easily picture me riding a camel to school! With a jar on my head perhaps, fetching water from the well?

Electrical appliances and paved streets do not admit you to the modern world, the English boy's infatuation is telling me. Father believes that education does. Khaled's father is more ambivalent towards the West and its so-called modernism. At times he praises its medical and technological progress, its industry, and its commitment to the written word. Other times he reviles the West as imperialist, morally decadent. It depends on what suits him at the time.

—As our house grew smaller and smaller for him, we made a hole in the ceiling so that poor Jemil could stand upright somewhere. The opening cut into my room on the second floor. But the camel's head sticking out from the floor didn't disturb me at all. I did my homework, and he stared into space for hours, chewing time away.

I pause, waiting for my English neighbour to protest, but he is speechless, enthralled by my life.

—His favourite place was the window in my room. He'd stand there for hours, his neck and head stretched outside, watching the comings and goings in the street.

I hear our car purr. Our gate jangles open. There is not much time left.

—In the garden, he devoured everything. Trees, flowers, climbing plants. It broke mother's heart to see the garden turn into a wilderness, but still she put up with it, because, you see, Jemil was in a way her baby, too.

Laurence smiles sympathetically. He knows nothing of mother's aversion to animals.

—Serious trouble began the moment he moved on to the neighbours' trees, which, as I've shown you, got shorter each day.

I point to the loquat trees across the wall, the way I did at the start of my story. This time, he nods in acknowledgement. Our car is moving into the front yard.

—We did our best to reason with them, but they refused and pressed for one and only one solution—that we get rid of the camel within a month. Otherwise they'd poison him. Actually they swore it by the Prophet. No, no, not Khaled's father, he has a heart of gold. It was the tenant before him. He terrorized us. Poor Jemil, who never went into tantrums, never bit anyone, never hurt a fly. I didn't close my eyes for nights. Father got in touch with the zoo, but they wouldn't bother about a camel. Then a rumour spread that the neighbours were planning to slaughter him and give a street banquet. My stomach turned at the idea of Jemil boiling in a pot. I insisted he sleep in my room from then on. Miraculously, one week before the deadline, an Egyptian film director called us. He was urgently looking for a camel for a film on the battles of the Caliph Omar. Perhaps you've seen it? No, the film didn't come to England? Anyway, it was decided that day, and when I returned from school, Jemil was gone.

I stop to take a breath.

—For days, my tears were running like a water tap. My eyes were so . . . large, what? Swollen? All right, my eyes were so swollen that I could hardly do my homework. Mother tried to cheer me up by saying that we now have an actor in the family. Knowing that Jemil was being treated kindly and that he was having an exciting life eventually consoled me. And believe it or not, I do catch a glimpse of him every now and then in Egyptian films on TV.

When father appears, the English boy stands up. Man and boy stare at each other, the man at the boy's *kaffiyah*, the boy at the man's suit and tie. Then they both gape at me. I remain silent, at a loss myself, too drained to offer an explanation to either of them.

—Glad to meet you, young man, father says in English at last, and stretches out his hand.

—Laurence, my pleasure, sir! Our neighbour introduces himself and shakes father's hand.

—Nice you've found yourself a new friend, Lina, father continues in English. But isn't it getting dark out here? Why don't you two go up to your room and have a game of Monopoly?

THE ENGLISH CLUB

Drained of water, the swimming pool in the English Country Club looks like a purposeless excavation. The wiggly black stripes have straightened, and the blue no longer floats but adheres to the walls and to the ground. A stone wave marks the transition between the shallow and deep ends. Eucalyptus leaves and carob pods, fallen from the surrounding trees, are scattered about. The ladders are cut short above the bottom of the pool. The diving board charcoals its shadow between two black lines. In the absence of water, depth and height have united into one dimension.

—A thirsty sight indeed, Laurence remarks.

A remark he will repeat the whole season.

—Unbelievable how dry your winter is. Put this pool in the centre of London and you'd have it filled up with rain by now.

Put it in the centre of Baghdad and you'd have it flooding with urine by now.

—It looks like a house turned upside down, I hasten to say, to drive away the stench rising in my head.

—Great! Come down, let's walk on the ceiling.

The ground gradually disappears from view as I climb down the ladder after him. Unlike the boys in my class, Laurence has the decency not to peep at my thighs from below. From the last rung, he jumps into the shallow end. Carefully I follow suit. The pleats of my dress open up like a parachute. He is heading to the deep end. A chain of clouds skims overhead and shields the blue winter sky. The dry container feels like a drawer sliding into its compartment as the sky darkens above.

Thirst saws me from within.

Although acquainted with English ways by now, I still shake my head politely each time Laurence's mother offers to treat me to a sandwich or a fizzy drink, fully aware of the consequences. Oblivious to our manners, Mrs. Langley still takes my no for an answer instead of repeating her proposal several times until I utter my consent.

No, I am neither hungry nor thirsty, thank you very much. And not greedy enough either to jump at your first offer. Why ask? Why not impose a fact upon me, the way Selma's mother does? Order a muffin, a pie, a scone, or an ice-cream soda, and see if I have the cheek to refuse? Or a Coke at least.

Laurence lies on his stomach flat on the floor. His chin and hands press against the ground while his elbows are bent upwards.

—Tell me what d'you see?

A tidy, handsome, twelve-year old is resting on the ground, not bothering about soiling his white shirt or his jeans, the blue jeans which every boy in the neighbourhood envies—as denim is not available in Baghdad. An impulse to stroke his long fair hair seizes me, not for the first time. I clasp my hands behind my back.

His hands advance, his arms pull his body forwards. The hindquarters do not cooperate though. As if a screw has come loose, his lower legs suddenly spring in the air and cross each other, reminding me of an uncoordinated grasshopper.

—A grasshopper?

—Wrong. You've got no imagination. It's a lizard, crawling on the ceiling, slowly approaching a light bulb, and just about to snatch a moth. You should have seen it in our yard yesterday. It captured twenty-three moths in one evening!

The idea of watching lizards and counting moths as an evening entertainment appalls me. Why has television been invented, after all?

—If you have to crawl, put some power into it. Be a croc-odile at least.

He frowns. He is about to tell me that I have missed the point.

—Laurence, watch out! Stop! I shriek.

His nose has, by a hair's breadth, escaped collision with an anthill. His two pupils face dozens of creatures of the same size and colour, pouring in and out of the sand. He sits up. I squat down. The ants proceed with their activity. In great haste, as if their industry is shaping the future, unaware of their liquidation at the end of the season with the first jet of water.

Laurence has been playing with similar fantasies.

—I wonder what they'd do if I pissed into their mound!

—Do boys everywhere pee in the open?

Laurence snickers and tells me about the bronze stripling who pees into a fountain in the old city of Brussels. Can I still blame Baghdad for what is equally celebrated in Brussels? I stand up to collect carob pods. Laurence declares,

—What an ideal shelter! It's a trench we've got here!

I refuse him the attention he is requesting and go on pick-ing up carob pods. Cautious not to stoop and expose my thighs, I keep sitting and standing and sitting down again. Laurence paces the length of the pool, his hands behind his back, soliloquising.

—If only the boys were around, we'd have played at sol-diers. What a battle it would have been . . . we'd have carried on for days without interruption. Imagine, days without food or sleep, just like men at the front.

Does he truly miss such childish games with his English friends or is he only trying to make me jealous?

Unlike other English children whose parents work in Baghdad, Laurence does not go to boarding school in England but studies at home, by correspondence. Though he obviously prefers my company to that of the other children in the street, he never gives me the feeling that he actually enjoys it. He does not smile when he drops by, but greets me with a nod and a hello. Hardly audible, lest his voice be wasted on a banality. Sometimes he holds out his hand, like somebody who has come to do business. And even then, he draws it back in the middle of a shake, as if afraid I would walk away with it.

—Down here, in this vast pool? I reply. You must be kidding. One air raid and all your boys are dead soldiers. They'd be lying side by side, head to foot, like sardines in a tin.

Laurence relinquishes the ditch and proceeds to the next round.

Once upon a time, a Greek fellow descended to the underworld in order to recover his deceased sweetheart. After a series of exploits and hindrances he manages to find her. On their way back home, however, he commits a fatal mistake. He turns round and looks back—like Lot's wife, I suppose. Needless to say, his beloved vanishes on the spot, and he returns alone to the world of the living.

Laurence wants me to play the dead girlfriend!

It would be just like him to scour the ends of the world for a lost love, particular about his belongings as he is. Not only does he withdraw his hand before it is properly shaken, but he also recovers his jigsaw puzzles before I have finished assembling them, and feels the urge to browse in those particular comics he has lent me.

Am I prepared to die for him?

I dismiss the game as unlikely and propose that we play at Jonah. The prophet has been swallowed by a whale and has had to wait three days and three nights in its intestine until the beast burped and catapulted him out into the ocean.

Will he agree to be locked in with me for three whole days?

The game sounds dull to him. Why not a submarine? I do not object. He takes a piece of chalk out of his pocket and breaks it in two. We draw round white windows on the blue walls of our submarine, through which we will watch underwater life.

For a whole winter, the waterless pool will serve us as a toy box, a container for our games and fantasies.

Laurence chalks a round fountain on the wall of the pool. I draw an octopus beside it. Its arms creep underwater and emerge at the circumference. The eight tentacles curve inward, and pour out water into the centre. The octopus is taking a shower, Laurence says, and adds a few coins at the bottom of his fountain. On the largest of them he sketches the profile of a woman with a crown on her head.

—Is your queen thirsty?

It is a wishing fountain, like the one he has seen in Rome. Its floor was covered with coins from all over the world. People, children and grown-ups alike, flipped a coin and made a wish. He tried it a couple of times himself, and the wish always came true.

My turn. I sketch a coin falling into the water. It has a scalloped circumference and "10 *fils*" marked in the middle. I close my eyes and make a wish.

My checked dress is being torn apart, cut with scissors into hundreds of small green squares. They are floating, like leaves, on the surface of the water. Hundreds of brass and silver coins, profiles of celebrities, are watching the scene from the bottom of the fountain. My new blue overall has two large hip pockets into which my hands can slide whenever they feel observed. Laurence and I are strolling in the English club. Nobody grumbles that it is improper for a girl to run around in jeans.

I open my eyes again. Laurence is staring at me. His brows are very fair, almost white. His unruffled expression is harder to decipher than his father's. Reveal my wish? I am taken by surprise. Why me first? No, I don't argue about everything. What about you? No I'm not, I'm not a chicken.

I tell him I was dreaming of a walk through London. Where exactly? Mayfair, Park Lane, Regent Street, Bond Street, all in the same neighbourhood. How do I know? That's how they're arranged on the Monopoly board. Why is he laughing?

—Is that true? Is that what you were really thinking of just a second ago?

—I don't know. All my dreams collapse when I open my eyes. I can never put them together again. Like, like what's his name, that egg of a man?

—Humpty Dumpty?

—Right. You now. You tell me, what was your wish?

He was dreaming of a gold medal in the next diving competition. It would be his fifth. It is my turn to doubt his words.

—Barmecide medals!

Then I have to explain. Barmecide was an emir in The Arabian Nights—about which Laurence is such an enthusiast. Today, his name stands for exaggeration if not deceit, as he, Barmecide, used to serve empty plates to beggars and claim they were full of food.

Laurence is not amused by the comparison. He sneers at me, then swaggers out of the pool, onto the diving-board.

He advances to the end of the bouncey plank, some fifteen feet up—the height of the board added to the depth of the pool. I move to the deep end of the pool to get a closer view of him. While I am still on my way, Laurence, without warning, makes a handstand, and before I have had time to take fright, he has sprung back to his feet again. I applaud him fervently. His fearlessness alone has won him my admiration, I shout, beckoning him down. Laurence takes off his shoes and twirls them flirtatiously, before tossing them down to me. His show has only just begun, he announces. I pick up his shoes and plunge my hands inside, feeling the warmth of his feet. He is wiggling the board, testing its flexibility, tempting fate, I dare say. My heart is pounding. I can neither look at him nor look away. He is jumping, each time bouncing higher in the air, his straight soft hair like the flapping wings of a bird.

—I'll show you a swallow dive.

Before I have asked what a swallow dive is, he bends his legs, and throws himself still higher. In midair his body pikes, his back arches, his arms stretch out to the sides. When called by the force of gravity, Laurence straightens himself and lands back on his feet on the board.

I clap the soles of his shoes, applauding him again, longer than the first time. None of the boys in my class are capable of such a performance. Certainly not of such courage. He can keep the coin in his pocket, the gold medal is his without doubt. He's a true diving champion. And an acrobat. Can't he quit the dangerous game and come down now?

—Now a jackknife!

And the golden boy takes to the air. Once, twice, and three times, before his waist bends and his arms stretch overhead. His fingers touch his toes. His legs, his arms, and his back draw a triangle in the blue sky. Immediately the triangle opens up, and its sides unfold into one vertical line again.

In spite of his nimbleness, Laurence's movements do not suggest haste. Apparently, speed has not so much to do with being in a hurry as with stretching time!

I blurt out my infatuation for his illusory slowness. It incites him to demonstrate one last jackknife. In slow motion, he tenses, and flits upwards. His waist twists, his fingers and toes touch. A cry escapes me. Terrific! His head slightly rises, his eyes meet mine for a fraction of a second. Time enough to steal away his concentration. His arms are waggling. His legs are fluttering. His body has seemingly forgotten what to do next: return with the feet to the board or plunge headlong into the concrete box?

In less than no time his bones will crash at my feet. His teeth will roll, like dice, about the pool. His mother will kill me. And I don't even know my way to the underworld . . .

Fortunately, his feet remember. He is back, safe and sound, on the plank. But just then, seized by a sudden fear of heights, he starts tottering. About to lose balance, he crouches down and, shivering, crawls along to the firm end of the board.

The flexing of the diving-board slowly dies down. Laurence's face has turned grey, like those immortal profiles scattered in the bottom of the fountain, waiting on the wishes of the living.

December is the month when his wishes are most likely to come true.

A Christmas tree three times my size, trimmed with tinsel, is placed beside reception to adorn the entrance hall of the Club. Bright balls dangle from its branches, as well as winged angels, dressed or naked, singing or lazing on a cloud. I am fascinated by the heap of wrapped presents at the foot of the tree. Laurence assures me that the packages are empty.

Paper bells and lanterns and golden stars and motley garlands and balloons festoon each room in the Club. In the tearoom, the French windows are dressed with cotton snowflakes, like the shop windows of Christians in our neighbourhood.

—It's not Christmas without snow, Laurence explains.

On the blue wall of the pool he draws a white tennis ball that keeps on swelling as the chalk grows shorter. He uses them up, one piece after the other, until the whole box ends up chalked on the wall. Three white balls are placed on top of each other. The one at the bottom is the largest.

Laurence rubs his finger in the chalk and removes it from a few places. Two cavities emerge, a carrotlike nose, a muffler, a stick.

Like him, the snowman has blue eyes.

I try my hand and rub more chalk away. New features in blue appear: a few hairs on the forehead, two eyebrows, a mouth. The snowman is not smiling. I add a corrugated beard to his face.

—That's Bluebeard! Do you know the story?

—Sure! Any rooms in the Club I'm not allowed into? I reply, playfully.

He bursts out laughing.

—The gentlemen's lavatories! Three of them. But if you're keen on exploring them, be my guest!

I do not reply.

—Honestly, it's not forbidden. Nobody's going to behead you.

My ears feel hot. I may well be blushing.

—Come on, I'll give you a guided tour!

And like a gentleman, he offers me his arm. *Bras dessus, bras dessous*, we have spent a whole lesson practising the distinction between the French 'u' and 'ou'. But I have never seen it for real, a man and a woman walking arm in arm. Only in foreign magazines and foreign films. A courteous gesture, if only he were not mocking me. I push his arm away and slap his shoulder. He snickers and offers his arm again, elegantly, as if it were an invitation to dance. Again I push it away and punch his chest. He does not condescend to ward off my blows. I try to poke his ribs with my fingers, but he deflects them with one arm. I would do anything to wipe that confident smile off his face. The more amused he looks, the angrier I am. How do the boys in our street tease him?

I flick my hand at his long locks and make the sound of a long kiss.

—Sissy!

Before I realise it, his arm has surrounded my neck while he drags me backward. My knees give in. I lose balance and fall. He plops down on my belly and pinions my arms over my head.

—Say sorry.

—You should say sorry, you started it.

So what? He is the stronger. Nevertheless, he is ready to compromise for a peaceful surrender. Over my dead body! I slash back, fuming with pride and making a new attempt to release my hands. Flounder, buck, worm, wiggle. Nothing doing. His grip is too tight. Cemented. While every square of my checked dress is itching at the back and at the thighs.

—You have no choice, he whispers

I scratch his hands with my fingernails and pierce his flesh. A cry of pain escapes him, but his expression does not change. Carefully, his grip crawls down to my wrists, out of my nails' reach. Then he grins again, secure enough to find my resistance cute.

Two blows in the back take him by surprise and thrust him forwards. His eyes roll as he drops on me, squealing. I pull up my knees and fling myself upwards, taking advantage of his momentary upset. My arms shove against his. My shoulders join forces and push. Blood rushes into my head. It is now or never. Sweat drips down my back. His elbows are bending. Our eyes meet on the same level at last. His head slowly slopes backward. I am winning! His face is flushing from exertion. I am the stronger. I'd love him with his ugly grimaces too, I tell myself, already thinking with the generosity of a winner.

A sudden bellow ends my short-lived glee. Startled by his battle cry, my arms loosen. One moment later, his head jerks and faces mine. Two moments later, it is looking over me. My backbone recognises the cold concrete. My head bangs on the ground. His arms force mine to my sides. His legs pin down mine. Our limbs stop struggling, all eight together, bundled in twos.

—Say sorry.

He is breathing on my neck. His warmth covers me like a blanket. A lock of his hair grazes my forehead. I can smell him sweating. The odour is foreign, blond—lighter, sharper than my own. His heart flutters between my breasts—hot and flat like two slices of toast.

—Go to hell, I answer back.

Surrender. Hands off me. Say sorry. You say sorry. I hate you. And other exchanges of this sort divert us from the closeness of our bodies and from the hard swelling in his groin. Is that his penis resting between my thighs? But why so bulky?

I never thought . . . Are we doing something wrong? What if mother saw us? Will father disapprove terribly? It is not my fault! He is the one who started it, and he is not getting an apology from me.

I should resort to passive resistance. Try it Gandhi's way. It worked with the English, they say. Let mind and muscles relax, let me sink under him, and let him sort it out. It is the least a winner can do. The checked dress is chafing every inch of my skin. His hip joint is prodding at my flesh. A drop of sweat slides down his cheek and lands on my lower lip. His legs are pressing against mine. A wave of heat flits through my belly. My throat is sore. I am dying for a glass of water.

—Say sorry . . .

He is almost begging. I keep quiet. If he can prolong time with his speed, I can stop it with my silence. He is fidgeting. My eyelashes have tickled his neck. It is tense and vulnerable. It succumbs to the strain and his head falls beside mine. He is shivering. His forehead is all sweat. He is about to burst.

—I'll hold you down forever, he cries out impatiently.

—I'll cry for help, you big fat bully.

Damn it! I should have kept my mouth shut instead of committing myself to action. Suppose my voice crosses the playground and the lawn and startles Laurence's mother in the bridge room, or worse, disturbs his father, who is leafing through pink newspapers in the library and biting at his pipe as if it were the Kirkuk pipeline itself? Never again will they invite the loud Iraqi neighbour to their orderly club, where members tiptoe through the premises, open and close doors as gently as if they were in a hospital, play bingo and watch tennis matches with incomprehensible listlessness. Not even under curfew would a residential sidestreet in Baghdad be half as quiet as the English Club on a normal day.

Was it with the same quietness that the English dominated half the globe only a century ago?

—Help, I bawl at last into Laurence's ear, loud enough to perforate his eardrum.

It takes me three such screams to hurl him to the ground.

—It's prickling everywhere, all over my body, he yells.

Black ants are racing up his legs and back. A few inches from our feet, they are running erratically in and out and around their battered fortress, the way the old Judeans must have mourned their destroyed temple two thousand years ago. Have Laurence and I trampled down their hill during our struggle? Suddenly I realise that it was not my dress itching after all, but the ants, in dozens, meandering about my body and biting my flesh.

Laurence clambers up the ladder and runs howling towards the changing rooms. I bolt after him. The two wooden doors are locked. He crawls through the wide opening underneath. I hesitate for a moment before the silhouette in trousers nailed on the door, then duck my head and follow him into the men's room.

His clothes rapidly pile up on the floor. Dozens of ants are skittering in and out, down and up, covering routes similar to the ones their sisters must be tracing on my skin. If I do not immediately undress, they will eat me up, reduce me to a heap of clothes beside Laurence's.

He darts naked under the shower. He is yelping, now because of the cold water. I scrutinise his hairless body from top to toe, as white as chalk. His hair has turned brown and sleek. His penis is bouncing up and down like the diving-board. He is raining ants. They swim and whirl around his feet before draining away into the plughole.

—It's getting warm, he says, relieved, his voice fenced in the patter of water.

Hearing no answer, he peers at me from under the shower. His hands instantly twitch and cover his privates.

—Go away! he hollers. Go to the ladies' room.

—You said I was your guest!

—Get lost I said!

—The dress ripped as I took it off in the changing room, I tell mother later that evening, tucked up in bed. Driven crazy by the bites, I couldn't wait to unzip it. Even after the shower, I caught two ants in my left ear, one between the layers of my eyelid, one between the folds of my navel, and another . . . in my genitals.

Mother sits on my bed and mends the seam in sombre silence. I hug Teddy-Pasha who whispers her unspoken thoughts in my ear. Why did they fool about in the changing rooms? The girl's too old to be playing with a boy. I should speak with her father. We ought to put an end to this relationship before it is too late. Before the neighbours start talking. I wonder if she has told me the whole story. I have a hunch that she is keeping something back.

I gulp down the bottle of water on my night table.

—Mama . . .

She raises her brows, about to squeeze a confession out of me.

A sneeze comes to my rescue. An ant rushes out from the

hem of the dress. Mother and I burst into laughter. She blows the lone beast away, the mite of evidence of my incomplete account.

—Mama, I spoke English the whole day.

She stands up and hangs the checked dress in my wardrobe.

—You're old enough to be mending your clothes by yourself. Girls your age sew their own dresses and knit their own pullovers. Now cover yourself well. I hope you didn't catch cold.

She kisses me on the cheek and turns off the light.

When thirst wakes me up in the middle of the night, I find poor Pasha strangled between my thighs.

PURIM

In the sixth century B.C., Judea falls to Nebuchadnezzer. The Temple is destroyed, and the Judeans are deported en masse to Babylon. Five decades later, Babylonia in her turn is conquered by the Persians. Cyrus the Great allows the Judean captives to return to Jerusalem and rebuild their temple. But Persia is tolerant and the Judeans are wealthy and assimilated. So they remain in Persia and send money for the reconstruction of the temple in Jerusalem.

Can anyone imagine a Jewish queen in the diaspora? It could only happen in Susa, the capital of Persia, when King Ahashwerosh fell in love with and married the beautiful Esther.

Without inquiring about her origins.

Now Persia is rich and liberal, and Mordechai, Esther's uncle, is a devoted courtier. But he is careful, too. He advises Esther to conceal her true identity and keep quiet about their family relationship. In case a new wind blows.

In case trouble knocks at the door of history.

Trouble comes in the form of Hamman. He is the personification of evil and he has just been made a grand vizier. Mordechai refuses to bow to him. Hamman is insulted. Not only is Mordechai a traitor, Hamman whispers in the King's ear, all the Jews are a threat to the Persian empire. A crazy argument, but Ahashwerosh listens. Not only should Mordechai be hanged, but all the Jews will have to be destroyed. A fanatical proposition, but the King agrees.

Mordechai urges Esther to intervene on behalf of her people. She hesitates. The Queen is not to meddle in the King's affairs. Mordechai does not relent; the danger is imminent. Esther despairs. The King executes whomever steps into his inner court unsummoned. Mordechai reminds her that her fate is bound to that of her people. Hamman casts lots to determine the right day for the destruction of the Jews. Esther calls on the King. Mordechai fasts and prays. Esther uses her beauty to open the King's eyes. Hamman is the one who is hanged the next morning and not Mordechai. Esther has gambled with her life and rescued her people from destruction.

—And that's why we call it Purim, which means lottery, *ustad* Heskel explains, the way he does each year after he has related the story of Beautiful Esther, Pious Mordechai, and Hamman the Wicked, as if they were characters in a puppet show.

—The Book of Esther demonstrates the vulnerability of the Jews in the diaspora. No matter how safe their situation seems to be, they...

And each year the moral of Purim is drowned by the school bell, piercing the premises for twenty seconds, delivering twenty-five classrooms from the tyranny of education. No authority, not even a biblical one, can hold back the children after the bell. The savages fling chalk and date pits at each other and roar at the top of their voices. *Ustad* Heskel strokes his white three-week-old beard, which gives him the appearance of a Jew in permanent mourning. Only through the abrupt wildness of the children does he realise that his time is over. He has become almost deaf lately and does not even hear the bell. A Hebrew prayer book drops to the floor. He is about to remonstrate, but the pupil picks up the book, kisses it, and slips it into his satchel.

Ustad Heskel puts on his *sidarah*, the headwear that only elderly Jewish men wear nowadays. The classroom is already empty. He smiles. On Purim, fun and merriment are commanded. The Feast of the Mjellah belongs to the children after all. For two days, they are allowed to do what Esther did—gamble.

His head goes on shaking. He is no longer in full control of the muscles of his neck, but he still carries his body straight, an ancient *ustad*, the oldest of all teachers, father of the century.

When the century was born, they say, *ustad* Heskel begged his father, the rabbi, not to send him to a yeshivah but to secondary school, like the other boys in the neighbourhood. The boy's wish was painful to the man. Yet how could the son marvel at the promises of electricity more than at the coming of the Messiah, and not break his father's heart?

When the century was eight years of age, *ustad* Heskel graduated from secondary school. In October of the same year, the Young Turks proclaimed that all the subjects of the Ottoman Empire, Muslims and non-Muslims, would be equal citizens and treated alike.

Were the Ottomans truly prepared to abolish the Islamic law regarding the *dhimmis*—the protected, socially inferior religious minorities—and exchange it for novel ideas such as liberty, equality, and fraternity? *Ustad* Heskel had good reason to ask.

His encounter with equality began with a drawback, compulsory military service. In the middle of the First World War, he found himself in uniform, untrained, on the way to the Caucasian front. His unit was so ill-clad and ill-supplied that it had little chance of survival in the

Caucasian winter. He deserted at the first opportunity, escaping the cannons of the Russians and the rifles of his own Ottoman officers. In one of the villages, he traded his uniform for food and a rag of an overcoat, which helped him to pose as an Armenian refugee whenever he came across a Russian regiment, and as a Kurd when the troops turned out to be Turkish. They did not believe his ruse but found him too lousy to waste a bullet on. So they set him free, battered, starving, and disoriented in the mountains of Persia. Luckily, he was knocked down by a jeep full of English missionaries who felt so awfully sorry about the accident that they offered him a lift to Kurdistan. From there he set off on foot to Baghdad, and reached it in February 1917.

His own mother did not recognise him. She handed the stinking *derwish*—beggar—bread and a bottle of water from between the bars of the gate, and told him off.

One month later, General Maude marched at the head of the British army into Baghdad.

The Ottomans blew up the Talisman Gate and retreated. Maude entered a desert city, destitute of palaces and pleasure grounds and orchards and pavilions and harems to entertain one thousand and one soldiers. They say no traces of the original Abbasid capital were preserved after the Mongol invasions in the thirteenth and fourteenth centuries. A miserable phoenix rose from the ashes, bound to a legendary name it would never live up to. The city Maude entered was a patchwork of living quarters based on religious and ethnic divisions—Sunni, Shia, Jewish, Christian, Kurdish, Armenian, Persian, Turkish, all strewn along the two banks of the Tigris. Each neighbourood had its *suqs*, *hammams*, *khans*, and houses of prayer. Each was a maze of twisted alleyways that tunnelled through crowded houses, seeking shade under the overhanging balconies. And then, of course, there was the citadel, the boat bridge, hospitals, private schools, a telegraph service, and an unfinished railway station whose track had once been destined to end in Berlin.

When flood protection dykes were in place, Baghdad soon expanded under the British colonial administration. British architects, who worked with a triangle and a ruler, laid out new streets, broad and straight, parallel to the river and to each other. They were crossed at right angles by sidestreets, similarly straight, wide enough to allow the passage of *arabanas*, horse-drawn carriages. The Round City was stretched northward and southward; two pontoon bridges were added. The straight line changed the sense of distance in the city; the four wheels challenged its sense of time. The main road, Khalil Pasha, was regraded and paved. Arcades and shaded pavements were built on its two sides. It was renamed New Street, and became Baghdad's modern commercial centre, on which the city galloped into the twentieth century. The wealthy and the educated took off their *kaffiyahs*, *dishdashas*, and *zbouns*, and slid into white shirts, ties, and suits. They held a cigarette in one hand, thumbed worry beads with the other, celebrating the *effendis* they were—vain gentlemen of the East.

To be or not to be . . . How familiar the question must have sounded in Maude's Irish ears, even in Arabic, when the General attended a performance of *Hamlet* in one of Baghdad's Jewish schools as guest of honour.

To his misfortune, General Maude was stricken with cholera two days later, and ceased to be.

As for the Jewish community, which constituted one quarter of Baghdad's population, its life was revived by the British occupation. British laws were as straight as the streets they cut and, unlike the Ottomans, they applied them to the letter. They taxed impartially and were unschooled in the art of bribery. The predictability of their rule safeguarded life and guaranteed personal property. Business improved after the war. Opportunities for the educated, regardless of their religion, opened up in every field. The brave new world was knocking at their door and they were not going to send it away.

Ustad Heskel got married and set up his own import–export business. From his office window in New Street, he would keep his finger on the pulse of the city for decades to come.

His first son was born in 1921. He called him Faisal, after the first King of Iraq, crowned in the summer of that year. Shortly after the British had placed the king on the throne, the Jews of Baghdad held a reception in his honour in the Great Synagogue. King Faisal I, son of Hussein, the Sharif of Mecca, astonished his hosts and all the other notable guests by kissing the Torah Scroll and embracing the Hacham Bashi, the chief rabbi of the community. Then he delivered that unforgettable speech in which he acknowledged the con- tribution of the Jews to the development of modern Iraq, and added that both Arabs and Jews were Semites, related by their biblical forefather, Shem.

The entire community was fed on the King's words, and his liberal spirit was to breed a generation of patriotic Arab Jews. Arab Jews, what a paradox. It would be hard enough for the children of the sixties to picture an Iraqi parliament, no less one with seats for the Jews! They also could not have imagined how in the twenties and thirties and as late as the forties, Jewish poets had written love poems to Arabic, their mother-tongue, and how Jewish journalists had aspired to shape the new kingdom, their *watan*, their homeland. *Watan*, what is it, the Jewish children, born half a century later, would question? How could one possibly be infatuated by earth, plain dirt under one's feet?

Horses clopped on the paved streets, electricity and tele- phone poles stood up as tall as palm trees, from which hung cables, as if to start a game of eat's cradle. Streetlamps burned all night, making starlight superfluous, and, much later, romantic. Sewers were dug under the earth, houses were numbered, a new currency was introduced, and postage stamps printed. Order was slowly emerging from the shambles.

In 1932, the British ended their fifteen-year mandate. Iraq was the first Arab state to gain independence and to be admitted to the League of Nations. From his office window in New Street, *ustad* Heskel watched the last of the British troops leave.

Please don't go away... don't leave us alone with the Arabs, a voice cried after them.

It issued from the back of his office. *Ustad* Heskel turned, but he was alone in the room. The recently installed telephone was ringing.

Patches of green sprouted in the capital. Public parks were built in the new residential areas. Walled gardens surrounded the new houses, replacing the inner courtyards, the heart of the oriental home. Circular lawns were planted at street intersections, flowers and shrubs coloured the centre of avenues, and eucalyptus trees lined the pavements. But the desert city did not turn into an oasis, nor did the greenery induce halftones in the vision of the Baghdadis or coolness into their temper.

The modern neighbourhoods based on social classes broke up the centuries-long tradition of religious and ethnic divisions. Like hundreds of other Jewish families, *ustad* Heskel moved with his wife and six children from the Jewish quarter southward to a mixed middle-class district.

In 1933, King Faisal died and his son, Ghazi, succeeded him to the throne. The procession of the young King passed in front of *ustad* Heskel's office in New Street, which was about to be renamed Rashid Street.

But no sooner was the city restored to its owners than armed tribesmen from the Middle Euphrates roamed its streets, protesting against national conscription and land reforms. The Iraqi army was dispatched throughout the country to crush the uprisings and to force the tribes to submit to the authority of the state. On their return, the victorious soldiers paraded through the streets of the capital. Flowers and rosewater showered from the rooftops onto the smart boys in uniform. Politicians, too, would resort to the army to settle disputes in the cabinet. Military planes often roared in the sky. A putsch was announced, the fall of a government, the emergence of a new leader. Five coups erupted in the second half of the 1930's. The radio blessed each in turn. Rumours elaborated upon the mistrusted official reports. People slighted their politicians, joked about their speeches, gossiped about the intrigues in the palace, and put all the blame on the English. Then the dice clacked, coffee was sipped, and radio music resumed.

They say that Baghdadis will dance to any tune you play them.

But they danced most fervently to the anthems of nationalism, and drew their example from Nazism. Hadn't the Fuhrer united the German people and rescued them from national disgrace? *Mein Kampf* appeared in Arabic as a serial in a local newspaper. Prams with baby boys named after Hitler and Himmler and Rommel proliferated. At the barber's, while the razor was scraping smooth surfaces along his foamed face, *ustad* Heskel suddenly realised to what the radio was tuned. Swifter than any railroad, radio waves brought Berlin's broadcast in Arabic directly to Baghdad. Street demonstrations against the British increased, against their policy in Palestine, and against Zionism. Heads of the Jewish community publicly distinguished between Judaism and Zionism, and repeatedly dissociated their community from the latter. To no avail. Assaults upon Jews in the streets persisted.

Never trust a Muslim, not even in his grave, says a Jewish idiom.

Had it been a blunder to move out of the Jewish quarter? Did a Jew stand out in a mixed neighbourhood? A fear older than himself was dug out from *ustad* Heskel's heart. For centuries, the Jews were prohibited from bearing weapons and from striking back at a Muslim, even with a bare hand. No wonder that the image of the Jew in the Muslim world was that of a weakling, a despicable coward. But where could he learn fighting? In the war *ustad* Heskel had learned only to flee. Perhaps he was a coward after all. So who would defend his family if the need arose? The British army was too far away, and, although he was still an observant Jew, he had long forgotten how to pray with his heart.

In the spring of 1941, Radio Baghdad proclaimed a sixth putsch. The new cabinet consisted mainly of Nazi sympathisers. Italy and Germany supported the new government. Controversies with Britain escalated into an armed conflict. Iraqi and British aircraft were seen in air battles above the capital. A month later, when British planes rose all alone in the sky, the government of Iraq had to fall.

During the two lawless days that followed, a pogrom against the Jews broke out.

Pillage, rape, havoc, and murder make up the universal language of pogroms. The Jewish quarters of Baghdad were assaulted by Iraqi soldiers, by tribesmen and by townsmen, by growling men, women, and children. Within two days, they murdered hundreds of Jews and wounded thousands.

Ustad Heskel and his family were not hurt. No hostilities had taken place in their mixed neighbourhood. On the contrary, Muslim families had offered them refuge. As for the British army, it turned out to be not so far away after all. It stood on the outskirts of the city, under orders not to interfere.

It became clear at last to *ustad* Heskel that the British would not lift a finger unless it was in their own interest. But nobody could deny that the streets were safer when the British troops were present. And the streets remained safe until the end of the war, as troops of the Allies were stationed in Baghdad on their way to, and back from, North Africa.

Subsequently, when Europeans queued for food and European Jews lined up for the gas chambers, business boomed in Baghdad and *ustad* Heskel, among thousands of other merchants, made his fortune.

In the meantime, his children had grown up with minds of their own, deeply marked by the *farhood*, the pogrom. If it had lasted a few days longer, none of the mixed neighbourhoods would have been spared, they assured him. They blamed him for accepting pogroms as an inevitable part of life. They claimed that he had the soul of a *dhimmi*, who turned invisible whenever a Muslim foamed at the mouth. The more harshly they flayed him, the more sophisticated they appeared in their own eyes. As a youth, he had himself broken his own father's heart by not devoting his life to the study of the Torah. But had he cut the old man to pieces only to feel free to go his own way? *Ustad* Heskel did not remember.

Half of them joined the *Tnuah*, the underground Zionist movement, where they were trained to shoot and defend the community if necessary, and where they learned modern Hebrew—in preparation for *Eretz Israel*. The other half identified with the oppressed masses in Iraq and found their answers in communism. Two ideologies under one roof, two revolutions in one dining room—what clashes *ustad* Heskel had to put up with. How rebellious and righteous they all sounded, even the girls—he could side with none. Meddling in politics would bring nothing but disaster, not only to themselves but to the whole community.

His words were heeded no more than the babble of the radio stations they swept across in search of news.

Without prior illness, his wife passed away one night, leaving *ustad* Heskel alone with half a dozen offspring who, each day, ceased to look like his own. Loneliness he could slowly learn to bear, but his life was bereft of meaning. Why had he neglected his devotion to God, he asked himself over and over again.

In 1948, the state of Israel was founded. Mullahs cried "*Jihad*" in the mosques of Baghdad, students went on strike, and demonstrations urged the government to take up arms. Iraq followed the decision of the Arab League and sent its regular army to the front.

Martial law was imposed throughout the country. Thousands of communists, Zionists, and Jews were arrested and detained in a special camp in the southern desert. A wealthy businessman, Shafiq Adas, who lunched with ministers and dined with the Regent, the richest Jew in Iraq it was said, found himself accused of communism and of Zionism at the same time. Though the military court presented no evidence of his arms trade with the Zionists in Palestine, Adas was sentenced to death. He was publicly executed in front of his mansion in Basra. Crowds gathered to watch the spectacle and their cheers incited the hangman to a repeat performance. The next day, close-up shots of the hanged man covered the front pages of Iraqi newspapers. His neck was broken, his corpse dangled over his puddle of excrement. He was labelled the Serpent, the Traitor, the Spy, the Zionist, the Jew, while his estate worth millions was appropriated by the Ministry of Defense.

But he did not bequeath any Arabic Émile Zola.

And the wave of arrests continued. All government departments dismissed their Jewish officials and employees. The Ministry of Commerce refused to renew licences for Jewish merchants. The Ministry of Defense forbade Jewish bankers to conduct transactions with foreign banks. The Ministry of Health would not issue medical licences to newly graduated Jewish doctors. The Ministry of Education reduced its quota of Jewish university students. The official language used the terms Zionist and Jew as synonyms. Street hostilities against the Jews increased. A synagogue was desecrated by a group of demonstrators. Nuri al-Said, the Prime Minister, called the Jews of the Arab World hostages. Illegal emigration of young Jews who refused to be hostages of Arab moods increased.

And *ustad* Heskel had to deal with a son in prison, two underage daughters on their way to Israel, and a business licence about to expire.

Unable to control the illegal emigration, the government finally decreed a *taskit*, a law of denaturalisation in 1950. It allowed the Jews to emigrate to Israel, provided they gave up their Iraqi citizenship.

The first weeks, hardly anyone deigned to consider the offer seriously. Tension would soon abate, they all said, and life in Baghdad would resume its normal course. Who, apart from some rash youngsters, was eager to emigrate anyway? Could middle-class merchants turn into farmers within one lifetime? Who was keen on having his sons drafted into the army, and who could tell if the new state would survive the next war?

They were the Babylonian Jewry, they did not forget. They were the First Exiles, whom God had sent back to the native land of Abraham. They had been living in Mesopotamia for the last twenty-five centuries, for one hundred generations, one thousand years before it had occured to the Arabs to invade it. It was here that the first synagogue had been erected. It was in the academies across the river that the Talmud had been put together. Didn't these contributions carry any weight? Didn't their history commit them to continuity?

Was it possible that all *ustad* Heskel's friends were indifferent to *Eretz Israel*? Israel, he repeated to himself, what a sonorous sound! It had obstinately persisted throughout the centuries, a Holy Promise transformed into a tangible reality. A piece of land and a flag, a cloth whipped by the wind and defended by a row of tanks.

All its stores, without exception, closed on Saturdays, they said, as Saturday was the official day of rest. Over there, even housewives scribbled their shopping lists in the holy language. Over there he would fill out forms, sign cheques, call a cab, have a haircut, read a newspaper, gamble on a horse, order a drink . . . all in Hebrew. And each sentence would sound like a prayer.

He could not help it; Israel made him sentimental.

They said that over there even the policemen were Jews. No, he would not be content with tolerance. In the Jewish state he would belong, he would be a citizen. His rights would not be bestowed as a favour, he would take them for granted. He would be nobody's Jew any more. After twenty-five centuries of exile, *ustad* Heskel was given the chance to part, once and for all, with fear.

Is home merely the place where he can fall asleep in safety? The rash youngsters signed up with enthusiasm. They swept along their friends, who dragged their siblings, who blackmailed their parents, who convinced their relatives, who left no choice for the grandmother, who shocked her neighbours with her determination. The chain reaction was expanding beyond all expectations. And then a bomb exploded in a café frequented by Jews, followed by another in a synagogue, a warning sent to the other half of the community, to those minds who were not set on leaving.

A rumour circulated that the Zionist underground had a hand in the bombings. The Zionists in their turn put the blame on Arab nationalists. But whether Jewish- or Arab-made, the bombs brought about a turning point in the attitude towards emigration. From that day on, it was departure that became self-evident, while staying required a decision and a series of justifications.

Within a year, over 100,000 Jews gave away their Iraqi identity cards and prepared themselves for the transfer, or the exodus, as they would rather call it. Among them were *ustad*

Heskel's children, Zionists and communists alike, some eagerly, others reluctantly. His elderly parents were packing as well, possessed by the idea of being buried in the Holy Land.

As if the earthworms had turned holy too.

Ustad Heskel was caught up between the piety of his parents and the pioneer spirit of the youth. He felt neither old enough to celebrate his death nor young enough to rely on the promises of the future. Carefully he went over his daughters' letters from Israel until he reached his own conclusion. Pioneers his children might well be—as for him, he would only end up as a refugee in the new country.

In 1951, on the day that the *taskit* expired, the Iraqi parliament passed a new law which froze the possessions of all the Jews who had registered for emigration.

He laughs best who laughs last—what a jolly session the parliament must have had. The Zionist bandits, who boasted of greening deserts and drying marshes, were now defied to perform one last miracle and survive the onslaught of 100,000 naked newcomers.

Ustad Heskel watched plane after plane airlift his children, his parents, his relatives, his friends, his business associates, his business rivals, his clients, his doctor, his lawyer, his barber, his butcher, his baker, his banker, his beggar, his tailor, his shoemaker, his maid, his cook, his favourite poets, and the musicians he would never hear play at parties again. Only a year ago, every sixth Baghdadi had been Jewish. Now, the Jews were flying away, with 50 *dinars* each, and an extracted root to replant in the desert.

Schools, synagogues, *suqs*, stores, banks, clubs and whole neighbourhoods stood, one after the other, empty. But Baghdad wasted no time wailing over her Jews. Business and trade were at last open for Muslim merchants to take over. Some of the vacant houses were handed over to Palestinian refugees. The rest, the frozen possessions in cash and real estate, were appropriated by the state.

Ustad Heskel paced the house, cluttered up with piles of bed linen, towers of china, stacks of books, bundles of clothes, and whatever else his children had left behind. He picked up a pearl necklace resting in a basket between balls of wool. His present to his eldest daughter on her eighteenth birthday. Couldn't she have hidden it inside the heels of her shoes, the way banknotes were smuggled! Fingering the necklace as if it were worry beads, his eyes fell on the Book which he had laid aside for the last fifty years. When *ustad* Heskel started to read, he remembered. And once he remembered, he came across those historic roots, preserved between the pages like the dessicated wings of a dead butterfly.

He read on for months, for years perhaps, until he brimmed with thoughts and queries which he longed to share with people of his kind.

He went out to seek the remains of Jewish life in Baghdad.

There were but a few thousand Jews, who lived in middle-class mixed neighbourhoods. Their vulnerability as a Jewish minority in an Arab country made them avoid politics and all manner of ideologies. As a consequence, or just out of laziness perhaps, they neglected values altogether. Their Jewish tradition was too loose to support them, their Arab heritage all too ready to desert them. They were people who had been spat out of place and time. Facing a cultural void, they turned to modernity, not unlike their Muslim and Christian middle-class counterparts. And not unlike them, they consumed only its shell.

They said sorry, *merci*, please, *vraiment*, with a thick Arabic accent. Some gave their children European names: Linda, Edward, Ramsey, Lisette, Vera, distancing them from their environment from birth and preparing them for a future abroad.

They devoted their lives to work, to the family, and to poker—their main leisure, their addiction, and only culture. They played it in clubs or at home, men and women alike—modern enough to sit face to face. Dressed in their best at the card table, they trumpeted their aristocratic origins, the prestigious posts their fathers had held in Baghdad before the *taskit*, and their children's brilliant performances at school. Between hands, they flirted with one another and gossiped about the marital problems of the players at the other tables. Although they were living out their fat years, they were well aware of their mistake in opting for Baghdad. They had bet on the wrong cards, they admitted to each other now and then. Their bluff had been called by fate, time, or just history—they could not even name their antagonist. And in spite of the relative security they currently enjoyed, they were always on their guard, warning themselves against staying too long and losing their entire stake.

And what gambler leaves the table in time? *Ustad* Heskel found their existence too superficial, their company too pretentious to bear. Determined to share the bliss of the Bible with others, he called on the Jewish school.

Yes, they would be glad to assign him a few hours a week.

What, had he forgotten that the Ministry of Education had, years ago, curtailed religious teaching in Jewish schools? No, by no means—reading the Bible in Hebrew was forbidden. The students read only from prayer books, without translation or interpretation. True, religion must bore them to death!

But when he closed the prayer book and recounted biblical stories, their ears pricked up, as if he were a first-hand witness to Samson's extraordinary powers, to the prophetic dreams of Joseph, the crossing of the Red Sea, the miracle of the light. Sometimes he deviated, to other stories about great Jews like Einstein, who, before his death, had declared his belief in the existence of God. The mixture of compassion and respect he read in their eyes told him how antiquated he looked, how old he had become. The spoiled brats! It pleased

him all the same that they called him *ustad* so naturally, as if
he had been born a teacher.

Although my father strictly disapproves of gambling, his
principles make an exception for Purim. As he does every
year, he brings us shining new coins from the bank to gamble with on the two feast days. As he does every year, he
builds coin towers on my desk. Two towers of ten silvery
dirhems each. Only one *dinar*? A *dinar* was my Purim gift
last year, but now that I am twelve years old, father has
promised me a raise. Has he forgotten? With an oblique
glance I follow his hand as it slips into his pocket. Small
change! He has not given me small change yet. I fidget with
the *dirhem* towers to hide my expectations, while father, pretending not to notice anything, unwraps more cylinders and
builds five additional shining towers with scalloped edges—
made of ten coins of ten *fils* each.

A total of one and a half *dinars*!

I fling my arms around father's neck and squeeze him
with all my strength, longer than last year. Then we toss my
shining coins into the green felt pouch that mother has
sewed for me, especially for Purim.

It is Selma who is throwing a card party this year, and she
has been talking about nothing else for weeks. As soon as her
mother opens the door, I smell *sambousak* pastries and hear
the jangling of a machine nearby. A babble of whistles and
laughter pours out from the guest room as I step inside. So
many attractions, all at once! Hastily I take off my jacket, and
peep inside the small room beside the entrance. Selma's father
is demonstrating the fruit machine he has rented for the occasion. Spellbound by the rotating pictures, the children are
staring without blinking lest they miss the moment when the
five lemons come up, or the five cherries or the five bananas.

The chances of getting four or five of a kind are extremely
low, father explained to me yesterday. But the children are

saying that no fives have appeared for a while, and are there-fore expected any minute. Father would have certainly con-tradicted such a statement, "because the machine does not remember," and because at each turn the chances of getting five of a kind will be as low as ever.

And I am saying that the five cherries have been waiting for me all morning.

I insert my first ten *fils*, pull the metal handle, hear the coin fall and set the machine in motion. Slowly, the pictures in the small windows come to a standstill. Pineapples and lemons and ice-cream cones and clusters of grapes turn up, but why all together, damn it! In no time the machine swal-lows four coins, five, six, spits back two, only to win them back in the next rounds. All too quickly I have used up my ten turns and lost how many coins? The brief thrill has only whet my appetite for more. I plead for another chance, just to get my money back, but the girls in the queue do not give way. Reluctantly I let go of the handle and move over to the guest room.

The spacious room has been converted into a gambling den, as on Saturday nights I suppose, only this morning, the players are spruced up eleven- and twelve-year-old school-children. They are sitting at small rectangular tables spread all over the room or standing at two round tables in the mid-dle, one for roulette, the other for *dossa*, a card game. I wave to Selma, who is standing by the roulette wheel, but she is too caught up in the game to notice me.

A familiar burst of laughter draws my attention to four players sitting in the corner. Dudi and other children are playing Liar Dice. I approach their table. Dudi announces a full house, while shielding his throw with his palms and wearing a straight face. Dora peers at him through her thick spectacles. Her narrow eyes have narrowed further into two slits. Dudi blushes at last, bites his lower lip as if to suppress a smile. Dora's face lights up. "Liar!" she cries out, like a judge in a revolutionary tribunal. Dudi slowly removes his hands and uncovers his dice: three fours and a pair of twos.

I snatch a cheese *sambousak* from the finger buffet by the window, and proceed towards Selma to congratulate her for the best Purim party I attended in years.

—Just like Las Vegas, isn't it? she asks.

—Like what?

—Never mind, she says and shows me the mound of coins in front of her. She claims that the roulette ball has been following her from red to black and vice versa all morning. No sooner has she said that than she loses her bet on red. She persists in backing red and keeps losing for a few rounds. She abandons red, bets on even and wins. She wins a second time. She shifts to odd, loses, returns to even and loses again. Now it is Selma who is hopelessly chasing the ball. Soon she loses what little patience she has, grabs the heap of coins in front of her, and hurls it all on red. The mini wheel spins. Red and black mingle into one dark ring. The ball twirls and rattles and multiplies to make me feel a bit dizzy. Brown splits into black and red divisions again. The ball slows down, skips from slot to slot until it drops into a red one, still swinging but settled. Selma's money is doubled. She is about to place the whole sum on black. Take your money and leave the table right now or you'll lose it all, I tell her, and pull her by the arm. The last of the baked cheese has melted on my tongue. I am longing for the touch of playing cards and for their colourful pips and pictures. Selma collects her coins, but does not budge. The wheel slows down. The ball hops into a red slot. Selma casts the handful of coins into her purse and follows me to the card table. Only then do I notice that it is Laila who is keeping the bank.

It has taken me a moment to recognise her. Laila has powdered her face, made up her eyes with brown kohl and rouged her lips in a radish pink. What is she doing at Selma's party anyway? The two quarrel over every trifle and waste no opportunity to annoy each other. Last week, they had a row about who deserved to be class monitor. They told the teacher so many mean things about each other that she ended up punishing them both. They were assigned to write: "He who digs a pit for his brother will eventually fall into it" one hundred times.

Selma and I squeeze our way between the other children and make ourselves a place in front of Laila, who is collecting the cards from the table. She dryly acknowledges us while shuffling the cards, and starts dealing. Cards are laid face down, one for each player and one for the bank. Laila arranges them in two rows of five in the middle of the table and puts two directly in front of us. Ignoring her hint, Selma stretches out her hand and places 10 *fils* on a card in the middle. I do the same. After each player has selected a card, Laila draws the remaining one towards her. She turns it up, and grins. The ten of clubs. The players groan and grumble. If your card ranks lower than a ten, you must pay the bank double your bet. Most of the bankers allow the players to take care of their own cards. Not Laila. She would not let anybody touch anything. My two shining coins disappear into her mountain of a bank. Selma's card is turned up last. The ace of clubs, the only ace in the round, spoils Laila's fun.

The ace is worth three times the bet placed on it. Laila pitches three coins to Selma, as if she is doing her a favour.

—How come you invited her? I whisper in Selma's ear.

—Mama said I had to. Just because she plays regularly with Laila's mother at the same poker table...

Laila shuffles the cards, longer than last time. Again she lays out twelve cards, ten in the middle and two under our noses. Again we ignore her hint. Selma selects the card closest to Laila and draws it all the way across the table towards her. Laila glares at Selma in a way that makes me understand how gangsters in films overturn tables and shoot one another because of a card game. Laila turns up her card. The players cheer her seven of diamonds. One by one, she pays out the bets placed on cards higher than seven, and takes in the ones on cards ranking less. I get a dull 10 *fils* coin for my jack of clubs. Selma's card is picked up last. Ace again! The ace of spades.

Selma receives another 30 *fils*. I wonder how much of her delight derives from piquing Laila and how much from winning for its own sake. Laila puts on a poker face and shuffles the cards. But her hands shake as she flicks the knife-edged corners together. The pack is cut at last. Laila lays three rows of four cards in the middle. Selma places 10 *fils* on a random card. Laila turns up her card and clears her throat as she displays the ace of clubs. This time, she darts to Selma's card first.

The ace of diamonds catches Laila off guard. A player whistles in wonder.

—Hey, Selma, you're getting nothing but aces today, says another.

Laila blushes. What is the probability of getting an ace three successive times? I try to calculate while Laila and Selma stare for a long moment at each other. Their fists are resting on the table. Everyone has stopped talking. I do not know what would have happened had Selma's mother not called her daughter at this very moment and asked her to fetch glasses from the kitchen.

—No luck today? Dudi says, putting his arm around my neck. Come, let me show you something.

I push his arm away, startled by his sudden presence at my side. Since when has he been looking over my shoulder? I let him drag me to the buffet to witness the unlimited capacities of his nose. As asked, I blindfold him with a table napkin. His hands behind his back, he stoops towards the buffet, while I seize the collar of his jumper to guide his nose between the dishes, keeping a hair's breadth between the food and his nostrils.

—Cumin! I'm smelling cumin, and it's wafting from cooked chickpeas . . . so that must be fried *sambousak*, right? You see! The next's no problem either, it's cheese *sambousak*. The smell of its baked dough with the smack of aniseed and caraway is filling the house. Tell me one thing, Selma's parents aren't that observant, are they? All right, there can be no doubt then that the allspice is coming from rice balls, yellow rice balls to be precise—stuffed with meat. Yes, I know that turmeric has no smell, but rice balls are yellow by definition, aren't they? I've missed the *kubba*! That's a shame. I'll try and sniff again. No, it's of no use, let's go on. Now what do we have here? *Amba*, mango pickles, and lemon pickles, and Persian garlic, and to top it all, *mechallelah*, red turnip pickles in brine. When it comes to *mechallelah*, believe me, I can even smell red. No, I'm serious. I sometimes do smell colour; I can prove it. What, I've passed over the *burek* rolls? Stop! This tartness is definitely tamarind, but damn it, what else is there? Yeees, a fragrance of cinnamon, and true, a tang of lemon juice, too. No, don't tell me, it's on the tip of my tongue . . . it's *dolma*, stuffed vine leaves, right? God, my nose is getting sharper every day. Nonsense, Lina, your hints have been minimal. Oh, now we've landed in another world, this is the smell of paradise after rain. All right, I'll be more concrete, it's rose water, but you have to tell me the rest. *Zingula* spirals? Goodness, my mouth is watering. You know I can't resist sweets. Now that we're at the pastry let me make one last guess. My nose must be right above *malfouf*, puff pastry fingers stuffed with ground almonds, right?

—Wrong! Selma says, and pushes Dudi's head down.

His nose sinks into the *man-al-samah*, soft nougat cakes lying in flour. Selma and I laugh until we cry as he sneezes inside the dish and flour spreads out all over the table. Dudi takes off the blindfold, sneezes again, and runs to the bathroom, cursing us and sweeping the white dust off his face.

Selma and I pile our plates with a bit of everything.

—The buffet's superb, Selma. Delicious.

—You should tell Mama. She's been working on the savouries for the last three days.

Steam flows out of Selma's mouth as she bites her *kubba*.

—Mama says that as a hostess I have to entertain all my guests, but I just can't wait to return to the *dossa* table. It wouldn't be proper to stand up the ace of hearts, would it?

—Selma, you won't get it even if you played till tomorrow morning.

I repeat what I have retained from father's introduction to the laws of probability. Selma agrees that the chances of getting an ace, any ace, from a deck of 52 cards is 52 divided by 4, and that is 1 in 13. It takes her some chewing and finger licking before she accepts the ensuing statement that the chances of getting an ace, any ace, in two successive rounds is 1:13x13, and in three successive rounds is 1:13 x 13 x 13, and that must be less than 1 in a thousand!

But hers were not just aces. Selma has drawn a different ace each round, which is a far less probable combination. How much? It needs pencil and paper to calculate; the chances must be 1 in 4/52 x 3/52 x 2/52, one in thousands, I suppose. The figures hardly impress her. Selma halves a dried date lengthwise, replaces the stone with a walnut, and bites the tiny sandwich in the middle. Did she get my point at all, I wonder, as she studies the rest of the date in her hand and examines its stuffing as though she had not filled it herself a moment ago.

—Tell me, why all this headache when the actual outcome is in any case determined by chance? Selma finally asks. And if chance has sent me three different aces successively, do you really think that it's your calculations that are going to stop the fourth?

—It's a chance of one in 4/52 x 3/52 x 2/52 x 1/52! It's most unlikely to occur, don't you understand?

Unimpressed, she replaces her empty plate on the buffet and returns to the card table. Laila is suddenly all smiles. She passes Selma the deck, and politely explains that she can no longer resist the sight and smells of the fabulous buffet. Selma cheerfully beckons me, rubbing her hands, eager to keep the bank. I go over to her side, puzzled by Laila's abrupt retreat, and still more by her unusual friendliness. Selma takes off her sweater, empties her purse on the table, and shuffles the cards.

She has been perspiring, my nose tells me. But the smell is tart, as though of fermented sweat, an odour which Selma's pores have never emanated before.

She has grown so tall lately; she has definitely overtaken her mother. Her buttocks are bulging out, about to burst her skirt, as if they have been raised by yeast. Her shoulders have widened and her breasts have swelled, so that they keep jiggling whenever she deals or collects the cards from the table. I bet she will be wearing a bra very soon.

I daresay she is menstruating already.

Her pile of a bank soon accumulates into a hill, not without the ample contribution of my shining coins. Nevertheless, neither the ace of hearts nor any other ace has appeared in any hand yet.

Selma suddenly stops shuffling and fans out the deck on the table, the cards turned face up.

—Someone has removed the aces from the deck! I exclaim.

—Lailaaaaaaaaaaaa. . . . Selma yells, and sets out to retrieve her aces. Dudi's convulsive laughter erupts from the Liar Dice corner.

TALES TOLD BY THE TIGRIS

The wave washes my feet then recedes. My toes tickle as the sand pulls away from them. The sky is still dark blue. Hai tells me to remove the two last cork cubes from my waist. I untie the strings and hand him the life belt. Fortunately, the light is dim and the others are too sleepy to notice my excitement. Our swimming instructor casts my lifejacket into the rowboat. With this unceremonial gesture, Hai has declared me a qualified swimmer.

I am seven years old.

The other children let out cries of hesitation, that moment of reluctance before letting go. I plunge in knee deep, wade, and pause to feel the swiftness of the flow. The dark water gurgles and releases a nocturnal smell, like that of sleep. Without a lifejacket, the Tigris and I are meeting on equal terms at last. Hai shoves the boat into the deep water.

We set about our daily route across the river, heading to the west bank, swimming northward in order not to drift downstream. Hai rows behind, corrects us, warns of riptides and unpredictable whirlpools, chats and argues and hardly stops talking.

—Jackie, your arms are caressing the water. No, now you're flailing. You want to do the crawl, then listen to me boy, will you? I'd been doing it for forty years before you were born, so I can teach you something, right? Your arms should be working like oars. Stretch them forwards. Good, now pull them back through the water. That's fine. Why are you lifting them so high in the air? Who are you waving hello to? Selma, if you have to be the fastest, then you've got to use your legs properly. Kick girl, push yourself with all your might, like a frog springing with joy, madly in love. That's it, that's my Selma. Shame on you boys, to let a girl beat you just like that. Kids, what's the matter with you? With a pace like yours, we'll never reach the west bank. Where's your energy this morning? At your age I used to cross the river twice a day, once at cockcrow and again at night. If you don't believe me, ask your fathers. We were much stronger and healthier than you are nowadays. Dudi, if all you want to do is to float lazily on your back, then do me a favour and stay at home in your bath. Did I tell you to turn over? You may swim on your back, son, if that's the position you prefer, only show me your backstroke. Don't close your eyes. With this current you'll find yourself in Amara when you open them again. So what if I'm exaggerating! Can one speak Arabic without exaggerating? Life's so dull, children, you may spice it with some imagination without immediately being called a liar. Ronnie, your legs are suspended, are you swimming or are you walking? Don't worry, you won't sink, that's what the cork is there for. Hey, you're still wearing four cubes. It's time we reduced them; you'll manage with two, won't you? Kids, did I tell you that ages ago, before the bridges were built, the two banks of the Tigris, Rasafa and Kerch, were connected by a bridge of boats? No, not like my rowboat, but with *guffas*. You don't know what *guffas* are? Really, you've never seen one? My God, you make me feel like an old boy. Thirty years ago we still had *guffas*, round boats, a bit like bowls, half as big as this one, but they were made of woven palm branches. Now can you tell me how many of them you needed for a bridge? Come on, it's not so hard to estimate. How wide is the Tigris? What, you can't use your brains and your limbs at the same time? You're a funny generation, you know? Go on, laugh at what I'm saying as if I were here just to amuse you. When I was your age ... What, that's right, two hundred *guffas*, very good Reuben. At least two hundred. Dudi, if you continue this way, I'll remove your lifejacket. You're not lying in your bed, and I'm not ready to slow down just for your sake. Children, now that we've got some light, you keep your eye on the date palm over there. Don't be silly, Dudi, of course it's not fainting; it's always been bent like that. Let's see you stand straight in this heat, and you're not half as tall nor half as old as it is. How old? How'd I know? It was there when I opened my eyes. How old am I? Hmm ... no, no it's no secret, it's only that ... well, if I told you that I didn't know myself what year I was born, you'd laugh again. See! Now kids, be serious for a moment and listen, will you? This palm's your guide. Remember, as long as you keep it in view and swim in its direction, you'll never lose your way.

A sandy beach stretches along the opposite bank. It is broken by abrupt rows of old oriental houses, built directly on the water. Random date palms impose verticals on the flat skyline. Our palm crops up from some concealed spot on the shore, slightly slanting to the south. My arms and legs bend and stretch according to the rhythm of my breath. My head dips and emerges. The slanting palm vanishes and reappears accordingly. The pruned stubs of old leaf bases mark her stem with indentations. At last I understand why our drawing teacher taught us to outline the trunks of palms in a zigzag.

A man suddenly enters the picture and clambers up the palm. A dark belt binds him to the stem. How small he looks beside it, like Teddy-Pasha in my arms! His baggy trousers are rolled up to his knees. He uses the leaf stubs as hand- and foot-holds. After a couple of steps, the belt falls to his buttocks. He adjusts it to waist height and proceeds upwards.

Will I get to the shore before he reaches the crown?

Selma has caught up with me. I spurt forwards but she does not fall back. There is no point in competing with her, Selma is robust, all limbs, and very long ones. She is overtaking me, splashing water all over my face. It's at times like this that I ask myself whether I should still call her my best friend. I slow down and let her pass, tired of being washed by her used water.

The light is shifting from blue to purple. The voice of the *muezzin*, singing out *Allahu akbar* and calling the faithful to dawn prayer on the loudspeaker, must be resounding in our neighbourhood by now. The flies have raided our roof and are hovering with disappointment above my empty bed. Shuli is cursing God and His creation. His head is buried under the pillow in a futile attempt to protect his sleep from daybreak.

The man is at the crown of the tree. He must be able to see the sunrise from up there. But certainly he has not scaled the palm for the love of nature. Supported by the belt, he leans backward, pulls out a sickle and strikes at the dates, dangling under the crown. A bunch of what seem like hundreds of yellow and amber dates falls rapidly.

My foot hits the riverbed.

On the beach, Selma is digging a pit large enough for her to fall into. The other children gradually emerge. Hai arrives last and moors his boat. His canteen of water passes from mouth to mouth. Hai does not say much when on dry land. Selma, Ruthie, and I are silently counting the curls of grey hair on his brown chest. A golden medallion hangs from the chain around his neck. On it, two Hebrew letters are engraved. They read "Hai."

Sixty-two, Selma whispers. Sixty-four, I challenge her. Sixty-seven, Ruthie insists. Hai turns to us.

—Hey . . . what kind of auction are you holding, girls?

The girls burst into laughter. Hai claps his hands.

—*Yallah* kids, our break's over. Don't grumble, look how fast the sun is rising, we'd better get back before the heat breaks out. You can start dreaming of the royal breakfast Mama's preparing for you. And don't forget to remind her that tomorrow's the first day of the month, and that's when Hai's fees are due. And whenever she has a dish of *salona* in mind, she should call good old Hai and he'll catch her a fat *shabbut*, fresh from the river. Laila my girl, your strokes are perfect, but you swallow too much water. I know you've had your vaccinations, but they still shouldn't turn you into a water buffalo, should they?

The sun is rising in the pale sky before us. Its rays are searing, preparing to flog another day to delirium.

Abu Nuwas street runs along the eastern bank of the Tigris in Rasafa. Coffee houses, or *casinos,* have been set up on the bank. They consist of fenced lawns furnished with wrought iron tables and chairs, painted in green and blue and red— the same colours as the light bulbs strung over the fence. Sometimes, a myrtle hedge serves as the boundary between two adjacent *casinos*. In the summer, after dusk, Abu Nuwas turns into a promenade while the coffee houses on its riverside fill with customers.

We have just had our dinner in Semiramis, a *casino* for families, together with Zeki and Dunia and their two daughters, Suad and Huda. The waiter is clearing the table. He is heaping the pressed lime segments and the eight skeletons of fish into one dish. Their heads are still sweating from the fire that had grilled them. Although open, their stony eyes are impossible to meet, no matter from what direction I try.

Father orders eight *finjans* of Turkish coffee. Dunia agrees to read our fortunes in the coffee grounds. Zeki asks for a second glass of *arak* and some raffia fans.

The mouths of Suad and Huda are painted red, the same

red as the bubble gum they have started chewing. Like real women, they will stamp the brim of the white *finjan* with red imprints of their lips.

Although they are only one and two years older than I am, the girls have recently grown into young ladies who pluck their eyebrows, paint their nails, remove the hair from their legs, swim only in pools and only on women's days, abstain from bread and biscuits, and avoid the eyes of young men, including my brother, with whom they have been friends since their childhood. Their abrupt metamorphosis made us lose interest in each other, even though I am twelve years old and am bordering on puberty myself. But my breasts are still too flat to fill the cups of a bra and the hair under my arms is too sparse to be shaved. Mother reassures me that her menstruation, too, was late, unaware how thankful I am for the delay.

—Their hair's so beautiful, mother tells Dunia and fans her face. Long enough for them to sit on.

—Long enough to let them do without toilet paper, Shuli whispers in my ear.

After I have drunk my coffee, I place the saucer upside down on the cup, and turn the two over. The coffee grounds are streaming down. The traces they will leave on the sides of the *finjan* will serve Dunia as inspiration for her reading.

Her nose is poked inside Shuli's *finjan*. I pull my chair beside hers, hoping for an initiation into the secrets of fortune-telling.

—A new page is opening up for you, young man, Dunia begins with an airy tone. I can see them clearly, your grandiose plans. You've resolved to take your place in the big world, and nothing less will satisfy your ambition.

Shuli sits up.

—Come on *Um* Suad, you don't need the *finjan* to tell me this. You know I've just finished school. It's pretty obvious that a new phase is about to start.

—He's too clever to be fed on vague statements, Zeki chuckles.

Dunia ignores both Shuli's and her husband's remarks. She turns the *finjan* slowly between her red-nailed fingers and studies the amorphous blots from every possible angle. Zeki takes a sip of *arak*, stretches out his legs, and yawns loudly.

—Be patient Abu Suad, father says with a measure of irony. Visions need time to reveal themselves.

—It's all right with me, Zeki replies. As long as the future doesn't precede its prophecy.

Dunia does not blink. Mother lights a cigarette. Huda's bubble bursts and chewing gum gets all over her made-up face.

—Forgive me, Shuli suddenly resumes. All I really want to know is whether this page will be read from right to left or left to right?

It is unlike my brother to apologise. Besides, he is too rational, like father, to take fortune-telling seriously. Has Dunia disarmed him with her composure, or is he so desperate as to resort to coffee reading?

—There's more than one possibility, Dunia speaks at last. Some are at hand, others are very far away. But you definitely prefer the faraway ones.

Shuli clams up.

—Where? Show me? I ask.

Dunia points her finger at what look like snakes to me, creeping up and down the cup.

—See all these lines? Look how narrow this one is, messy, too, a dirt road I'd say. It's made exclusively for individualists—egoists who believe their lives belong only to themselves. Here's a highway, wide enough to hold a demonstration, for those who take no single step without the backing of the whole clan. The dark one over there is a blind alley. It's reserved for the despairing. This line's as straight as a ruler to suit the needs of the practical, while the one next to it is winding, most attractive to adventurers. This is no more than a thread, almost transparent, one that only ascetics can discern. If their self-denial is sincere, their traces, too, will fade on the way. As to this long street that goes beyond the brim, it is taken mainly by the ambitious, those who go so far away that even if they looked back, they wouldn't be able to spot their origins any more. Now do you see this figure? The big head's your brother, right?

It looks more like a concrete brick with a protruding nose, sitting on a wheel.

—See how ready he is to move? The wheel's small, though, and not particularly convenient for a long ride. But note the direction to which his nose is turned, to the longest of all paths.

—M-I-T! I cry out.

—Can't you ever keep your mouth shut? Shuli barks at me.

—Don't worry, young man, the *finjan* doesn't need your sister's assistance. Your American university is very distinct. Here . . .

And she indicates a dark lump, stuck to the outer brim of the *finjan*. But Shuli's cup is always smeared! He has never learned to sip the hot thick coffee or to pause after each sip and wear that grave look that denotes nothing more than oral pleasure. No, he gulps it down like water, as if only to quench his thirst, and spits out the dregs caught on his tongue onto the brim of the *finjan*, providing Dunia with clues to his career.

—It's positive! Take my word for it, *wallah*, you'll be admitted.

Her full voice is a temptation to believe. Her tone conveys authority, pride, too, as if he were her own son. Shuli's face gleams with warmth for a moment. Then he frowns, folds his arms, and looks away.

—How do you know? Where? Show me.

—Enough of your prying, Lina! She's not on trial, she's only reading the *finjan*, mother says.

—But how come the *finjan* knows...after all it's only coffee grounds.

Dunia's fishlike eyes open wide.

—Fate drops you messages everywhere, my girl! On the palm of your hand, in cards, in the stars, in coffee grounds, and in your dreams. Fate is not a foreigner. On the contrary, it's a lifelong companion—though not necessarily a friendly one. Now let's return to the *finjan*. See this letter flying above your brother's head? That's the new page I mentioned at the very beginning.

It looks more like a flying saucer than a sheet of paper.

—Examine the space around it. Is it cloudy? Are there any signs of an impending storm? No, the sky's clear. The letter can only be good news.

Shuli bursts out,

—It won't make any difference! Whether I'm admitted or not, I won't be allowed to leave the country.

Dunia glances at Zeki, then goes on.

—Yes, my boy, but...things might change...Just a few weeks ago we agreed to a cease-fire with the Kurds. Who would have dreamt of that last year? For the Jews, too, better days will turn up, I'm sure of that. You know how it is—regimes and ideologies rapidly burn themselves out like an American cigar.

—I'm sorry, it's not the American cigar we're dealing with here but the Arab moustache, Shuli retorts.

—Now you've carried it too far! It's neither the place nor the time to discuss this anyway, father says to hush his son.

Cars swish and honk along Abu Nuwas street. Men whistle at girls strolling alone. Dogs bark in reply. A donkey heehaws from nowhere. Domino tiles clack at the table beside us. The family to our right is cracking pumpkin seeds, while the eight of us grow silent, lest more words be said that could not be taken back.

Dunia's brown eyes sink into the dark coffee stains again, in search of better days. But the *finjan*, too, keeps quiet. Zeki gulps his second glass of *arak*, and wipes his moustache with the back of his hand. Shuli is staring at the river. I know where his thoughts are wandering.

In the south of Iraq, near Basra, the Tigris and the Euphrates join into the Shat al-Arab waterway, whose southern branch serves as the border between Iran and Iraq.

Three years ago, in 1963, shortly after Abd al-Karim had been overthrown, the new regime decreed laws against its Jewish citizens. Their property was frozen and they were denied the right to hold passports and to travel abroad. Since then, those Jews who wished to leave for good packed their suitcases and went for a cruise on Shat al-Arab. Within less than an hour, they landed at Abadan, on the coast of Iran, where they were admitted without difficulty. From there, they were free to proceed to any destination they chose.

Since last year, Shuli has been flirting with the idea of crossing Shat al-Arab once he has finished school. But he is still underage, and father would not hear of letting him flee by himself. Shuli stands up to him, threatens to break away without his consent, succeeds in irking him but takes no action.

—Do you see any heart in the *finjan*? I ask Dunia. Is he by chance in love?

Suad and Huda burst into laughter. Shuli nudges me with his ankle. Dunia surveys the *finjan* once again.

—Yes, he is. He's in love with his freedom, with his future, and with himself. What else would you expect from a young man?

And she waves the raffia fan to cool her neck.

PART II

SIX DAYS, A WAR, AND A TRANSISTOR RADIO

The morning break seems never ending. Teachers have gathered in the headmaster's office. War has broken out, students are saying. War with Israel. My mind tries to classify the news into the familiar range of internal disturbances, somewhere between uprisings and government collapses. Yet the excitement that such occasions usually provoke is missing. Excitement makes me light, but this tension sits like a weight on my chest. Strange, it is the description mother uses whenever she is engulfed by worries. Are we exposed to a closer threat now or have I simply grown older? The headmaster is glued to his revolving chair in a daze, as if he has sunstroke. The meeting is destitute of words, I notice, as I peep through the gap between the curtains of the office.

At noon, Abd drives us back home. The school will be closed until the war is over. I am not ungrateful for the break. The bus radio is on, blasting out national songs, war songs, victory songs. Baghdad, too, is taking the day off. School children, students, factory workers, and office staff are relieved from their duties and dispatched to sing and dance in the streets, in support of our troops helping out on the Egyptian and Syrian fronts. Abd is unusually quiet. Whatever he is thinking, he is keeping it to himself today.

Father comes home shortly after me. He and mother are anxious to have Shuli back from the university.

They are having lunch in the dining room, while I am browsing through the newspaper in the sitting room. "The Battle of Revenge," says the headline. Smaller headlines follow underneath: "Soon, our brave soldiers will tear the hearts from the bodies of the hateful Jews and trample them in the dust," "In a few days, valorous Arab armies will convert Palestine into the graveyard of its greedy occupiers." At the bottom of the page is a cartoon. The Wailing Wall is razed to the ground, a flag with a six-pointed star is burning, and three crooked-nosed Jews are drowning in the Mediterranean.

The conversation in the dining room has developed into a row. He is blaming her for having opposed emigration many times in the past. She denies her responsibility and claims that he has always been the decision-maker in the house. He reminds her of that missed opportunity, years ago, when they had resolved to leave—had she not at the very last minute refused to budge? She shoots back the familiar justification. Here at least the boy is studying and not peeling potatoes for Polish Jews in some kibbutz. Here, the boy is not conscripted. Would he rather have his only son break his back in some Jewish army and perish in somebody else's war?

Shuli shows up at last.

—An insult to intelligence, these students! They've gone wild, delirious with joy over the war. Their bloodthirsty speeches would turn the stomach of a cannibal. If only they had the guts to bear arms and go to the front themselves.

He grabs the transistor radio and throws himself on the sofa without removing his shoes. I wonder if today mother will let it pass.

He switches on the radio. *Kol Israel*, the Voice of Israel, reports in Arabic that the Israeli Defense Forces resisted artillery and air attacks from the Egyptian and Jordanian borders this morning. Father walks into the sitting room, chewing his last mouthful, frowning. Shuli's feet dart to the floor. Father rebukes him for the high volume of the radio. From now on, he should listen to *Kol Israel* under the staircase where he cannot be heard, and remember, as always, to turn down the sound each time the broadcaster announces the name of the station.

—My life as a mouse, Shuli remarks theatrically on his way out.

Father shakes his head in disapproval and leaves for his room. Mother joins me in the sitting room, the second transistor radio in her hand, restlessly switching from one Middle East station to the other.

Radio Baghdad claims that Iraqi warplanes are raiding Zionist towns and that the traces of the enemy will soon be erased. The Voice of the Arabs reports that Egyptian armed forces have penetrated occupied Palestine and that fire is devouring Zionist settlements. Radio Amman maintains that seventy enemy planes have already been shot down and that the cancerous growth will at last be extracted from Arab soil. Radio Damascus calls on its soldiers to be the first bullets to pierce the Jews' cowardly hearts.

Radio Cairo is broadcasting an interview with Um Kalthoum. The Nightingale of the East promises Egyptian troops a concert in Tel Aviv in the near future.

Father returns to the sitting room with some documents and asks mother to check them. Without casting an eye on them, mother impassively consents to their destruction.

—What about the picture on your night table?

—What about it? I don't care. You can have it too. Burn it if you want.

—What's wrong with the picture on your night table? I protest. It's only your sisters, and they're living in New York.

Father and mother exchange glances.

—Tell her. She's no longer a child.

Mother's two sisters do not live in New York, father reveals. In fact, they have never been to America. Neither has Uncle Baruch, Uncle Moshi, Uncle Naji, or Aunt Rebecca. All mother's family, as well as father's, are living in Israel, in the suburbs of Tel Aviv.

—But their letters, they definitely came from America! I tore off the stamps myself. Always the same small one with the picture of Abraham Lincoln . . .

What did I expect, mail service between Israel and the Arab countries? Correspondence with our relatives was only possible through a third party, and it went without saying that such contacts were strictly illegal. Consequently, a letter from Israel should by no means provide clues as to its place of origin. Nothing in its appearance or content should ever suggest that it had started out from Tel Aviv; that it had crossed the ocean to reach the hands of a friend in New York; that the friend replaced the envelope with a new one, wrote down our Baghdad address, affixed an American stamp, and mailed the letter back to the Middle East.

Their letters were always dated ten days in advance, to fit the date of postage from America. They hardly said anything—it dawns on me now—apart from banal reports, as if addressed to the censor. Everybody was always well, so and so got engaged, so and so was graduating. Sometimes they enclosed a photograph of a boy standing in front of his birthday cake, or a girl celebrating her bat mitzvah in a sitting room which could have been anywhere.

Did Shuli know this? Since when? That's not fair. So what if he's six years older? Now it's too late, just before you burn them, I know. No it's not a trifle. I don't care what you think. No, I couldn't find a better moment for such a scene. Oh, yes, it is, it's the right moment and a half.

I grab my bicycle and ride onto the street, flee my foolishness and the smell of burned paper spreading in the house. War songs are blaring from radios all over the neighbourhood, from shops, roofs, gardens, and courtyards. From passing cars. The grocer across the street is shaking his fist to the martial music. It used to electrify me, too, especially the marches. But now that it shuts me out, the cannons and missiles evoked by the music seem to be aimed in my direction. If only I could flee Baghdad and its blatant soul. I ring the bell of my bicycle and overtake the lettuce vendor's handcart. The old man waves back cheerfully. The road is vibrating under my wheels. The days of playing hopscotch on the roadway while soldiers are slaughtering each other a few streets away are over. My feet keep sliding off the pedals—what is the matter with me? Selma's house is only a few streets away, and nothing in my appearance gives me away as Jewish.

She is cutting roses in the garden, listening to a play on Radio Baghdad. "Heskel surrender...," the Palestinian *fedayee* and the Iraqi soldier are bellowing by turns. Heskel is a common name among Iraqi Jews.

—How can you listen to such bullshit! I exclaim and silence her transistor.

—It amuses me. Besides, what else can you listen to out here, Hebrew lessons from *Kol Israel*? Selma replies, without forgetting to drop her voice at the last two words.

—I can't listen to their abuse any more.

—Better get used to it, we'll be hearing a good deal of this stuff for a while, she says, sounding as wise as a prophet.

I ask her for a few back issues of *Nous-Deux*, the French photo-romance magazine.

—Suddenly you're interested in love! Congratulations. Decided to grow up at last?

As Selma goes inside, I switch on the radio again. Not that I am curious about his fate—it is evident that Heskel is done for—but I am keen to try out Selma's philosophy. Can one ever get used to abuse? Can I hear the name on the radio and remain composed before its ugliness? Heskel, Heskel, let me just listen to the sound, as if for the first time, as if Arabic has not distorted my ear-drums. Forget old *ustad* Heskel; forget the two unbearable Heskels in the back row of the classroom and let me hear a neutral sound. Heskel, you are nothing but two gutturals, separated by a dry whistle, esssss, after which the mouth promptly opens and keeeeel, it dribbles your second half, like the yolk of an egg dripping onto an old Jew's beard.

Damn the old Jew, damn all Heskels, and damn every Arab on earth. I switch off the radio again.

Selma fetches me a stack of *Nous-Deux*. Just before pedalling away, I begin,

—Tell me Selma, we don't want Israel to lose, right?

—Right.

—But then, do you think . . . is there any chance that . . . we, here, will be hurt?

Selma's grimace makes me instantly regret my question. All I wanted to hear was a carefree remark that would brush away my apprehension.

—Well, Mama thinks that if the Arabs win they'll certainly leave no dog alive over there. But if they lose . . . hmm, she reckons they might well *yeberdon samem*, cool their poison on us.

—Do you mean we'd . . .

—No, they'd kind of . . . come on, you know it yourself, they'd persecute us, she replies in an impatient tone and reverts to her roses.

What exactly did Selma have in mind, I wonder as I cycle back home, exploring the connotations of persecution. Will they beat us up, throw us in jail? For how long? Certainly not women and children. What is the range of persecution? Does it imply murder? Related terms like "maltreat," "oppress," "harass," and "abuse" come up, but fail to elicit concrete images involving me or anybody I know.

I reach home with an empty mind. A foreign car bearing a

cd plate—*corps diplomatique,* is parked in front of Laurence's house. Laurence's mother is speaking to the man in the car who looks as English and as upset as she. I wave hello but she does not notice me.

In the evening Dudi's parents drop by. Mother serves a snack of toast, cold peeled cucumber, and hard Kurdish cheese steeped in tea. The four adults wallow in self-reproach. They should have left long ago, they keep saying. They should have known better—it was evident that we would never be safe in this country, not after the birth of Israel.

—Now we're stuck in a war that we can neither escape nor take part in, a war which we can only lose. Lose Israel and all our relatives if Israel loses, or lose ourselves if Israel wins.

It is the second time today that I hear this dark prediction. They do not bother going into details as if the sequence were all too obvious. Persecution, I presume, as I bite at the Kurdish cheese. Mother casts me a compassionate look and blames herself out loud for having raised her children in this turbulent country. I enjoy being declared the victim of my parents' foolishness. Let's hope they remember it next time they tell me off me for my moods. Now she is counting our male relatives likely to be drafted over there. When their concern shifts to the family members in Israel, I sneak away, bored and fed up, unwilling to swallow another dose of gloom. Shuli is sitting on a stool under the staircase, listening to the forbidden station and manipulating his slide rule. Nothing new, he signals as I pass by.

—I couldn't care less, I yell back and climb up to my room, fling myself on my bed, and sink into *Nous-Deux,* the French world of love and passion.

Radio Baghdad wakes me up the next morning, pelting insults at Britain and the United States, accusing the two countries of a conspiracy against the Arabs and of direct intervention in the war in favour of Israel.

—You'll have to go under the staircase next time you listen to the BBC, I tease Shuli at the breakfast table.

—You'll have to keep clear of your English darling, he replies with a sly smile. Otherwise they'll accuse you of espionage for the British enemy.

—Don't be silly, we're only children.

—No, you aren't, mother retorts.

—She behaves like one though, Shuli says.

—Stop this persecution, you two! I cry out.

Mother and Shuli gaze at each other, openmouthed. Have I misused the word? Was I rude to mother? Shuli bursts into laughter. He is just having fun at my expense, I assume, whereas mother is using the war to separate me from Laurence. She has been growing ill at ease with our friendship lately, and has on several occasions maintained that, at thirteen, girls should no longer be playing with boys. I try to catch father's eye, but he is immersed in the bowl of cornflakes before him. If only some important news were broadcast right now, then the Laurence issue might be postponed for a while.

Father wipes his mouth with a napkin.

—Children or not, you might well put ideas into some informer's head. Stay away from Laurence, will you?—just to be on the safe side. He's a reasonable kid, I'm sure he'll understand. Don't play with him, don't speak to him—not in the street, not at his place, and certainly not here. Is that clear?

As clear as the end of my world.

—And the telephone, is it also . . . forbidden, dangerous I mean?

—Don't haggle, daughter, not in such matters. I said don't speak to him? Don't speak to him. Period.

—No love letters either, and no clambering up walls to the balcony, Shuli merrily adds.

—Until when?

—Till the coming of the Messiah, Shuli answers.

—Shut up Shuli, nobody asked you anything! Baba, please tell me, how long do you want me to stay away from Laurence?

—Until further notice.

The coming of the Messiah was no exaggeration after all. I sigh as noisily as possible to demonstrate my distress, but I am drowned out by the news bulletin.

We have won the war, we have routed them, the great day has arrived, the Voice of the Arabs is gasping. *Our troops have penetrated the Negev desert and are spreading despair amongst the armed forces of the Zionist bandits.* Radio Baghdad claims the enemy has lost one hundred and sixty-five planes, half of its air force within one day, and that the brave Arab infantry is marching towards Tel Aviv. Radio Damascus says the Syrian tanks have taken control of the Hula Valley and are advancing towards Safed. Radio Amman proclaims that Jordanian warplanes are strafing the suburbs of Tel Aviv and that, seized by panic, the Jews are rushing out of their houses into the streets.

Mother and father exchange dismayed glances. The Tel Aviv branch of the family must be on their minds. Father breaks his soft-boiled egg, tapping it nervously with his spoon. Only now do I notice that mother has taken nothing but tea for breakfast. She looks like a bundle of nerves. Did she spend a sleepless night?

—I don't believe a word they say, Shuli growls. They never report facts, just wishful thinking.

He turns on the second transistor radio, which emits a deep and delicate female voice, melancholy and yet detached. It's Feirouz, my favourite singer. Before he switches to another station, I snatch the radio and dart behind father's chair, challenging Shuli with my nervous giggles.

—It's not your radio! Baba, tell him the radio belongs to the family. It's not fair...

Father says nothing. Shuli gets up, advances toward me. I jump behind mother's chair, screaming and giggling.

—Lina, Shuli, stop this nonsense. Let us have our breakfast in peace.

"Let them eat it up . . . let the fires eat up Israel," Feirouz
is singing.

Shuli grabs the radio from my hand.

—My beloved singer has deserted me, I mumble, back at
the table.

—Don't be so pathetic, she has never sung for you! Shuli
replies as he shifts the station to *Kol Israel*, and lowers the
volume.

The Israelis claim to have destroyed four hundred Arab
warplanes on all fronts.

—Four hundred in one day, wow! Israelis don't lack imagination either!

—Shh! . . . can't hear a word.

While Shuli is thrilled by the news, father in no way looks
happy about the four hundred destroyed warplanes. I doubt,
though, that it is the fate of the Arab armies he is concerned
about.

—I'm totally confused, mother falters. I don't know what
to feel, who and what to believe.

Father acknowledges radio reports as facts only after they
have been broadcast by the BBC, preferably in English. Shuli
swears by *Kol Israel*. But while the two men judge with their
hearts, mother's own heart keeps drifting among radio
waves, homeless and confused.

The telephone rings. A Jewish friend warns us of a mass
demonstration in the centre of the city and advises us to stay
at home. Furious crowds are heading for the U.S. Embassy
and the British Council, he says, to denounce the so-called
Zionist-British-American conspiracy.

—All the more reason, father concludes as he lays down
the receiver. I must do some shopping today. Who knows
what the next days will bring?

In the afternoon, the demonstrators run out of Union

Jacks and Stars and Stripes to burn, and after hours of raucous cursing, they begin to lose their voices, too. As the crowds dissipate, father and I venture out to the market. We buy a dozen cans of Kraft cheese and luncheon meat, tea and sugar, radio batteries, washing powder, toilet paper, tranquilizers and laxatives to last for months. And a supply of rice bags and watermelons to erect a barricade.

On the third day, the BBC reports that the Israeli forces have gained ground and penetrated deep into the Egyptian Sinai Peninsula and the West Bank of Jordan, causing Arab armies heavy casualties on both fronts.

Father turns down the radio as the broadcaster announces the name of the station. Shuli cries from under the staircase,

—Come here, they've conquered Jerusalem! The Wailing Wall . . . Israeli soldiers have occupied Old Jerusalem, come quick . . . The four of us huddle under the staircase and listen to a direct broadcast from *Kol Israel* in Arabic. The Israeli Defense Minister, Moshe Dayan, the one-eyed war god, arrives at the Wailing Wall. The Israeli national anthem is played while the broadcaster describes each move the General makes. Dayan is standing at attention. Reviewing the guard of honour. Scribbling a wish on a piece of paper. The General is folding the paper and inserting it into a crevice between two ashlars of the Wailing Wall.

Father's eyes are wet. The massacre conceived and prematurely celebrated by the Arab world has proved false. Israel, will continue to be.

—Father, have we got some wine? Shuli cheerfully says. What are we doing in this mouse hole? It's an historic day. Let's get out of here. Let's celebrate the conquest of Jerusalem. Let's celebrate the defeat of our native land!

In the evening, the BBC reports the burning and looting of Jewish houses, cars, and shops in Tunis. The same is said to have taken place in Tripoli. In Aden, a number of Jews have been murdered by rioters. In Egypt, four hundred Jewish men between the ages of twenty and fifty have been arrested.

Father is in his late fifties and Shuli is barely nineteen, I tell myself, hardly reassured, now that the variations of the word persecution are unfolding themselves. While Egypt is openly punishing its Jewish citizens for Israel's victory, other Arab governments are setting the man in the street against them, instigating a sort of improvised, do-it-yourself revenge. Taking both possibilities into account, my parents revert to the standard measures of precaution. Mother conceals her jewels under a wobbly tile in the bed-room while, at father's request, Shuli installs a new pad-lock on our gate—without sparing us his doubts about its effectiveness.

At his wits' end, father does more burning—more letters, more pictures, including the last portrait of his mother, who died in Tel Aviv alias New York two years ago.

—Look at us, he says as he dumps the ashes into the toi-let. We're achieving what the Arab armies have failed to do: we're erasing the traces of the enemy...

The toilet flushes and sweeps father's personal documents down the drain, along with the security he once provided me. It does not seem such a long time ago that I used to hide behind him as if he were a mound of sandbags, hold onto his knees, and watch the world from between his legs. Later, I would ride him piggyback and, my arms clasped around his neck, order him about the garden, hunting clouds and butter-flies, detecting woodworm in trees, listening to the buzz of bees, and chasing swallows as far as India and China...

The next morning, a shrill meowing issues from our garden. A red tiger-striped kitten! He must be starving. I sneak to the kitchen and pour milk into a bowl, quietly, hoping to escape mother's sharp ears.

She catches me in the corridor, bowl in hand.

—For God's sake, how many times must I tell you not to walk barefoot outdoors? An insect will bite you one day and only then will you learn a lesson . . . Wait, you can't have this bowl, take the green one instead; we're no longer using it. And be sure to keep it outside, as well as this loudmouth of a cat. Heavens, did it swallow a microphone or what!

Not even a speech about filthy street animals being carriers of all sorts of disease and epidemics? Mother's strictest rule has been toned down overnight. Should her abrupt leniency upset or please me? I cannot decide. I cross the damp grass barefoot, apprehensive of a sting shooting up from the dubious earth. The red kitten approaches, his tail upright. His colour ranges from orange to ginger and from carrot to curry.

He laps up the milk, licks his whiskers, then his paw, with which he scrubs his face clean. After that he rubs his humid snout against my legs. I kneel down. He shuts his eyes and leans his warm purring body against my thighs. I scratch him under the chin and run my hand down the nape of his neck. His fur is so sleek, he cannot possibly be ill. Curry opens his sleepy honey eyes and licks my toes with his prickly tongue.

Khaled has been watching us from their balcony for some time. I lift my head and acknowledge him at last, after which we both hasten to look away. I do not call him over to see my new kitten; he does not spray me with his water pistol. At this moment, it flashes through my mind that Zeki and Dunia have not rung us up or dropped by, as they usually do whenever a local upheaval breaks out.

During the following days, while the map of the Middle East is changing, I divert my attention to my French romances and forget myself in the embraces of lovers who long for and betray each other. Quite often, I am tempted to peek at the reassuring kiss or wedding cake on the last page.

Now and then I hear Radio Baghdad asking its citizens for blood donation; *Kol Israel* inviting Um Kalthoum to give her promised concert to the thousands of Egyptian prisoners of war in Tel Aviv; Nasser admitting defeat and resigning. Between one romance and the other, I grab a bite in the kitchen and overhear that Iraq is severing its diplomatic ties with Britain and the United States, that masses of demonstrators throughout the Arab world are calling on Nasser to retract his resignation.

—*Sacham wichew*, Nasser has sooted his face. They've all sooted their faces, mother says.

The streets in Baghdad are packed with more people than they can hold. Demonstrators are neither dancing today nor running riot, only marching. Students, workers, bedouins, intellectuals, *effendis*, and *fellaheen* are walking side by side, hand in hand. Their faces are gloomy. They are weeping over their defeat, aching with wounded pride.

Dangerous are the tears of proud men, mother murmurs.

They gather in *Sahat al-Tahrir*, Liberation Square, stamping a thousand times, and more. The Square sags under their trampling—the pulse of people in fury.

They will call it *al-naksa*, the Dejection. In the rest of the world it will be known as the Six Day War. It will take me longer than six days to put it on paper, thirty years later, when I will speak of it as my first war.

On the sixth day, Dudi's father is arrested.

SUMMER '67

—Wake up children, quickly! Hurry up. Collect your bed-clothes and come inside . . .

Slowly, I open my eyes.

—Watch out! Don't open your eyes.

What's the point of waking up just to keep my eyes shut? I sway in and out of sleep, while mother's paradoxical instructions repeat in my ears. Between her words, windows are rattling, trees rustling. She is shaking my shoulder.

—Hurry up, Lina, the sandstorm is about to break.

Mother rushes back inside. Shuli is rising to his feet. I stretch out my arms and release a lengthy yawn. Hot dust blows into my mouth. Shuli is removing his sheet, hastily folding his mattress. Coughing in the yellow haze I leave my bed and do the same. A gust twitches the sheet from my fingers. Shielding my eyes with my hand, I chase the white sheet, snatch it, and lose it again to the storm. It pierces the yellow night, swirling along in the howling wind like a ghost, flapping and twisting with stomachache. I grope towards the door, dragging the rest of my bedclothes inside.

Sand grains will patter against my windowpane for the rest of the night.

The next morning, the pale sky has come into view again while the floor of my room has been covered with a carpet of dust. In spite of the closed windows and doors, the storm has left its traces all over the house. Before breakfast, mother assigns us our duties. Father is to shake off the dust sheets, wipe the door handles, the window sills, the picture frames. Shuli is to clean his room. Mother and I are in charge of the floor. After brushing away the sand, we rinse and mop the tiles, again and again, until the fresh water in the bucket is no longer muddy.

Only hours later will mother discover the sand strewn like curry over the chicken in the freezer.

Distracted by the cleaning operation, I lift the telephone receiver to call Selma. The absence of the dial tone reminds me that our line is dead. I press and release the two black pegs, but nothing doing. What's dead is dead. The black set is as useful as a toy telephone.

Last month, shortly after the war, when the first lines were cut off, a rumour circulated that the government was depriving its Jewish citizens of the luxury of communicating with the outside world. It took us a few days to discuss the plausibility of such a far-fetched idea until, one after the other, our telephones were silenced.

—Better no line than a tapped one, said one.

—It spares us anonymous calls in the middle of the night, added another.

—But what if there is an emergency... argued a third. What if one needed an ambulance in the middle of the night?

I slam down the receiver. What's the use of a telephone when all my friends' lines are dead?

Shuli vacates the bathroom at last. I hurry to occupy it and lock the door, resolved to take a bath, like the actress in the foreign film yesterday. She was the picture of pleasure and relaxation. I insert the plug and turn on the water. As I get undressed it occurs to me that the bath in the film was brimming with soap bubbles, which concealed the body of the actress—except for her head and arms. I add some shampoo to the water, but it does not foam.

I plunge in all the same, eager to wash the grains of sand out of my pores. Scenes from the days when the bath used to be spacious enough for Shuli and me along with a few toy ducks and turtles return to my mind. What's the point of growing up if the world only gets narrower? I stretch out my legs and open Louisa May Alcott's *Little Men* at the page with the folded corner.

The book fails to grip me. Before the chapter is over, my mind has wandered away from New England, my gaze landed on my toenails—red and glistening, poking out like beacons from the water. A dark thought closes on me. Of all the faraway shores I long to explore, I fear the remotest point my feet will ever reach is the opposite end of the bath.

A knock at the door followed by Selma's voice dissipates my melancholy. I put *Little Men* aside, get up, slip into my bathingsuit, and unlock the bathroom door. A disheveled Selma bursts in, panting.

—A plague on them, she grumbles, and unbuttons her shirt, revealing her dark green bikini underneath.

How did she know I was in the bath, I wonder, and plunge back into the water, which by now is as turgid as the Tigris.

—What happened?

—Our Sports Centre . . . it's gone . . . the bloody army has confiscated our Sports Centre!

Without asking whether I minded, Selma plunks herself into the bath opposite me—her long legs on either side of my body—throwing up waves and slopping water on the floor.

—What army? Why? How come?

Her curls are floating like paper boats.

—Three officers went to the Jewish Community Council yesterday and asked for the keys of the Sports Centre. And do you think anybody stood up for our club? Our *Hacham Bashi* opens his big mouth only at press conferences, and only to proclaim that we're first Arabs and then Jews, and least of all Zionists, and all this obsolete stuff which impresses nobody. But when it comes to something important . . . Anyway, Abu Lias was in the office at the time, and he thought at first they'd come for him. Their uniforms alone made him wet his pants. I swear by God, I'm not exaggerating. Baba knows him and he says the man's scared of his own shadow. So it wouldn't surprise me if this Abu Lias not only handed over the keys to our club without any objection but ended up thanking the three officers for their visit.

—Pity he didn't hand over the keys to our school.

—Iraqi officers learning to read and write? You must be kidding! It would ruin their reputation!

We roar with laughter. Selma's wet curls are sinking one after the other into the water.

—Anyway can you imagine this vacation lasting forever? First it was no swimming at dawn, and no open-air cinema in the evening, in case we drew the attention of some bullies. Then picnics were crossed off, in case we appeared to be having fun and celebrating the Arab defeat. And now it's no basketball in the afternoon, 'cause our great army. . .

And we are not even committed to *devoirs de vacances* this summer, since Mlle Capdevielle will no longer teach at our school. In fact, she has left the country for good, God knows why, because she definitely has no reason for fear—France and the Arab countries seem to be getting along like *dihn udibis*, like butter and honey.

Selma is fluttering through *Little Men*, looking for pictures. She keeps fidgeting and spilling water out of the bath, then resumes her raging.

—Ashes on them! Some heroes! How dare they take it over? With what right, the premises belong to us. They've always been ours. Ours and a half!

And she drops *Little Men* on to the wet floor.

—Selma, that book belongs to the school library. Why can't you treat it more gently?

I lean to pick it up, and throw it on to the dry tiles in front of the door.

—Hey, you've grown hair in your armpits! Let me see, one second, what's the matter with you? I won't tickle you, I promise. All I'll do is check the colour, please? Hmm, that's what I thought, straight and black, like a paintbrush. Mine are red and curly, see!

—Like rusty steelwool.

—Don't be mean, they aren't repulsive, only sweaty, especially when I play... May their fortunes fall. I'll go nuts doing nothing all day. It's like being under house arrest!

—Stop it, Selma, you're overdoing it! You were so calm during the war, and now you lose heart just because you have to give up basketball for one summer?

—Easy for you to say it. You haven't set foot in our Sports Centre ever since you began to frequent the English Club with, what's his name, Florence?

—Laurence! Why can't you remember his name?

Selma chuckles.

—Because of his hair perhaps. I took him for a girl the first time I saw him—the only time I saw him in fact, as you've been keeping him to yourself.

Her remark startles me. Was my possessiveness that obvious?

—Let's drop it, I don't feel like arguing. And what's the point now that both the English Club and the Jewish Sports Centre are equally inaccessible to us?

I lay the stress on the Jewish Sports Centre, hoping to divert her mind from Laurence and restore his memory to me, back into English, so that my thoughts and feelings might stay hidden safely in his language.

Selma picks up the soap, smells it, puts up her leg, and starts soaping her foot.

—I don't know how I'll manage without our basketball team the whole summer. By the life of Baba, I'll break up cars... I'll chop down trees... I'll...

The bathroom door is pushed open. I must have forgotten to lock it after Selma's arrival.

—You'll simply bang your head against the wall, Selma. Just like the rest of us.

Dudi laughs brokenly while his soiled shoe tramples over *Little Men*.

—Mind the book, Dudi, you're damaging my book! Damn it, it's not even mine. Why don't you just get out of here, don't you see we're...

—*Nkal'e*, get lost! Selma yells, and flings the bar of soap at him.

Dudi ducks. The soap rebounds off the wall and plops into the toilet bowl.

—Goal! Good shot, Selma!

Dudi kicks the book into a dry corner, steps inside and slams the door behind him, sniggering, as if we were two of the five sisters he could always pester. His shoes are muddying the water that Selma has sloshed about the bathroom. Wait till mother sees the mess. Let her utter one complaint, and I will give her a piece of my mind. How many times did I tell her to ask me before sending Dudi upstairs? It is thanks to her that he has been taking liberties at our place recently. So what if he happens to be our neighbour. Is it a reason to tell him "you may drop by whenever you like, this is your house"?

—You think your father owns the place? Selma snaps, and reaches out for the bottle of shampoo.

Dudi raises his hands in the air, as if in surrender.

—Listen to this piece of news: we're no longer being watched! It's been two days already. Mama has driven the Smoker away.

Last month, on the sixth day of the war, three security men raided the Lawys' house, and took away Dudi's father from the breakfast table. The next day, the Smoker was patrolling our street. He paced up and down the pavement as if he had all the time in the world. Which he did, we soon realised. The Lawys unchained their dog, a black Alsatian, who barked nonstop and chased him frenziedly from behind the front wall. But the man remained unruffled. It took the poor guard dog three days to give up after which it sprawled behind the gate, its snout slightly protruding from the gap underneath, its ears pricked up and turning in the direction of the footsteps.

The security man wore a pencil moustache, had narrow black eyes and narrow lips. He was always shaved and tidily dressed. But his waist did not bulge with a pistol, and he was never seen taking notes. Nor did he ever read a newspaper, accost a passerby, bite into a sandwich, or pee against the wall. Only chain-smoked, which is why he was nicknamed the Smoker.

His coffee breaks and telephone calls at al-Muchtar's, the grocer on the main road, Hindiyah Street, started the rumour that the latter was an informer. Since then, for fear of getting into his bad books, mother sends me to his store once a week with a list of minor items: a pound of sugar, a container of sherbet. Hoping to hit a patriotic note, I also buy one or two national dairy products that have recently been launched onto the market. But al-Muchtar does not give himself away so easily. The broadness of his smile and the joviality of his voice are more conditioned by the prices of my purchases than by their country of origin.

The Smoker's appearance spread immediate alarm among the five other Jewish families in the street, each of us anxious that we were also under police surveillance. Shuli would stand behind the window and study the Smoker's comings and goings. Did his pace slow down and did he suck deeply at his cigarette when he passed our gate? Did he peer at our windows or did his eyes only brush past them? Within a few days it was evident that the only Jews who made the Smoker's head turn were the Lawys. At them he stared so steadily you would think he had no eyelids at all.

As if caught up in the scope of a sniper, they anticipated a shot—a word, a move, a blow. Six weeks passed and nothing of the sort happened. Yet his gaze remained as unremitting as on the first day, and even when he was off duty after ten in the evening, the Lawys felt no relief. His unblinking narrow eyes trailed them to their rooms and disturbed what was left of their peace of mind.

When the fear for her sanity surpassed the dread of his stare, Dudi's mother was ready at last to face the Smoker.

He was walking down the pavement, moving away from her. She waited at their doorstep, a glass of water in her hand. Neither a fizzy drink nor coffee, only water, as plain as a white flag. A few steps past our house, he turned on his heels and set out in her direction again. A tremor went through her body, she would later tell her children. It was sheer folly, she thought, but her legs went numb and refused to carry her inside. Step by step, he drew nearer, and the closer he came, the more distinctly she could make out what we had all failed to notice. That his cigarette was not lit. That his cigarette was not a cigarette, but a broken pencil at which he kept biting and sucking.

Dudi, oh my Dudi, our Smoker is no smoker! she felt like crying out, as if this trivial detail made all the difference, as if she had already won her first battle. And if the Smoker isn't a smoker, she began, hopelessly seeking the missing words on which she could base her elation. Because if he isn't a smoker, she began again, and again completed the sentence with feelings which could have carried her to the verge of tears or, just as well, to a burst of laughter, had she only had the time to indulge in either.

He stopped before their gate. She held out the glass to him. Her hand was so steady that the water remained still.

—We're all flesh and blood, she said softly. Drink, Brother! Nobody can go without water in such heat.

He reached out for the glass, but at the word Brother, the Smoker shamefully dropped his eyes.

—My husband's in jail, as you well know, and my son's
still a boy, too young to head a family. That puts the responsibility of five daughters entirely on my shoulders. What else
can I say, I'm in your hands. We're all in your hands.

As she paused to catch her breath, the Smoker drank the
water. Dudi's mother took it as a goodwill gesture.

—By your honour, by the life of that which is dear to you,
promise me, Brother, that no harm or disgrace will fall upon
my girls.

What self-respecting Arab with a notion of dignity could
turn his back on such an appeal? Poor fellow. The Smoker
not only pledged his word on the safety of the girls, he
swore to it by his personal honour and by the life of his
own children.

After which he handed her back the empty glass and
strode away. As Dudi's mother went straight back into the
house, she did not see the Smoker proceed to the main road
For her part, one dark cloud had dissipated. The man she had
just encountered was neither a smoker nor a sniper nor a
vulture. He would not lay a finger on her children. They
could even start greeting each other, as people normally do.
It did not occur to her that after their talk, the watch would
be lifted and the security man would never again show up in
our street.

The Lawys are taking more than their share of the punishment afflicted on our community, mother maintains, and
bids me, for the sake of their plight, to be more patient with
Dudi. Open, tolerant, even warm—as if I were running a
welfare service, as if I did not have worries of my own. As if
I were the one who informed against his father. If you ask
me, I reply, Dudi looks anything but distressed. But mother
is adamant. She is convinced that, unlike women, men tend
by nature to conceal their most intimate feelings.

Dudi a man? What a joke.

—Don't you miss your father? I ask him one day in

order to test mother's theory about the other gender's hidden feelings.

—Miss him? he replies, perplexed as if the term were altogether alien to him. Well . . . to be frank, we used to see very little of him even before his arrest. Baba was already at work when I woke up, and by the time he was back, I was on my way to bed again. Except for Saturday mornings of course, when we had our family breakfast.

If there was a note of grief in Dudi's voice, I failed to hear it.

People say that a former employee of Peres Lawy had reported him to the police at the outbreak of the war as "a dangerous element." Although no charges were brought against him, Dudi's father has been detained since then in the Central Prison of Baghdad. He shares a large hall with about seventy other Jewish men, all arrested within the last six weeks. Dudi's mother is allowed to visit him once a month, and to take him food, clean underwear, medicine, and cigarettes. He has been interrogated only once, and even then it consisted of bureaucratic questions, as he later told his wife, undertaken for the sake of appearances rather than inquiry.

Before the sun has set, and long before the heat breaks, I join Dudi for a walk—a habit we have taken up this summer out of boredom. One afternoon, I hear Lassie barking in front of our gate. By the time I have come out of our house, a frightened Curry has leapt over the wall and swooped into the neighbours' garden. Dudi is guffawing, proud of the superiority of his beast.

—Don't tell me you're bringing him along? I ask, stealing a glance at the house across the street, wondering if the dog's barking has called Laurence to the window.

—A friend of Mama said dogs needed exercise. I hope you don't mind. He'll stay on the leash, of course.

—It looks odd, walking with a dog. Everyone will stare, but never mind!

No sooner have we set out than Dudi stops at al-Muchtar's for a bag of pumpkin seeds. The grocer-informer fondles the dog's head and whispers who knows what instructions into his ear. Then he adds some extra pistachios to our paper bag, and to be certain his gesture has not escaped our attention, he seasons it with a flowery description of his affinity with the Lawy family. Dudi thanks him for his generosity and we proceed, cracking the seeds, while Lassie roots among the junk on the pavement, sniffs and pees at every electric pole. When we get to Abu Thumas' hamburger kiosk, Dudi offers me a treat. Best in the city, he assures me, but I politely refuse. He treats himself to a double burger. Lassie keeps barking and bounding about until Dudi pitches a ring of fried onion to him. With his own mouth stuffed, Dudi begins a long joke, which turns out to be the same one he told yesterday. I do not bother to remind him of that, for I find it easier to ignore a joke I have already heard than a new one. A passing taxi honks and the driver blows me a kiss. I look away, feigning interest in the shop windows. They display the same swimming costumes as yesterday.

On the spur of the moment, I walk into the Masbah Bookshop, leaving Dudi and dog behind. Dudi devours the second half of his hamburger in one go, wipes his hands on the inside of his pockets and follows me into the store. In my favourite place, under the ceiling fan, I browse through the new *Mad* magazine. Next to me, Dudi flicks through the latest *Semir*, the Egyptian comic. Is he still interested in this childish stuff? The dog's wet tongue lolls out and he wags his tail as if he has not seen me for two years. The bulky tail is thudding Burda and Elle on the shelf below. The shopkeeper is scowling at the three of us. I bury my face in *Mad*, disowning Dudi and the dog. Dudi shakes my shoulder. What's the matter, I mutter. He plants the comics in front of my nose. On the cover, the two schoolboys, Semir and

Tihtih, have changed into army uniforms and slung rifles over their shoulders, cheerfully taking pride in their war effort. Dudi taps his forefinger on his forehead, meaning they're cuckoo. I replace Mad on the shelf and skip out of the bookshop before it occurs to him to make louder comments on the subject.

The smell of fresh bread draws us into the Masbah Bakery. The baker is sliding a tray out of the oven with a wooden paddle, and emptying the flat, rhombus-shaped bread into a container. Dudi fishes one out and instantly drops it into a brown paper bag.

—It's piping hot, he says waggling his hand. I love the ends!

—Mmm, so do I. They look like elbows, don't you think?

Reluctantly, Dudi offers me one end of the bread. The crumbs are steaming.

—Pity we like the same things. We won't make such a good match, he says, biting off the other end and passing the rest of the bread to Lassie.

The street feels almost cool after the bakery. I raise no objections when Dudi orders two cones at the ice cream stand a few yards further up Sa'adoun Street. It is the last time I am accepting a treat from him today, I tell myself. The vendor pulls down the handle and turns the cone under the tap to compose a spiral of soft white ice cream. The young man sprawled out in the chair beside the machine winks at me. I do not react. As we walk away, he slurs something like "nice legs." He is making a pass, I tell myself, uncertain whether I should feel flattered or insulted. I examine my skirt. It is just above the knees, by no means too short or provocative.

Suddenly it strikes me that I haven't seen Dudi in shorts once this summer. Is hair already spreading over his legs? I doubt it. His cheeks are as smooth as a baby's and like me, he has hardly grown this year. What is more, a layer of fat has grown around his body, slowing down his movement and giving him the heavy walk of a drunkard.

Now that he has finished his ice cream, he is dying for a drink. We extend our stroll as far as Baghdad Stores, the largest supermarket in the city. A soothing air-conditioned draught blows into my face as I push the revolving door. Bright cans and neon light are reflected on the clean glossy floor. Dudi lingers by the sweets section, handles each box and reads out the names of Swiss and Belgian chocolate. Mlle Capdevielle must have something against me, he concludes, otherwise I don't see why I always get bad marks in French. There's no match for this glittering English blue, I murmur, stroking the Cadbury bars with my forefinger. I've got a checked handkerchief exactly this colour, Dudi replies. We walk between shelves of Scotch whisky and French wine, Californian fruit salad, Ceylon tea, English biscuits and marmalades, German sausage, Italian ravioli. The jolly foreign faces on the packages prompt us to play "Airport." We fancy ourselves sauntering amid hundreds of handsome, healthy, and happy travellers on their way to the plane. Dudi has a ticket to London, where he will buy a Sherlock Holmes cape and, together with Lassie, hunt anarchists in Hyde Park. I am flying to Paris to write letters in cafés about all the lovers kissing on public benches. Dudi insists on offering me a parting gift. While I am thinking up a proper reply by the soft drinks section, he makes a fuss about Iraq's recent boycott of Coca-Cola, following the licensing of Coca-Cola in Israel.

—Why doesn't your Mama do something about it, I ask mockingly. Smuggle Coca-Cola into the country, or speak with the Prime Minister perhaps?

—She did.

—What?

Dudi chuckles.

—*Wallah*, I swear she did. A delegation of Jewish women were admitted to the Prime Minister two days ago.

—To the Prime Minister! Why didn't you tell me this before? What did he say?

—He was frank, for once. He said there's no question of releasing any of the detainees in the near future. Then he claimed that our situation would have been much worse if not for him, that the measures taken against us are for our own good, so to speak, as they appease the mob and...

—Liar. Heavens, what a hypocrite! Who asked him to poison the masses with hatred in the first place?

Dudi puts his arm around my shoulders in an almost fatherly way.

—Perhaps you'd like to tell him that yourself?

I push his arm away, ill at ease, uncertain whether Dudi is allowed to hug me, let alone whether I like being hugged by him. Boys, men, and physical contact have become a delicate combination lately, and I am at a total loss as to how to distinguish between the affectionate touch and the greedy one.

Father is on holiday this summer, or that at least is his way of putting it. In other words, he was sacked last month from the firm where he had been employed for the last twenty-two years. The chairman summoned the five Jewish chartered accountants to his office. He had always valued their service and he deeply regretted their departure, but he had no option, he swore. He was only succumbing to the directives of the Ministry of the Interior. When they brought up the question of severance pay or some other compensation, the chairman swallowed twice but did not reply. Apparently, he could not bring himself to swear that the Ministry of the Interior had also forbidden him to pay compensation to his Jewish employees.

Father assures me that we will not turn poor overnight, that our savings will last a long time. How long, I dare not ask. The maid is already cut back to twice a week, and my parents consider selling the car. Father spends most of his time in the living room, with postage stamps heaped in front of him and a catalogue at his side. Through a magnifying glass, he studies each stamp and compares it to the illustration in the catalogue. On the days when neither Zeki nor any other former colleague pays him a visit, he engages in his solitary activity for hours. But sometimes I catch him staring into space with a blank gaze which I am unable to bear, and into which I intrude with a *finjan* of Turkish coffee and our mother-of-pearl *tawli* board.

It is Shuli who scornfully points out to me that neither coffee nor a *tawli* game could ever make up for what father has lost.

At least mother is spared the daily ordeal of waiting for his safe homecoming, or so she tells her friends. Otherwise, I dare say, she is not that happy to have him hanging around. In fact, they seem to be doing their best to keep out of each other's way. While he pores over his stamps in the morning, she locks herself in the kitchen—except for a cigarette break that she takes in the living room while waiting for the pressure cooker to whistle. Just then he steals out and hoses the grass to cool the garden for the evening. On his return, he finds the shopping list smoothed under his magnifying glass. At breakfast and at lunch, it is the radio that does the talking. At teatime, they hide behind the daily papers. Only after sunset, relieved perhaps of the fear of daytime clashes, do they start relating to each other in a natural way again.

As we all have time to while away this summer, Jewish friends drop by almost every evening, and quietly exchange the latest news in our garden. The Jewish pharmacists were forced to close last week. Our school graduates will not be admitted to universities this term. The three country clubs in Baghdad have barred their Jewish members from entering their grounds. Yesterday, our president praised the new translation of the *Protocols of the Elders of Zion* into Arabic. The telephone department will soon be collecting our telephones. Curry wanders from one leg to the next, rubbing his striped body and meowing for attention. Somebody's neighbour, who works in the French embassy, passed her a clipping from a French newspaper. It reports that the Jews of Libya and Aden are being allowed to emigrate to Italy and England.

A military jeep draws up in front of our house. A fly swat halts mid-swat. A sentence forgets its end. An unpeeled pumpkin seed remains poised between two canine teeth. Two soldiers jump down from the jeep. Father is petrified in his chair. Mother appeals to God. I lift Curry onto my lap. The soldiers head to the front of their jeep, lift the bonnet and examine the engine.

After they have driven off, mother fetches another round of sherbet from the kitchen.

—*Wallah*, I'd leave on the spot with nothing but the clothes I am wearing, if only they'd let us.

"If only they'd let us...," everybody keeps saying. But nobody will take the risk of travelling to Basra to check out the possibility of an illegal trip through Shat al-Arab to Iran.

Tired of their *kinah*, I go inside and listen to pop music from Radio Monte Carlo. "The Young Ones." "Help." "You Are My Destiny." "Diana." "Tell Laura I Love Her." But the thought of departure recurs in my mind. What if we were indeed to set out this very evening and leave everything behind? What about my comics? The stamp and key chain collections? My new coat? And all the knickknacks and board games? Before going to bed, I inspect my closet and sort out, for the first time, my most important belongings.

The fat albums are stacked on the upper shelf. How many stamps they must contain! I wince at the hours invested in soaking and detaching them from paper, drying, smoothing, and arranging them in the album. Four albums. Hundreds of sets that have taken years to build up, and still more waiting to be completed. I would never be able to drag them along. Father was sensible enough not to purchase a house, as if he were preparing for this day. Why didn't he warn me against collections? Even a miniature such as a postage stamp turns bulky when multiplied by thousands.

I wipe the dust off my photo album and browse through the black and white family pictures and snaps taken on excursions. The album preserves my thirteen years. Even memories end up as a collection. Each picture is affixed with four golden corners. Each celebrates a moment in life. I am posing in front of the Arch of Ctesiphon, the ruins of Hatra, the spiral minaret of Samarra, the Palace of Assur, the lake of Habbanyah. The carefree smile worn during the early years contracts into a self-conscious smirk as the pages progress. The gaze, though still alert, is now rather more anxious to please than to explore.

The last pages are blank. We have taken no pictures this summer. No moment has merited safekeeping. And blank they will remain, the last pages of my Baghdad album, marking a period which, in spite of my farewell, has only now begun.

They practised the use of sirens last week. This evening we have a blackout even though the war is over. From our roof, Baghdad looks entirely black, as if stormed by soot. Even the Dora, the oil refinery, is put out. The sky, on the other hand, is spilling over with light.

Shuli unfurls his star chart.

As he has scarcely slept lately, Shuli has been spending the small hours of the night locating and identifying heavenly bodies. What appears to be an arbitrary scattering overhead is grouped in clusters and constellations on the chart. Besides, the stars are numbered and connected to each other with lines, forming geometrical shapes and bearing fancy names: *al-kaid*, the leader, *al-markab*, the boat, *al-dubhe*, the bear, *al-tair*, the bird, *al-gol*, the demon.

Stars are a collection one can never lose, I conclude, because no matter where one goes, one will always recover them overhead.

—Wrong! Shuli says. The sky isn't identical all over the globe. The sky above Buenos Aires for instance is entirely different from the one above Baghdad. But even the sky above your bed is variable, and not only throughout the year, but during one single night.

I have never noticed it.

—And, anyway, suns and stars aren't eternal. They either explode one day or are extinguished. Some of the stars you see up there no longer exist. While their light has traveled for years to reach our earth, they have in the meantime been obliterated. This is why looking at the stars is, in many cases, like looking back at the past. That's why starry nights can make you feel so nostalgic.

Nostalgic about what? His last sentence sounds remote, as if spoken to the stars. I nod all the same, without really understanding how a light we can see no longer exists.

—One day, our earth will complete its cycle and burn itself out. Oh, don't worry, this will happen when you and I and our descendants and perhaps the entire human race are long dead. It could take millions of years. Not that time really matters, for a lifecycle is a whole, whether it lasts 30 days or 30 billion years, be it the lifespan of a flower, a bird, a man, or a planet.

I wish he would stop speaking of death and go to sleep.

My eyes return to the earth, across the street, to Laurence's house, which is as dark as an extinguished star.

ONCE UPON A TIME

In the late afternoon, when the heat relents and the sky recovers its blue, I climb up to the roof and open our beds, mine and Shuli's. Father and mother stopped sleeping outdoors years ago, giving up the stars in favour of air conditioning as father likes to say. I pull away the sunshade, unfold the mattresses, spread the sheets and spray them with water, which will evaporate by night and cool the beds. Before going downstairs again, I steal a glance at Laurence's house across the street.

Dozens of coloured underpants are hanging out on the clothesline on their roof.

Crimson red, navy blue, dark green, yellow, black. What festivity! White underwear must be out in England. They are painting them bright, like Easter eggs. I lean over the parapet to examine the underpants from a closer range. Their size leaves no doubt. They belong to the son of the house.

Blue would certainly match his eyes. Yellow should go with his hair although it could also make him look pale. In red he would acquire sex appeal. I giggle, embarrassed by the intimacy I have lately cultivated with respect to Laurence's clothing and underclothing. Black would accord him an older, grave appearance. As to green . . . The door on to their roof is pushed open. The Kurdish washerwoman trudges out with a mound of washing, screening her down to the waist.

I vanish inside.

Mlle Capdevielle once told us the story of a French artist who had painted the same cathedral over and over again. It was the light at different hours of the day that he had studied, she explained. But now I am convinced that the pursuit of light and colour had been a pretext and the cathedral on the canvases only half the story. The other half was that the artist had been secretly watching for someone, a woman needless to say, at whose glimpse his heart leapt, no matter at what hour or colour of the day.

At night, the light behind Laurence's translucent window is yellow-orange. As the street quietens down, the small silhouette of the night watchman scuffs about the dimly lit neighbourhood. His rifle, slung over his shoulder, pulls down the right side of his body. He greets father, who is locking our gate. Father returns the greeting and, as usual, hands him a coin. A *dirhem*, I suppose. May Allah protect you, the old watchman replies in a humble tone. A shadow sweeps past Laurence's window. The light in his room dips to pale green. He must have switched on his table lamp. How long is he going to read? I recline in bed, stretch out my arms and legs to savour the first touch of the cool bedsheet.

"*Que sera sera . . .* whatever will be will be." The band's vocalist has started singing in the Embassy nightclub nearby. They often play Doris Day, Frank Sinatra, Tom Jones, and Elvis Presley till the small hours of the morning. Shuli complains that they disturb his sleep, whereas I enjoy listening to them while lying under the stars. "Strangers in the night . . . exchanging glances . . . " Did a window just squeak? I lift my head and check Laurence's light again. Out at last. Now he must be all ears, listening to Sinatra with me, as if music has contracted the straight line between us to one point that we inhabit simultaneously.

Sinatra pauses. The barking of stray dogs answering each other from different spots in the neighbourhood shifts into the foreground. Our doorbell rings. Laurence is asking for me. Go away, father says, the last thing we need is to be accused of espionage. Laurence is heartbroken. My father does not relent. My eyelids get heavier. The green grass of home is getting fainter. The air feels cooler. The dogs have joined Tom Jones in a single chorus. My breath plunges deeper, attuned to doze.

Tomorrow, perhaps tomorrow, Laurence will ring our doorbell and inquire after me.

One tomorrow afternoon, standing by my window, I catch a glimpse of my English friend crossing the street and walking to our house. I sprint downstairs, my heart beating fast. I, and only I have the right to turn him out. The bell rings. Wait, father warns. My hand is immobilised on the door handle. I didn't call him over. I've no idea what brings him here, I shrug, feigning indifference. Mother shows up with curlers in her hair. How did she hear the bell from the bathroom! Don't let him inside the house, you hear me? Father asks me to make it brief. Mother stresses it is the last time. Father reminds me to tell him that it is not personal.

—Are you letting him wait till tomorrow morning? mother cries out at last. Go before somebody sees him at our door.

I stroll to the gate, as if I possessed the world and not only the exclusive right to send Laurence away. My guest smiles his way in and follows me to the garden, to a corner which the *nabug* tree and the climbing plants have screened from the street. His hair has grown longer still. It is now gathered with a red rubber band into a ponytail. Is he wearing red underpants, too? I am dying to ask. His cool gaze tempers the emotions about to run loose inside me. Our eyes meet. His freeze into an opaque, artificial blue, like that of a Barbie doll. I stare into his irises and capture the distorted reflection of my own features.

I should be saying something, the speech I have prepared.

The War . . . the six days . . . Jerusalem . . . petrol . . . damn it, what does all this have to do with us? Make it brief. Tell him about the watch, surely they must have noticed the Smoker. About Dudi's father . . . about our telephone. Has he tried to ring me up by the way? Well, yes, I have become inaccessible! Why? Because . . . I should watch my words. A hint will do. Israel and Iraq? No, that's no concern of his. It's rather Iraq and Britain . . . Right, Britain and Iraq—so what about them? A verb is missing. Have I forgotten? A verb is indispensable in the English sentence, whereas the Arabic needs no action for its right to be.

—I've come to say goodbye, he announces.

Two verbs, so simple, so easy. And I don't even have to drive him away. He is flying to England in a couple of days. For good. Boarding school. His parents will visit him during the holidays. He will never return to Baghdad. The country is no longer safe for us foreigners, he says, like a man of the world. Our parting does not seem to upset him in the least. Laurence has the world at his feet. Why should he linger before our closed gate? Soon he will be flying across the sea, far above the clouds. What made me think that in the abyss of my despair he would seek an adventure?

His arm is rising. He is about to hold out his hand to me. My hands grab each other behind my back. He checks his hand halfway and slips it down into his pocket.

Your ticket is ready, your passport is in your pocket, what are you hesitating for, you lucky foreigner? Life has already separated our paths, so why don't you stop dithering, say goodbye and go?

But Laurence shows no hurry. He ambles by the myrtle hedge, stoops over the sweet peas, jumps into the hammock, and clambers up the *nabug* tree until nobody in the neighbourhood has failed to notice him. I remain stiff and still behind the climbing plants. Hasn't he got the faintest idea of what fear is? He folds his legs and, clutching at a branch, throws his body upside down. His two arms are dangling, his golden ponytail in between. If he falls and breaks his neck, I will pinch his passport and fly British Airways.

His rubber band loosens. His hair falls free. Effortlessly, he pushes himself into a sitting position, then jumps down to the ground. The two lines of sweat streaming down his temples remind me of his former acrobatic performances. I am longing for him already. Should I brush aside my pride and admit how much I have missed him? Would it be proper to ask for his address in England, or had I better wait for him to make the offer?

—Gosh! Your orange trees are growing fast...he remarks, as he collects his hair into a ponytail again.

—To hell with our trees! I don't care a pin for anything growing around me anymore.

Laurence gapes at me, as if my indifference to the orange trees has offended him personally, and advances slowly towards our gate. I accompany him, resolved not to hold him back. Let him be shaken by the violence inside me. Let him perceive the rift between us. Let him at last play Orpheus and flee hell. Go off, hero, save your skin and don't you ever dare to look back. Go, I am far more at home in my own hell than in your innocent sensitivity to orange trees.

Laurence opens our gate.

A DDT lorry enters our street. Each summer it rumbles through the city and sprays insecticide to relieve us from bugs, gnats, and all sorts of mosquitos for a few weeks. Windows open to let the vapour in. Small children are chasing the truck, shouting with excitement, running in and out of the thick fog.

Laurence snatches my hand and hauls me inside the mist.

Two rubbery lips are dabbing my cheek. Is he kissing me? I cannot discern a thing in the whiteout. His mouth slides down my nose and lands on my lower lip. I close my eyes. I ought to open my mouth. I have often seen such kisses in the cinema, but the taste of DDT does not motivate me. Having somehow managed its way inside me, Laurence's tongue bumps into mine, scrapes itself on my teeth, reluctant to come to rest. Isn't it time for a declaration of love instead of this dancing and gurgling? I open my eyes again. The haze is dissipating. Laurence's nebulous features are emerging. I push him away. His soggy tongue darts back. His eyes open. Two lapis lazuli discs are glistening in the evanescing cloud. Like a *jinni,* he would have said, had he seen himself in the mirror at that moment.

Like a *jinni* going back into the bottle, I murmur, aching farewell, as I wipe my mouth and run home.

Laurence and I will never see each other again.

The story, however, does not end there. While he was kissing me inside the DDT cloud, Laurence slipped a folded strip of paper between my fingers. His address in London, I presumed.

We were invisible inside the DDT. Nobody, not even the children who were playing around, could have taken notice of the gesture. No sooner have I quelled one worry than I think up a new one. What if our house is ransacked by the security police? To be on the safe side, I ought to learn the address by heart and—following father's example—burn the paper and dump its ashes into the toilet. But could I rely on my memory, months, perhaps years from now? With two security officers at the back of my mind, I go over every nook and cranny in our house. Would they check inside every reel of thread in mother's sewing box? Would they dig up our garden, dismantle our transistor radios, unroll the bandages in our first aid kit, search between the slices of our bread, peep behind the pictures in my photo album?

Going over the spice and herb jars in the kitchen, I remove the lid of a cracked teapot standing on the same shelf and hit upon a wad of green banknotes tucked inside. Two notes of a quarter-*dinar* and some coins. Mother must be keeping them at hand for occasional street vendors. On the upper right corner of one banknote, a name is scribbled in red ink. Imad. A name on a banknote, how unusual! Who is this Imad? When did he part with his quarter? Banknotes circulate all their lifetime, change hands day in and day out, without bearing the personal traces of a particular owner.

Would it occur to a security man to check a quarter folded in the purse of a schoolgirl?

Grateful for his tip, I kiss tiny red Imad and steal him into my pocket. Back in my room, ready to copy Laurence's address under Imad's name, I unfold the paper slip:

> I was walking through the desert
> when I saw a mirage. Instantly
> I reach for my camera
> and shoot
> the sheet of water.
> In the darkroom, to my
> wonder,
> your figure emerged
> on the sheet of paper,
> swimming in the water.

I read it a second, a third, a fourth time, but detect no cipher or covert address between the lines. Laurence has left no trail behind, only a keepsake, a poem that questions my reality and veils my face behind the mystery of the Orient.

Mother calls us for dinner. I pull myself together, get up, and cast a look outside the window. Our English neighbours have lit the candles in their dining room. Why light candles when the IPC pays their electricity bill? I will never understand. Have I been listening all alone to Frank Sinatra at night on the roof? I will never know. The address in London has itself turned out to be a mirage. But one load is off my mind: I have nothing to hide any more.

THE STAR

—Hey, weren't you supposed to be back in the afternoon? Father asks Shuli as the latter unlocks the door.

He barely finishes his sentence when two men follow my brother into our sitting room. The room suddenly appears crowded, as if a stranger occupies double the space of a family member. They are young, neatly dressed. Perhaps they are only university friends, I tell myself, using the last moment of doubt to our advantage.

—Lunch is ready, mother calls from the dining room.

Shuli's face is pallid. He smiles wryly at me the way he does when he loses a bet or admits an error.

—We want to go over his things, explains one of the men, as if he needed father's permission.

Father opens his mouth, but finds nothing to say. Shuli leads the two security men to his room. Father follows. Mother darts from the dining room, alarmed by the unfamiliar male voices and the multiple footsteps thronging the stairs.

I tell her.

—*Sa'at al soda*! Our black hour has come! she murmurs and clatters with me upstairs to Shuli's room, her kitchen apron still tied around her waist.

The taller of the two men is ransacking Shuli's books,

stacked on the floor under the window sill. His hands are smooth and delicate, as if they have never beaten anybody up. He is wearing a wedding ring. The other security man has pulled out the desk drawers. Shuli is leaning against the wardrobe, his arms behind his back, watching silently. My parents are standing on either side of the door, like retired guards, no longer licensed to protect their offspring. The security man is reading admission letters from American universities. Under his left eye is an *oukht*, a patch of eaten up skin, as large as an eye socket, the scar left by the Baghdad Boil. His face reveals neither respect nor disapproval. He returns the letters to the drawer and picks up a booklet illustrating signatures of famous people. He unfolds a paper stuffed between the pages and examines the stylistic signatures Shuli has been trying out. My brother's hands slide inside his pockets. The man with the *oukht* pitches booklet and signatures aside. He looks neither puzzled nor amused. His gaze brushes the ziggurat, creeps up to the pictures pinned on the wall, inspects the coloured space ships and the two black and white NASA photographs of the moon. Suddenly he grabs the transistor radio and fumbles for the on-off switch. I hold my breath. It is too late to ask God anything. Shuli either followed father's instructions or dismissed them as too cautious. He either did or did not change stations last night after he had heard the news from *Kol Israel*. Um Kalthoum's voice rises, resonates like never before in Shuli's room. I avoid my brother's eyes, lest a sigh of relief gives us away. The security man looks neither disappointed nor satisfied. He turns the radio off and proceeds to the books on the desk, standard textbooks on the rudiments of architecture.

—What are you looking for, Brother? mother dares to ask.

As she speaks, she notices her apron and hastens to untie it.

—Zionist propaganda, he replies, in a matter-of-fact way, without interrupting his search.

The three of us gawk at Shuli.

—Fetch your father a glass of water, mother quavers.

I hurry to the kitchen and remove Laurence's poem from between the sheets of *kamardin*, dried apricots, in the larder. Why have I hidden the poem in the first place? It evokes a vision in the desert and not a lure to Zion—even a security man can tell the difference. What am I up to now, have I lost my common sense altogether? One hand has turned on the tap while the other is drowning the piece of paper under the running water. The verses pale as blue ink oozes and flows down into the sink. His blue tears. His blue beard. His blue underpants. Our empty blue swimming pool. It is hardly the time for grief or regret. I bury the wet leaf in the bottom of the rubbish bin and race upstairs with a glass of cold water.

Father, slumping in Shuli's chair, swallows two white pills with the water.

The man with the *oukht* is now searching the wardrobe, examining Shuli's sweaters, shirts, pyjamas, fiddling with his balled socks and underwear. When he pauses to light a cigarette, mother beckons me to bring him an ashtray. I feign not to notice her gesture. He is not our guest, and he will not be treated as one.

—Excuse me Brother, but can you be kind and tell us what wrong did our son do? she asks.

The man with the smooth fingers sends her an astonished look, as if she has asked for a search warrant.

—Spread Zionist propaganda, replies his partner, again in a matter-of-fact way.

Shuli frowns. Whoever asks ludicrous questions deserves ludicrous answers, he would have told his mother in other circumstances.

—For God's sake, she says, imploring her son. Why don't you open your mouth and tell us what happened?

Shuli glances at the two security men alternately, waiting for their permission. Both are ransacking the books now. Squatting amid the piles, the man with the smooth fingers

looks like a bust placed on a stack of books. The other man is
leaning against the window. They check each title, riffle
through the book, then discard it on the heap in the corner. As
they ignore his inquiring look, Shuli hesitates for a moment
then relates his story. In the Muslim dialect—the way we
usually speak in the presence of non-Jews.

Two days ago, a fellow student, an asshole of a nationalist
(Shuli will save the last detail for mother, some hours later),
asked him what the Zionist star looked like. Shuli drew his
answer on the blackboard: a six-pointed star. No, quite a large
one, but what difference does it make now? The student summoned two so-called witnesses from the adjacent classroom,
pointed at Shuli and the star, and made his accusation. Shuli did
not deign to argue or deny anything. He just told his fellow
student to eat shit and went away. No, he didn't tell us about it,
what for? He considered it a trifle, a bad joke which he himself
tried to forget. Today, at the end of the second lecture, the two
security men waited for him outside the classroom.

—I've found something! The man with the smooth fingers flaunts the pale blue paperback while rising to his feet.

Shuli's lips are shivering. He seems thrown off balance.
Does he have anything to hide? A book that he borrowed
from an American professor last year flashes through my
mind—*The Dead Sea Scrolls*. It contained pictures of
ancient tattered documents, parchment I guess, as well as the
photograph of an Israeli shepherd by the Dead Sea. The
word Israel, appearing uncensored, dozens of times, filled
me with awe. Although it dealt only with archaeology,
father asked Shuli to keep the book at home for as short a
time as possible.

—This pamphlet here. It's written in Zionist! the security man gasps, speaking to his partner and dragging at his
cigarette.

I recognise the cheap prayer edition issued by our school
for religious instruction.

—Hebrew, you mean? the man with the *oukht* dryly corrects his partner.

Shuli glances at me and suppresses a mocking smile. I hasten to look away, for fear of bursting into hysterical laughter. Wait till they hear it at school. Written in Zionist...in correct Zionist spelling. It will be the joke of the month. I turn to mother. She does not seem to find the scene funny. On the verge of tears, she approaches the man with the smooth fingers.

—Brother, it's a prayer book. Nothing to do with Zionism, by my life. It's for elementary school children. The boy never throws anything away. Let me show you...

Smooth Fingers shakes his head with a snigger that says, "Don't try to fool me, woman!" His partner snatches the book from him.

—The first page, Shuli coldly dictates, hardly concealing his scorn. The title's printed in Arabic. At the bottom, there's an authorisation stamp from the Ministry of Education.

Without looking up, the man with the *oukht* nods to acknowledge Shuli's words. Smooth Fingers flings his cigarette to the floor and treads on it roughly, as if he were crushing a cockroach. His partner, still browsing through the Hebrew text, draws out a Rafidain packet from his pocket and hands it to him. Something in the prayer book seems to be giving him second thoughts.

—Let's go! says the man with the *oukht* to my brother in a decided tone, as he lays, with care, the prayer edition on the window sill.

They went over three out of eleven stacks of books. They did not search his bed. They did not check the tubes and flasks in the chemistry box above his wardrobe. They did not dismantle his camera or listen to his tapes. They did not carry out a thorough search.

—Where are you taking him? father stands up, reasserting his paternal claims.

—To Rashid Camp. You can take him a mattress this afternoon.

He is saying they are not releasing him today. Without a word we accompany them to the gate. The man with the *oukht* sits at the wheel. Shuli waits, as he is told, until Smooth Fingers gets into the back before he takes the passenger seat. Nobody waves as the grey Volkswagen Beetle drives away. No sooner has the car turned into the main street than father bursts out.

—How foolish of him, he should have known better...

—Now you're back to yourself! Your son has just got arrested, and all you do is blame him for it.

—Jews are being arrested for nothing these days. We can't afford to be off our guard. And here he is, drawing the Star of David in public. He could have just as well turned himself over to them.

—He's only a boy, nineteen years old...

—Nineteen's long past childhood. At his age, I carried the responsibility of...

—You were hungry a while ago, what about lunch?

—How can I put anything into my mouth right now? I've got to find Zeki first, at home or at work.

They divide their tasks. Father will seek Zeki, and together they will go over their connections. One of Zeki's cousins is a high-ranking officer in the army, while a distant relative is married to the daughter of a prominent official. Father is acquainted with some magnates whose accounts he audited in the past. If we are lucky, we might reach someone who has access to someone among the top brass, who might in his turn be willing to pull strings. Otherwise, we must reckon with bribery. Whatever works will do, they both agree. In the meantime, mother will drive to the Rashid Camp and see to Shuli's needs. By no means, he is not letting her walk into an army camp all by herself. No, she is not having him go with her. It's out of the question; what if they took it into their heads to throw him into jail, too?

They settle on an escort, a female one, Dudi's mother preferably, due to the mass of experience she has assembled recently. For the last three months, our neighbour has been knocking at doors, lingering in dusty corridors, waiting for a minister or a party member to admit her for a few minutes, hear her pleas, and send her away with vague promises to intercede for her husband.

—What about you, Lina, want to come with me? Mother asks.

—Who, me? I can't . . . I've got homework. Geometry.

—I don't know when your father or I will be back. Go to Dudi's or to Selma's. Leave a note where you are and we'll pick you up later. Don't stay alone in the house, all right, dear?

—Don't worry, Mama, I'll be fine.

The door bangs. A second time. Then silence. I have never been alone in the house before. I climb up and down the stairs, wander in and out of the rooms, erratically, as if I've lost my way, running into the same thoughts in each room. Another Jew was arrested today. This time I did not hear the news from anybody. This time, the news happened right here. They came, they searched his room, they took him away. All too fast, all too close for me to grasp.

They came, they searched his room, they took him away. The sequence recurs in the sitting room, in the guest room, in the bathroom, in the dining room. There, the table is set for lunch. Food is served. We were supposed to have finished our meal by now. Unbroken by our spoons, the mound of rice stands intact, jeering at our timetable. It gives off no steam. When I was a little child, I once asked mother to cover the rice, because the white grains were turning into steam and flying away. Everyone laughed, except Shuli.

—Count them, he suggested contemptuously. Find out for yourself whether they are really escaping.

I climb up to his room. Squashed cigarette butts, still wet from their lips, are scattered on the floor and window sill. An ashtray would have saved us the mess, but these barbarians did not ask for one. I replace the drawers inside the desk and close the wardrobe, as if covering a naked body. As if rewinding the film, to the moment before they burst in, when their arrival was still a possibility hanging over us.

My fear is no more, it suddenly strikes me. Taken away, together with Shuli. All in vain, all that fear in vain, I repeat, as if the fear of this event was supposed to create an immunity against it.

I stumble, almost sprain my ankle. Goddamit! The ziggurat? When was it knocked down? I pick it up and check that it is still in one piece. Its stairs are tickling the lines of my palm. A forgotten sensation. Now that he is gone, I can play with the statuette as long as I wish. My hands twitch at the thought, as if stung by it. The ziggurat slips and falls down again. I bolt out of the room. Let him pick it up himself when he is back.

Mother was right perhaps. I had better not stay alone.

I lean against the window. It is twilight. Khaled and Hassan are cycling in the street. I wonder whose mother will call out first to remind her son of his homework. It was not long ago that I used to cycle out there myself. We hardly speak to each other nowadays. Did they give me the cold shoulder after the war or did I keep my distance? I cannot remember. The street looks hazy. My breath has steamed up the window pane. With my forefinger I draw a straight line on the fogged surface. Connect it to a second line. A third. A fourth closes the quadrangle. A diagonal divides it into two triangles. The sum of the angles of every triangle equals 180°. So far, so good. Anything else we can deduce about them or about their relationship? No idea. Geometry has never been my strong point. I wipe off the drawing, steam up a new patch on the pane, and start off with a straight line again. It meets a second. A third intersects them. A capital A comes forth. What next? Allah? Aaron? Adam? Adieu? A fourth line closes it into a triangle. No, two triangles, one enclosing the other. Back to geometry. Let's see now, a triangle within a triangle: they must have a few features in common. It is their angles, if I'm not mistaken, but this lesson is not due before the end of the term. I rub out the drawing and trace a larger triangle. What problem can I assign myself now? My little finger sneaks and draws a second triangle. Across the first. Equally large. Standing on its head. Khaled and Hassan are cycling in and out of the hexagram. If only they knew it! Look everybody, I have drawn the Zionist star. Up here! Above your heads. In spite of you and in spite of your fathers and your fathers' fathers. Before anything happens I hasten to wipe off the outlawed star. Fool, why didn't he erase it from the blackboard in time? Was he too proud or just too slow to react? I steam up the adjacent window pane and draw a six-pointed star again.

Shuli once said the hexagram was an ancient symbol of balance and harmony. The two triangles represented the above and the below, the divine and the human, spirit and matter, intermingled. I contemplate the interlaced triangles, but all I can see is a troublesome star.

I add a pair of thin triangles. A pair of fat triangles. Two triangles with zigzagged sides, like stamps. Two triangles with loose sides. A star with extended corners. A star with sharpened corners, like thorns. A star with convex sides, like a balloon. The window pane is replete with stars, as if it were Christmas. A Zionist Christmas.

Somebody is fumbling with the lock. Either mother or father is back. I wipe my window designs away. The street is dark. The sound of high heels heads to the bathroom. She puts on the lights. I am hungry at last. With only the three of us, supper will be incomplete, like a table with a missing leg

YOM KIPPUR

Hungry?

The question pounces on me as if it has been perching on my bedpost all night, waiting for me to wake up.

I feel a slight pressure under the navel. A flash of heat around my belly. A draught of air. But nowhere hunger. My lips part, my tongue creeps out and sweeps them wet. As is does every morning, and no matter what flavour might have been left by my dreams, a foul aftertaste of sleep lingers in my mouth. I open my eyes. Nine-thirty. Last time I looked at the watch, it was seven. The front door was closing; father was obviously on his way to the synagogue. I have shortened Yom Kippur by two and a half hours.

I leave bed, slowly get dressed. Had I drunk another glass of water yesterday afternoon at the prefast meal, my mouth wouldn't have been that dry now. Are we allowed to wash our faces at least? Certainly not, mother would say. Father, on the other hand, does not hesitate to shave or even brush his teeth on Yom Kippur. But I don't think I would go that far, for what if I swallowed, just by accident, some drops of water while rinsing my mouth?

The doorbell rings.

—It's Dudi, mother cries. Can he come upstairs?

—No, let him stay exactly where he is. I'll be down in a minute.

Quickly I sprinkle my face with water and run down to the sitting room.

Curry is meowing in the yard.

—Your cat's starving, Dudi says.

—Curry's always hungry. He had a huge meal yesterday evening. Tell me, do you believe what they say, that the wishes of your first fast are likely to come true?

—Much the same as the first falling star you see, or the first wishbone you break. So, you've joined the hunger strike too, congratulations.

I do not reply. I am not up to an exchange with Dudi today.

—What's the matter with everybody this year? Even our little one is determined to fast till noon.

—Good for her.

—Nonsense, fasting's making people uptight and sullen, anything but forgiving. This morning, I felt like fried aubergine, and instead of asking Mama or one of the girls, I did it on my own, out of consideration mind you. You should have seen how they paid me back. They freaked out because I forgot to close the kitchen door and the smell wafted into their bedrooms. One by one, they made an appearance in the dining room to tell me how selfish and tactless and mean I was.

—Fried aubergine . . . this morning? You aren't fasting?

—I happen to have a delicate constitution. I just can't go without food for long.

—Dudi, you're thirteen, everyone starts at thirteen, everyone can make it! Unless of course you're sick or something.

The screen door bangs. Curry pules. He pierces the net with the nails of his forepaws, retreats on his hindquarters, and draws the door open. As he retracts his nails from the net, the door slams, rebounds and slams again.

—But he's not thirteen! And his squealing is heartbreaking. Let me give him some milk myself if you can't bear the sight of food, all right?

And without waiting for my reply Dudi springs to his feet with the energy of a well-fed boy and fetches Curry's bowl from the yard. Curry begins meowing his loudest. Dudi heads to our fridge.

—What a gorgeous dinner is waiting for you here, chicken pilau, good God, I can't resist the smell of allspice. The only thing I envy you fasters is the appetite you're building up for the evening. Hey, that's a toffee box I've never seen before. May I . . . ? Thanks. Mmm, it's a mixture of . . . Sorry, I'll keep my mouth shut. Come on, I said I was sorry. So I have hungry eyes, so what? Heavens, everyone's on edge today!

Dudi carries the bowl outside, sucking and chomping. Curry circles between his legs, his head upturned, meowing.

—There you are, Curry boy, I've brought you some milk so you won't say that the wicked Jews are starving you. Hey, I almost tripped over you, will you step aside and let me put the bowl on the ground?

While the toffee is shifting from one side of his mouth to the other, showing no signs of melting away, Dudi asks me to lend him some comics for the long boring day.

—Selma's picking me up around noon. We're going to the synagogue. Want to come along?

Dudi slurps his saliva.

—What for? Everybody will lay into me with inquiries about Baba, and within five minutes they'll have killed my day. Apart from that, it's the animal world which fascinates me at the moment, not the spiritual.

He pauses, as if expecting to be overwhelmed with questions. I remain silent, refusing to grant him the feeling of importance he is begging. Not today. Not while I am fasting and he is not. Dudi does not wait long before he goes on,

—I'm preoccupied with two questions, day and night.

—Two?

—Suppose, just suppose, dogs stopped barking and started speaking . . . they'd mainly discuss smells, right? Now, imagine all the words they'd come up with to describe smells without referring to whatever gives them off.

—I don't get you.

—All right, let's take it step by step. For example, we humans speak of white, red and green, without the need to say the colour of milk, the colour of blood, the colour of grass, do you follow? Good. Now if Lassie could handle smell the way we deal with colour, he wouldn't have to go into concrete details like . . . the smell of the drumstick of a young turkey, cooked in curry and mace, or . . . the smell of the first morning pee of a sixty-year-old who has stones in his kidneys. Two, perhaps three, attributes from the vocabulary of a dog would cover the range of these smells and specify their combinations . . .

He crunches on the toffee, then adds,

—Only we wouldn't understand them, I'm afraid, because we lack their equivalent in our language.

Dudi's ideas often remind me of *suq al-haraj*, the flea market in the old city, where most of the goods can be discarded as junk. And yet, in one case out of a thousand, you come across a real find.

—Did you read this stuff or did you pick it up somewhere? I ask just to annoy him.

—No, by the life of Baba! Why? What'd you mean? You think I'm incapable of such ideas?

—Sure, sure, go on. And the second one?

Dudi hesitates,

—Well . . . it concerns Lassie too. I keep wondering what my dog thinks about while he's masturbating. Ha, ha, ha . . . I'm off now. You'll get back your magazines as soon as the feasts are over, I promise.

He shambles through our yard, chuckling at his own non-sense, and chased by a yowling Curry. As he slams the gate behind him, I let out a cry. The red tail has escaped getting caught in the door by a whisker. No sooner have meows and laughter subsided than listlessness descends upon me. The foul taste in my mouth spreads under my skin, exudes its smell through my pores. My bones feel rusty. I would have willingly skipped the synagogue this year and crawled back to bed, if not for mother.

The idea of spending the day alone in her company, listening to her lamentation, is unbearable.

Curses on me if I find sleep in my bed when my son must lie on the floor! Ashes on me if I breathe fresh air when he's denied a window. Do I have the heart to take a stroll while his moves are restricted, watch television while he is staring at four blank walls, chat with friends while he is all by himself?

And so on and so forth.

Any attempt to lift mother's spirits is met with hostility, as if it is something precious she is being asked to renounce. He's my son, too, but you're overdoing it, father once said, unable to contain himself any longer. You can't fathom a mother's heart, she coldly retorted and refused to speak to him for two days. Since then, the anatomy of my mother's heart intrigues me. At times, it thunders like a combative knight, at other times it whimpers like a convict serving a life sentence.

I suspect father to be, in his heart of hearts, jealous of the devotion and concern which mother bestows upon her son. But unlike me, father is sensible enough not to slip into comparisons and competitions which he is anyway bound to lose. His presence at home exacerbates Shuli's absence. And no matter what I say and do or refrain from saying and doing, Shuli will, from the distance of his cell, always win.

A taxi honks. I plant a kiss on mother's cheek and run off.

I'm not hungry, Selma says with a note of pride as she moves up to the middle of the back seat to make space for me. Next to her, Selma's mother greets me cheerfully behind her sunglasses. Her dress is new, her white shoes are shining, her cheeks evenly powdered. I wonder whether mother would have been upset by the festivity of her attire.

—Isn't your Mama coming?

—No, she's not feeling well.

Selma's mother asks the driver to pull away.

A textbook is lying on Selma's lap: *The Living Organism*. Has she brought homework! No, she has borrowed the book from Ferial, our new biology teacher, and forgottten to return it. Selma expects to see her at the synagogue. Selma's breath tells me that she has not brushed her teeth this morning. I wind down the window, allowing in a gust of hot air. Although it is mid-October, autumn still looks far off and rainfall as real as science fiction. The taxi soon pulls up at the door of the Alwiyah synagogue. We get out. Selma's mother thanks the driver and bids him farewell.

—We paid him yesterday, Selma points out.

—Why?

—'Cause Jews aren't supposed to drive or to spend money on Yom Kippur, remember?

I smile to see our car parked at the end of the street. Unconcerned with our laws, father does not even take the trouble to play tricks or haggle with them.

He has picked a seat at the edge of the men's section. He looks out of place with his straw hat and green eyes and with no prayer book in his hand. Remote too, immersed in his own thoughts. I cross the courtyard, where the service is being held, to the men's section. Father's face lights up. I fling my arms around his neck. His hug almost smothers me, as if he were squeezing a daughter and a son at the same time. I refrain from detaching myself too soon, lest I hurt his feelings.

—How are you taking it? he asks after he has let go of me.

—So far so good, apart from a parched throat.

—Don't run around too much, daughter. It's quite hot and you're constantly losing fluid, even though you won't feel it right away.

I nod to spare myself further advice. Our headmaster, unshaved, wearing a skullcap, suddenly comes over and sits beside father. Even in the house of God and in my father's presence, I am intimidated by this skinny man. Even when he is only inquiring after Shuli. *Allah kerim*, God is compassionate, father replies, insinuating that there is no news. In contrast to mother, father expresses his grief through silence, which is often misleading, as people take it for an eagerness to listen. The headmaster shakes his head in sorrow, and pours out the story of his brother-in-law's arrest, two weeks ago.

I sneak to the garden and join Selma, chatting with a girl two classes above us.

—She's not here.

—Who?

—Ferial, who else! They're saying she usually attends the Shemtob Synagogue. It's on the edge of Bettawin, half an hour's walk away. I've got to see her. I had promised she'd get her book back before Yom Kippur. Will you come with me? Please? It's boring here anyway; none of our friends are hanging around.

We set off along sidestreets empty of pedestrians as if the sun has imposed a curfew. Iron kiosk shutters have been rolled down for the midday break, tantalizing us with bright billboards of Seven-Up, Sinalco, Canada Dry, and other refreshments.

—What wouldn't I give for a cold glass of sherbet, Selma says.

—Orange or mulberry?

—Pomegranate, with crushed ice as plentiful as the kernels.

We seek shade but all the streets provide is the shadow of

electric poles. So we stretch out our arms to the sides and balance along the dark line, pretending to be acrobats walking on a wire. A tall and fleshy blonde woman stomps out from a sidestreet, and marches towards us. In spite of the yellow umbrella she is holding above her, her skin is flushed from the sun. In harsh broken English, she asks for the way to the Goethe Institute. Selma and I vie with each other in guiding her, only to falter in turn, as Selma is familiar with the route whereas the foreign words belong to me. The woman grumbles that it is time we issued a street map for our city or at least took the trouble to name our sidestreets. Selma's stomach suddenly rumbles. The two of us burst into hysterical laughter. Looking insulted, the woman grumbles some incomprehensible words and marches off in her original direction.

In no less than an hour, we reach the Shemtob Synagogue. After a glimpse into the backyard where only small children are romping, we climb up to the women's gallery. Dressed up ladies, young and old, are following the service or just chatting. No trace of Ferial. While Selma works her way through the seats I lean over the balustrade, air my head under the ceiling fan and observe the hall below, the large arched windows, the fans and chandeliers hanging down from the ceiling. The *bimah*, the reader's platform, rises in the middle of the hall, surrounded by an iron balustrade bearing designs identical to that of the gallery. The men are sitting on wooden benches dispersed about the hall. How different is this synagogue from the Alwiyah one, which is a mere courtyard provided with portable chairs arranged in two sections around the reader's portable lectern. A synagogue out of a suitcase. My eyes search for the Ark and find an old wooden cupboard carved with Hebrew verses standing against a wall to the far left of the platform. Inside it the Torah Scrolls, the holiest objects in the synagogue, are housed.

And how did they display the *Muallaquat*, I wonder, suddenly reminded of our Arabic lesson from last week. It is a collection of seven distinguished Arabic odes—each considered to be its author's best piece, and representing the finest of pre-Islamic poetry. A legend maintains that in the *Jahiliyah*, the Age of Ignorance, as the pre-Islamic era is called in Arabic, the Seven Odes used to be hung on the pagan shrine of Mecca.

The idea of worshipping poetry instead of law fascinates me.

But I still cannot imagine how the desert Arabs actually hung their verses. Definitely not in the trivial way we dangle nylon stockings on a clothesline, as Selma suggested. Where is Selma? I fail to discern her red head amid dozens of white, brown, and black perms. The made-up faces reveal no signs of hunger, thirst, or any physical deprivation whatsoever. Can they all, nevertheless, be fasting? Two elderly women by the aisle are beckoning to me.

—Come here, child, aren't you the daughter of what's his name? We've heard that your *khal* got engaged lately, over there. Congratulations, my girl, may your day turn up soon.

I shake my head. You've made a mistake, I am about to explain, I've got no *khal*, no maternal uncle, neither here, nor over there, nor anywhere. But the woman breaks in,

—What do you know, young lady, time goes by much faster than you can tell and it waits for no *emir* nor *wezir*. I'm related to the bride, you see, a good catch, take my word for it, renowned family, and wealthy too. Between us, Hanina, they should have married her off long ago. She was nearly thirty. But if you ask me, her father was the one to blame! He had a soft spot for this daughter, and you know what happens once you give in to their whims. The poor matchmaker exhausted her list, but there was no suitor to the *khatoun*'s liking. This one had a high-pitched voice, that one had no sense of humour, the third had an old bat for a mother, and the fourth was a chainsmoker. Hell she gave them until she had no suitor left to find fault with. Anyway, all's well that ends well, thank God.

Assuming that my interrogation is over, I take a step backward, intending to tiptoe away and once at a safe distance, politely bid farewell. But the other woman, Hanina, grabs my arm.

—Aren't you the sister of Shuli, the one who drew the Star? Poor boy, may God look after him, may he be among you on Succot, *inshallah*.

And she throws up her two hands.

—But, to be frank, girl, wasn't your brother looking for trouble? I mean, why did he have to cover the walls of the classroom with Stars of David? Who's saying this? Do you remember where we heard it, Joza? Never mind, go on my child, you tell me what really happened.

I relate the incident, as I have done dozens of times before, briefly and flatly, to prevent further prying while I scan the gallery for Selma, or anyone who could serve as my pretext to break away.

—Now isn't that a different story altogether, Joza? Goodness, the rubbish people make up. Hopefully he hasn't been beaten up or something? Thank God. Forgive me child, but I always weep when I'm depressed, I can't help it. Such a young man in the prime of his life, may God pay them back for all the sufferings they're inflicting on us. Plague on them. All the ten plagues of Egypt in one day, amen.

Not today, Joza whispers. Such thoughts are strictly forbidden on Yom Kippur. Yom Kippur is a day of forgiveness.

Hanina draws a handkerchief from her handbag and wipes away her tears. After she has studied the two dark dots on the white mousseline, she flaunts them as evidence of her agony. Joza reaches for her own handbag, pulls out a mirror and applies another layer of orange lipstick over her dry lips, their sole nourishment for the day.

—A brilliant boy, they say, Joza resumes. I heard your

brother was to have been admitted to the best university in America and that his mind was set on crossing Shat al-Arab last year. Only your father objected and . . . what? You've got an appointment! And only now you remembered? What a pity, it was nice chatting with you, but go if you have to, child, we won't keep you back. Are you fasting by the way? Good for you then, may you be sealed with happiness.

—Did you see that, Hanina? We're old enough to be her grandmothers, couldn't she have waited for my sentence to end?

I dash down the stairs, out into the backyard, cursing and holding back my tears, until the children's curious looks send me inside again. Longing to be alone, I huddle up on the bottom stair while Joza's words keep swirling inside my head.

—Hey, did you evaporate or what, I've been looking for you all over the gallery, guess who I met?

I turn back, nonplussed, as if Selma has landed from some other Yom Kippur.

—Her mother!

—Whose mother?

—Ferial's mother, what's the matter with you? An old chatterbox, goodness, all the rubbish she dumped on me. She claimed Ferial would have been better off in a Muslim school, where the pupils tremble with fear at the mere sight of their teachers. Then she admitted that Ferial had no other alternative. For nobody's going to employ her, and nobody's going to ask for her hand either, that's word for word what she said, I swear by God. In her view, as long as our destiny in this country is not clear, no Jew's gonna get married, but I didn't really get the connection. Do you think Ferial's already twenty-five? If I were a man I'd marry her on the spot. She's so beautiful, don't you agree?

I shrug, weary of Ferial and of weddings.

—Eventually she told me that Ferial had attended the

morning service here then left with a friend for the Ezra David Synagogue. Have you ever been there? It's by the river, ten minutes' away, why don't we drop in and have a look?

On our way out, we run into a cheerful Hai, dressed in white. He strokes our two heads simultaneously.

—I miss you awfully girls, let's hope we'll go swimming next summer again, *inshallah*.

A bunch of young men and women have gathered in the courtyard of the Ezra David Synagogue. Most of the faces are familiar. Some I associate with the Jewish Sports Centre; others I remember from school, years back. As Selma obtains no definite answer from them with regard to Ferial, she proceeds to the women's gallery while I loiter outside, under the date palm. To distract myself from the gnawing in my belly, I listen to the group's discussion.

—Have they entirely gone out of their minds? When in history could losers ever afford to set conditions?

—When they're swimming in petroleum and when they've got the Soviet Union, and all the communist bloc behind them.

—Isn't there anything Jews can talk about nowadays, apart from our fate or politics?

—Full of hot air, so pleased with their Three Nos, I'm surprised they didn't issue stamps in commemoration of their bright summit conference. A set of three, a stamp for each No.

They burst out laughing.

—Drop your voices, we can be heard from the street . . .

Prayers indoors, jokes outdoors, I wonder which mood is more apt to appeal to our God. The man who suggested issuing stamps for the Three Nos is moving towards me.

—Aren't you Shuli's sister? he asks, peering at me over his sunglasses.

I nod my head, apprehensive of a new interrogation.

—I'm Adel, remember? You came over with your parents to see me after my release. I had been detained with your brother in the Rashid Camp.

Now I remember him.

—He was the propagandist, I was the treasurer, that's how we joked about it when we were in a good mood. I was accused of collecting donations for Israel, but the moment Major Abu Azzam laid his hands on father's two hundred *dinars*, the charge stopped being an issue and within two hours I was out. I still have to report to the police though, once a week. But I really shouldn't complain.

He is wearing a golden pendant: the Two Tablets of the Law shaped like an open book.

—Any progress? Any prospects of . . . of his release? he asks, voicing the last word with a measure of inhibition.

Release?—our daily source of hopes and disillusions. I shake my head.

Father's endeavours to intercede through senior officials have proved worthless, while Zeki's connections soon reached a dead end. Abu Azzam is as shrewd as a fox, one intermediary concluded, the sort of fellow "who'd lead you to the river and bring you back thirsty." Apparently, Shuli is a special case, more than 200 *dinars*' worth—at least in the Major's eyes, who might well be saving him for who knows what profitable occasion,

—You've got no idea how supportive his presence was to me. God, it all happened too fast. Within a few minutes, my existence became as trivial as that of an ant. I was still dazed when they shoved me into the stuffy cell and locked the door behind me. Anything could happen inside those four brick walls, I thought, and nobody would see it or hear of it. I was entirely at their mercy. On the bricked up window, there was a calendar. The picture on it was of a cosy interior with a pot of flowers on a round table, and a dog napping on a rug. Suddenly I felt like tearing everything to pieces. It was then that . . .

Adel stops talking, and swallows hard. I wonder why he is telling me all this.

—Shuli had asked for the calendar to keep track of the days he would cross out of his life, I say.

—After I had sobbed my heart out, your brother went through the daily routine of the camp with me, and told me which guards to be careful of. He kept reassuring me that I'd be out within less than a week. And how right he was, poor chap. It must have been desperate to watch us get arrested and then released, while his case came to a standstill. Funny, I used to take him for an arrogant fellow. But there, in that room, where he was too dejected to put on his airs, I came to know him.

Adel takes off his sunglasses and rubs his eyes. His eyelashes are so long he could have combed them.

—Next time you see him, send him my best wishes.

I have not visited Shuli even once during the last six weeks. I do not have the heart to see him locked up in that hole, downcast like a ten-year-old who has wet his pants. But how can this Adel understand that I prefer the impetuous, antagonistic spirit of my brother to the despondent friend he felt so much at home with?

A scowling Selma shows up, the biology textbook tucked under her arm.

—She was here a while ago, but left again for the Meir Tweg Synagogue. Now isn't that tough luck? Anyway, Meir Tweg's not that far, near the YMCA, a question of . . .

—No, no, no, I cry out, I've been to more synagogues today than in my whole life. I'm fed up and worn out, and we still have the trek back to Alwiyah.

—But we've got plenty of time. Look, the *Haftarah* hasn't started yet.

—You're not listening, I said I'm done in, enough is enough! You go ahead as far as you wish, I'm off back to Alwiyah, with or without you.

—But wait a minute, maybe . . .

—Maybe you tell me why you didn't hand her mother the book in the first place? Maybe because you're keen on chasing our teacher from one synagogue to the other? Or maybe you're just enjoying the heat, testing our own biology?

Adel grins. Is he siding with me, or just amused at our girlish dispute?

—Nonsense, I couldn't have trusted her with the book. I've got to put it into Ferial's hands myself. I've promised her.

Selma cradles the old dog-eared textbook as she whispers the last three words. Her gentleness strikes me as unusual, almost suspicious. Eager to extract one more smile from Adel, I push on.

—I don't think it's the book you're worried about . . .

—Never mind what you think, she cuts me short. Let's shove off.

—But . . . but what about Ferial? You've promised . . .

—None of your business! Let's go now.

Adel pats me on the back and bids us farewell. Selma beckons me with her head. At the gate, I am seized by an impulse to glimpse at the long-lashed man under the date palm one last time. I turn back to find his gaze fixed on me. My heart leaps. Adel's face lights up. I look at his curly black hair, his Clark Gable moustache, his olive-green complexion, and wonder whether other girls find him attractive.

We strike out along Abu Nuwas, walking on the river side of the street. The sun is half way down, like a tyrant forced to bow. The heat must have abated, but I barely feel the difference. My head is burning, my throat is sore. Not far from the river's edge, I discern a barrellike object drifting downstream. A corpse, a cow perhaps, is floating on its back, its limbs thrust up in the air. There's something which has drunk itself to explosion, Hai used to joke each time we encountered the blown-up corpse of an animal in the water. Nauseated by the sight, I ask Selma to take a shortcut. She does not even bother to reply. Her face is flushed, from heat, strain, or fury, I cannot tell. She must be terribly frustrated at having missed Ferial again and again. Goodness, what a futile pursuit it has been, and on top of it I let her down and entertained Adel at her expense. Who is he to me after all? Who cares about the length of his eyelashes, and so what if he discovered my brother's soul in prison?

While I am thinking up an apology, Selma, without warning, crosses Abu Nuwas and turns into a sidestreet. If she has complied with my request and is taking a shortcut, why doesn't she say it?

—Wait, I scuttle after her.

But Selma, acting deaf, is striding along as if resolved to lose me. I would certainly go astray if I were left on my own. Damn you Selma—furious or not, you still owe me the way back to the Alwiyah Synagogue. I summon up my strength, run to catch up with her. We pass a grocer's, a barber's, a haberdasher's, a mosque, girls skipping.

—Three Lucky Sticks for the price of two, only today, only for you! the vendor behind is harassing us.

—Some other day, Selma barks back.

He snuggles his cart up to our behinds. We make off across an unbuilt space, weave through piles of rubbish, and deserted *serifas*, until the ice cream tune is out of earshot. The muscles of my flat feet are stinging, as if about to tear. I lag behind Selma as we go from one sidestreet to another, with an inkling that our journey at noon was much shorter than the way back. We walk past a Pakistani boy polishing shoes at the threshold of a house. His green plastic sandals increase my doubts. Am I raving, or did we in fact pass this shoeblack a while ago? We must be going in circles, I complain, but Selma ignores my remark. Has she lost her way and will not admit it, or is she determined to drag me through detours until I collapse?

The moment we set foot in the Alwiyah Synagogue, Selma and I split up. Pangs of hunger are tearing my belly. Father has not moved from his place and is listening now to the stories of a former colleague. *Ustad* Heskel is reading the *Haftarah*. I fetch myself a prayer book, and sink into a chair in the shade. The women around me constantly fan themselves, as if it were part of the service. I search for the passage *ustad* Heskel is reading. His full voice sends me back to elementary school, when the *ustad* used to tell us Bible stories while we licked lollipops behind the lids of our desks. Everyone is standing up and facing west. I follow suit. The fasters are turning around me. My legs feel like pencils with sharpened points. They cannot hold up my weight any longer. I grip the armrest, but the congregation is whirling faster and faster. The blown-up cow recurs, lying face down on the shore, while water drains from its eyes, ears, nostrils, and genitals. Nausea overwhelms me. Somebody shoves me into a cube of a room. Unable to distinguish the brick floor from the brick ceiling, I lose my balance. The next moment I find myself sprawled on the floor, my head caught between two chairs.

—The girl's fainted!

—It's dehydration!

—These kids shouldn't be roaming the streets on a hot day like this. They wander from one synagogue to the other as if they were coffee shops.

—Whose daughter is she? Where's her mother?

Some other mother picks me up. Her voice is familiar, but I cannot place it. She sits me up, gently pats my cheeks and sprinkles my face with rose water. I press my lips together lest a drop sneaks into my mouth. How would Dudi's dog describe this smell? Sweet? Refreshing? A soft wind is blowing on my forehead. A breeze? I open my eyes. The old lady fanning my face heaves a sigh of relief. All the other women have turned to me now instead of facing the

Ark. Let one of them try and worm information out of me and I swear I'll fetch the hose from the garden and shower the whole congregation.

—It's nothing child, it has already passed. Just take it easy.

Everyone is seated again. I can barely hold my head upright. If only I could rest it on a pillow, suck my thumb, and surrender to the emptiness within me. My eyelids close. *Ustad* Heskel's resonant voice rises, as if all the prayer books in the courtyard were his loudspeakers. I can hardly follow his melodious reading. If only he would tell us a story instead. There he is, the good old *ustad*, distributing books in our classroom. Selma has taken her usual seat beside me, but what are Shuli and Adel doing in our class, and how can our headmaster make a fool of himself and sit on a school bench again? "Every Jew is entrusted with a book," *ustad* Heskel says while Shuli examines a hardback as fat as a dictionary. "But why so many pages cut out?" my brother cries out with indignation. "No book is new, my boy, and none is flawless, " the *ustad* replies. Now Shuli must read every written word in the world in order to retrieve his missing pages. Our headmaster gets a telephone directory where the parents of all the pupils are listed. "To lose it is to lose yourself," the *ustad* warns, wagging his forefinger, but Selma pushes away the paperback placed on her desk and defiantly clutches the biology textbook to her breast. Joza and Hanina are tittering like schoolgirls in the back row. Their books are sealed and will open only at the utterance of a magic word. That is why the two women are so garrulous and must chatter about every topic, from *she-hon* till *behon*, until the magic word accidently passes their lips. The pages Adel is turning are scorching, unless he cools them constantly with his tears. Father's diary is written in a language only he can read, and therefore my father is bound to lead a solitary life. *Ustad* Heskel motions to me to pick the booklet with the brown leather cover lying on the table. My photograph, which is not really my own, is stuck on the first page. "What's this?" I ask the *ustad*. "A passport!" he replies, and at that moment, they all disappear and I am left all alone in the classroom—which is no longer our classroom.

Where is the *ustad*, why has he stopped reading? I open my eyes to twilight and to some other, younger voice. How long have I dozed and since when has Selma been sitting beside me? The biology book on her lap is open on the fifth lesson, but she is squinting in my direction, with the rueful smile of someone who has broken her mother's crystal vase. I yawn, stretch out my arms, leaf through the prayer book, and take my time before I condescend to glance at her. After which, Selma immediately bends over me and smacks a loud kiss on my ear.

—It's the *ne'ila*. We've got only three stars to wait for and then we're through. We've made it, Lina, we've made it through our first Kippur!

The fasters are standing again. I push myself up to my feet. You really don't have to, everyone saw you collapse, Selma whispers. No, no, I retort. No special favours, not on my first fast.

The last supplications are recited. I hope mother remembers to warm the chicken pilau in time. Silence follows for the *shofar* to break through. The ram's horn, blasting from all the synagogues on earth this evening, blows our penitence before God and proclaims that we too are a part of this world—whether the world appreciates it or not.

The first stars are shining overhead. More than three, more than ten.

—Next year in Jerusalem, somebody murmurs. I glance left and right, resentfully. Nobody's moving from here, nobody's going anywhere, neither to Jerusalem nor to America. Not even to heaven. Not before my brother is released and among us again.

"May you be signed and sealed for a good year." The Day of Atonement is over. The fasters are congratulating and embracing one another. The rows of chairs soon zigzag, the two sections unite into one turmoil. In a spurt of energy, I run to father and jump at his neck. Together, we weave our way through the crowd to the canopied part of the court-yard, where the Ark is standing. Its doors are open, the Torah Scrolls are displayed in their silver cases. I stand on tiptoe, crane my neck forwards to kiss the silver and breathe my wishes.

A taxi honks outside the gate of the synagogue. A lighter snaps. A woman is weeping in her brother's arms. An old man is washing his unshaved face under the tap. Someone is telling a new joke about the Prime Minister. They are distributing glasses of sherbet to the fasters. Father intercepts one of my two hands reaching out for the tray.

—Take it easy, daughter, one's enough! Drink it slowly, don't overload your stomach. You may have your second glass at home, and the third after the meal.

The Seville orange sherbet soothes my throat and spreads a cool bitter aftertaste in my mouth. The flavour of atone-ment, I suppose.

ON STAMPS AND SWALLOWS

Baghdad, 9 June 1968

Dear Clifford,

To my embarrassment, I can't remember if I ever thanked you for the First Day Cover you sent me two years ago. Please forgive me, although no excuse could justify my delayed reply. I can even recall how carefully I studied the set of British Birds, but of the four only the black-headed gull rang a bell . . .

I saw gulls for the first time when I sailed on the Anglo-Indian cargo ship from Iraq to England, forty-five years ago. Among the few passengers on board, I was the youngest, fifteen years old, travelling on my own and, scared to death. But soon the sea distracted me from my fears, that is, I was sick most of the journey. Eager to tread on solid earth again I'd cry "land" together with the English sailors whenever we spotted a harbour on the Arabian Sea, the Red Sea, the Mediterranean, the Atlantic Ocean, or the Bay of Biscay. But when the gulls of Portsmouth joined us, heading to the horizon, gaggling and hovering above the ship, the sailors just whispered,

"England."

I fell for her at first sight, although the sight was no more than a streak parting the sea from the sky.

But why am I telling you all this? It happened a long time ago, and we are not through with stamps yet. I am enclosing two sets: the International Tourist Year, issued in December 1967, and Iraqi Birds from January of this year. To the best of my knowledge, no other stamps within the range of your interest have been issued in Iraq in the last two years.

Now that I think of it, I must admit that my stamp collecting is, like England, a borrowed love— one for which you may hold yourself entirely responsible! Stamps are birds, you used to say at school forty-five years ago, the carrier pigeons of the twentieth century. Your collection at the time barely exceeded thirty: portraits of King George V and older ones of King Edward VII and Queen Victoria, to which I contributed Babylonian bulls and winged cherubs—that won me your friend-ship, I dare say. Or that was at least how I read your unique farewell present––the photograph you con-verted into a giant stamp. It must have taken you days to cut the frame into delicate perforations, mark the five shillings at each corner and the date of my departure at the bottom, 12.8.1927, crowned by the double half-circle of the postmark.

It was the photograph of our rowing team, dressed in caps, jackets and shorts—if you remem-ber. It was shot during my last term at school, when nobody took me for a foreigner any longer, not in that picture nor in real life. My English was impeccable. My looks did not give me away either, unlike Ramesh, the Indian boy, who was thrown into the river by the other boarders "to wash off his darkness."

Until last year, our rowing team photo was pinned up in my wardrobe, behind my shirts. Not in the sitting room, lest our guests would misread it as flaunting, nor on my desk, lest my wife would tease me and call it "my corrective institution." It was rash of me perhaps, but I destroyed it, out of cautiousness, on the first day of the war.

The last sentence is crossed out.

After four years at Oxford, I collected my degree and set off for Iraq. So many ballads sing of the longing for home, but give me one that depicts the despair of an exile bound to return. Crossing the Suez Canal, I prayed that the sands would fall back into the waterway and stop us from reaching Basra. As the groves of date palms loomed on the horizon, I whispered "Iraq" and waited for the name to awaken my homing instincts. Again and again I uttered it, until the guttural sound estranged me from my own voice. I was no sailor, I understood at last, only a deserter posing as an English gentleman.

But let us leave my rootlessness and return to stamps. As your farewell present predicted, it is most probably our collections that have kept us in touch all these years. Still, today, our worlds overlap whenever we pore over a pile of stamps, whether it is you, sorting out the damaged ones, or I, hunting for "errors." It was not for nothing that I became an accountant, my wife likes to say with regard to my obsession with philatelic errors. Not that I totally disagree with her, only I would rather compare it to a quest, the pursuit of treasure at the bottom of the sea. And I did chance upon quite a few treasures, the most recent of which was a British one, whose perforation cut Her Majesty's profile in the middle. But as life often claims back what it has once granted, for lack of cash I may soon be compelled to sell them as I sold our Kashan carpet last month.

Clifford, I turned sixty yesterday.

Men my age have built houses in the suburbs, cosy nests for the golden years—as they are called nowadays. I, on the other hand, am living out of a suitcase, preparing the family and myself for a journey. Where did I go wrong to end up an immigrant, if not a refugee, at sixty?

The two last paragraphs are crossed out.

Yesterday, on my sixtieth birthday, my wife and daughter surprised me with a new magnifying glass—which just reminds me that the names of the enclosed "Iraqi Birds" are printed only in Arabic. So here is their translation, in ascending order of value: the bulbul, the hoopoe, the jay, the white stork, the marbled duck, the swallow. Being a bird of passage, the swallow shouldn't be included in this series you'd say, and I would totally agree. It is even called *sind-ou hind* in Arabic, the one from the lands of Sind and India.

Their departure caught me unawares this spring, the swallows I mean. Suddenly I realised that the days were longer, that the smell of orange blossom was wafting through our garden, that birds were copulating on the branches, that the breeze was blowing, announcing the new season.

It is quite painful, I'm afraid, to watch the world flower while I myself am growing dull, as time stops for me and life stagnates.

I have been out of work for the last eleven months, sacked two weeks after the Six Day War. Besides, it has become quite difficult for me as a Jew to draw money from my own bank account. Fortunately, my former colleague, Z., one of the few non-Jewish friends who did not shun us after the war, secretly brings me work and reports it as overtime. If not for him, I wouldn't like to think what would have become of us.

The last paragraph is crossed out.

My son S. was arrested eight months ago,

The last sentence is crossed out.

Shaul, my nineteen-year-old son, has been detained for the last eight months. The sequence of events which had led to his arrest is too painful for me to relate and too absurd, I'm afraid, for your English mind to grasp. My wife, who visits him once a month, says that he has free access to a toilet and a tap. He is also allowed books, thank God. Nevertheless, I am quite concerned about his powers of endurance. Shaul has never been particularly tough, and, although quite intelligent, he is still immature and by no means sensible. But to be honest, it is mainly I who am to blame for his current misfortune. Had I not been overprotective and imposed my will upon him, he would have now been studying at an American university instead of languishing in some army cell . . .

Naturally, you can't expect civil rights in a country ruled by military dictatorship, justice in a society still struggling against feudalism, or integrity in a people torn between a tradition in standstill and imported modernity. But after their defeat in the last war, our rulers lost the little moderation they still possessed. There are not more than three thousand Jews in this country, what threat can we possibly present to a population of eight million?

Believe it or not, we still get some foreign papers, but since the articles on the Middle East are censored, their relevance to us is significantly reduced. I'd give anything to know, for instance, if any attempts are being made in the world to pull us out of here, or just how long we will be kept like hostages in this country. For the sake of my family, I do my best to display an optimistic face, but whenever I wallow in despair, it dawns on me that a decade is a very short span, not more than a twinkling in terms of history.

History itself looks like a chain of inconclusive, unfinished episodes . . . is it possible that such a diffuse author is our God?

Father did not sign the letter. I crumple the creased sheets back into a ball and toss them into the wastepaper basket. Like his previous letters, they will end up as ash flushed down the lavatory.

He folds a sheet of stamps along the perforation lines. The swallow is illustrated with pointed narrow wings, a short bill, and a forked tail. Father divides the sheet into ten rows, splits each row into ten stamps, and inserts the hundred identical squares into a blue envelope.

Not even a jigsaw puzzle for beginners. Just a flight of migratory birds dispatched to Oxford without a return address.

PART III

.

ONE MORE REVOLUTION

*Z*ebil! Rubbish! He cries out as he rings one doorbell after the other. It is collected on Mondays, Thursdays, and Saturdays, early in the morning. Mother asks me to take out the bin. I do as I am told without arguing this time, keen myself to have it emptied. The roofless lorry advances slowly towards our house. From either side of the street, a man is picking up the bins waiting before the gates. A third is standing inside the lorry, up to his ankles in litter.

Dustmen, Laurence used to call them. A delicate term, I thought, and pictured English rubbish to be odourless, pale, and airy—like sawdust.

—Ready? *Abul zebil*, the rubbish man asks.

Ready is echoed from above. The Langley's bin is flung up. The man in the lorry seizes it, empties it to his side, and drops it into the hands of the man below. Then he bends down and manipulates the greasy pile, searching for some item of value in the English refuse. Stale bread, egg shells, chicken bones, orange peel, garden clippings, broken bottles, balls of paper, torn nylon stockings, and a number of empty food cans. I feel uneasy at the thoroughness of his inspection. The rubbish man fingers the contorted bristles of a toothbrush, runs a single scissor blade over his chin, then tucks the two articles into the pocket of his rolled-up trousers.

—Ready? shouts the man below, and hurls up our bin, the first in a series of three.

Now that it is buried under two bucketsful, nobody will have the chance to scrabble through our refuse.

The rank smell of the lorry is receding. I shake our empty bin to chase away the fly inside, whizzing and whirling around the yellow grains of rice stuck to the sides. Two bangs against the wall and the fly finds its way out. Too late for it to catch up with the lorry, which has reached the main street.

I breathe a sigh of relief. They have disposed of my first sanitary towels.

It caught me unawares yesterday—a lump of blood smudged on my pants, so thick and dark that I let out a cry of awe, then screamed for mother to come urgently to the bathroom. She neither smiled nor frowned at the sight, but her voice sounded tired as she instructed me to wash away the blood stains with cold water, and showed me how to hook the two ends of a sanitary towel to the pink belt which I was to wear under my knickers. Her matter-of-fact demonstration annoyed me. When I asked if it was definite, if there was really no way out, she fondled my head briefly—for the last time, I assumed—and said we were now in the same boat. Then she left me to my lot.

What had made me so certain that I, of all females, would be spared?

I hate to be in the same boat as you, I wanted to yell back, urge her to put a stop to my bleeding, postpone it for a year, perhaps two, for I was by no means ready yet for such a life-long commitment.

But when the warm liquid trickled from my vagina, the sensation was far from unpleasant, and although sharp, the odour was in no way repulsive. On the contrary, I even recognised a vague familiarity about it. Moreover, the idea of an inner wound that did not hurt was a paradox which endowed my body with an aura of mystery. If only I were not bleeding so much. Covering up the mess gave me a hard time, wrapping the sodden towel in a newspaper—as mother had suggested—proved insufficient. Its smell might be detected, I feared, or else its shape might give it away. So I wrapped it further until it swelled to the size of a shoe and laid it under Curry's nose, who sniffed it all over and meowed inquiringly. I swathed the package with additional sheets and tried again. Only when the cat lost interest in sniffing and started playing football with the parcel did I relax and dump it at last into the rubbish bin.

Adah, habit, we call it in colloquial Arabic, as if it were any other habit one may take up or abandon of one's own accord.

In the same boat, I mumble, as I put the empty bin back in the kitchen. Suddenly my swimming date with Selma dawns on me. I cannot make it tomorrow morning. Not in my state! I ought to bike to her place and cancel our appointment. Didn't I tell you it was contagious, she will mock me, as if my bleeding were another accomplishment of hers. Our child has finally made it, she will tell all the other girls, for I was the only one in the class who had not menstruated. Such secrets leaked out in the summer, whenever a girl missed three or more successive days of swimming. At first it puzzled me that their absences did not coincide, for I had imagined all women in the world bleeding on the same days, the last five of each month.

But who said I ought to announce my menses at all? All I need is a credible excuse—not a headache, not a sore throat, and definitely not a cold. None of the stories which girls use during their period, grinning in a mixture of mischief and apology.

Selma's mocking words haunt me all day. Yet no matter how I ponder the problem, I fail to find a sound explanation that would mislead her.

At night, I set the alarm for quarter past five and place it under my bed on the roof. If they do not find me at our gate

at five-thirty tomorrow, Selma and her father will honk and
honk until they have woken the whole street. I lie in bed and
observe the full moon overhead. The milky face and its smile
remind me of a bedtime game that Shuli and I used to play
on full-moon nights. We had to disassemble the features of
the face and replace them with landscape—hills and valleys.
I visualise the hills, but my eyes are still blind to them. I
make a new attempt. The white smile persists, fatuous, like a
white lie. I am about to give up when, without warning, the
disc in the sky changes into a sphere—a radiant planet suspended in a dark, infinite universe. The sky is no longer
above, but all around me. The moon has moved closer. I've
made it, I can see the moon! I would cry out, fixing it with
my gaze, lest it would slip away. Good! Now drop it and try
to catch the face again, my brother would dictate. The quicker
you shift, the more points you'll get. But my eyes are too
possessive to let go of the planet, which is slowly freezing
into a still life.

A star falls. A wish is released into the night.

It must be a hangover from childhood to believe in shooting stars, I tell myself and turn over, my back to the moon.

The hour hand hits three. The alarm could not have gone
off. It sounds more like machine gun fire, coming from the
west bank. The Presidential Palace? Now it is cannon shots, I
am sure of it. I pick up clock, pillow, and blanket and rush
indoors. Mother meets me on the stairs, on her way to call
me inside. Father is trying to tune the radio in the bedroom,
but all the local stations are silent.

—God be with us, it's a military coup! Who could it be
this time? mother exclaims.

—Go back to sleep, daughter, father says. Whoever these
gangsters might be, it will eventually come to light—by
morning at the latest.

I retire to my room and turn off the alarm, reconciled with
the world again. It is beyond doubt that all tomorrow's

appointments will be suspended—no matter on whose side the star has fallen.

I wake up with a start the next morning and check my sanitary towel. Soaked again. My knickers too. It's a miracle that the sheet has remained clean. Then I see that I am in my room and not on the roof, and last night's shots flash through my mind. I look out of the window. The street is dead, as if there is nobody left to shoot. I join my parents at the breakfast table downstairs. Radio Baghdad has come to life again. It is broadcasting communiques given out by the Council of the Revolution. The former Nationalist regime consisted of illiterate and corrupt men, thieves, opportunists, and Zionist spies—the new voice is snorting. The change our country has been craving for is at last attained. Not a single drop of blood was shed last night, the announcer assures us. The former president has already been dispatched by plane to London this morning.

—Good for him! I sigh.

"*Wahda, hurryiah, ishtirakyiah,*" unity, liberty, socialism. They are repeated at the end of each communique and again between the martial songs. I pour hot tea on a hunk of hard Kurdish cheese, and pierce it with my knife to check its softness. "*Wahda, hurryiah, ishtirakyiah*"—always in the same order. Even I can recall the slogans of the Ba'ath, who seized power in 1963, five years ago. Although they did not rule longer than ten months, their name has become associated with the notorious national guard and blood baths.

A new President is appointed. Portfolios and key positions in the government are being redistributed among the adherents of the new regime. Lists are being read—names of new generals, ministers, general managers, ambassadors. Enough names to fill a telephone book. The Ba'aths are calling the exiles home, pledging to stamp out corruption, to pave the way for democracy, and to release political prisoners.

Mother glances questioningly at father.

—Don't build up hope, he replies. By political prisoners they mean members of political parties, and this, too, will most probably begin and end with Ba'ath cronies and activists.

—*Waqa' mezzalem*, may their fortune fail! Couldn't they have waited for a while? Why now, when our situation has just begun to improve?

A month ago, forty Jewish detainees were released without prior notice. In the same week, the Minister of the Interior promised our *hacham* that the rest, about sixty, would be discharged within the next days. No wonder Jewish morale immediately skyrocketed. We believed that the worst was already behind us, and that our star would soon be on the ascendant again. A rumour circulated that the authorities were on the point of issuing *laissez-passer* documents for those who wished to leave the country for good. Although weeks passed and the Minister of the Interior did not fulfill his promise, the Jews, all the same, felt secure enough to return to some forgotten activities, such as frequenting coffee shops and promenading along the river bank. Some students even went to see *Un homme et une femme* at the Nasr Cinema. Selma's father hired a boat for the summer. I was allowed to join in.

—No matter what policy the new regime adopts towards us, father goes on, I wouldn't expect any drastic changes in the coming weeks. They've got more urgent matters to settle, interior opposition to begin with. What's the future of three thousand Jews in comparison?

A twenty-four hour curfew is imposed throughout the country. Time enough to arrest opponents, suspected opponents, and potential opponents. Dudi's mother drops by to share her worries with us. A few days ago, the Minister of Justice in person promised her that all the Jewish detainees would, in no time, be released.

—I had a hunch that this time he really meant it. And silly

me was dreaming already. I saw Abu Dudi out, I saw us celebrating the bar mitzvah of our son at last. Woe is me. I suppose the Minister himself is sitting in jail now!

I notice a pimple above her upper lip and wonder if Dudi's
mother is having her period, too.

No matter how obscure the situation is, it requires
patience. More patience. Any attempt to contact party members is premature. It might bring about more harm than
good. Like the rest of the country, we have no option but to
wait and see.

Selma and her father wait a week then resume their swimming schedule, regardless of whether it is the Nationalists or
the Ba'aths who occupy the Presidential Palace. In spite of
my nagging and begging, father does not allow me to go with
them—not yet, not under the present circumstances. Not
before he is positive that the street and the river and the
wind and the fish are absolutely safe for his daughter.

Paper patterns, pieces of red and white cloth, shears, pins,
needles, and reels of thread are spread out all over the living
room. Mother hands me the summer dress she has just
stitched to try on. Since father is reading the newspaper in
the living room, I go and change in the guest room. A needle
scratches my chest, then my side, as the sleeveless dress
slides down my body. I let out a cry of pain, loud enough for
mother to hear. The uneven frayed hemline reaches the middle of my shins. Now it is my belly that is tingling.
Cautiously I pull out the forgotten dangling needle and sulk
back to the living room. It's not the first time! I grumble, displaying the needle before casting it into its box. Mother
beckons me so that she can check over her handiwork.
Reluctantly, I obey. With a bold sense of ownership, she
straightens the shoulders, rights the collar, strokes the bodice,
goes over the seams of the bosom. Pulling the skirt down, she
asks me to turn.

—Fine! The back too! These Burda patterns always fit you! Now go upstairs and have a look in the mirror before I sew on with the machine.

I move my legs apart to test the width of the skirt.

—It's too narrow! I'll never be able to climb stairs in it. Definitely not two at a time. Anyway, I prefer shirts and skirts, like Selma. They're more like sportswear, and there's always the possibility of a new combination.

—Lina, you're not the same build as Selma. You're short and waistless. A skirt and a shirt cut you in the middle and make you look even shorter. In a dress, you look petite.

Petite? Does the French petite imply short and . . . delicate? Short and cute perhaps? Or just small, with no prospect of growing up? Nonsense, short is short, no matter in what language one is short. Short and stocky, although not plump. If not for my missing three inches, my protruding buttocks and my full breasts would have been in perfect proportion to my height. But at fourteen, my body still refuses to grow, as if it had left childhood but is heading nowhere.

And I who thought that after childhood came America.

—What about the length?

—I haven't fixed it yet. Come here!

She sticks a few pins between her teeth, kneels down, folds up the fabric, and fastens the hemline above the knees. Then she walks back a few steps, tells me to turn round.

—You should really look in the mirror. You look so elegant, a young lady for once.

—And where am I supposed to display my elegance? We hardly ever go out! I need something cool and comfortable for every day.

—It's chiffon, touch it! You don't get such fine fabric nowadays. English made. Cost two *dinars*, and that was years ago.

I scratch my shoulder blade.

—It's itchy!

—Lina, the fabric's so thin, you'll have to wear a slip undereath. It surely won't itch then.

—But then it'll be too hot. I'm already burning inside it.

—Daughter, it's not morning wear. It's for the evening, for the garden, when the air's cooler. Look what an unusual red it is. And these white flowers, aren't they gorgeous?

—I hate flowery designs.

—Heavens, you're prying my soul out of me! Here I am sweating and slaving to make you happy, and what do I get in return?

—Mama, did I ask for an elegant dress?

—This time it's elegant, last time it was old-fashioned. You're always finding fault with the clothes I make you . . . instead of learning to sew yourself! Girls your age make their own wardrobes.

—Girls my age are wearing miniskirts this summer! You should raise the hemline, if you want me to wear this dress. Two inches at least. Otherwise, chiffon or no chiffon, it'll hang untouched in the wardrobe. I swear!

—I'm fed up. You should settle this matter with your father!

Father's newspaper rustles.

—I told you we should have slaughtered and eaten them at birth.

—For God's sake, will you be serious for a moment?

Father puts down his newspaper.

—What's wrong? What are you two arguing about this time? The dress? It looks cute to me!

Mother rolls her eyes.

—Cute! What has cute to do with it? It's dressy, don't you see? Can't you tell the difference!

—Baba, it's too long. You should see what other girls are wearing. Up to here! Believe me.

I point to the middle of my thigh.

—I believe you. Girls are prepared to walk naked in the street if you tell them it's in fashion.

—One or two inches shorter won't make me naked! Honestly, you're exaggerating. Even the Muslim girls are wearing miniskirts, Nawal, Rehab, Ilham, Iqbal, all our neighbours. Their hemlines are one hand above the knees, and nobody thinks it's wrong or indecent. It's just the new fashion.

—Hey, isn't that Selma coming? mother says.

—What a godsend. See how long her legs are and how short her skirt is!

Selma storms in, her hair wet, her eyes red, her lips white. Without greeting us, without introduction, she blurts out that she has witnessed army officers arresting Hai at the river bank this morning.

—He was fixing his fishing net. Baba and I stopped to chat with him for a while. He said he missed us kids, and what a pity it was that our parents were still reluctant to send us swimming. I told him about my determination to learn to drive and he whistled in wonder. Then Mrad Aboudi showed up, carrying a clumsy fishing rod. That's right, the same Mrad who's three classes above us. He came with his bike, but sleep was still in his eyes. We said goodbye and went to our boat. I asked Baba to let me do the rowing. He didn't object. He sat opposite me and told me how to row. I rowed in a straight line from the start, away from the Rusafa shore. Baba said I've grown stronger than him. We were in the middle of the river when Hai was approached by three men in army uniform. Officers I suppose, because of their caps. Two of them seemed to be interrogating him. The third was looking inside the boat, turning over this and that, as if searching it. The next moment, he was striking it with an axe—or with some similar tool. Hai tried to stop him but he was held back firmly by the two others. Then that son of a dog, that officer, may God take his life, got off the boat and fell on Hai, punching and kicking him.

—Beat up Hai? It's not true!

—What about the youngster? father asks.

—Mrad just stood and watched.

—Poor boy, to be trapped like that! He must have been shocked! mother says.

—It was obvious that they'd come for Hai. Mrad had the bad luck to be there at the wrong moment. They probably didn't even know who he was or what he was. They were busy pummeling Hai, may their names and memories be wiped out! Mrad couldn't have done anything for him anyway. He had a bicycle. I would definitely have cleared off.

Selma takes a breath then slowly continues,

—But what do I know? We were some way off. I couldn't make out every detail, that's what Baba says. Perhaps they were armed. Perhaps they did ask Mrad's identity in the first place.

—Your father's absolutely right. You wouldn't be able to judge unless you had seen the whole episode, father says.

—Mrad kept glancing in our direction, as if wishing to cry out for help. But he didn't utter a sound. And neither did I. Although my heart was pounding, I just went on rowing—to make sure Baba stayed out of it. But my eyes kept returning to the shore, to see Hai's wrecked boat sinking, and the officers hustling Hai and Mrad away.

But Mrad is only seventeen, a boy, three years older than us!

Two classrooms have always stood between us—worlds, in terms of elementary school. We spent our breaks in different playgrounds, we were invited to different birthday and Purim parties. Two years ago, by chance Mrad and I were both at a ping-pong table in the Centre. He grimaced at the bat in my hand. I was a girl, he grumbled, and on top of it much younger than he! It would be neither fun nor fair to beat me. But he did not mind us playing until his partner showed up. He was a calm, cunning player. When his friend arrived, Mrad dismissed me, but said we should meet again in a couple of years and have a real match together.

—Imagine, if they had come twenty minutes earlier, they would have picked up Baba too, Selma says.

—True, mother agrees, *Allah setar*, God saved him!

—Come to think of it, I was close to getting arrested myself! Selma adds, with a touch of self-importance.

When her statement is not confirmed, she goes on,

—Anyway, only after we'd reached home did I tell Baba what I had seen. He was extremely upset. We skipped breakfast and drove to Mrad's family, then to Hai's sister. I had to repeat the story all over again, twice.

—I wonder if they haven't been taken to the Rashid Camp, like Shuli, mother says.

When Mrad's father and Hai's brother-in-law appeal to the army spokesman, he will deny any involvement in the episode. Furthermore, Hai and Mrad will be found neither in Baghdad's central prison, nor at police, or security headquarters. Some people will say they are being kept at intelligence headquarters. Others will claim they are being held in special prison cells near the Presidential Palace, where they are being put to all kinds of torture.

We will be torn between news and rumours during the months to come, as if the two were playing tug-of-war with our nerves. More Jewish men will be arrested in Baghdad and in Basra. Young and old, wealthy, prominent, and poor—the choice of the victims will seem erratic. They will be picked up from their homes or from work—those who still have it. Some will disappear from the street at any hour of the day or night, as the spirit moves the security men. None of them will be traceable in any of the known prisons. Why are their whereabouts kept secret? Why are their families denied contact with them and treated like dirt, as though they were but the refuse of the revolution? Our *hacham* attempts to meet influential

Party members, but nobody is willing to receive him. A rumour circulates that the son of the *hacham* himself has been flung into jail.

Mother draws up at our gate. She and Zeki are back at last from the Rashid Camp. Like Dudi's father, and like all the Jews arrested before the Ba'ath's seizure of power, Shuli continues to be granted a monthly visit—as if the regulations of the overthrown regime were still applicable to him. Every month, mother implores father to stay at home, for fear of his safety. Three times out of four, father concedes, but on condition that she does not set foot alone in the army camp.

I turn off the tap and stop watering the garden.

Mother lingers in the car. Zeki lights a cigarette. He looks out of place in the passenger seat, especially with a woman at the wheel. Our screen door slams. Father dashes out to meet them. Mother and Zeki exchange their last words. Why can't they wait two minutes and share them with father? I catch a glimpse of her glance as it brushes Zeki's forehead and slides down to his chin. Her features soften. Her eyes sparkle too urgently to stand for gratitude alone.

Father opens the door for her. Mother steps out of the car, smartly dressed, still particular about her appearance—even when she goes to prison. Father rests his hand on her shoulder, while Zeki, in his turn, slowly gets out. A stately man, I notice for the first time. His sleek black hair is untidy around the forehead and the temples. He arranges his tie, tucks his white shirt properly into his trousers, then feels his paunch as if sizing it up.

They cross the courtyard, heading for the house. Father is walking in the middle, listening to mother's account. His grave, deliberate tread has set the pace for the three of them. He looks grey and defeated. Curry has run to mother's side and is meowing for his meal. Zeki is puffing at his cigarette, carrying himself in a leisurely manner, like a knight off duty.

I observe his thinning hair, his black eyes, his full cheeks, his fleshy lips, his thick moustache, his broad shoulders, and wonder...if mother would go for him.

Would she go for a *majnoun*, a crazy one, as Zeki was dubbed in his youth?

It must have been an allusion to the famous modern play, *Majnoun Laila*, Crazy About Laila, by the Egyptian poet, Ahmed Shauqi, who is renowed as the Prince of Poets. The play takes up an ancient desert legend, the love of Qays and Laila, a love whose impossibility drove Qays to poetry and madness.

It must have happened about twenty years ago when Dunia was in secondary school and Zeki was possessed by her beauty. He used to follow her to school and back home every day, they say. But he always kept to the opposite side of the street, to let the cattle and the pushcarts and the occasional cars pass between them and bear witness to her virtue. Nevertheless, he walked close enough to set tongues wagging, and when the gossip reached Dunia's family, her brothers set on Zeki with their knives. They would have chopped him into pieces that day if he had not been rescued by a pack of stray dogs that happened to be nearby. Stirred up by the commotion, the dogs rushed to the scene and burst into the brawl, barking with excitement and biting indiscriminately. After the event, Zeki stopped tailing Dunia and resorted to the composition of *ghazal*, love verses. He taught them to the street vendors, whose merchandise he used as a metaphor for his lovesickness. Early each morning, the woman who sold *geymar*, cream skimmed from buffalo's milk, would compare her fresh snowy wares to the soft untouched skin of the beloved. *Tekki a sham*, black mulberry, tasted like the forbidden lips of the desired one. *Semit* rings, pretzels, were the engagement rings the wooer dreamed of sliding on to her fingers, while onions hid sad secrets as tearful as her heart. "Remedy for all the wooers, remedy for all the weepers, " sang the chickpea vendor on cold winter nights, offering hot *lablabi*. Dunia would wait by the window for the vendors to walk past and deliver Zeki's love messages. And they sang them all day, in every lane and alley, and multiplied their profits by the hundreds. In no time, not only Dunia but the whole Waziryiah quarter was humming and carolling Zeki's songs of food, love, and virtue.

Aljenoun fenoun, madness is art, as the saying goes.

Some claim the songs eventually found their way into the heart of Dunia's father. Others attribute the happy end to the devices of his sister, a well-known fortune-teller. She was reading her brother's *finjan* one day, the story goes, when she cried out in astonishment and started slapping her face and beating her chest as she showed him the outline of a head traced out in his coffee dregs. Even Dunia's father recognised the profile of that *majnoun*, that crazy young man, with his football of a skull and potato chin. The rest of the *finjan* was virtually empty, except for an unevenly thick ring resting at the base. Wasn't it clear as daylight? All was written and predestined. What sense did it make to wage war against almighty *qadar*, fate?

Dunia's father did not wage war against the decree. They say Zeki has remained his favourite son-in-law to this day. So why should the old man ever doubt whether that prophetic *finjan* had truly been his own or whether his late sister had played tricks on him?

I join them in the sitting room. Zeki has slumped into father's armchair and stretched out his legs. He is lighting a new cigarette, lost in thought. Is he thinking up a poem for mother? She is recounting the meeting with Shuli from beginning to end, dwelling on every detail concerning Shuli's physical condition and morale until father's anxiety is appeased. Then, as if suddenly reminded of Zeki's presence, father turns to him and says,

—We owe you so much, Zeki! I'll never be able to pay you back . . .

—*Eib aleik*, Abu Shuli, shame on you! Aren't we brothers and isn't Shuli like a son to me?

Zeki expels smoke from his mouth and nose, and says quietly,

—What dark days we're going through.

—Any news? father asks nonchalantly. I haven't been through today's papers yet.

—You can forget our papers. They'd rather discuss the students' revolt in Paris or the Russian tanks in Prague, as if there were only rabid dogs and car crashes to report in Baghdad.

Father, who has long ago given up on a free press in this country, does not reply. Furthermore, he does not seem in the mood for a political discussion.

—They're destroying whatever they lay hands on, may Allah destroy their homes! Did they have to renew the war with the Kurds after a two-year cease-fire? And this hideous wave of arrests?

Zeki raises his voice although nobody is arguing with him. Not only Jews, but prominent Muslims and Christians are being arrested too, he says. Industrialists to begin with, together with their factory managers. Similarly a number of army officers and former ministers have been thrown into prison. It is rumoured that some of these men have already perished, tortured to death.

—People would rather feed themselves on rumours than grope in the darkness of uncertainty, father comments.

Zeki flushes. I recognise the same sumac red which floods his face whenever a young man makes eyes at his daughters.

—They're not only rumours, Abu Shuli. The general manager of the Zahra factory is an old friend of mine. He's been picked up, too. Now that's a man who feared Allah and who cared only for his work and family. He wasn't in the least involved in politics. They let him out some days ago, and I went over to see him. I was shattered by his state. Poor fellow. You can't imagine what they've done to him in three weeks. He's no longer the person he used to be. In fact, he's no longer a person at all. For two hours, he couldn't utter one meaningful sentence, just babbled to himself and fidgeted in his armchair as though seeking the least painful position in which to sit. When the telephone rang, he jumped in panic and howled like a dog.

Is it only in films that, after being in prison, a man becomes more of a man?

—His wife's determined to leave the country. Their passports are ready, but they're still waiting for their visas for England.

I decide to heed mother's signals at last, and go and brew Turkish coffee in the kitchen.

When the coffee foams, I spoon out some froth and distribute it among the *finjans*. Then I let the coffee simmer for as long as possible. Only at the last minute, before it boils over, I remove the pot from the fire. I repeat this three times. The first for unity. The second for liberty. And the third for socialism. *Wahda, hurryiah, ishtirakiyah*, always in the same order.

SPIES

Muddy drops of rain pitter-patter on the windscreen just as mother turns the ignition key.

—The washing! My God, all our washing's on the roof!

She opens the door, about to step out of the car. But she continues to sit, undecided whether to save the washing or to proceed with our schedule.

—It wouldn't occur to your father to bring it inside, would it?

—I don't know, I reply, lying for father's sake.

A woman walks past us, a small child skipping along at her side. The child looks up and thrusts out his tongue to savour the water falling from the sky. Lacking the words for his first rain, he jumps about, clapping his hands, and letting out cries of wonder and excitement.

—To hell with the washing, mother decides and slams the door of the car.

The drizzle soon intensifies into a heavy rainfall. We cross the city in the direction of the Rashid Camp. Grocers are hastily dragging their goods inside while pedestrians are seeking shelter in shops or jumping into buses and taxis. Mother turns the windshield wipers on full. I switch on the radio. Najat al-Saghira is singing *la takthubi*, "Don't Lie."

—I'm so glad you're with me. I hate to trouble Zeki each time. He's already done so much for us.

Does she really prefer my company to Zeki's, or is she saying this to cover up her true feelings?

—I always have to be on my guard with him, she goes on. Always keep my mouth shut when he criticises the government. Because even his own words, coming from me, would sound different.

La la la la, la takthubi, inni raeitukuma ma'an. Don't don't don't don't, don't lie, for I have seen you two together...

Mother switches off the radio.

—Why don't we just listen to the rain? I love the force with which the first rain comes down.

Who else does she love apart from Shuli and the rain, I am dying to ask. If she had tried to dissuade me last week when I expressed my wish to visit Shuli in detention, my suspicions would have been confirmed, and I would have been positive at last about her secret romance with Zeki. But my mother's reactions are elusive. Although taken by surprise, she did not betray any sign of annoyance or discomfort at my request to accompany her to prison.

Was she putting on a show of innocence or have I been reading too many *Nous-Deux* magazines lately?

—Your brother will be delighted. It's over a year now that you haven't seen each other!

Delighted? After one year? I would not blame him if he refuses to look at me. Mother steers to the right and lets a military lorry overtake us. I haven't noticed that we have joined the motorway.

—By the way, Mama, is Shuli dressed in that...that pyjamalike...what do they call it, prisoner's clothes?

Mother shakes her head, annoyed at my image.

—No! Not at all. He wears his own clothes. Didn't we pack his clean shirts and trousers yesterday?

—And his head? Is it shaved like prisoners in . . . in films?

—Believe me, he looks just the same as when you last saw him. A bit thinner perhaps. A bit paler for sure. He has been alone in his cell too long, and it's doing him no good.

The squeaking of the windshield wipers fills the silence that follows. Left, right, left, right, like a prisoner pacing his cell.

—Will you tell him about the new arrests and all the recent developments?

Mother purses her lips.

—We can't keep it back from him forever. At some time he'll have to be informed. So he'd better hear it from us than from a guard. Who knows what they might tell him.

—I can't imagine anything more monstrous than reality.

We take an exit, at the end of which the military camp comes into view. Mother pulls up at the gate. A soldier springs out of the sentry box. He seems to have recognized our car, for he lifts the barrier and, without asking for identification or an entry permit, motions us to pass. Mother rolls down the window and hands him a *dirhem*. Wet already, the sentry inspects the coin and nods, as though acknowledging a parking fee.

—See! Even soldiers don't like to stand long in the rain. I told you there's no need to worry.

We drive along a dirt road inside the camp. I try to figure out how to turn the dreary landscape into the vivid account my classmates will be expecting tomorrow. Rows of barracks spread over a flat wasteland without any apparent order. A few date palms are dispersed at random, bearing no connection to the barracks. Military jeeps and lorries are speeding in all directions. A line of soldiers, overloaded with rifles and kit bags, is marching towards a muddy horizon.

Mother parks in front of a long white building. We unload the two baskets and the bundle of laundry from the backseat and run in the rain towards the barracks. She pushes the door marked "Enquiries," and we enter a small empty hall. A wall-to-wall wooden counter separates the reception desk from the oblong waiting space. Mother drops her baskets to the floor.

—It might take a while, she warns me, crosses her arms, and leans against the wall in the posture of someone who is expecting nothing to happen in the next twenty-four hours.

Too restless to stand still, I pace up and down the reception area. The wind constantly slams the entrance door, and although the noise soon gets on my nerves, I dare not interfere with any military order or disorder around me. A telephone rings in the adjacent room. A gruff voice answers.

—So the telephone isn't entirely extinct in this country!

Mother ignores my remark.

—Aren't you cold, Mama? Has your headache gone? Don't you feel like a cigarette?

—I'm dying for one! But I'd rather not smoke here. They might take it the wrong way, you understand?

The voice stops talking. The adjutant should be coming out any minute to organise our visit. After he has blown his nose boisterously. After he has opened a bottle of fizzy drink. After he has finished burping. After he has punched holes in who-knows-what documents. After he has rubber-stamped them. After he has torn masses of paper, pulled out dozens of drawers, swatted hordes of flies on the desk.

After he has snapped closed his lighter, he starts talking and guffawing again. I missed his dialling.

—Mama, are you sure it's the right place? Who are we waiting for? Perhaps you should go and announce us to him?

—Relax, daughter. This isn't a grocery with opening hours at our convenience. It takes time. Didn't I tell you to bring something to read?

Her stoicism reminds me that she has been going through this procedure once a month. Ashamed of my fussiness all of a sudden, I stop complaining and squat on the bundle of laundry beside her legs, sinking down into the familiar smell of her damp nylon stockings. According to my watch, my class must be attending the chemistry lesson right now, and my classmates counting down to break time.

At the thousand and first slam of the door, a Sergeant appears. I jump to my feet, almost standing to attention. He greets mother like an old acquaintance and inquires after her health.

—Waiting for the Major? he asks and points with his thumb to the next room.

Mother nods. The Sergeant knocks on the Major's door. The gruff voice barks out permission. The Sergeant opens the door, shouts two syllables which I fail to catch, clicks his heels, salutes, and only then does he enter. Soldier and officer exchange information. The Sergeant returns and takes us to his commander. His small proportions strike me as inconsistent with his harsh voice and his discordant noises. Surrounded by dusty folders, the officer slurs a greeting, hands mother a form to sign, glances past me, and fumbles at the books, the fresh laundry, and the items of food in the baskets. When the search is over, he dismisses us with a sweep of his hand.

—No, that wasn't the notorious Major, mother whispers as we squat on our baskets in front of the reception desk, unattended again.

After what seems like hours, the Sergent reappears and gestures us to follow him outside. The rain has stopped, the sky has turned blue.

—Alone this time? he asks mother—as if my presence did not count—and offers to carry her basket.

She delicately turns him down, and explains that "our good friend" could not make it this time. Proudly, the Sergeant tells her that he is learning English. As we zigzag between the puddles of mud, he starts to count in English from a hundred backward. We walk past a kiosk around which a group of recruits have gathered. Catcalls and whistles shoot in our direction. The Sergeant stops and hurls abuse at them, insulting their sisters, their mothers, and their grandmothers. The soldiers shrink under their khaki caps. The Sergeant apologises as we go on—whether for the soldiers' behaviour or for his own foul language, I cannot say. Then he jumps from sixty straight to forty, but mother does not correct him. When we draw near a double-storeyed barrack, he whistles for the guard, who immediately comes out of the building, a rifle slung over his shoulder. The Sergeant orders him to take us to the student. That's right, the Jew. He thanks mother for the green banknote and takes leave, floating on air, like a schoolboy who has just received his Purim gift.

At the end of the corridor, the keys clank.

The smell of stale air and static time creep into my nose. The cell is larger and dimmer than I had imagined. I step slowly inside, hiding behind mother. Shuli is leaning against the wall behind the door, arms folded, wearing his ironic smile. It takes me a fraction of a second to recognise him. He has grown a thick moustache, similar to Zeki's.

The keys jingle behind us. As Shuli moves towards me, I hold out the basket of food, trying to conceal my embarrassent. Shuli flings the basket to the ground, pulls me into his arms, and lifts me up in the air.

—You're still as light as a feather! No intention of growing up, Lina?

Apparently, mother has kept her promise and said nothing about my menstruation.

—Your face's prickly. I swear I wouldn't have recognised you with this moustache.

Mother and son hug each other for a long time. *Bdalek*, may all the misfortunes meant for you fall upon me, she repeats. I survey the cell and Shuli's reduced possessions: a mattress, a small travelling bag, a stack of books arranged like a night table, a family-size bottle of Coca-Cola filled with water. Shuli's familiar blue bedspread lends the place a painful illusion of domesticity. The unplastered brick walls are covered with names, scratched by former inmates. The calendar above the mattress is two months out of date. In the corner lie a raffia broom and an old sheet of newspaper on which a heap of dust is piled. Shuli must have just swept the floor in anticipation of our visit.

Mother manages to control herself. They squat down on the mattress while I use the pile of books facing them for a seat.

—Raining outside? he asks, pointing at our wet hair.

Then he showers questions on us, concerning father, Zeki, friends, neighbours, and acquaintances for whom he has never cared before. He inquires about my subjects at school, my marks, my classmates, my teachers, greedy for news, as if it were the very fresh air his cell is lacking.

When he pauses to catch his breath, mother remarks,

—There are dark rings around your eyes, my son . . . You look so pale. Don't you . . .

—No, as you can imagine, I don't get to sunbathe!

Mother's attempt to shift the focus of the conversation to Shuli has been untimely. Anxious to rectify her mistake and win back his favour, she urges her son to examine the contents of the baskets which she packed meticulously the day before.

—Our time's too short to be wasted on such trifles!

Mother wears a face of *tisha' bab*, the day of mourning for the destruction of the Second Temple. Shuli does not look too happy with himself, either. In a conciliatory tone, he asks whether she has remembered to bring him candles. Whether real or contrived, his interest immediately breaks the ice. Radiating pride, she takes out the package of white candles from the basket, and displays it as evidence of her devotion. Shuli concedes a smile.

—They switch off the light at eight in the evening. I told

them I can't get to sleep so early, but they act deaf. Last week, the light went out twice in the middle of the day. Fuse, I reckon, but it lasted hours. You should have seen the fuss I made. I went on a hunger strike. No, I'm not joking. They were so helpless, they didn't know what to do with me.

—Shuli, please, be sensible. Don't be rude to them. Don't provoke them, they might . . .

—They might what? What else can they do to me? Beat me up? Keep me here forever? They can't hurt me any more. Not these degenerates. I've become so immune, you can't imagine.

The noise of crackling paper irritates me. I lift my eyes to its source. A shiny brown cockroach is crawling over the calendar on the wall, its feelers exploring the month of August in the Swiss Alps. Goose pimples spread all over my body. Cockroach feelers used to scare me out of my wits as a child, because I took their swaying for a display of defiance.

I pull myself together and return to the conversation. Mother has managed to poke a cheese *sambousak* in Shuli's mouth.

—Anybody released? he asks, chewing.

In short bursts of speech, she tells him about the new arrests, about the alleged Zionist spy ring, and about the wireless set which the authorities claim to have found in one of the houses.

—They're accusing them of sending military information to Zionist and CIA agents in Iran, top secret information that caused Iraq to lose the war last year.

Shuli wrinkles his brows.

—So what the guards are saying is true! The poor bastards, they must be really in the shit. But who's going to swallow this rubbish? Iraqis never believe the tales their governments fabricate. They don't take their rulers seriously. Remember all the jokes they used to crack about the Thief of Baghdad?

He quietly mouths the nickname of our former Prime Minister and giggles.

—You're wrong, Shuli, the spies are working wonders, like a pain killer!

—Remember *ustad* Juad, our history teacher? He tried to convince us they're spies! I add.

—Pain's pain, whether you're a peasant or an intellectual, mother goes on. Whatever has gone wrong in the country over the past years, they've got the spies to blame now. The government must be up to something—I dare not think what—otherwise the press wouldn't be harping on this subject. Last week, the radio was warning the public against Jewish agents, saying they were about to commit acts of sabotage all over the country and urging citizens to be vigilant and to notify the police of anybody acting suspiciously. It's a wonder, I must say, that so far only a few people have exploited this situation and in fact informed against Jews. But the air is charged, and I'm afraid that eventually something will burst.

Although no footsteps are heard outside, mother has lowered her voice to the extent that I must bend toward her in order to hear every word.

—A Jewish kitchenware merchant from Basra is supposed to be the leader of the network and the mastermind behind it. An old man in his sixties. They're accusing him of having illegally sent young Jews across the border to Iran, where they were trained by Israeli agents to commit acts of sabotage in Iraq. Can you imagine what's awaiting these young men? Most of them are schoolboys and university students.

Shuli's already pallid lips turn deathly. His teeth are chattering.

—What's the matter, Shuli?

He fails to utter a single word. Mother persists.

—Did anyone tell you anything? Speak to me. Speak up! Say something!

Shuli breaks off a piece of plaster protruding from the wall and uses it to draw a pale Star of David on the floor, on the tile between his foot and hers. His legs are shaking. Mother considers the drawing for a moment then dusts it down with her shoe.

—Nonsense! They won't implicate you. They wouldn't want to share the honours with the former regime, don't you understand? Besides, you don't fit into their plot. Your story belongs to another era. They won't touch you, my son, believe me, you're safe here, safer than all the men outside!

Shuli buries his face in his arms. Mother's hand ventures towards him and touches his head. As he does not rebuff her gesture, she begins to stroke his hair. She looks so happy you'd think she had won the national lottery. The cockroach has climbed up to the top of the calendar. Its feelers move up and down, back and forth, like the arms of a conductor celebrating the drama of human life.

The guard suddenly shoves the door open. Shuli starts up. Not even he has heard the keys. The thirty minutes have elapsed already. The three of us stand up. Mother hugs her son and starts talking fast, as if to fill the last seconds with as many words as possible.

—You didn't tell me what you need. Something to be darned? More books? What should I bring you next time? Medicine? Fruit juice? They let everything pass recently. Nuts and dried fruit last quite long; they're better than baked goods, perhaps. You look thin and pale. You shouldn't go on a hunger strike any more, you'd upset your father. What about chocolate? You used to . . .

—Please, Mama, Shuli interrupts impatiently. Don't bring so much food. It's a waste. I don't eat that much and . . .

Whispering, he adds,

—. . . and anyway most of it gets stolen.

—You never told me!

Shuli pulls away from her and gives me a fast farewell

hug. Suddenly, he seems eager to get rid of us. Mother and I follow the guard out. See you, I cry out as the wooden door closes on him. Too late to pass him Adel's regards from Yom Kippur last year.

After the guard has received his *dirhem*, we make our way back with empty baskets to Enquiries.

—Not only do they lock him in, they also steal his food! *Wlad al haram*, bastards, haven't they got a conscience? Haven't they got any dignity?

Mother's complaints cease at last at the Enquiries. When he has signed our way out, the adjutant remarks,

—It's all right for you to drive down here. Only don't forget, *oukhti*, Jews aren't allowed to travel more than thirty miles from their city of residence. You're aware of that, aren't you?

—Thirty miles? Since when? That's a new regulation, isn't it?

—Don't ask me. I heard it only last week, from an officer friend. Thought you'd better know and keep yourself out of trouble.

Zeki slides his hand into the pocket of his sports jacket. Assuming it is the keys of his car for which he is reaching, I stand up, as I am taught to do when bidding our guests farewell. But the three grown-ups continue to sit and Zeki's hand soon reappears with a new packet of cigarettes. I remain on my feet, embarrassed by my *faux pas*. If I sit down again, my misunderstanding, or worse still, my secret wish to see our guest leave, will be exposed. Quickly, I clear away the empty teacups and carry them to the kitchen. On my return, father asks me to switch on the television. Zeki, who has hardly taken any notice of my actions, raises his brow in surprise. It is too early for the news, and we are not in the habit of having the TV on unless we are watching it.

Is it possible that he has not heard about the special broadcast scheduled for this afternoon?

A Lebanese commercial is shown. Abu Zeid is back from bird hunting, his white *sherwal* is drenched with mud. Instead of resuming my place, I pull up a chair beside father, leaving the middle cushion on the sofa, the space between mother and Zeki, sagging and empty. Zeki's puzzlement is about to turn into irritation, when Abu Zeid is succeeded by a TV announcer.

"In a few minutes, ladies and gentlemen, you will be transferred to the Tribunal of the Revolution, where you will see with your own eyes the traitors who made us lose the war."

Zeki goggles at father and mother alternately. He has indeed missed the newspaper headlines this morning, as well as my rude hint ten minutes ago. His watch tells him that it is too late to start for home. As required by oriental hospitality, father implores Zeki to stay longer. To make up for his half-hearted tone perhaps, he asks me to fetch a bowl of pistachios that he places—together with a glass and a bottle of *arak*—on the tea table, within his friend's reach.

Zeki rests his back against the sofa and puts on his spectacles, getting ready for the show.

A song by Feirouz, adapted for television, follows. While the vocalist is singing, shots of refugees are shown, shots of Jerusalem, of flags fluttering in the wind, of strafing planes and advancing tanks, of more and more refugees. Feirouz's picture is superimposed, at times full length, at times only down to her waist. Feirouz is interrupted in the middle of a verse, and the plight of the Palestinian victims is replaced by a court of justice, obviously the Tribunal of the Revolution. The camera moves from one man to the other, mutely introducing the main characters. Sitting on the tribunal is the judge, a colonel, with an assistant officer on either side. On a lower platform, another officer, lower in rank—apparently the public prosecutor. In the box opposite them, men in civilian dress are whispering to each other. They stop talking when the camera is aimed at them and stare at us with childish wonder.

—The journalists, Zeki remarks.

Mother sticks a cigarette between her lips. Zeki snaps open his lighter, and stretches out his hand, slightly leaning towards her. The familiarity with which she accepts his light without looking at him brings my old suspicions to life again.

—*Mahkamah*, a deep voice cries out, announcing the opening of the trial.

—That cry makes my skin crawl, mother murmurs. It reminds me of those awful Mahdawi trials.

Although she was muttering to herself, mother nevertheless spoke in the Muslim dialect. It occurs to me that we Jews never keep to our dialect when we are in the presence of non-Jews, although our Arabic is as comprehensible to them as theirs is to us. The unwritten rule applies to friends, officials, subordinates, and strangers alike. At school, not only does a class of forty students shift to the Muslim dialect in the presence of one Muslim teacher, but the headmaster does the same, too, in spite of his being the teacher's superior and employer. It is comparable to the rules of gender in French grammar. Let one valet stand amid four hundred dames and the entire group will be designated as *beaux*, *élégants*, *charmants*.

The defendants are led into the court in a line while their names are read out by the judge. They are dressed in dark suits, white shirts, and ties. As they march towards the dock, I jump up. Hai Rahamin! Did he say Hai or Haim? Couldn't it be another Hai? My wish barely outlives its articulation. There he is, my very own Hai, limping, seventh in the line. I have never seen him in a suit, never heard his full name before. With heavy steps, he climbs up to the dock. The camera focuses on him, displays his sunken cheeks and his freshly shaven face, then flits to the man behind him.

—My swimming instructor, I inform Zeki, to warn him away from ugly thoughts.

—At least we know now that he's alive, father mumbles.

Why should he be grateful for Hai's life? Is he withholding some crucial information from me? Impossible! I am the one who brings most of the news and rumours from school. The name Mrad Aboudi restores my attention to the screen. I recognise his silhouette, third from the right.

The rest of the men are strangers to me. Many are quite young. Most of them bear Jewish names, which my parents keep linking to friends and acquaintances. Zeki listens to their associations in silence.

The prosecutor reads out the bill of indictment. The spy ring was founded by the Zionist enemy two years ago and charged to work for the interests of Israel and imperialism. Since then, the ring has been collecting military information and dispatching it to Israel and the CIA through Iran. Its further aim was to sabotage bridges, pipelines, private cars, and other civilian targets in order to undermine the socialist regime and distract our army from the liberation of Palestine.

Zeki pours himself another glass of *arak*.

The judge summons each man for an initial interrogation. The defendant is asked his name, his religion, the date of his birth, his profession, and his place of residence. Then the prosecutor reads out the charges against him.

They start with the alleged ringleader, a short elderly man, the Jewish kitchenware merchant from Basra. He is charged with setting up the spy-and-sabotage network, recruiting its members, and collecting top secret military information. By means of a wireless radio, the ringleader had been regularly transmitting to the U.S. consulate in Abadan reports about the positions and movements of our military units in Basra, about the navy and airbases in Basra, and about Soviet weapons in use by the Iraqi army.

When the kitchenware merchant pleads not guilty, laughter rises from the media section.

Hai looks haggard, as thin as his own skeleton, as if he has lost thirty pounds in the five months of his detention. To the standard questions put to him, he replies that he is Jewish, that he was born in 1920, that he is a fisherman, that he lives in Baghdad. Thank God, he has left the swimming lessons out, mother murmurs, stealing a glance at father. Hai is charged with receiving a sealed message from the ringleader in Basra and delivering it to a member of the ring in Baghdad. The content of the message remains untold. It is my turn to thank God. Hai's case sounds moderate. He has not been directly implicated in military information or in terrorist activities.

Zeki lights another cigarette. His smoking and drinking seem to know no end. His countenance, however, refuses to reveal his position.

It is Mrad's turn to stand for interrogation. In his large suit and with his fallen face Mrad has acquired the looks of an aged youth. At each question, his lips tremble, as if he is about to burst into tears. But he does not. He holds himself together and forces his answers out. That he is Jewish, that he was born in 1949, that he is a secondary school pupil, that he lives in Baghdad.

—That's not true! mother cries out. The boy was born in '51, in the same week as Lili, Dudi's sister. Um Dudi told me that yesterday. She said she had shared the room with Mrad's mother in the hospital. The boy's definitely under age. He's only seventeen, *haram* on you!

Mrad is facing serious charges. He has allegedly been trained in the use of explosives and timebombs by Israeli agents in Abadan; has participated in blowing up a bridge in

Basra, and received money for it. He keeps shaking his head and swallowing and pleading not guilty.

One after the other, the seventeen defendants—thirteen Jews, two Christians, and two Muslims—all plead not guilty. The prosecutor insists on their guilt again and again and promises to supply the court with enough evidence in the coming sessions. In the name of the Revolution, and in response to public pleas, he demands the death sentence for each member of the ring. Their execution will frustrate the dreams of the Zionist-imperialist alliance, and will provide moral support to our heroic armed forces at the front.

—Just what do they teach them at Law School, the judicial system or nationalism? mother bitterly remarks.

Zeki glares at her. What is he defending? Certainly not the reputation of the Law School in Baghdad. Nor this new regime which he himself loathes. Mother glowers back defiantly, showing no consideration for his feelings this time. Fully absorbed in the proceedings of the court, father seems unaware of the silent battle taking place between the two edges of the sofa.

The appearance of the defense counsel draws them back to the screen.

The defense counsel, a civilian appointed by the court, pays his respects to the judges and opens his speech with an apology for having to plead for the traitors of the country. He promises to fulfil his assignment and defend the spies, but assures his audience that he does so only out of legal necessity and not because of any doubts he has as to the justice of the Tribunal of the Revolution.

—Who needs a prosecutor with such a defense? father mutters.

The judge adjourns the trial. The journalists cheer the Tribunal of the Revolution. Mother switches off the TV. Father and Zeki do not budge. As our guest makes no sign of leaving, mother invites him to have supper with us. Zeki ignores her offer and, without removing his eyes from the blank screen, starts to speak, slowly and carefully, lest one unnecessary word slips from his tongue,

—Six months ago, my brother, Hashem, passed through Abadan on a business trip. Hashem imports spare parts from the States by way of Iran, and somehow, at the last minute, he needed an official stamp from an American government office. But there wasn't any in Abadan. So he had to travel to Khorramshahr, or Ahwaz, I don't exactly remember, but that's not the point. What I definitely remember was his complaint about the absence of an American government office in Abadan.

Father does not reply. He knows better than to let emotions or opinions on this matter come between him and his friend. Zeki goes on,

—What I'm saying is that this story . . . well . . . at least this part of the story, can't be true. What was his name—this kitchenware merchant? He couldn't have transmitted his messages to the American consulate in Abadan, because . . . because there isn't any!

—You're unusually cautious with your conclusions today! mother retorts. Is it the only flaw you noticed during the whole session, Zeki?

Zeki wears the face of a child who has been treated unfairly. How much more does she expect of him? Is he supposed to condemn this show trial in plain words? To identity with the defendants the way we do, and not even question their innocence? Father frowns at his wife but does not put in a good word for his friend. Zeki gets up and quietly bids us farewell. Father rises to his feet, too, ready to accompany his guest to the car. Mother says to remember her to Dunia. With one foot outside, Zeki turns, casts her a hungry look, and mumbles some decorous formula in return.

If their romance was merely a fiction and I was its author, I would find no better moment than this to end it.

—What do you think? Does he believe them? I ask her while we prepare supper.

—Hard to tell. I'm afraid he doesn't know himself what to believe and what not to. Basically, Zeki's an honest man, and by no means naive or narrow minded. But when it comes to Israel, he's no exception. Israel's like a wishbone stuck in his throat. As he can neither swallow nor expel it, it continues to strangle him with hate and delusion.

By the time father is back, tea, toast, cheese, and luncheon meat have already been served at the tea table. Mother asks why he took so long. Father explains that Zeki had not parked his car in front of our house, as he usually does, but in front of an empty plot, two streets away.

TAHRIR SQUARE

No sooner have I cracked my soft-boiled egg than Abd blows his horn in front of our gate. Mother rushes from the kitchen, wrapping the sandwich she has just prepared for me.

—You haven't even combed your hair! How is it that the rest of the children manage to be on time while you always have to be honked out?

—It's not true! Abd honks in front of every house, I protest and glance at father imploringly.

Coolly, he winks his consent to drive me to school. Grateful for the extra minutes, I go to the front door and wave Abd away.

We get to school shortly before eight. School buses coming from different neighbourhoods have jammed the street. The car in front of us is honking. Without unloading her children, Dudi's mother is reversing and gesturing to us to do the same. What is she doing? Father is perplexed. The scene in the street strikes me as like the end of the school day rather than its beginning. Pupils are streaming out of the gate, onto the buses, while the older boys are cycling away. Something is wrong, father says. Dudi hops out of the front passenger seat and dashes towards us. I roll down the window.

—Go home! Quickly, he gasps. They've executed them ... they've hanged the spies! ...

—I see, father murmurs without moving his lips, and immediately backs up the car.

I switch on the radio. The first local station is broadcasting martial music. The next is blaring out an interminable speech: "Today is your feast, great people of Iraq. Leave your work, take the day off, and go to your Liberation Square to celebrate the demise of our traitors. Traitors who have maliciously prepared the ground for the Zionist bandits to realize their aggression in June '67. Traitors who have exploited the generosity of the country that has tolerated them, fostered them, and treated them as her equal citizens. Traitors who . . ." On the third station, the announcer is reading out the torrents of telegrams that are flooding the radio station from all over the country, congratulating the government for its brave revolutionary action.

Father switches off the radio.

The opening of the trials was transmitted live on TV four weeks ago. After that there were only snatches of sessions, tape-recorded and broadcast on radio. For security reasons, the trials were conducted behind closed doors. In fragments, we heard the taped voices plead guilty to the charges against them. Mrad confessed that he had been trained in explosives in Abadan; that he had taken part in the bombing of a bridge in Basra; that he had been paid a hundred *dinars* for his assignment; and that he had further orders to sabotage another civilian target in Baghdad. Similarly, all the other defendants confessed their crimes, testified against and implicated each other. Except for the old kitchenware merchant from Basra, the alleged ringleader, and Hai, who both persisted in pleading not guilty.

We stop before a bookshop. I jump out to buy two local newspapers.

Father asks me to read out the headlines. "Death Sentence passed on Fifteen Spies! A Real Revolutionary Start." "No Spy Will Stay Alive on Noble Iraqi Earth." "The Traitors

Convicted By the Revolution Have Stabbed Us in the Back and Assisted the Filthy Zionist Monster to Suck Our Blood." "The Fair Trials Have Proved How the Spies Were the Direct Cause of Our *Naksah* in June '67." The names of the fifteen men sentenced to death are published in both newspapers. Hai Rahamin and Mrad Aboudi are among them—the elderly kitchenware merchant from Basra, too. According to the newspaper, the verdict was announced on Radio Baghdad at two o'clock this morning.

At home, mother is sitting by the window, waiting for us. Ululations of joy emanate from the transistor radio on her lap. Since dawn, the corpses of eleven of the executed men have been hanging in Tahrir Square in Baghdad while the other four bodies were flown to Basra to be similarly exhibited in a public square. Crowds of demonstrators are marching through Rashid Street, heading towards Tahrir Square, cheering the executions and shouting their support for the Council of the Revolution.

Father's face contorts, as he begins to cough in short raucous bursts. Only when he convulses on to the armchair and tears well up in his eyes do I realise that my father is weeping. It is the first time in my fourteen years that I have witnessed him in tears. And so loud! Father has always kept quiet about his sorrows. Not even the news of his mother's death several years ago could extract a groan from him. I recall him watching television the entire evening while furrows kept accumulating on his forehead and the veins bulging in his temples throbbed with an alarming ferocity.

Today he has finally exploded.

Mother kneels at his side and attempts to appease him with words of hope and wisdom which even I no longer believe. Unable to watch him cry his heart out, I make off to my room and close the door. But his unrestrained sobs pursue me to the first floor and pour out, all in one morning, his unspoken grief of sixty years.

I seek refuge on the roof.

A cold, dry wind slaps me in the face. The sky is bright blue, as in children's books, limpid, indifferent to the atrocities on earth. The sun has risen, as it does daily, to announce a golden winter morning. Not a grain of dust blurs the clarity of today's light, not a cloud throws doubt upon its integrity.

No, I was not expecting a solar eclipse.

The list of the hanged men recurs in my mind. I have gone over their names so many times in the papers that I have learned them by heart. And still I fail to grasp that the same Mrad who sweltered in his oversized suit on TV last month is no more, that our date for a ping-pong match is cancelled for good. That Hai is dead, executed, hanged, perished for-ever. Not even the sentence makes sense. Hai means life, or alive, in Hebrew. How can he-who-is-alive be dead? It is hardly surprising that our hangmen do not bother their heads about Hebrew, but God, our beloved and only Lord, don't You hear the paradox in Your own language?

In the small hours of the night, Hai's last wish, unuttered, unfulfilled, perished with him.

Hai's capital offence consisted of receiving a sealed enve-lope from the alleged ringleader in Basra. No matter how hard I try, I fail to reconstruct his face, fail to dress him in his trunks, tan his shoulders, hand him the two oars, glue his boat in one piece again. Only his black suit comes into my mind—the one they made him wear for the trial. It is damp, punctured with holes, bearing traces of the needles with which they had injected water into his body before they assaulted it with electric shocks. I grab the tortured suit and cast it into the river. The trousers skim over the water, their legs outstretched, their flies gracelessly unbuttoned, their pockets pulled inside out. The sodden jacket lingers behind, its shoulders swollen, its sleeves twisted and distorted. Its collar soon catches on the stump of a tree near the shore. As the trousers drift rapidly downstream, the distance between the upper and lower halves of the suit increases. When the horizon settles between them, they take leave of one another and of their obligation to the human image.

Treacherous waters. What of Hai's shirt? Where is his tie? His shoes? His undershirt? Where are Hai's socks?

The river ripples and gurgles and burbles and swallows its answer. Underwater, the fish are celebrating the fall of a fisherman.

I curse man and nature and their common Maker in heaven until the chill of January drives me indoors. Father's sobs have subsided and a dubious silence has fallen upon the house. Not knowing what to think, I tiptoe down the stairs, fearing to intrude on the peace or to stumble into the abyss awaiting me in the living room. The sight of my parents, sunk safe and sound in their armchairs, reassures me. Father's green eyes have turned grey and hollow. Mother is smoking, her cloudy gaze staring past the walls. On the small table between them a bottle of Valium stands empty.

—Do you need anything? Water? Tea? Shall I fetch you a blanket?

They shake their heads, without uttering a word or looking at me. As long as their eyes stay open, I decide not to worry—no matter how many pills are heaped in their stomachs. They might as well take the day off. I switch on the electric heater, lock the front door, and leave them to themselves, sagging in their solitude, each too shattered to endure the shock and despair of the other.

Back in my room, I open the first book at hand and absorb myself in my homework.

I start at the doorbell. For a fraction of a second I wonder what has kept me at home on a weekday, then I remember. I hear the front door open. My watch says it's just past two. The guest is mounting the stairs. Heavy steps. Dudi staggers into my room, sweating, out of breath, and flings his hundred and sixty pounds on to my bed. The springs screech. I already regret the past hours when I was unaware of time and place. Without taking off his shoes, Dudi rolls himself up in my bedcover and wipes the sweat off his face with the corner.

—Mama would kill you if she saw this!

Dudi rests his hands under his head, and grins,

—Your mother's in love with me. She received me with such a mysterious look just now, you'd say she's been waiting for me for years.

—There's nothing behind Mama's look, Dudi. Neither meaning nor feeling. Nothing but Valium.

Dudi twiddles with the fringe of my bedcover,

—Only Valium? What a pity. And your father? He looked like a philosopher reflecting upon the meaning of life. He didn't stir a bit when I greeted him. Did he stuff himself with Valium too?

I do not reply. The last thing I feel like doing is striking up a conversation with Dudi. I glance demonstratively at my watch, hoping he will take the hint and shorten his visit.

Dudi kicks the bedcover off and gets up, but only to look over my shoulder.

—I don't believe it! You're solving physics problems! Aren't sensitive girls supposed to keep diaries in which they confide their secret wishes and feelings?

I immediately slam the exercise book closed, as though it were in fact my diary. Dudi drops himself on my bed again.

—The government has granted us this sunny day off, and here she is shutting herself up in her room and doing homework!

It clicks at last.

—Why didn't you say it right from the start? You're dying to be asked about what you've been doing today, right?

Dudi starts chewing my bedcover again.

—All right, go ahead, tell me how you spent your morning. Only be short and keep to the point. I've got plenty of homework to do.

In a casual tone, Dudi says that he has just returned from Tahrir Square.

—*Tah* . . . !

A smile of triumph flashes over his face.

—All Baghdad is celebrating in Tahrir Square. Schools and shops and factories have closed. Buses are free today. Thousands of people are swarming through the streets, ululating, hailing the heroism of their leaders, shaking their bodies in a frenzy . . .

—Dudi, I could watch TV if I felt like seeing horror stories.

He goes on as if he has not heard me.

—Three hundred thousand participants, the speaker in the square announced over and over again. He kept increasing his number as if at an auction. Two hundred and thirty thousand . . . two hundred and fifty thousand . . . two hundred and eighty thousand . . . I guess I was the only Jew there. The only one alive, I mean.

He waits for me to respond, but I am too stupefied for words.

—Can you imagine—one in three hundred thousand? I've just savoured minority in its naked physical aspect!

—They could've torn you to pieces.

—How would anybody recognise me as a Jew? I don't write it on my shirt, like . . . like . . .

—Like who? What on earth are you talking about? What's written on whose shirt?

Dudi giggles,

—Not my own, *wallah*, not my own! The patent belongs to our Council of the Revolution. Every convict had a sheet of paper pinned to the front of his shirt. They'd written his full name on it, preceded by the title, "The Spy." The Spy, Hai Rahamin. The Spy, Mrad Aboudi. Wait, I'm not finished yet. Title and name were followed by profession. The Spy, Mrad

Aboudi, student. After that came religion. The Spy, Mrad Aboudi, student, Jewish. Then their place of residence. The Spy, Mrad Aboudi, student, Jewish, resident of Baghdad. Eight Jews, two Muslims, and one Christian. At least in one respect we are in the majority.

—Spare me your humour. How could you bear such a scene? Why did you go in the first place?

—There were children, five- and six-year-olds, riding pig-gyback on their daddys' shoulders to get a better view. Are you suggesting their hearts are stronger than mine?

—Stop prattling, for God's sake!

—All right. I wanted to see our President! Unfortunately I missed him by half an hour. When I arrived it was only the Minister of Youth Affairs, the Minister of Defense, and the Minister of Culture and Publicity who were on the platform. Each of them gave a long speech.

—I don't want to hear it!

—I didn't bother to listen, either.

—No? So what did you do?

—I wormed my way through the crowds. You see, the square was packed with unions and associations—the teachers, the workers, the scouts, the soldiers, the stu-dents—all roaring victory and carrying banners. "Today Marks the End of One History and the Beginning of a New One"—proclaimed by the Students' Union banner. Terribly academic, don't you think? I wonder how many years it requires to develop such critical faculties. However, the Union of Women and Mothers of Soldiers surpassed the students in their insight. Their slogan went like this: "The Execution of the Spies is the First Step to Liberation." Now that phrase finally convinced me that the fair sex can be as intelligent as us! Don't stare at me as if you were about to devour me, Lina, I'm just quoting what I've read. Not the trivial ones, only the sayings which left an impression on me. Take this for instance: "The Fatah Revolution and the

Ba'ath Revolution Walk Hand in Hand Against Imperialism and Its Agents." The Palestinian commandos put in quite an appearance, by the way. They were rollicking and romping—so elated, you'd think they were at last at the gates of Haifa and Yaffa.

—Stop it, Dudi. I can't take any more.

He clears his throat and continues.

—I haven't told you yet about the masses of Bedouins and peasants who kept spilling into the square. Illiterate as they are, they carried no banners—thank God—only food baskets for the picnic in the capital. Oh yes, and there were the Ba'ath's flags, how could I forget them? Please Lina, one more sentence, the last, I promise. I beg you, just listen to the Ba'aths' slogan. Theirs was at least to the point: "This is Only the Beginning. The Squares of our Noble Iraq Will Be Filled with the Corpses of Spies." That's what they wrote, word for word, I swear by my father's life.

It strikes me that Dudi hardly ever mentions his father, apart from swearing by his life.

—Imagine such a revolutionary spectacle three or four times a year! Promising vision isn't it? One detail still excapes me though: what will they do when they run out of Jews to hang? They can't import us like . . . like lampshades, can they?

—Dudi, I'm tired of you. Do me a favour and get lost. Go and tell the rest to your mother and sisters. It's their fate to put up with you, not mine.

Dudi frowns.

—No, it's to you that I want to tell my story. You and nobody else.

—But why? I raise my voice.

—Because I love you!

I heave a deep sigh.

—No! Oh no. It's because you're a nuisance, a pain in the neck, a thorn in the flesh, an enema in the arse. This is the worst day in my life, in your life, in the life of every Jew trapped in this accursed country. And even on a day like this, you can't help making a fool of yourself?

—No! Dudi coldly replies. Not even on a day like this.

Staring at me with defiance, he carries on:

—The crowds were dancing under the corpses, swinging them, hitting them with sticks and palm branches. Boys my age were catapulting stones at them—the way they sling them at birds and pigeons. I saw men, city men in shirts and trousers—not barefoot *shirgawis*—jump in the air to touch the toe or to tickle the sole of a hanged man's foot. Just for fun, for the sake of boasting to their wives and amusing their children.

—People climbed up the scaffolds? The spectators were allowed to come that near?

—What scaffolds, what *bettich*? Their feet were swaying above my head.

—What do you mean above your head? How close did you get?

—I went near each one.

—But . . . what for? What's the point?

—Because their heads were twisted. Because their necks were broken. Because their tongues were sticking out, like idiots in an asylum. Because their faces were deep blue, like your beloved Cadbury bars. Because their eyes were bursting out, about to pounce on you any moment. Because they reeked of . . . shit, yes, it was shit. Because their stiff lifeless bodies reeked of shit.

—You're lying! Hai never . . .

—Lina, allow me to impart some general knowledge to you. Maybe we'll be taught this subject at school. When you hang a man—any man, Jew or Muslim, innocent or guilty, handsome or ugly, without exception—when you hang a man, his bowels open immediately afterward. That's all!

I cover my face with my hands, and wish the earth would swallow up Dudi forever. Then, to my astonishment, it is my own voice that breaks the silence and asks about Hai, about whom I was most dreading to hear.

—Yes, I've told you already. I saw them all. They were spread out around the square, dressed in red linen pyjamas. I dragged myself from one corpse to the other until I came full circle. Hai and Mrad were hanged on the same gallows. Both were facing our gigantic *nasb al-hurryiah*, our Liberty Monument. Mrad was wearing a white cotton glove on his right hand.

Dudi pauses, scowls at me with hatred.

—Well, aren't you going to ask "why"? What happened to your "whys"? Did you run out of them? Come on, don't tell me you can't spare a "why" for Mrad's white glove. Go ahead, Lina, ask! Ask me "why"...

—I don't know... why what? What'd you want of me? What's the matter with you?

Dudi quavers with rage,

—Just ask me "why" for God's sake! It won't cost you anything. Are you afraid to ask all of a sudden?

—Fine. Why?

Dudi responds with an ugly smile.

—Now that you've asked, I owe you an answer! You see, I asked myself the question, "Why the glove?," because it certainly wasn't there to warm Mrad's frozen hand. So I hung around, busied myself with fizzy drinks, cracked pumpkin seeds, and kept an eye on the white glove. As the mood of the demonstrators got more and more heated, two boy scouts started to shove the corpses against each other. One used a flagpole, the other a broomstick. Hai and Mrad collided like dodgems in a fun fair, swinging and spinning, before they were pushed at each other again, each time with merrier whistles and wilder applause from the onlookers.

Dudi clears his throat, then goes on, stammering for the first time,

—After a few prods the cotton glove... dented. I refused to believe my eyes at first, until... not only the fingers but the palm itself was flattened. Do you get me? There were no fingers, no thumb, no palm, no wrist . . . the white glove was hollow . . . Mrad's right hand had been chopped off.

I push my desk away and rise to my feet. Dudi raises his voice,

—Do you understand now why they wouldn't show the trials on TV? Security reasons, my arse! We all knew it was bullshit. We assumed they just couldn't be bothered to invent a coherent story. We could only think that far. But did it occur to us that some of the defendants were disfigured or mutilated while they were still alive and standing trial?

—Dudi, if you're not leaving, I am!

I cross the room towards the door. Dudi starts to sing,

—*Ssemiiit, hay el-semiit!! Semiiit har.*

I look back at him.

—Familiar, isn't it? So familiar that for a moment I thought I was at school. Yes, it was our little pretzel hawker in the flesh, struggling to keep the tray straight on his head. One heroic word from him and I would have been lynched by the masses.

—*Al-a'awer*, the one-eyed, was there! Did he see you? Did he say anything?

—Wait, wait a second! A moment ago you were trying to get me to shut up, now you're impatient to hear every gory detail. Relax. Sit down. Don't worry about me. Am I in one piece or am I not?

—Don't try my patience, Dudi! I know you won't calm down before you've told me everything, so spit it out once and for all.

—All right, all right. I moved further into the crowd until I couldn't hear him anymore. What a relief it was, as if I'd been granted a second life.

Dudi sighs like an old man.

—But I soon heard another urchin crying out "*semit*," and, although I'd never seen this one before, I was just as alarmed. I was sure every *semit* vendor in Baghdad knew who I was. I was sure one of them would point at me and scream "*yehudi*" instead of "*semit*" at the top of his voice. The picture stuck in my mind the way chewing gum sticks to the sole of your shoe. I kept bumping into *semit* hawkers, and was startled each time as if they were the security police and not just slum kids. Imagine, Lina, if you can't hide in such a massive crowd, where on earth can you ever be safe?

I return to my seat.

—Why didn't you just leave?

—Why! Why! You and your irrelevant whys! "Why" makes no sense today, don't you see? Because it was impossible. Because I was scared to death. Because I was so agitated that I wouldn't have walked away but run away, and that would have looked suspicious. It would have been asking for trouble.

—As if going there in the first place wasn't asking for trouble! But never mind. You made it after all. How?

Dudi pulls out his wallet from his pocket and shakes it to make the coins clink.

—I stopped the next *semit* vendor and bought up all his stock. I was ready to pay anything for his silence. The bastard grinned all over his face and said the spectacle must have aroused my appetite. I was so revolted I could have thrown up. On the edge of the square, an ill-looking man was reciting patriotic verses in front of a circle of admirers. I threw the rings at his feet and walked off.

He takes a deep breath and quietly concludes:

—I ran off in fact, all the way back. I came directly here. It was like swimming against the current. Everyone was pushing against me in the opposite direction. Everyone was heading for Liberation Square.

Dudi lies on my bed, drained and dejected, finished at last. I go down to fetch a container of sherbet from the kitchen. On my return, I find him playing with a matchbox, a cigarette in the corner of his mouth. When he sees me, he sits up and sucks deeply.

—Don't you have an ashtray? he asks, waving the spent match, his eyes tearful from the smoke.

—You may use the wastepaper basket. Since when do you smoke?

—I bought a packet in the square this morning. It's my fifth already. Who said smoking affects your health? I ran three miles without a break.

Gripping the cigarette between his thumb and forefinger, he takes a long drag, and is seized by a fit of coughing. I pour him a glass of sherbet.

—After I saw what I saw, I felt as if I'd aged by ten, no, twenty years. So I thought I might as well start to smoke. You get the point?

—More or less. If you're fourteen and your face is still as smooth as a bread roll, then you should go and watch public hangings. End the show with a cigarette, and, sure enough, the calf has grown into a bull.

—That's not fair! It's not what I said. My intention was . . .

—Your intention was to show off! Walk in here like a hero and talk me into listening to your horror stories pretending to be concerned about the victims and . . .

—Lina, you're twisting my words. You owe me an apology.

—You make me sick!

—You're not in your right mind!

—Look who's talking! As if you were in a position to distinguish a right mind from a warped one.

—Perhaps Valium wasn't such a bad idea after all! I wonder if your parents can spare you a pill. It seems to run in the family.

—And it seems it's time to kick you out. Yes, you've heard me right. Just lift your ass off my bed and *welli*, get lost! Right now! I don't want to see you ever again.

Dudi spits out a shred of tobacco, wipes his lips, and grins.

—You forget we're neighbours? It's quite difficult not to run into each other twice a day.

He guffaws in disbelief as I thump him and pull him out of my bed.

His heavy body thuds to the ground. His cigarette falls and rolls towards the door. Slowly he rises to his feet, coughing and chuckling by turns, limping and groaning, pretending to be in pain.

—What a fuss about a packet of cigarettes! What do you have against smoking? Your mother herself's a walking chimney.

I shove him out of my room.

—Hey, watch out, my shoulder, you're hurting me! You're supposed to be the gentle sex, remember! Goodness, where've you gotten all this strength from? Your hand's as hard as iron, nobody will dare ask for it. Even I will have to think twice. Lina, are you crazy, I almost tripped. I could have broken a leg. Let go of me! Wait till your father...

—Leave my father out of this, all right? He's busy reflecting on the meaning of life, did you forget, you creep? Baba can't cope with anything today. He's not cool and brave like Dudi. Dudi! There's a daredevil, a real man, beardless perhaps, but you should see his balls!

Dudi yelps as I push him through the living room, and boisterously implores my parents to help. They watch the scene nonchalantly, without batting an eyelid. Once in the courtyard, Dudi lowers his voice,

—Lina, wait, you've got me wrong. Honestly, I didn't tell you the whole story. I held back one detail, a crucial one. Remember you kept asking why I went to the square, and I wouldn't answer?

—I don't give a damn about your motives any more.

Dudi suddenly stands still, folds his arms across his chest, and is immovable. No matter how fiercely I strike and push and kick, he does not budge an inch.

—Lina, I swear, I went to Liberation Square to make sure that my old man wasn't hanging there.

His new confession throws me off balance.

—You want me to swallow this now? The names of the executed have been repeated all day on the radio. They were in the papers. Your father's detained in the Central Prison. His name has never been mentioned in the trials. Your mother visits him every month.

—This is word-for-word what I told myself, a thousand times and more, and still my mind couldn't rest. It sounds mad, I know, but I couldn't help it. I had to go and place myself beneath every corpse in order to believe it wasn't my father's. Then I asked the hanged man's forgiveness for the relief that his misfortune granted me and dragged myself to the next gallows.

A tremor runs through my body. Whenever Dudi reveals a new face, it turns out to be more elusive and upsetting than the previouse ones. I could have hugged him in my confusion, or, just as easily wrung his neck.

Eventually I hear myself say:

—You must have a screw loose somewhere, Dudi.

He does not reply, but pushes the gate open and walks away.

His cigarette dropped at the door of my room has burnt into an ashen cylinder. Doubts start looming in my mind. Was Dudi's fear for his father genuine or did he invent the confession on the spur of the moment as a trick to win me over?

I fling myself on my rumpled bed, bury my face in the pillow. But Dudi's smell has invaded the bedcover. I kick it away, get up, air the room. Civilization was sacrificed in Baghdad this morning. I wonder how long the stench of its excrement will stick in our nostrils.

PART IV

ANATOMY OF HOPE

Ferial drops the frog into the transparent plastic bag which Selma is holding. Selma hastily closes up the opening, leaving a tiny hole for the yellow liquid our teacher is about to pour in. The frog flaps nervously about, flinging itself against the supple wall only to slide, time and again, down to the bottom. The yellow liquid rises to its ankles. The animal jerks up and bangs its head against Selma's hand. "Pow!" the boy beside me exclaims, as if we were watching a cartoon. The frog lifts a weighty head then stretches out its forelegs in a last attempt at a leap. Betrayed by its hind legs, the body slumps back into the sedative, and the bulky eyelids fall, like curtains at the end of a play.

Selma retrieves the numb animal and places it face up on the dissection table. As she spread eagles its fore and hind legs for Ferial to nail them to the wooden board, I have a flash of insight. The dual form in Arabic grammar must have derived from the symmetry of the body! My old question, long pursued, then forgotten, has suddenly found its answer, lying right in front of me. How evident it appears now that the rules of speech should reflect the rules of anatomy. I look around, eager to share my thought with somebody, but the attention of my classmates is captured by the two pairs of hands engaged in teamwork. Ferial seizes a scalpel and slits the amphibian down the middle, starting from the loins and moving upwards to the neck. The green skin opens, the tissue parts underneath without spilling a single drop of blood. Selma peels away the skin with a pair of tweezers then nails it to the board. Ferial pulls back the flesh until the innards are neatly exposed. Boys crack macabre jokes. Girls let out cries of pity and disgust. Our biology teacher calls for quiet.

—Boys, girls, what do we see, here? What organs can we identify? Who wants to start?

I recognise the heart by its stubborn rhythm. The throbbing reminds me of mother's recent words: "One should never lose hope, not as long as the heart is beating."

And yet, things do look pretty hopeless for this amphibian.

The bell rings. The students leave for morning break. Selma asks me to wait for her until she has helped Ferial clear up the laboratory. I stroll about the corridor, basking in the winter sun. In the yard below, smaller children are playing seven tiles. Passing by Dudi's classroom, I catch a glimpse of his empty desk. Dudi has not been to school since last Monday, the day of the executions. His absence had escaped my notice until Thursday, when, after school, *ustad* Heskel led a group of forty students to offer condolences to Hai's bereaved family. Two of Dudi's sisters came along and they told the *ustad* that their brother had a high fever and could not join in. They did not sound as if they knew about his hazardous wanderings in Liberation Square.

—Ferial told me I have the hands of a surgeon, Selma says, flaunting her long white fingers, smelling of laurel soap.

At the bottom of the stairs, dozens of pupils are thronging in front of the staff room, barring its entrance, elbowing one another aside to get a view from the window.

—We must have foreign guests again! So early? Have they already gone 'round the synagogues!

Infuriated by world condemnation of the spectacle in Tahrir Square, our government is repeating that the spies had been proved guilty by strictly legal trials, that they were hanged for being traitors and not for being Jews—as Zionist propaganda is claiming. To prove it, foreign journalists are being allowed into the country to judge for themselves whether the Jews are being persecuted and to see if there is any trace of discrimination in Iraq.

Selma and I squeeze through the crowd to the window and peep into the teachers' room. Ferial has just stepped in and let herself fall into the armchair beside *ustad* Heskel. He is still wearing his torn jacket, although the seven days of mourning are over. Across the room, two tall blond men are interviewing *ustad* Faouzi, the English teacher in our elementary school. He seems to be faltering in the company of our headmaster, the two foreigners, and the two security men accompanying them.

Will he find a way to convey to the visitors that his cousin, who had been arrested three weeks ago, was sent back home yesterday morning as a corpse in a jute sack?

Ustad Faouzi shakes hands with the foreign correspondents and draws up a chair towards Ferial and *ustad* Heskel, his speech flowing freely now. He throws up his hands in a gesture that says "what could I do?" *Sit* Fahima, another elementary school teacher, has joined them. *Ustad* Juad, our history teacher, is sipping his tea, aloof yet not inattentive to the agitation of his Jewish colleagues at the back of the room. He has the grace not to stare too long, but to hide his face behind a newspaper. He is all too ready to cast it aside when *ustad* Riad, the civics and Arabic teacher, taps his newspaper and pulls up a chair next to him.

The headmaster leads the visitors out.

The journalists smile in wonder at the restless mass of children waiting for them outside. Followed by the four men, the headmaster makes his way through the crush, distributing his usual scowls of reproof. No sooner have they disappeared inside the office than Selma nudges me and gives me a thumbs-up.

—Not again!

She nods her head affirmatively.

—But when? They went past so quickly...

—Didn't I tell you I was gifted? Selma mimes an *oud* player with her left fingers.

—Which one?

—The beardless one, with the yellow hair and blue eyes. He looked so smart in that brown leather jacket, don't you think?

—Oh yes, he's terribly handsome! Pity they didn't show them around the classes. Imagine if they'd have interviewed us!

—God forbid, my heart would have stopped beating on the spot!

—Come on, Selma, don't exaggerate!

—He's like a prince from a fairy tale. But too old for me anyway. And married too! He was wearing a wedding ring, did you see that?

—Say, you've really fallen for him! Did you write him a love letter or what?

—Oh no! she giggles. I just scribbled the same message I used for yesterday's visitors: Please, help us leave Iraq!

—You're sure you sneaked it into the right pocket? What if the security man finds it in his jacket this evening?

Selma giggles again, pleased with her feat, then gasps.

—Imagine, they're travelling all the way from France, Belgium, Italy, Holland... just for our sake! If the West intercedes on our behalf, it might work miracles. We could well be holding passports soon! Passports, Lina, passports, can you believe it?

—Not really. Come to think of it, I don't even know what a passport looks like.

Another miracle is waiting for me at home. Shuli, in flesh and blood, is leaning over the gas cooker in the kitchen, spooning out sauce from the steaming pan and slurping it from the ladle. Startled by my cry of joy, he drops the ladle into the pan, splashing red sauce on his shirt and fingers. I jump on his neck, while he waggles his scorched hand, convulsing with laughter.

—I thought they'd never let you out. What happened?

—Don't ask me! Maybe the lock of the jail broke and none of the guards knew how to repair it. Maybe there was a revolution and all the guards were shot.

—Shuli, don't tease me, please!

Instead of receiving his tepid tea at dawn, he was told to dress and was led to the prison commander. In disbelief, he listened to the officer inform him how he, Shuli, had been wronged by the former corrupt regime, but now that the revolutionary government was setting things right, he was free to go. Without bail, without signing any statements. With or without my star? He was tempted to ask, but fortunately kept the quip to himself. In no time, he packed his things and set out from the camp, disoriented like a bat in daylight. Military jeeps raced past him along the dirt track. Sparrows sang above his head. The sun was rising. A new day! There was more to time again than the position of the hands of his watch. His senses were waking up. But only when he reached the motorway did he start to feel safe. So they had not planned to shoot him in the back after all. On impulse, he began to run. No, he was not impatient to be home, he was just running as far as possible from the ugly chapter behind him.

I carry the bowl of *kubba* and beetroot—Shuli's favourite dish—to the dining room. Father uncorks the bottle of red wine that he bought this morning especially for the occasion. We gather around the table, the four of us together again. It is as though we are about to have the lunch we missed one-and-a-half years ago. As we raise our glasses and before father has said a word, the bell rings. How strange to hear the doorbell again, Shuli remarks. Father frowns, ill at ease. Recently he has been treating every signal from the outside world as an alarm bell. Mother goes to the door. Shouts of excitement soon emanate from the courtyard. She returns arm-in-arm with a boisterous Dudi—cheerful, full of life, and anything but feverish.

Since when has he grown two fingers taller than my mother?

—Abu Dudi's released, too...

—Together with all the Jewish men in the Central Prison...around sixty...all those picked up before the Ba'ath came to power, Dudi adds.

—*Alhamdellah*, thank God! What a day! Congratulations, my boy, father says, and shakes Dudi's hand.

—You must drink a toast with us, Shuli proposes.

—What do you mean drink, he's having lunch with us! says mother. Have a seat, my son. Lina, fetch him a plate from the kitchen, will you?

Averting his eyes from me, Dudi declines her invitation—as required by politeness—assuring us he has had lunch already. When mother insists, he corrects himself and claims the opposite, that they're waiting for him to have lunch back home.

—Are you refusing Mama's *kubba*? I say, getting up.

—Of course not, I didn't mean to be rude. I'll try a piece and keep you company for a while, but not for long. By the life of my father, I promised to be back in a minute.

After the toast, while fishing for the *kubba* in the red sauce, Dudi asks,

—Say Lina, what happened at Hai's *saba'a*? I heard *ustad* Heskel created turmoil. My sisters came home with their jackets torn. Some parents were outraged. Everybody's telling a different story. And what the hell did Job have to do with it?

"Slain like a dog, and mourned like a dog," repeated Hai's sister. "Do you call this a proper *saba'a*, when security men—may their eyes be gouged out—are patrolling across from our house? The criminals, what are they after now? His soul? His ghost?" Sitting beside Hai's sister, *ustad* Heskel was trying his best to comfort her. He assured her that nobody on earth could ever deprive a man of God's compassion. Quoting the *Zohar*, he said that Hai's soul was wandering to and fro between the house and the grave, mourning his body for seven days. He said we should pray for it with all our hearts before it departs to the eternal world, and he read out all sorts of verses from his holy books. In one ear and out the other, as far as Hai's sister was concerned. She did not even pretend to be listening. Her flippant reaction gave the *ustad* to understand that if he was to reach her, he had no other option than to join her in her disconsolate grief. So he stood up and, with his pocket knife, he tore his jacket from the right lapel down to the chest.

The *keri'a* is a mourning ritual reserved only for close relatives. Hai's sister hugged the *ustad* and called him her brother. But as soon as the other guests had recovered their speech, they got into a heated argument with him. A young woman maintained that it was wrong to tear one's shirt when—*Allah leykul*, may God not utter it—none of one's own family members were deceased. An elderly man added that once misused, such a ritual called forth bad fortune. It was—*hasha assema'a*, may the listeners be spared—as if asking God to take somebody's life away. Weren't they confusing religious belief with superstition? The *ustad* answered calmly. Did they really think that the Almighty was so susceptible? Did they forget how manifold our Torah was? To prove his point, he read out the passage from the Book of Job, in which Job's three friends rent their garments to commiserate with him over the death of his children.

—So she gets carried away by the Bible and ruins her brand new woollen jacket! mother complains. We buy it for her at the beginning of the season, no matter how tight money is, because we won't have our daughter dressed shabbily. And what does she do? She goes and cuts it with a knife.

—Everybody did it! All forty students. We all stood up, and, one after the other, tore our jackets for Hai. It was the only thing we could do: wear our wound.

I turn to Shuli, seeking his approval. He smiles back, faintly, with an air of detachment that makes me doubt whether he has been listening at all.

—What's done's done! father concludes with a measure of discomfort. Didn't we agree to close this subject?

Mother reaches out for Dudi's empty plate and, without asking if he wanted it, serves him a second helping.

—You haven't heard yet how Baba was released. The commander of the prison himself put in an appearance in their cell early this morning and delivered a speech about how they had been wronged by the former regime and how the revolutionary government was...

Our meal lasts until Dudi's sister comes over and drags her brother back home. His family has, in fact, been waiting for him to start lunch.

Mother calls me to the kitchen. She needs my help, she says, and thrusts a bundle of rags into my hand. Shuli's room has not been cleaned for over a month. Carrying a bucket of water and a blue rubber glove under her arm, she marches upstairs. Reluctantly, I follow. Shuli is standing by his window, absorbed in some scene outside. From his stiffness, I can tell we are not welcome. His good humour at lunch has sunk into melancholy. Mama, you really don't have to, he falters. But she has already put on her glove and is rubbing the headboard. The night table. The table lamp. First with the wet rag then with the dry one. I am in charge of the windowsill. Mama, it can wait, please do it later, do it tomorrow, he implores. Everything will shine in a minute, she replies, moving him gently aside, to proceed with the cupboard.

Brown water is dripping from the cupboard. Mother wipes it dry, then plants the bucket on the desk. Shuli's colour changes. Not the desk, he cries out, and grabs the cloth from her. And who did he think had been cleaning it all this time? Or did he imagine that dust flew back the way it came, all by itself? Mother laughs. Shuli does not look amused. He declares in a firm voice his wish to be alone. Alone? Hasn't he been alone long enough? Can't he wait five more minutes? NO! Don't shout at your mother, she replies and snatches the dust cloth back from him. Now they are wrestling for that ragged muddy undershirt, half playfully, half in earnest. The undershirt sails out of the room, followed by the blue rubber glove. My hand, stop twisting my hand, you're hurting me! He grips her by the shoulders and forces her to the door. *Barrah*, out! She is tittering like a little girl. Let go of me! You've broken my hand, she groans, displaying her unscathed wrist. He removes the bucket from his desk, slams it down beside her foot. *Barrah*, he repeats to the bucket, and bars the door with his arm. Mother beckons me.

—Didn't you hear what your brother said? He wishes to be left alone.

I shrug my shoulders. Shuli utters no word.

—Come with me, I said! I need your help in the kitchen.

—Later! I reply, and rest my elbows on the window sill.

—Later, everything can wait for later when you're fourteen! she grumbles, shakes her head in disapproval and flounces away.

He, too, is shaking his head, in much the same way, until he turns round and lets out a cry of alarm. A circle of dark water on the desk is crawling towards the nearby folder. I throw my rag on the formica desk, rub it until the water is soaked up. Shuli picks up the folder, feels its base. Dry, thank God. He browses through the loose scraps of paper inside—notes, addresses, bibliographies, and many smudged sketches. Such a fuss over a trifle, he murmurs, as he replaces the folder on the

table. He then picks up the pencil case, unzips it, scans the row
of pens and pencils, and zips it up again. He repeats the procedure with the ruler box and the compass box. He undoes the
top of the ink bottle, and, shutting one eye, peeks inside. What
are you looking for? I ask. Nothing in particular, he mumbles.
Looking for nothing in particular, he squats down and starts
pulling out the desk drawers. Just pulling them out and pushing them in again, as if the friction of the wooden drawers
sliding in and out evoked some remote memories, the way
music does. Wearied with the music of drawers, or maybe just
with himself, my brother gets up, pads to his bed, and lets
himself fall. Absentmindedly, he stretches out his hand, and
clicks the table lamp on and off, like a little boy. Suddenly he
sits up and clutches the transistor radio.

He moves the dial left and right, right and left, mumbling
numbers to himself, as if having a discussion with his memory.
Only when he has precisely located the station, does he turn
on the radio. The deep-throated female voice restores pride in
his leaden face. After one-and-a-half years, he can still remember the wavelength of the forbidden station. They are broadcasting a lengthy agricultural report. The pips on the hour are
sounded at last. The newscaster announces the time—one
hour behind us. The name of the station is about to follow.
With a vicious smile, Shuli turns the volume up full blast.

—Let's see how long it takes Baba to run upstairs and...

—Shuuuuliiiii... mother yells from downstairs,

—All right, all right! he yells back, and switches off the
radio.

Then he winks at me.

—We don't want the old man to have a heart attack, right?

Missing a sign of complicity from me, Shuli placidly
returns the transistor radio to the night table.

—What am I sulking about? It's so much easier to silence
the radio announcer than to shout for the guard each time
I've got to shit.

I go over to the window. Shuli continues:

—I suppose you people still wet your pants when the bell rings late in the evening, right?

—No! We switch it off at nighttime. Baba says if it's the security police, nothing will stop them anyway, but if it's a mistake or a bad joke, then we're spared the fright in the middle of the night.

A look of horror passes over his face. He has not taken such routine into account. He joins me at the window, leans his elbows on the sill, and stares dreamily outside.

—Did you see my new jacket? I say after a while. Mama has stitched it, but the cut still shows, like a scar!

—Since when? he asks, pointing at the construction site in the street behind us.

The building is surrounded by ladders and scaffolding. The brickwork of the outer walls of the ground floor has been completed, with holes left for the doors and windows. A concrete ceiling has been laid on top, but above that there are only projecting steel reinforcements. The place looks deserted. The workers must be having a break somewhere in the shade. When did the excavation begin?

—Sometime in the autumn. Semidetached houses.

—I can see that. The standard shit. When will they understand that such buildings are no good for the climate here? Thanks to those French windows the inhabitants will grill in the heat most of the year. In the old oriental houses, there was always shade because of the *hosh*, the inner courtyard, and you had the cellar if you wanted a cool place for an afternoon nap. They're both out now, sacrificed to modernity. I bet you, in a few decades, when they finally wake up to the alien city they've created, they'll put the blame on imperialism again.

—You can't wait to start your own thing, right?

Shuli is taken aback.

—My own thing? Here? You're kidding. Who'd let me? And even if they did, what would I build? New palaces for the new dictators? Larger avenues for their military parades? More squares to stage still more spectacular executions? Or should I devote myself to building cozy houses for the middle class while I myself am living out of a suitcase?

I do not reply. Shuli goes on after a while, quietly, as if talking to himself,

—How can their history be filled with such meditative architecture and yet so much violence? This will always be a riddle to me.

Mumbling indistinct curses, he bends down and goes over his books, jerking from one stack to the other, selecting the large, hardcovers, beating the dust out of them, then slamming them down on the window sill. No, he is arranging them along the sill—putting them down flat, one next to the other, spine inward. The second row is laid in such a way that the books overlap those underneath, and the gaps at the edges are filled with smaller paperbacks. Only by the fourth layer do I realise that my brother is bricking up his window. Volumes of history, archaeology, philosophy, eastern and western architecture, Renaissance art, and various dictionaries and lexicons, pile up and bar the daylight. Except for those sunbeams that sneak through the gaps between different sized books, and reveal the motes of dust fluttering in the air. After he has laid the last row, just beneath the curtain rail, Shuli considers the variegated structure with a mixture of pride and irony.

—There you are, I've set up my own thing, my own Wall of China, for now and until our last day in this place.

Why is he fuming? A wall of books has always stood between Shuli and the world. I draw my forefinger into a shaft of light and adjust its position until the nail shines.

—We may not be here when the new neighbours move in! Selma says we're likely to get passports pretty soon.

—Passports? Tell your Selma she's living in a dream-world. Why would they allow us to leave? We're breeding spies for future conspiracies. Forget it, Lina. They won't let us out. Never in a million years.

—Don't say that. I don't want to grow up here.

—And I don't want to rot here. That's why we can't wait until this or that regime feels revolutionary enough to grant us passports. We've got to find our own way out.

He goes over to his desk again, pulls the drawers open.

When he finds the map of the Middle East, he nails it to the wall. I switch on the light. Shuli emphasises Iraq's frontier with a red Magic Marker.

The concrete mixer outside is rasping again. The noise will last until sunset. Shuli is too busy painting the frontier to be disturbed.

—Needless to say, we can rule out an escape to the west and to the south. We certainly have no wish to jump out of the frying pan into the fire.

I follow the marker as it wanders along the border with Syria, Jordan, Kuwait, and Saudi Arabia and nod attentively, as if he were teaching me something.

—Our good fortune won't come from the north, either. Turkey's known for its tough policy towards fugitives. If they catch us, they won't hesitate to hand us over to the Iraqis.

Shuli's arm sags as he eliminates one alternative after the other.

—Our only chance is the border with Iran, thanks to the Shah—may God grant him long life.

This is no news either. Shuli taps on the blue line in the southeast, *Shat al-Arab*.

—Unfortunately, the way over the stream is no longer possible for us. There are large armies on both sides of the southern frontier, and they'll stay there as long as the conflict over the oil fields hasn't been resolved.

I wonder how his information has been updated within half a day.

—That means only the northeastern frontier is left,

through the Kurdish provinces. The region is mountainous, and it won't be as smooth as crossing a river. But I'm sure . . .

—Shuli, you know how cautious Baba is, I interrupt him impatiently. You think he'll ever take such a risk?

—I don't care. I only know that I'm taking off at the first opportunity. With or without Baba.

—But how, for heavens' sake! Since war has broken out with the Kurds, just travelling to the north in itself has become next to impossible.

Shuli gazes at me with stupefaction, then despair.

—In that case, I'm afraid we're trapped . . . inside this map, he mumbles, flinging the red marker on the desk.

I spare him the news of our thirty-mile restriction.

DICTIONARY OF HATE

New school books are heaped on my desk: physics, chemistry, algebra, biology, and other volumes of boredom. A shaky tree of knowledge. The term has just begun, and already I am fed up with school, tired of learning and tired of pretending to learn.

Contemporary Arabic Literature lies open at the table of contents. I go over the collection of short stories, essays, poems, and plays, trying to remember the assignment we were given last week: "The Call of the Soil," "Salute to the Iraqi Republic," "Homeland of Fog," "The Martyr," "Valley of Blood," "The Arab Woman and National Life." The titles sound almost identical to last year's. No wonder, the Arabic reader is edited by the Ministry of Education and prescribed for both state and private schools. I yawn, tired of reading books not written for me. Tired of not belonging and tired, just as much, of belonging, I leaf through the pages of the book, ready to pick a quarrel with the first popular word I encounter. *Watan*, homeland, a key word in our contemporary literature, easily lends itself to my declaration of war.

It is repeated eleven times in the first text, a short story about a mother who receives the news of her son's death on the battlefield with alternating grief and pride. No, underlining will not do, I draw a circle around each *watan*—as if to prevent it from escaping. Then I move on and comb the next pages for further homelands. His, hers, yours, mine and ours. Homelands of gold, homelands of grass, of sand, of salt, of light. Homeland as father, as lover, as womb, as victim, as martyr. Ancient homelands, fertile homelands, homelands betrayed, and homelands retrieved. I locate eighty-six of them, strewn between pages 1 and 192.

Who needs eighty-six homelands—all in one book?

I start erasing the homeland on page 1, gently, lest the paper tear. To my surprise, the ink does not resist and the letters pale under my fingers. The smell of the abrading rubber reminds me of our first alphabet lessons in the kindergarten when we kept correcting our drawings until they resembled the characters on the blackboard. What work it was to sketch the final *nun*, the letter n! It's like a chamber pot, with a dot dangling atop, I whispered in Selma's ear, but it did not temper our despair. The paper under *watan* is also being scraped away. The chamber pot is fading. My first homeland is on its way to oblivion. Who said the printed word was immortal? The neutrality of the blank space soothes me. I wonder if the clerk who deleted the Jewish names from the telephone directory experienced a similar gratification. My parents are climbing the stairs. Mother reminds me not to stay up too late. After washing in the bathroom, they put out their light. At dead of night, I plough on through the book, eliminating one *watan* after the other, delicately, like a soldier dismantling bombs in a minefield.

Enemies end up getting fatally bound to each other, father once said—a saying which might well explain my urgency to check the Arabic reader the next day, as if to make certain that the banished word has not returned. The wounded surface reassures me. But why are terms like earth, soil, land, country, state, republic still around? What about the wealth of hyperbole, the stock of superlatives and turgid verbs guarding the blank spaces and nourishing the spirit of *watan*, even after its elimination?

Armed with a half-dozen erasers, I set upon the textbook again and remove each word that evokes homeland or associates it with heroism, chivalry, nobility, honour, faith, virtue, martyrdom, motherhood, manhood, brotherhood, life, freedom, blood, beauty, loyalty, soul, and glory.

When the omitted words have outnumbered the remaining ones in my *Contemporary Arabic Literature*, the design of the pages collapses. The order from right to left and from top to bottom has been shaken. Margins are hardly discernible and paragraphs no longer conspicuous. Sentences are frequently interrupted by long silent blocks, which, in their turn, are punctuated by commas and full stops that break up the silence into a series of minor pauses. Here and there, question and exclamation marks erupt, like misplaced intonation. Prepositions designate vague connections, while adverbs and adjectives linger, substituting time where no motion is, and suggesting a mood in the absence of a subject. Personal pronouns haunt the scraped pages, like amnesiac fugitives seeking their identity among the rubble of the past.

Only the page numbers have remained intact, designating a sequence which no longer makes sense.

I have at last forced Arabic to stutter.

—I've censored our Arabic reader, I confide to Selma, when she pops in at the weekend, and show her the expurgated version of our textbook.

She riffles through the pages, then casts the book indifferently aside.

—And? What's next?

—The dictionary! I hear myself say.

But when Selma jiggles her mother's car keys, I realise we are at cross purposes.

—All by yourself! You never told me . . . Selma, since when?

Shattered by Hai and Mrad's arrest on the river bank last summer, Selma and her father could not but give up their swimming schedule. They continued to get up before dawn, however, and drove to the suburbs instead. On the empty motorway and in middesert, Selma's father fulfilled her wish and let her take the wheel.

—But you're underage, you're only fifteen!

She grabs my hand and drags me downstairs, then outside. Her mother's green Beetle is waiting at our gate.

—You know how easily I'm taken for eighteen. Let's go for a drive. Not as far as the centre of town though. I've promised Mama to stay in the neighbourhood.

We drive to her place, proceed to the market in Rikheta, and drive back to our street. We repeat the journey, taking various routes and detours until Selma has displayed her skills in reversing, making U-turns, overtaking other vehicles, and parking in extremely narrow spaces. Finally she pulls up in front of our house and explains, in a flow of technical vocabulary, the function of the lights, knobs, gauges, and counters on the dashboard. As if that were not enough for a first lesson, we hop out again, go round to the back of the car, and look inside the engine.

—Do you know how the car starts? As soon as you turn the ignition, the carbureator mixes air and fuel together, and this brings about an explosion. Isn't it exciting? Every journey begins with a tiny explosion. Most cars have radiators, but Beetles are special, they're air cooled, and the engine is where the boot should be. The disc lying over there is the air filter, and down on the left, you'll find the oil filter. The battery's also in an odd place, under the back seat. Do you know how it works?

When she has at last finished her demonstration, I divert her back to my own interests.

—Selma, do you think we're capable of an active, deliberate forgetting of what we have learnt?

Leaning over the engine, fiddling with some oily wires, she says, absentmindedly,

—Active forgetting? I don't know. Anything in particular you want to forget?

—The Arabic language!

Selma throws me a curious look, then bursts into laughter.

—Selma, I'm dead serious.

—But Arabic's your mother tongue!

As if I have been waiting for these words to fuel my anger.

—With such a mother, we can envy the orphans! How are we to live with the abuse they pour on us: bloodsucker, vulture, poisonous snake, cancerous growth, child of a whore, agent of the devil, error of humanity—just take your pick, you'll end up hating yourself anyway.

Selma motions me to keep my hands away and slams the engine shut.

—Drop your voice, Lina, we're in the street!

—But that's precisely what I'm talking about! Arabic has been silencing us for the last fifteen years! It's my turn to silence it. I'm disowning it, it's as simple as that.

—I bet you've been seeing too much of Dudi lately, otherwise I can't understand what has possessed you. How can you imagine yourself going on living here and . . .

—That's the point, Selma, I can't imagine myself going on living here!

—You're talking nonsense, crap, from beginning to end.

—But why?

—I don't even want to go into it. Isn't it clear? Your language's not a piece of clothing you can just shed!

—How do you know?

Selma snorts with exasperation,

—'Cause Arabic's in your tongue and in your ears, p-h-y-s-i-c-a-l-l-y! Do words sound dirty or sweet unless they're in Arabic? Can you read between the lines in any other language? Can you laugh at English jokes, do you understand French puns? Can you multiply or even count, can you curse, can you remember other than in Arabic? It's as if . . . as if your whole life is stored in your mother tongue.

—Including fear. If I forget Arabic, I might forget what fear is . . .

—You'd still be sawing the very branch you're sitting on!

—I've got English and French at my disposal. I'll fly with them.

Selma snorts again,

—Or fall and break your neck! You'll never speak them as fluently as Arabic. They'll remain your second languages, second best, like crutches. You know what that means? Your memories will be scattered, full of gaps. Your heart will be divided . . . your feelings confused. You'll never have an opinion, but vacillate between at least two, one in English and one in French . . . both of which will be substitutes, none really your own. That's it, you'll always live in translation, forever a foreigner in your own mind.

Selma has never spoken with such eloquence before. In spite of her dark forecast, my impulse is crystallizing into a resolution.

—Better a foreigner in a free mind than a prisoner at home.

—You'll stutter in your freedom! You'll stutter day and night. Even in your thoughts, even in your dreams.

—Nobody dies from stuttering. Moses himself stuttered.

—Moses didn't want to be a journalist!

—So I won't be a journalist. I'll be something else . . . a photographer perhaps.

—That's not the same! she shouts.

—And who's the same after the executions in Tahrir Square?

Selma hops into the car, slams the door, and, without

rolling down the window, turns the key in the ignition. An explosion—the start of all her journeys. I am tempted to tap on her window, call her back, thank her for the ride, congratulate her on being such a good driver. But the only gesture I manage is to wave her off.

Selma speeds away while I slowly walk inside. She has not waved back. She looked offended as if I have spoiled her day. What did we quarrel about after all? Did I criticise anything close to her? Did I ask her to give up her driving? Why do arguments flare up so easily between us these days?

They say the closest of friends may diverge at some point. It seems to me that Selma and I are not only diverging but moving in opposite directions. She is absorbing the world about her while I am rejecting it. She is collecting, I am throwing away. She is adding, I am subtracting. Is our rift inevitable? The thought makes me shudder. If I ever walked away from Selma, it would only be towards solitude.

The dictionary at my side, I conceive a systematic programme of unlearning Arabic. It consists of twenty-eight stages which correspond to the twenty-eight letters of our alphabet. At each stage, I will omit from my speech and writing all the words beginning with a particular letter. The programme will start with the first letter and advance letter by letter, until the last.

I hope we will have left the country by then. Otherwise I would have to declare an everlasting strike on Arabic.

SECRETS

—This must be *suq* el-Bezzazin, mother says, indicating the entrance of the wood-roofed bazaar.

Like every old *suq* in the centre of town, the cloth market is dim, narrow, packed with shoppers. The stores have their fronts open to the road, their interiors girdled with bolts of colourful fabric, lined on shelves or stacked on the ground up to the ceiling. The owners squat on low stools before their thresholds, chatting or listening to the radio, worry beads in one hand, the *stikan* in the other. In their pose of leisured *effendis*, they greet the passersby, offer them tea, propose to display their goods—the best in the market—promise exceptional prices, bid them good day, wish them long lives, then crane their heads to welcome the next potential customers. Children keep weaving through the crowd, holding out small items like hankerchiefs, hairpins, zippers, clothespins. The vendor standing in front of the men's coffeeshop is dangling worry beads from his forearms. The old man beside him is holding out one red-eyed baby rabbit, shivering between his calloused fingers.

Mai el-zebib, mai el-zebib, raisin juice, cries out the boy in the brown *dishdasha*, wandering through the *suq*, rattling his brass bowls. I nudge mother.

—No! she retorts, forestalling my request. They never

wash these bowls. Do you know how many mouths drink from them every day?

My thirst is immediately quenched by the image of hundreds of lips bathing in the sweet juice.

—Mama, can you hear the hammering in the distance? It must be the coppersmiths of suq el-Sefafir!

—Impossible! We are nowhere near the copper market! If anywhere, we are close to *suq* el-Saray, the book bazaar. Believe me, daughter, I know these *suqs* like the palm of my hand.

The lane seems to taper, the throng to grow ever thicker. The brazen beating persists, defying mother's familiarity with the *suq*. The grey donkey, overloaded with tottering jute sacks, is coming toward us, claiming the entire road. His owner goads it on from behind, shouting his requests to let the donkey pass. I hasten to the side only to bump into the man with the blue shirt who rushes past me. Before I have realised it, he cups my left breast, briefly squeezes it before letting go.

—Mama! I groan, more in shock than in pain.

—What's the matter? Did he touch you? Show him to me. *Hassa asberu*, I'll soot his face right away!

But the blue shirt has disappeared in the crowd. I take hold of my breast, to reassure myself that it is still in place, in one piece.

—*An'al abouk, ibn al-gawad*, curse on your father, son of a pimp! By my honour I'll twist his neck if ever I lay hands on him . . . one shopkeeper roars in indignation.

Heads turn, first in the direction of the shopkeeper then towards me, brushing me with stern, disapproving glances— or so I imagine. I take my hand off my breast, blushing.

—Mama, I want to go home! Why don't we buy what we need and then go?

Mother clasps hold of my hand, kisses my cheek, then drags me with her deeper into the *suq*. Showing no hurry to do our shopping, she loiters, studies the stores, their owners, their distance from the last intersection, confirms their location in some tattered map in her memory. The drumming in my ears gradually dies out. When the road forks, mother takes the left turn. Her pace quickens. She seems to have regained her homing instincts. She stops before one of the shops. It bears no nameplate. No particular feature distinguishes it from its neighbours, not even the name of God hanging on the wall. The vendor is tending to two women. Mother inspects the old man in the brown *zbun*, who is squatting in front of the shop, consumed in his *nargila*. I follow her inside. The bolt of flowery violet cloth flows from the shopkeeper's hands, unrolling itself under the pale electric bulb.

—It matches the colour of your eyes, as if designed especially for them, he flatters while measuring the length of several yardsticks, then reaching for his shears.

Having made the two inch long cut just beyond the measured spot, he halts ceremoniously,

—*Mabrouk*, he congratulates his customer for her purchase before he plunges the shears into the fabric.

When they bid him farewell, the vendor turns to mother, pops his hands behind his back, like some mechanical toy reverting to its starting position.

—At your service, *oukht*i!

Mother shifts her dialect into Muslim.

—We're looking for *abayas*. One for me and one for the girl.

—I've got ready-made *abayas* in artificial silk. But if you wish to sew them yourself, I can show you plenty of fabrics in a wide range of prices and qualities.

—That's not necessary. The ready-made will do.

The vendor climbs up on the stool, fetches the heap of folded black cloth from the upper shelf. He unfurls it into two identical robes, displays them on the counter. Mother feels the material, cocks her head to one side, indicating it is worth considering. He holds the gown up to help her inside. No sooner has she slipped into it than she metamorphoses into one of those cloaked women who daily cross my path in the street, intimidating me with their grim exterior.

Mother calmly examines her reflection in the mirror, betraying no surprise.

—It's the right size, she says nonchalantly, focusing on her white high heels, which have escaped the totality of the shroud.

The dark silhouette in the mirror reminds me of some old sepia photograph of my grandparents, which we burned during the war. In spite of her blurred features, I recall my grandother's girlish figure, standing beside her husband inside his shop, bundled in the black sack. The black sheep of the family, you would think.

The vendor inquisitively eyes my mother while praising his merchandise. She takes off the robe then gestures to me to try on the other one. What's the point? With me being slightly taller than she, it is evident that the gown will look slightly shorter. So what? Didn't Sabah's father say we would most probably have no use for the things? I cannot protest now that the vendor is gallantly holding out the gown. If only he would hold it low enough for my hands to slide inside. The tips of my fingers finally peer out of the wide sleeves. The hemline sweeps the floor. The hood flops over my forehead.

—It's one size larger than the previous one, he points out.

—It's much too large! Don't you have another *abaya* in this size? mother inquires.

—But of course, I have them in all sizes.

He clambers up on the stool, rummages through the upper shelf. I pace the shop, feeling the different bolts, toying with taunts I dare not voice. What is keeping you up there, Brother? Is the rest of your supply motheaten, perhaps?

Suhtain, to their health! Let the moth be fed until every robe in the store has shrunk to the size of Barbie dolls.

—This must be the right size, the shopkeeper mumbles, climbing down.

My hands grope in vain for buttons on the front. Familiar on strangers, the robe feels strange once it sits on me, its tentlike dimensions swallowing me up. The vendor claims it fits me perfectly. The hypocrite. If he dares to say it has been designed especially for me. . . . When I shift my gaze to mother for her judgment, the hood slips down to my shoulders.

—We're taking them, she decides. How much do they cost?

He speaks his price. Mother raises her brows, feigns surprise. He swears that nowhere in the *suq* would she find such finish, that he has never made such discounts before— not even to his own relatives—that if the other shopkeepers hear of it, they would mock him saying he has given it for *balash.* Mother stands her ground, slowly brings him round to her terms.

—*Yallah,* let's hear your last price, I don't have the whole day.

—*Wallah* I'd lose if I went down by one more *fils.*

Standstill. Neither is willing to compromise. He replaces the flowery bolt of cloth on the shelf, puts the row in order, pretending to have lost interest in the deal. It is the right time for us to leave the shop, reckoning on being called back for some better bargain. My favourite stage in every haggling, but mother skips the strategy today. She speaks her last offer then opens her handbag with determination. The vendor continues to object, yet returns to the counter to pack our robes.

—You must be visiting relatives, somewhere in the *welayat?* he ventures, now that he is reaching out for the banknote.

—How did you know? My husband's family lives in Amara. They're sort of . . . well, I don't want to disparage them, but you know what the people from the provinces are like!

I fiddle with the reels of bright ribbon hanging beside the cash register, taking delight in mother's fluency in telling lies. The vendor hands me the brown parcel then grins in complicity, without speaking his mind on people from the provinces. Mother reviews the shop, dawdles over the silk section before she finally steps out.

—It used to be your grandfather's! she says, once outside. I used to take him his lunch basket every day. When he emigrated, he sold it for a handful of *dinars*, to that old man perhaps—but it could just as well have been somebody else. The warehouse must be a few steps from here. Who knows what's become of it. Nothing was the same in the market after the *taskit*.

I nod impassively, weary of old history—the mass emigration of Jews twenty years back. Mother goes on.

—Somehow, I felt like buying our *abayas* from here, as if asking for Baba's blessing.

Suddenly it occurs to me that the old photograph of my grandparents had been taken here, that my memory of the photograph is the extension of mother's memory of the shop. I turn for one last glance, wondering if her firsthand recollections would colour my sepia image of our familial past. The vendor is replacing the unsold robe on the upper shelf. The old man is making bubbles in the waterpipe. The bulb is sending out yellow light, timeless, just like that of the neighbouring stores.

Curry receives us with such nagging meows in the backyard, you would think he has not touched food for days. I pick up his bowl, carry it to the kitchen. While pouring the milk, I think of some trick I could play on him, rush upstairs to put on my disguise. The material feels pleasantly cool, surprisingly light, qualities which I had overlooked in the store. Slowly, I falter down the stairs, raising the black gown in order not to stumble over its hemline. In the kitchen, I veil my face up to the nose with the hood, then, the milk bowl in my hand, unlock the door to our backyard. Curry, who has been wailing, ready for the first opening crack, hushes in mid-meow. Instantly he recoils, swells to double his size. I must have scared him out of his wits! Sniggering, I uncover my face. Curry, who has never thought much of my sense of humour, stands his ground. I squat down to reassure him of my intentions. Too late. The cat has bent his back, ready for the fight. Curry! I call out, hoping he recognises my voice or his name. He hisses back, baring his teeth. I spill some milk on the floor to remind him of his hunger. Curry does not take his eyes off me. His irises, reduced to thin vertical lines in the sun, like the tubes of bar heaters, glare hostility, if not hatred. His blown-up tail continues to snake, thudding the ground. He is fewer than five feet from me. If I get up, he might well pounce on me. Carefully, I shift my hold from the edge of the bowl to its base, train it on Curry, then, throw the milk into his muzzle. Curry takes to his heels, scampering in terror. I call him back, convulsing with laughter. But the cat has skittered up the fence, fled to the neighbours.

I refill the bowl with milk, enrich it with cream cheese for the sake of reconciliation. Poor Curry. He does not suspect our plans. He thinks we will stay here forever, just to feed him. How betrayed he will feel on that morning. He will meow for hours without reply! The least we can do is compensate him with some farewell meal when our big day comes. That is, if Sabah's father keeps us in mind, remembers his word, before he, too, takes flight.

For no Jew's presence can be taken for granted nowadays.

The first of such undertakings began earlier this summer.

No sooner had the peace treaty with the Kurds been declared, than Sasson travelled to the north, people said. He wandered through the Kurdish provinces, frequented local restaurants, studied faces, struck up trivial conversations before he voiced his unspeakable request only to hear the inevitable replies, with which he returned, heavy hearted, to Baghdad. But Sass would not be daunted. Despite the thirty-mile restriction, the police checkpoints, the military patrols on the highway, he refused to relinquish his "suicidal plan." Two of his friends had been executed, his cousin had been tortured to death. Should he sit there waiting for his turn to be hanged?—he was said to have told his wife in one of their disputes. So he drove back to the north, who knows how many times, miraculously escaped discovery by the hordes of security men who roamed in the Kurdish regions, until he found the Kurd who was ready to smuggle the family out of the country. The man demanded four hundred *dinars* per person—to be paid beforehand—even though he could not guarantee the safety of their passage. Sasson could not guarantee the honesty of the Kurd either, but he took the chance.

The news of his safe crossing to Iran shook up our community. No Saturday service had been so restless, they said. Wrapped in their prayer shawls, the men whispered the news, recited it during the Sabbath blessings. When *ustad* Heskel was called up to read from the Torah, he could not refrain from exhilaration in godly recognition.

Our Sass had made it! He had been escorted by Kurdish cavalry, people said. His exploit had been supported by Mulla Mustafa el-Barazani, the great leader. He had surmounted the perils of the mountains. He had escaped the merciless hands of the security men. He had worked miracles. He had provided the script for our vision.

But whether this was in fact the turning point in our lives would be determined only by the reaction of the government. What if Sasson's brother had to pay with his head for the brave deed? What if the entire Jewish community were punished? Would the smuggler be trailed, sentenced, executed? Would the event have detrimental effects on the peace treaty with the Kurds?

One week passed. Two. Then three. None of our fears materialized.

In the meantime, one more Jewish family fled the country. They were friends of Sasson. He must have taken them into his confidence, people said. They had left the lights on, the hose trickling in the garden, the washing hanging on the roof, the mezuzot nailed on the doorposts. The radio, too, was on, not too loud, just to simulate human presence. What they forgot, however, was to cancel the visit of the plumber who, days later, rang their bell with persistence. Too stubborn to give up, he called the neighbour, insisting he had heard voices inside. The neighbour, in his turn, called the landlord. The landlord called his lawyer. The lawyer called the police.

The police called two lorries to load up the contents of the house.

Shortly thereafter, several families escaped, within one or two days of each other. Through Haj Umran, through Halabja—easier routes, people said. The prices, too, were reduced: three hundred *dinars* per person. It was obvious that new smugglers were involved. More experienced, better organised. They picked up their clients from home, drove them straight to the border. The only thing one had to do was to get out of the car, then walk over some planks towards freedom.

By midsummer, word spread that the thirty-mile restriction was no longer in force. Our people were perplexed. Elated. Suspicious. Unable to see through the schemes of the government. The repeal of the restriction could not have suited their purpose better. If they were stopped on the way, Jews could pretend from now on to be going on holiday to Salah el-Din or Shaqlawa, popular summer resorts in the Kurdish provinces.

Since then, four or five families had been disappearing weekly. Within the month of departure, the police would burst into their houses. Through the local newspaper, the families would be notified that unless they reported to the residents' registration office by this or that date, they would forfeit their Iraqi citizenship. Each crossing reassured us that the escape route was still in operation. With each escape the nervousness of those left behind intensified. Nobody could predict how long the government would maintain its closed-eye policy. Time was running out, faster each day. The race for information bordered on hysteria. People were evasive, uptight, reluctant to reveal their sources. Silence prolonged the life span of the source. Silence was the mother of safety. Secrets lurked in every Jewish house, yet hardly leaked out. The secret of the one was the rumour of the second, the pursuit of the third, the trade of the fourth. Only hours before one's own departure would one pass the name of the connection to one's relatives or best friends.

Like summer sales, cheaper bargains turned up. One hundred *dinars* per person, provided you made it to the north on your own. The train was highly recommended, especially for solitary travellers. The luggage should be minimal, one suitcase per person. One hundred *dinars* with one suitcase, it has never been so cheap! But how can one strike such deals? Where is it possible to meet the Kurdish smuggler? Who is the Jewish intermediary? How safe were these enterprises? People gossiped no end, but once concrete information was requested, silence fell, closing down the legendary travel bureau.

The closest we have reached so far is Sabah's father, my father's former colleague. It was rumoured that he was organising such journeys for ninety *dinars* per person. Sabah's father was quite indignant when my father brought up the matter to his face. May his hand be cut off if he had ever taken money from other Jews, he roared. He did not deny, however, that he himself was "enrolled" in some long list, initiated by someone whose name he could by no means reveal. Softened by father's pleas for help, he eventually consented to have us join his family when their turn came, *inshallah*. In the meantime, we had better pack our suitcases, buy plenty of canned food, medicine, black robes for the women "just in case . . . ," plus other necessary items for the road—for we might be given very short notice.

—But it's common knowledge, Lina! Escape routes are being sold like hot rolls in the *casinos* along Abu Nuwas.' The meeting place changes constantly, Dudi tells me, stroking the long thick sideburns he has finally succeeded in growing.

—You've seen too many thrillers! Who would bring up such delicate subjects in coffee houses?

—It's less risky than hosting smugglers in your own house. I'm on my way to the riverbank to see what I can smell . . .

—Dudi, come to your senses! If it was so easy, we would have been on the other side of the border by now.

—It's just a stroll along Abu Nuwas. You either return with some clue or you return empty-handed. We've got nothing to lose. Want to join me, or do you have a better way to waste your afternoon?

Dudi waits in our garden, eager to set out, while I go inside to tell mother of our stroll without revealing our real intentions. Mother gives me some change for the bus fare.

—Remember, no word to Dudi about the *abayas* we bought this morning! Don't let him pull anything from under your tongue.

I close the front door, carrying two secrets whose burden bears no relation to the little substance they contain. We stride up to the Masbah bookshop, from where we take the bus to the riverbank. I fidget in my seat during the whole ride, unable to stop Dudi—by hint or gesture—from going over the names of runaway Jewish families. True, he is not explicitly saying they have escaped, but I know him too well to trust his discretion.

However, it is only when we get off the bus that Dudi reveals his plan.

—We'll check every *casino* between Firdos and Semiramis. Just pop in as though we're looking for our friends and see if there are any Jews sharing their table with Kurds. You can distinguish Kurds from Arabs, can't you? They're tall, stout people, often light-skinned and brown-haired. Survey the corners in particular 'cause they won't be sitting in the middle of the lawn where everybody could listen to their conversation, right? We should also keep our eyes open for smugglers sitting alone. How to recognise them? Well, I guess most smugglers are chain smokers and heavy drinkers. Now, if you have a hunch that something's going on, pinch my arm. That'll be our signal!

Outside the Firdos, the waiter is hosing down the pavement to cool the entrance to the *casino*. Neither the neon sign overhead nor the colourful bulbs on either side of the gate have been switched on yet. We climb down the steep stairs. One large family of more than twenty people has taken up half the lawn. The only table in the shade, beside the myrtle hedge, is occupied by three greying men. To the best of my knowledge, none of them is Jewish. Their wine glasses stand empty, their cigarette-tray is filled with stubs. They seem engaged in some serious talk. The man who is sitting with his back to us is having his shoes shined. The young shoeblack is wiping his hands on his trousers—baggy, unmistakably Kurdish.

—Well-built and light-skinned, all three. The hairy man in the middle has red-brown hair. With some luck, they could be Kurds! Yours or mine? Dudi whispers, sounding like some senior detective.

—I'll take care of them.

I pad leisurely in their direction, my head lowered to the

grass. My earring is lost, I tell myself to enhance my make-believe. Crouching, groping under the table next to them, I manage to catch fragments of their conversation. Landlords, foremen, construction permits, lands in *Medinet el-Dhubbat*, Officers' City. Satisfied, I get up, pretending to have found some tiny object. The man who is having his shoes shined is eyeing me from head to foot. I bet his hair smells of lotion, his feet of shoe polish. Some dandy. I wave Dudi to the stairs.

—Contractors. Let's go!

The sun is halfway down, heading west, towards the other bank of the river. In the Corniche, the coffee house beside the Firdos, they seem to be making preparations for some private party. The next one, the Tarboush, is exclusively for men. Dudi prefers to skip it rather than inspect it on his own. The Golden Nest is closed for repairs.

Disillusioned, we drift down the promenade, looking over the chain of deserted green lawns.

—We're too early perhaps. Customers start coming after sunset. It's still useful though to . . .

—Sshh . . . I interrupt him, cocking my head to the side, pointing out the voices behind us.

We proceed quietly, our ears picking up some unfamiliar, incomprehensible speech. Unlike our harsh guttural tongue, this one is melodic, rich with soft round syllables which I immediately link to fleshy lips. I turn to see five foreign men walking behind us, perspiring in shabby, old-fashioned suits. Their complexion is pallid, nearly green. None of them has fleshy lips. In spite of their blond hair, they lack that replete, secure look, that carefree gait, so characteristic of the foreigners from England or the USA.

—My name isn't Dudi if these aren't the microphone experts!

—You mean Russians? *Shiyu'eyyeen!* Communists! I exclaim, my heart beating fast, my feet ready to run.

—Yes, the very assholes who teach our government to plant ears in the walls!

Before I have realised what is happening, Dudi turns round, greets them, so to speak, in our language.

—Say, *awlad al-haram*, bastards, are you planting ears in the river today? Feeding bugs to the fish? Or how do you do it?

The Russians stop walking, gape in surprise, exchange puzzled remarks.

—Dudi, for your father's sake, shut up!

—We need your help, you see. We're looking for smugglers. Perhaps you've heard in which *casino* they're meeting?

—Dudi, have you gone out of your mind?

—Come on, comrades, don't tell me it's your day off. Give us a hint. Don't be such misers, he says, closing his fist to indicate stinginess.

Surprise shifts to impatience, confusion to irritation—or that is what I read in their faces. Perhaps they have sensed the derisive note in Dudi's voice. The tall bald man in the brown suit, markedly older than the rest, says something which sets the others in motion.

Dudi walks backward, persistent in his teasing. I move closer to the river side of the street, wanting no part in his dubious game.

—They say you fellows are chronically constipated, guess why? 'Cause once it's out, you've got to share it with the other comrades, ha ha ha . . .

The bald man in the brown suit seems to have lost patience.

He quickens his pace towards Dudi, on the point of grabbing him by the shoulders, or pushing past him. The man, whose double chin sags to his collarbone, holds back his friend with some short comment while indicating Dudi's belly. The language sounds neither soft nor melodic this time. The entire group bursts into laughter. The short plump man speaks to Dudi, pats his shoulder, shakes his hand. Is it their polite way of dismissal? But then he grins—exposing two gold front teeth—makes some gag, I suppose, because it is received with renewed joviality. Dudi does not seem in the least bothered being the object of their ridicule. He emulates their horse laugh long enough to prove his invincibility before he launches into his own joke.

—When Karl Marx died, he was naturally sent to hell. He found two arrows at the entrance: one pointing right and reading "capitalist," one pointing left and reading "communist." What's the difference? he asked. The ugly little devil guarding the gate replied: in the capitalist hell they've got fire, hot iron, pillories, racks, etc . . . In the communist hell, it's basically the same equipment. Only on some days, they're short of fire, on others they've run out of hot iron, or the racks are broken, or the torturers are on sick leave, ha ha ha . . .

The bald man in the brown suit must have caught the name Marx, because he has been scowling since the beginning of the narration. The grimace made by the man with the gold teeth tells me he, too, has taken offence. Nevertheless, the entire group claps, with exaggerated ceremony, when Dudi has finished his story. Then the man with the double chin starts the next joke. I catch the word "sultan" within his flow of speech. Flushed crimson, the Russians roar, holding their bellies or stomping the ground. I wonder if their mockery, like Dudi's, is bordering on insult. Passersby stare curiously. I yank on Dudi's sleeve, whisper we should leave, but to no effect. I remind him of the urgent matters we have to settle, but Dudi is too busy preparing himself for the next joke. I walk onwards determined to dissociate myself from the boisterous group. Let them laugh each other down until the incomprehensible foreign words begin to hurt. Dudi's loud voice follows me, yelling nonsense in the Muslim dialect. The idiot! Will he never grow up? He is yelling out my name. I quicken my pace. In no time, he catches up with me, still tittering, wiping his tears.

—What a spoilsport you are, Lina! Why did you leave so abruptly? I can't let you walk alone, I'm responsible for you!

—You? Responsible for me? You're talking *dhrat*, farts, nonsense! You could have gotten us both into trouble.

—But why? They didn't understand a single word! When it comes to Arabic, all foreigners are alike. They never learn it, even if they live here for twenty years.

—What of the other passersby? Were they Russians too?

Dudi lets out one of his silly giggles which spurn the very notion of reason.

—You can have fun with them till tomorrow morning, Dudi; who's stopping you? I'm going home.

Looking for the gap in the traffic through which I could cross to the other side, I notice the police van—closing in from the opposite direction. The driver is giving us dirty looks. Or so I imagine. The van draws up some yards from us. By coincidence, *inshallah*. No, the driver is gesturing to us to halt. Have the Russians informed on us or have we been tailed from the very start? We stand still, waiting for the two policemen to get out of the van, shoot us.

—Son of a whore! So you think you're so smart? the driver bellows, before he delivers Dudi two sonorous slaps to the face.

Dudi staggers, then falls on me. Some little object drops from his pocket. I struggle to prop him up, but the two have grabbed him by the shoulders—one on either side—and dragged him to the rear of the van. The driver opens the two doors, exposing several young men seated on the benches inside. They thrust Dudi inside. He yelps in pain, stumbling over the feet of the boy with long hair.

But he is hardly sixteen, I want to protest when Dudi, having regained his balance, spins round with terror in his face.

When did his eyebrows grow so thick? He definitely looks older than sixteen—due perhaps to the stubble on his chin or to his long sideburns. The policeman shoves me down onto the pavement, then slams the rear doors.

—Let any son of a bitch try to escape and he'll regret the day he was born! he threatens, waving his fist, even though he cannot be seen from inside.

The police van takes off, disappears in the traffic. To Qasr el-Nehaya, no doubt! The Palace of No Return, where prisoners drop like flies, where men meet their end. "What happened?" inquires the young woman with the baby carriage, who has witnessed the scene. I do my best to stifle my tears. "Is that yours?" she says, picking up the flat square packet which Dudi has dropped. Cigarettes! I haven't seen him smoke since the day he went to watch the hanged men in Tahrir Square. Shamefaced, I reach out for the packet, slip it into my handbag with extreme care, like the last vestige of Dudi.

I should warn his family, tell them everything, now.

The red double-decker is nearing from the other direction. I cross the street to the stop. The bus pulls up, lets the passengers off.

—Hurry up, girl, we're not in a funeral procession! shouts the conductor standing by the door.

My feet hang back. The double-decker moves off, blasting clouds of dust in my face. I set out for the long walk back.

I reach home by dusk. The note in the living room says my parents will be back in the evening. Shuli has gone to the dentist's. I scurry upstairs, fling my handbag on my desk. I still owe the news to Dudi's family, but I have no idea what to tell them. Everything happened so fast that I cannot figure out myself what has led to what, or why. Did the Russians, in fact, call the police, or were the two encounters independent of each other? Had the police just chanced

upon us, then seen what we were up to? But then, why were
the other boys in the van picked up?—none of them was
Jewish! Nothing makes sense. Like pieces taken from different puzzles, no part fits into the other. Maybe I had better cut out the purpose of our walk from my story;
otherwise I will have to explain myself to my own parents.
What of the cigarettes? It might be sensible to spare Dudi's
mother this detail too, for, most probably, Dudi has been
smoking in secret. One more secret. How fragile secrets
become once their owner is not close by to watch over
them! I reach for my handbag, draw out the packet.
Player's. Navy Cut. Finest Virginia. Nothing less than the
finest for Dudi. Rafidain or some other local brand would be
beneath his standards. I lift the lid, then drop into the chair.
My stomach is shaking in mute laughter. I fiddle with the
packet. I examine them for the second time. I feel them with
my fingers. Of the six cigarettes lined in the box, only one
is real. Each of the others is candy—slim, red-tipped, white
sugar rods!

I treat myself to one of the fakes, wondering whether
Dudi is secretly smoking, or secretly pretending to smoke.
The blond-bearded sailor illustrated on the packet is not
smoking. The tip of my candy is melting, spreading its
flavour inside my mouth. I draw in the entire cylinder. My
tongue turns it, shifts it from side to side until the rod
breaks in two. Streams of sweet saliva bathe my palate, only
to vanish rapidly like water in the sand. I crush the rest of
the candy between my teeth. The ephemeral pleasure leaves
me empty, with the urge for more. Insatiability, or is it only
the neutral word for greed? Dudi, some sugar sailor!
Whether smoking or only pretending to smoke, he is, in
either case, trying to grow up the easy way. I poke two cigarettes into my mouth, crunch them to pieces. My shoulders
relax. My legs stretch out on the desk. Nothing could move
or disturb me now, neither Russians nor policemen. Now I

understand why father is so mistrustful of sweet eaters. "Pleasure seekers indulging in sweet idleness, " he calls them, once comparing grown-ups licking ice cream in the street to "infants sucking at their pacifiers."

Dudi's sweet tooth, coupled with his irresponsible, if not childish, conduct can only support father's premise. I devour the three remaining cigarettes. If the frequent consumption of sugar was in fact connected to self-indulgence, what per-sonality traits would be linked to the consumption of, say, bitter food? The image of father's grimace when sipping black coffee comes to my mind. Self-discipline! In father's existence, where confectionery is scarcely permitted, disci-pline has the last word. It is the source of his will power, the secret of his self-possession, the main constituent of his industry, walling him in melancholy.

I pick up the last cigarette, the real one, the Virginia. Shreds of tobacco stick out from both of its ends, like hairs protruding from the nostrils of hirsute men. I smell it, press its soft belly, then slant it between my finger tips. Elegant! I loosen my grip. The cigarette rolls down between my fin-gers. I play with different positions, try out the variety of styles they suggest. Cool. Confident. Pensive. Mature. Dynamic. The cigarette slips from my hand. I retrieve it, tuck it between my lips. Tobacco shreds stick to the tip of my tongue, bite it the way hot curry does. If sweet eaters were self-indulgent, bitter eaters self-disciplined, what would hot, spicy eaters tend to be? Restless, quick tem-pered, like Selma, or provocative, sharp-tongued like Shuli? I strip off the Virginia paper, crumble the rolled tobacco in my palm, then toss the entire pile into my mouth. The sharp tang mounts instantly to my nose, stinging my nos-trils like black pepper. Once I start chewing the tobacco, its sharpness magnifies, while some threadlike sour taste creeps from the edge. The peppery flavour is travelling from mouth to nose so freely that I no longer distinguish gustatory from olfactory sensations. The wetter Virginia gets, the more it burns. The sour thread has swollen, grown unbearable. Sour eaters must have self-destructive tendencies, I conclude, dashing off to the bathroom to spit the glob of tobacco into the sink.

No matter how thoroughly I rinse my mouth, the sourness clings to my palate, under my tongue, in this or that canal. In my parents' bedroom, I rummage through mother's dressing table, looking for the bottle of rose water. Mother says it relieves nausea. Drenched in rose water, I lie on her bed, my eyes closing, the toes of each foot removing the sandal from the other.

Wrapped up in her black cloak, the old woman, the only passenger in the bus, reluctantly gets off. "Last stop," the driver had blustered, giving her no say in the matter. No living soul is in sight. Even the bus shelter is missing. In front of her stands the famous palace. When did they fortify the tall mud walls with barbed wire? The red bus drives off, leaving her by herself in the middle of the desert. Mud is the colour of my skin, she tells herself, what is there for me to dread? She goes over to the iron gate, gives the bell one light press. Her forefinger is caught in the socket. She is not electrocuted, to her own surprise, but when she tries to tug her finger out, it remains stuck, ringing the bell without end.

I start. Did I hear the doorbell or was it only my dream? Father once said we were capable of sensing danger in our sleep. I try to retrace the last scenes, but they swiftly dissipate. Was it the Palace of No Return I dreamed of? Some name! They do not even bother to disguise its purpose. The bell rings once more, this time for certain. I get up. On my way down the stairs, it occurs to me to check who it is before opening the door. There is that spot in the corner of the sitting room from which we can look through the window without being seen. Damn it! The curtains have been drawn so meticulously that no slit is left to peep through. Nor could they flutter without betraying my presence.

I lope upstairs to my room. Even though our gate is not visible from my window, the street is in full view, which might enable me to identify our visitor by his car. Or just make certain that no grey Volkswagen Beetle is parked outside. But mother has drawn the curtains in my room too. In this case then . . . too bad for our visitor, but there is nobody home! I flop on to my bed, curl up my legs, reach out for the *Mad* magazine on my night table. *Mad* entertains me for twenty seconds, until the next ear-splitting ring. Now I understand what father means when he describes headache like some drill splitting his head in two. The ring that follows forces me out of bed, drags me downstairs to the front door, where I stand in dismay, too scared to open it, too disturbed to ignore the whole matter.

Our visitor is pacing the roofed yard behind the sitting room. The footsteps sound flat but heavy, men's shoes no doubt. He must have pushed our gate open, walked through our courtyard to the front door. Some intrusion! Even friends wait politely by the gate until we come out to let them in. What makes this man take such liberties? Why is he so obstinate? The footsteps draw near, then pause. He must be standing one or two feet in front of me on the other side of the door. Unable to bear this blind proximity, I tiptoe to the neighbouring guest room, place myself behind the similarly drawn curtains. His steps follow mine, directly to the windows of the guest room. Cold sweat runs down my back. He cannot possibly see me through the curtains. Do I still smell of rose water or can he hear my breathing? I hold my breath, listen hard, but detect no voice, no sigh, no cough, no exchange of words. Only the nervous gait, the heavy footfalls heading back to the front door.

Security men usually come in pairs. But who says his partner has not stayed in the car to keep watch on the street?

If Dudi has talked, I should be in deep trouble. I would not be the first Jewish girl to be sent to prison, but definitely the youngest. Norma, two years older than I, was held for one week last winter in security headquarters. When she was released, people said she had been beaten on the soles of her feet. Most of the episode remained obscure, however, due to the silence her family preferred to maintain. Mouzli's case was different. Picked up from the university, she was detained for several months in the women's prison—together with her mother—on the pretext that the two had moved without reporting to the police.

Three short, successive rings. Each is enforcing the intruder's will over mine. If he persists, I might well end up opening the door. Panicked by the thought, I slink upstairs, bury in the linen bin the black robes we bought this morning—just to be on the safe side. Then I rapidly put on my sandals, rush downstairs to the kitchen, open the door which gives on to the backyard. One foot outside, I linger in the doorway, hesitating. The luxury of hesitation! I chalk up the moments of silence, hoping the security man is giving up on us.

The next unfaltering ring drowns out my illusions. I click the backdoor quietly behind me. Curry's bowl is empty, but he is nowhere to be seen. I scale the wall of our backyard, with surprisingly little difficulty. The broken bricks provide first handgrips, then footholds. In no time, I jump into the neighbours' garden, from where I sneak out, undetected, to the street—the one directly behind ours.

What now?

My mind is empty. My thoughts must have stayed in the house. Still, I feel safe in this less familiar street. Safe for the moment. Safe from the doorbell. I slump down on the pavement, hide my face in my hands. If only the world ceased to exist, or even better, had never existed. If only God had immersed Himself in deep meditation instead of involving Himself in Creation. The honking of vehicles scorching through the main street of Hindiyah reasserts the voice of Creation. Other sounds invade my ears. The local news from several television sets in the neighbourhood. The fleeting radio music of cars. Young men pass by, offer their help to lift my spirits, then snicker like silly geese. Some woman, trudging behind them, comments on how girls from good families behave shamelessly in the streets nowadays. If there were litter bins for noise, I bet Baghdad would end up with the largest convoy of noise rubbish trucks in the world.

I do not know how long I have been in this position, when the familiar meowing reaches me. I raise my head. Curry! I cry out. My cat meows back from the front wall of the opposite house, surprised, in his turn, to find me in the wrong street. Curry, I repeat, urging him to my side. He springs down from the wall, unhurriedly crosses the street, tail upright, looking neither to the right nor to the left, with enough confidence for the two of us. Promptly he jumps into my lap, pokes his head into my belly, licks my hand, cooing with delight, bearing no grudge whatsoever for the pranks I played on him earlier today.

Since when have the streetlamps been glowing?

I dump Curry, stand up, determined to go back home no matter what is lying in store for me. Curry scurries to my side, making the detour for my sake, I suppose, by taking the pedestrian route instead of climbing walls, crossing private gardens. If only he stopped bounding between my legs, causing me to trip each time. In the main street, the grocer-informer is halving water melons with his knife, not in the least interested in my moves. I continue to our street, relieved to find no Beetle in front of our house. The courtyard is empty, but the gate has been left open, confirming the reality of the visit.

Curry leaps up to his regular place on our gatepost. In the

middle of the courtyard, it occurs to me that I have left my key inside. I ring the bell, several times, to no effect. Our house is suffused in darkness. There is nobody home!

Despondently I proceed to Dudi's place.

Dudi's mother's face lights up the moment she opens the front door. I curse myself for the news I have to break. She scuttles to the gate.

—Lina, at last! Nobody's answering your doorbell. Dudi's so worried, the poor boy's eating his heart out! He said you were completely shattered when they arrested him. We were just about to drive to Abu-Nuwas to look for you. Goodness, are you all right, you look bewildered . . . a bit tousled, what happened to you?

—Oh, nothing, I'm fine, just fine. But . . . how did you know? Isn't Dudi . . . ? Where is Dudi, for God's sake!

She draws me gently inside. Dudi, biting into grilled chicken, peers out of the kitchen. He waddles towards me in his undershirt, smiling broadly, in spite of the weal over his right eye, in spite of the razor cuts in front of his ears.

—Dudi, you should change your undershirt! It's torn and filthy, his mother says with embarrassment.

Something else has changed in his face. His sideburns have been shaved, up to one inch over his ears, exposing one finger's length of dry white skin.

—Dudi, what did they do to you?

—They kept collecting boys and young men from the street until the van was full. Then they dropped us at the police station and went off on a new hunt.

Within seconds, young policemen shaved off their sideburns then kicked them out of the station.

—They warned us not to resemble the Zionists. They said next time we grew sideburns they'd cut our ears off!

Zionists! Why Zionists?

Dudi bursts into hysterical laughter. His mother does the same, concealing her mouth with her hand.

—Seriously, Dudi, who did they mean this time? Marlon Brando? Tony Curtis? Jack Lemmon? Yul Brunner?

I try to recall more Jewish stars whose films have been banned since the Six Day War.

—Oh, no, they were referring to the ultra-Orthodox Jews! Dudi's mother finally replies. Those odd Jews from Eastern Europe who dress in black caftans and wear beards and funny side curls. They showed them on TV this week In "Know Your Enemy." Don't you watch the series?

—Baba, I saw Russians today! They were strolling by the river. They didn't resemble the English though, they looked sort of . . .

Holding his cup one inch from his mouth, father is neither sipping nor listening.

—What's the matter, Baba? Does your head hurt?

—Why are you keeping it back from her? She'll hear it anyway, if not today, then tomorrow, Shuli criticises, yet offers no information himself.

—What's the matter? Why's nobody telling me?

—*Ustad* Heskel has given you his life, mother says, in indignation.

—What!

Mother clears the coffee table, signalling that she has done her share, that she is not ready to tend to further inquiries. Father replaces his cup on the saucer.

—Yesterday night, *ustad* Heskel's name was mentioned on the radio station of Ahwaz, in one of these . . . reckless lists.

Though the station broadcasts from Iran, people believe it is being run by Iraqis who oppose the Ba'ath regime. Recently, it has been harping on some impending purge of the military, which, it claimed, the Iraqi government was planning. In this connection, long lists would be sent out every night, mainly names of officers, who were warned that they would soon be detained on charges of treason. Whether by coincidence or not, some of the men were, in fact, picked up the next day. Since then, whoever was mentioned in these ominous lists would rush, panic-stricken, to the passport office, to travel bureaux, to foreign embassies, to influential friends—to do the impossible: leave on the next plane.

For *ustad* Heskel, leaving on the next plane was literally impossible.

—His housekeeper found him this morning, father goes on. He was hanging from the ceiling fan in his bedroom. In the note he left, he bequeathed his holy books to his synagogue and begged God for His understanding and forgiveness. Poor Heskel, he's the last to deserve such an end. He was a real gentleman.

—He was much more than a gentleman! mother protests. He was a *zaddiq*, just a man.

Father unfolds the evening paper, spreads it round him like curtains. Bereft of words, he will spend the whole evening behind the world news without turning the sheets even once. Too tired to grieve or even to feel, I climb up to the roof, lie in bed—resolved to forget.

But my mind is far from empty. Ugly, cruel thoughts keep swirling round my head, hemming me inside their circle of evil. They disdain our worries, ridicule our hopes, call us nothing more than pawns in some game, manoeuvred by people much more powerful than we. I play with the idea, develop it into some boardgame of sorts—with colourful pieces, with dice, with various kinds of cards—not that different from Monopoly. Only my game takes place in prison since initially my players have been sentenced to death. Each player is handed fifteen day-cards to begin with, signifying the fifteen days until his execution. Survival is the ultimate goal of each player, that is, to win time. The dice should be cast by turns, the pieces moved correspondingly on the squares of the board, each redefining your current situation. On one square for instance, your lawyer has pleaded for stay of execution: you may collect five day-cards from the bank. On the next, your letter has been censored, you called the party nasty names, you pay two day-cards' penalty to the bank. On some other square, due to your good conduct, your mother has been granted one last visit, during which she tucks ten *dinars* in your pocket. Money, like tools, like information, falls into the category of reward cards. Not only is escape impossible without them, but they can be traded, too, for time cards, for instance. The game goes on. Due to your recurrent fits of violence, you have been placed in solitary confinement, that is, you miss two turns. It is the president's birthday, each player is to draw one chance card. Your chance card says your cell has been searched, you must replace your entire stack of reward cards in the pack. Sooner or later, you will either run out of time cards or stumble upon the square which shows the noose. Unless you bribe the chief warden with three reward cards, you will be executed on the spot. There is no way one can be pardoned or vindicated in this game. The most honourable way of winning is escape, but it requires the combination of certain reward cards plus seven day-cards. In that case, the game ends; the rest of the players go to the gallows. Otherwise, the winner is the player who manages to survive longest.

Some entertainment on sleepless nights! I turn over, open my eyes. Shuli's bed is still intact. He is not stargazing, either. It is two in the morning. I leap out of bed, go downstairs. The broadcaster's voice coming from his room tells me he is listening to the news.

Paris, 22 degrees. London, 18. Rome, 25. Madrid, 27. Brussels, 22. Zurich, 21. Copenhagen, 12. Frankfurt, 16. New York, 26. Vienna, 19. Istanbul, 32. Lisbon, 29. Luxemburg, 22. Paris, 22 degrees. London, 18. Rome, 25. Madrid, 27. Brussels, 22. Zurich, 21. Copenhagen, 12. Frankfurt, 16. New York, 26.

Vienna, 19. Istanbul, 32. Lisbon, 29. Luxemburg, 22. Paris, 22 degrees. London, 18. Rome, 25. Madrid, 27. Brussels, 22. Zurich, 21. Copenhagen, 12. Frankfurt, 16. New York, 26. Vienna, 19. Istanbul, 32. Lisbon, 29. Luxemburg, 22.

Is it my imagination or is the weather forecast repeating itself?

Quietly I open the door. His hands clasped behind his head, Shuli is rocking himself on the back legs of his desk chair, listening to his tape recorder, riding the meteorological waves in their trip round the world.

VACANT DESKS

—The kids will be running in as soon as the bell rings, Dora's mother explains. Thirty, forty at most. All you have to do is hand each of them two sandwiches and a lollipop in a plastic bag, together with a bottle of fizzy drink. Nothing can go wrong. You're welcome to a snack yourselves, there's plenty available. Please wash the knives thoroughly after use, and bring them back, together with the crockery, to *sit* Habiba's office.

I eye *sit* Habiba, our school secretary, in panic. Our task is ever expanding. To start with, she said we were to help the volunteers prepare sandwiches for the children. Then it turned out we were to replace them. Now, it is not only the preparation, it is the distribution, too.

—I'll send a third student to help you as soon as I find one, says *sit* Habiba, ignoring my look of entreaty. If you need anything, let me know, I'm in my office. Any questions, girls? Can I rely on you?

We simper, defeated.

—They're no longer children, let them learn to give for a change, *sit* Habiba mutters on her way out, loud enough for us to hear.

The moment the two women have left the school hall, Selma kicks the crate of fizzy drinks.

—Once in a lifetime a teacher's ill and we've got a free hour, and that's precisely when that woman's into education. Just another word for shelling hard-boiled eggs. *Abel a'aliyah*, may mourning fall upon her! She just can't bear the sight of young people enjoying themselves...

—Come on, Selma. The sooner we get down to this chore, the sooner we're through with it.

Still groaning, she gathers her shoulder-length locks into one red ponytail, rolls up her sleeves. We unpack the cartons, spread out their contents on the two tables. I shell the eggs, peel the cucumber, pit the green olives. Selma slices the tomatoes, the chunk of white cheese. The knife shifts from one hand to the other, her left gifted with precision, her right with strength. I keep nibbling the food I handle.

—Try the cheese, Selma, it's delicious!

—I can't. I'm fasting!

—Fasting! Why? Is it some holy day?

—No, no, it's a campaign to draw world attention to the plight of the Russian Jews. Some "Let My People Go" stuff Mama picked it up from *Kol Israel* yesterday, and I decided to join the fast on the spur of the moment. But frankly, now that we're talking about it, it sounds ridiculous. The Russian Jews are far better off than we are. Don't you think?

—I think it's the tang of mango pickle!

—Lina, I'm dead serious. They want to emigrate?—well and good, so do I. But they aren't disappearing from the street or being hanged in the squares of Moscow. Imagine us making claims for human rights and staying alive!

I uncap one Sinalco, take my first sip.

—You mean it would make more sense if the Russian Jews fasted for us?

Selma stifles her guilty smile. I pass her the Sinalco. She swigs the sparkling drink the way sportsmen passionately consume refreshments in commercials. Then, like someone who has not eaten for days, she snatches one roll, fills it with two fish *koftas*, spreads thick pickle inside. I repeat the procedure, in slower motion.

—The seasoning's great, it would have been a sin to miss it, she mumbles, her mouth full, hardly capable of clear utterance.

She sips more Sinalco to help the food down, then goes on in the same lighthearted tone,

—Say, Lina, did you know there were children in our school who can't afford their lunch?

The *kofta* sticks in my throat. Ironically, the piles of food have made me forget the very reason for its presence. I have indeed heard of plenty of Jewish families who were having financial problems due to their unemployment. I even saw the women volunteers, once or twice, heading to the school hall, carrying what looked like food cartons. Yet I never pursued that thought or those scenes in my mind to reach the obvious conclusion.

—Not really. Come to think of it, I wish someone else would take over the distribution. I feel quite uneasy having to face these children.

Selma casts the end of the roll into her mouth.

—Don't be silly. They aren't gonna eat us!

She waits in vain for my laughter, unaware of the tactlessness of her remark. My fault. Selma's insensitivity knows no limits; why raise the subject with her in the first place? Strange how the list of things I dislike in her has grown over the last months. Her vitality for example, which used to inspire me to stretch my own limits, now exasperates me with its insatiable need for recognition.

—*Yallah*, let's get back to work, she says, picking up the knife. Otherwise we won't be ready when the little monsters show up.

She slits the rolls open, casts them over for me to fill. I divide the sandwiches into three heaps: egg, cheese, *kofta*. Whenever too many empty rolls have piled up, Selma stops cutting to help me catch up. While we work in quiet coordination, my thoughts revert to the children. Once spoken of, my reluctance to deal with them has faded, while some old, underlying fear is surfacing: fear of the day we will run out of money. I imagine father, gathering the family to say that we have nothing left to sell, to elaborate on our deplorable state of debt. We listen in concern, expecting the practical solution to follow. Yet father shocks us with the conclusion that—no longer capable of providing for us—there is only one thing for him to do, resign from his paternal duties.

The door of the hall creaks open. Dudi's head pops round, intruding on our family conference. Cheerfully, he trundles towards us,

—So what I've heard is true! It's your day of *muswah*, good deeds.

—How come you're running around? says Selma dryly.

—I've asked permission to go to the 100, but I don't feel like going back to the classroom. English literature! Not my cup of tea, as the English say.

—And how will you account for it?

Dudi chuckles.

—There're plenty of vacant desks in our classroom this year. We keep telling *ustad* Ghazi stories about the flu circulating at school. He's not that gullible, of course, but still he gets confused as to who's off for good, who's ill, who's in the toilet, and who's playing truant. I don't think he cares any more. He doesn't even bother to call the roll.

If ill luck had not struck, I would not have stood here right now either. Last month, Sabah's father finally notified us that he would soon escape with his family, that we could join them if we were still determined. It sounded so definite that mother fetched the four suitcases from the storeroom, dusted them, put them in the sun, while each of us sorted out the necessary items to pack. The next morning, father woke with high temperature. It dampened our spirits to say the least. We tended to his needs with utmost devotion, hoping he would recover in time. Yet, in spite of the quantities of medicine plus the cold compresses, father's temperature would not drop. Flight within the week was out of question.

—How many students have already made it in your class? inquires Selma.

—Five! Nader and Ezra left in the summer. Rita got out shortly after term began, and Linda three days after her. Farid fled two weeks ago as you know. What a betrayal! We used to cry on each other's shoulder each time another desk stood empty, fearing we'd be the last to remain.

—Don't worry, Dudi, you won't be the last to leave, says Selma. Baba's not budging from here in spite of the scenes I make every other day. He tells me I'll be free to go when I've finished school and come of age. Period!

—You may not have to worry either. Last week's blow seems to have destroyed all escape routes until further notice.

Last week, some eighty Jews were captured in the resort town of Rawandouz in the north, on the eve of their crossing. Unfortunately, many of them were incautious enough to take their children's school diplomas or other certificates with them. Some women were wearing lots of jewellery. How could they explain to the police that they were "only on holiday" with this load of evidence? Nobody seems to know their whereabouts. Nobody has dared to take off since.

—By the way, girls, the smell of your sandwiches is irresistible. May I help myself to one or two? I'm dying of hunger.

Selma's forehead furrows. Dudi hastens to correct himself,

—I didn't mean for free. I'd pay, naturally.

—Tsk, Selma utters.

—In fact, I'm ready to pay double the price at the kiosk.

—Tsk.

—But why not? You'll have leftovers, and they'll end up in the rubbish as always. Mama's among the volunteers, and she doesn't stop complaining about the waste.

—No!

—Give the money to *sit* Habiba. Let her buy chocolate or chewing gum for the kids.

When Selma does not reply, Dudi treats himself to two pitted olives, testing out her compliance. Her knife darts threateningly over his fingers. Dudi tosses the olives into his mouth, munches them loudly, taunting her with his minor triumph.

—It doesn't even occur to you to offer help, you selfish spoiled brat! You think you can buy the world with your money? Well, you're wrong this time. We're not selling. Go and push your way through to the kiosk like everybody else, or go without lunch for all I care. It won't do you any harm, you're growing as round as a barrel.

If Selma's words have hurt him, Dudi manages to conceal it. Feigning innocence, he turns to me.

—What's the matter with her? Why's she eating and drinking me?

Selma is, in fact, unpredictable when it comes to Dudi. Sometimes, she will joke with him for hours, other times she will snub him or pick on him for no obvious reason.

—What if he earned his sandwich instead of paying for it? I suggest. What if he . . . told us stories for instance?

—You're kidding! Dudi snorts. I'm offering double the price and you treat me like a beggar! Why don't you ask me to stand on my head or dance like a circus monkey?

Selma's face lights up.

—That's a good idea! Tell us a story, Dudi.

—Come on, Dudi, it's second nature to you. Didn't you say you were dying of hunger?

Dudi clucks.

—May God never bring anybody to the state of needing

you! All right, I'll tell you a story. Your minds will fly when you hear it, but it's absolutely true.

—Anything will do, provided it's entertaining.

—It happened yesterday. The *amn*, security police, raided the market seeking Jews and other ill-fated merchants to torment. Does the name Naji Shumeil ring a bell?

—Who can forget it!

—Well, it seems there's another Jew with the same name, Naji Shumeil. The Naji who was publicly executed last year was from Basra, this Naji's from Baghdad. The Basrawi's dead, the Baghdadi's alive. No way to confuse the two Najis, right? Wrong! Yesterday, poor Naji was picked up from his store . . .

—Which one? The one still alive?

—What? Yes, of course the one who's still alive, don't spoil my story! Where was I? Oh yes, Naji Shumeil was picked up yesterday from his store and underwent a full day's interrogation at the *amn* headquarters. Guess what they kept asking him? "Didn't we hang you a long time ago? How come you're alive and still at work? You're supposed to be in the grave, *fi khabar kan*, you're in the past tense!"

The two of us laugh while Dudi dissembles earnestness,

—Girls, it's improper to make fun of a Jew's misfortune! Didn't they teach you that at home?

—I don't believe a word you say, Selma replies, wiping her tears.

—Suit yourself, but I've earned my two sandwiches.

—Two? Who said two? Selma recovers her hostile tone. We agreed on one story for one sandwich.

—Oh no, we didn't! You asked me to tell a story. You didn't explicitly say one story for one sandwich.

—Well, I'm doing it now: a story for a sandwich. Take it or leave it!

Dudi takes his time to examine the heap of rolls, fiddling with them, pressing them, opening those still unwrapped to peer inside—trying Selma's patience.

The strident ringing catches us off guard.

—Goodness, they'll be here any moment! Selma starts up. We haven't wrapped half the sandwiches yet.

No sooner has she finished her sentence than the swing door is shoved open with such force that it knocks the wall next to it several times. Three lads, seven or eight years old, storm inside, racing in our direction, shrieking with excitement, their echo filling the hall. The three of us huddle together, clutching sandwiches, like hand grenades. Some yards from us, the lads slide gracefully on the shining tiles. It is the one running fastest who notices the change. His eyes linger on us trying to place us, then shift to the table. The drinks, the wrapped rolls reassure him. The scrape of their shoes on the floor tones down. Seconds from each other, they halt smoothly, just inches from our stand.

—Wow, you're as fast as rockets! Selma exclaims. Are you the three musketeers?

They exchange puzzled glances. Dumas' heroes seem outdated.

—No, you're the three muskess...muskesteers! replies the fastest cheekily, pointing to us with his forefinger.

His friends press their hands on their mouths to stifle their fit of laughter, too similar to our own misbehaviour in the classroom. Do they consider us grown-ups, like the volunteers, to play like monkeys with us? When Selma requests orderliness, they pull themselves together, feigning shame. Having received their lunch, they sprint out, screaming, kicking each other, releasing who knows what urges they have suppressed for the last two hours in the classroom.

In no time, more children turn up, running in, running out. If I did not remember my own restiveness in those years, I would have thought children learn running prior to walking. They calm down, however, in front of our table, none of the usual jostling—not when they lack the coins to clink their demands. None of the gratefulness I had feared either.

They seem to take us for granted, counting on that vague rule of nature which commits the older ones to care for the younger.

Quickly I wrap the rest of the sandwiches while Dudi uncaps the fizzy drinks, lines them up on the table.

—Look how they're exchanging lollipops, Selma nudges me. They compare everything, just as we used to do at their age.

We did?

One slim child, his jacket too large, unwraps his sandwich in front of our table. His lower lip droops in disappointment. He peeps inside, holding it loosely, thinking of some way to drop it casually.

—If you don't eat eggs, I'll give you something else. What do you prefer, cheese or fish *kofta*?

He freezes, will not reply. When I offer him the two options, he picks the cheese sandwich without hesitation, hands me the egg in return. Then he smiles, half contented, half shamefaced, in no time saunters out of sight.

—Who said beggars can't be choosers! Dudi chuckles.

—Cute lad, I say.

—You mean boy? So the "Bs" are out of your vocabulary by now? Or did I hear you say bread or butter or bottles today?

Dudi's remark catches me off guard. Except for my family, who find the whole matter no more than some passing teenage phase, other people seem not to notice the change in my speech. Even Selma pretends not to hear it.

—Lina, why this self-censorship?

—Call it my private protest.

—I got that all right. But what if it rebounds on you, and ends up as a handicap?

—Well, it's draining, I can't deny it. On the other hand, censorship makes you more sensitive to the power of words. Sometimes it's even fun. You learn to say the same thing in more than one way. You realise that no word is irreplaceable, once you're willing to play with meanings or intentions. Can you see my point?

He sinks his teeth into the sandwich.

—So what do you call your father nowadays, if Baba's forbidden?

—Just father.

—And Curry will be . . . Spicy—I bet he wouldn't mind it either. And what about me? Have you figured a new name for me when "Ds" are out?

Sit Habiba suddenly turns up. Silence has descended upon the hall. Since when? The distribution must have ended with the same promptness with which it started. *Sit* Habiba engulfs us with sweet words we thought would never cross her lips. Elation seizes us. Selma hugs Dudi, in recognition of his unexpected contribution. Whoever saves one soul saves the entire world, *sit* Habiba continues, quoting the Talmud. Feeling like heroines who have just fed forty worlds, we succumb to her request to clear up the table. Dudi takes leave, gleaming with philanthropy, devouring his third, if not fourth, sandwich.

KAKA J.

Selma waves goodbye. I ring, push our gate open. Mother lets me in. The smell of roast meat is wafting from the kitchen. Quite unusual for this hour, for mother normally prepares our food in the morning. I remove my overcoat, throw it on the sofa. Then I sense some vague unfamiliarity lurking in the place. There is more wall, more emptiness in the living room than usual. Our television is missing! The gramophone, too. We must have run short of money once more. Mother has not greeted me yet. She is reading on my face the full report of my last two hours in town. Hoping to take her mind off me, I spill out the latest news.

—Mama, the Shamashes made it this week! Sami Nathan too. You know who that is, our new physics teacher.

—Good for them! she replies, sincere, yet unconcerned, lacking the inquisitiveness such news usually elicits.

Her look still fixed on me, she goes on,

—I've got news myself: Curry is due for his chicken!

My heart leaps the way it is supposed to when one's life-long wish is on the point of fulfilment.

—What! Heavens, when? Why haven't you told me earlier?

—Tonight! We were notified this very morning, shortly after you'd left for school!

Mother looks far from happy. The furrows on her fore-head read like the list of perils our undertaking entails.

—We'll be picked up shortly after midnight, she goes on. I'm preparing food for the journey. It's below zero in the north. Be sure to dress as warmly as possible. Are you hungry or did you stuff yourself with *semit* again?

—No, just peanuts . . .

—There's some pressed orange juice in the fridge. You should take a bath, who knows when we'll have hot water again. Wouldn't you like to give Curry the chicken yourself? Your father's packing upstairs. Go and see if he needs a hand. I'd try and get some sleep if I were you—we have a long night ahead.

I race up the stairs hardly feeling the ground under my feet. It is four p.m. Eight hours to go till midnight! How will I kill time without going mad? In his room, father is squatting, stowing winter wear into two suitcases. Towels, socks, slippers, soap, shaving equipment, various jars of pills surround him higgledy-piggledy on the ground. Plus enough toilet rolls to fill up two extra suitcases.

—Lina, at last! Go and pack your things, daughter. Pack what you need for the coming days. And remember, only essentials, there's hardly any space left.

Fortunately, he looks neither pale nor feverish this time. No pockets under his eyes, either. Quite the opposite. Without losing his natural serenity, father seems more vigorous than ever. I rush to my room; it takes no time select the warm wear necessary for the journey. While locking my wardrobe, it occurs to me that within one or two weeks, the police will unlock it for inspection. Later, they will put our possessions on public sale, the way they sold off the movable goods of other runaway Jews. I reopen the wardrobe, stand in the shoes of the police officer going over my personal effects—estimating their market value. My sandals. My garments. Knick-knacks. Stamps. *Mad* magazines. Games. No longer mine, they look unrelated to each other too, prepared to go their separate ways. Teddy-Pasha perches on the upper shelf, his eyes hanging loose.

I reach out for him, rest his head on my neck. His insides of straw have softened with the years. His scuffed sailcloth skin smells of faraway tears mingled with snot or saliva. His rich ochre hue has lost lustre. Old straw protrudes from the torn seam in his shoulder, from the lower part of his rear— making him look like someone permanently shitting. I kiss his muzzle farewell, stroke his remaining leg, reminiscent of that other leg, lost near the Monument of the Unknown Soldier, then replace him on the upper shelf

His scraggy neck gives way, his head inclines in resignation. He will undoubtedly end up in the rubbish. Pasha's glass gaze turns human, so similar to father's in the morning, when he faces up to his quotidian uselessness. I snatch Pasha from the shelf, shut the wardrobe for the last time.

—What of our photographs? I inquire, entering my parents' room, reluctant to let go of our past so easily.

—Already taken care of, father groans, trying to fasten the retaining strap of the suitcase. All our documents and family pictures will be sent to us, later.

—How? Who has them?

—They're in good hands. That's all you need to know for the time being, he replies, removing two woollen sweaters from the suitcase.

I think of pleading that my sixteen years should entitle me to more knowledge of—if not say—in family resolutions, when Shuli turns up with his own pile. He greets me with his malevolent smile, yanking Pasha's ear.

—Welcome back, old boy! So you're joining us? I don't blame you. Who'd like to be here when the police break in. Lina, are you sure he can make it with one leg?

—Very funny!

Father looks up, scowls so gravely that his two eyebrows meet,

—What have you got there! Didn't I say essentials? We can only take these two suitcases. Two and no more, for the four of us! And I still have to squeeze all this stuff inside.

—Lina, if a house is squeezed into a suitcase, the suitcase won't necessarily turn into a doll's house!

—Shut up, Shuli, nobody's talking to you! Father, Pasha's so pliable, we can tuck him into some gap, just like socks. Please, I'm ready to give up my slippers for his sake.

Father lifts his forehead, signalling rejection.

—We can hide jewels inside his trunk!

—Don't be a nuisance, Lina! We've got no jewels to hide, and when I say "no" it's "no"!

I throw my things on the floor, flounce out, Pasha's hand in mine. Shuli follows me. I take refuge in my room, fling myself on my eiderdown, unhappy with my foolish scene yet unable to restrain myself.

—Really, Lina, your brain's in your ass!

—Get out of my room! Nobody invited you in here.

—So you think you're the only person with feelings in this house?

—Spare me your lecture, wise guy.

—Baba's been eating his soul the whole day because he's leaving his father's grave behind. He blurted it out at lunch, he who never wastes a word on feelings. And instead of being considerate, there you are making a fuss over a stuffed animal, a handful of stinking straw...

—So what? Is there more to grandfather's grave than stone? I retort, my words sounding far more sarcastic than I intended.

No reply. No tit for tat. Shuli fails to retaliate. For the first time in our sibling rivalry, it is I who have had the last word. Serves him right, it is time he stopped patronising me. His speechlessness lasts too long. He is extending it into intentional silence. Silence is the standard strategy of extorting remorse in our family. I keep quiet, intent on prevailing over him in silence no less than in words.

—What's the holy difference between straw and stone . . . some nerve you have, he finally murmurs, stalks out of the room.

Heavens, why is everyone so fretful today? Why is nobody rejoicing? We waited years for this event to happen, yet now that no obstacle is in our way, each is setting up his own. Mother is loaded with uncertainties, Shuli is looking for trouble, while father, who has hardly mentioned his father for the last sixteen years, is suddenly hanging on to his grave. I should sleep, save my strength for the trip. When I wake up, I will smuggle Teddy-Pasha into one of the suitcases. Nobody will even notice. I slip under the eiderdown without removing my shoes. Let the sheets get soiled, it is the last time I will lie here. The thought flashes through my mind, yet the meaning escapes my understanding. My imagination, too, fails. Whatever will happen from midight onward will resemble nothing I have experienced so far. I pull the eiderdown over my head, the way I used to put the towel over Sultan to impose nighttime on him, to trick him into quietness. Night it is under the eiderdown, yet far from quiet. Some insect or fly is pacing my leg. I shake the eiderdown, tap the mattress. No fly. No insect. Nobody. I shut my eyes. There is noise in my ear, some trapped wasp? I fumble for the wasp with my little finger. Wrong. The sound is from within. My heart perhaps. I lie on my spine, try to relax. Is father summoning Shuli to his room? I push the eiderdown off my head, prick up my ears. "Take this, son, I don't want to have it all on me. You never know," father is saying. It is money he is passing on to Shuli, I suppose. My foot is sweating. These irksome shoes. How silly of me to make such mischief when the family is on the point of risking everything. Father remembered his father today. Shuli, in his turn, sided with father today, instead of proving him wrong. I keep rolling from side to side, finding no peace. Eventually, I kick off the eiderdown, get up to look for mother—the only person in the family with whom I have not yet quarrelled.

She is packing food in the kitchen.

—Mama, what of our pictures?

—What pictures?

—Our family pictures.

—Oh! Don't worry, they're at Zeki's. He'll send them over as soon as we are settled.

Zeki, naturally, how obvious. I hug mother, grateful for her trust. Her neck smells of Pond's, her hair of the variety of odours lingering in the kitchen. Hunger suddenly grips me. I let go of mother, remove the lid of the saucepan, pinch two morsels of mutton tongue.

—Mmmm, it melts in the mouth. Long live your hands, Mama! I say, uncovering the next pan.

—Why don't you sit down and have a proper meal like a human being instead of just nibbling?

She is filling two totebags with tea, sugar, marmalade, fruit, tins of food. The provisions should last till the journey's end—Teheran. In my imagination Teheran is some modern metropolis with exquisite Persian rugs spread on the pavements. What follows Teheran? Mother shrugs her shoulders. It is fun to go on one-way journeys, live with the unexpected, I remark. Mother fails to share my enthusiasm. In fact, she is growing impatient with my fluttering round her, thrusting my nose into every pot. I praise her rice pilau yet she remains indifferent to my flattery. I offer her half my peeled tangerine. She rejects it. I mention my long ride with Selma. Mother is not particularly impressed. I keep quiet, waiting for her to initiate the next topic. Her silence soon unnerves me.

—What's wrong, Mama?

—Nothing . . . why?

—You fear something might go wrong tonight?

—Not at all, by my life! It's not that!

—What is it then? Tell me, please!

Stacking flowered napkins next to the totebag, she stammers,

—Well . . . it was . . . painful, to part from them this morning.

—Part! Who from?

—From Zeki and Dunia of course, what's the matter with you!

—How should I know they were here this morning! How should I know you're saying goodbye to the whole world while stupid me keeps her mouth shut, following your instructions to the letter.

—Don't be silly, Lina. Zeki and Dunia are our best friends. We wanted them to have whatever they may need of our belongings before they get auctioned off by the government. Besides, with them, it's . . . different. We might never get to see each other again. Don't you understand?

Sometimes I think I understand too much. Other times I suspect I understand less than our tomcat. I scan my mother from head to foot, intent on tracing those feelings I swear she is harbouring. If only half of what magazine romances recount is true, then love, no matter how furtive, should show on her.

She is wiping knives, forks, spoons, selecting five of each.

—So you wept, or something of the sort? I test her, waitingfor her to swallow, for her eyebrows to tense, for the uncoordinated fingers, the unsteady knees . . .

One rare ironical smile slips out.

—Well, Dunia's eyes did water a bit, but I bet that's due to her . . . state. Anyway, refined as she is, you can be sure she didn't overdo it.

—True, she's ladylike, I say, peeling my second tangerine, waiting for the right moment to shift the focus to Zeki.

—She's pregnant, for your information!

Mother neither ranted nor yelled the information, only her voice quivered. Indisputably. She shot those shafts of rage, too, with which she intimidates every vendor she suspects of rigging the weights.

—Good for them! Let's hope it's the son they're longing for, I say, stabbing her in the heart.

Mother turns to hide her face. She is washing up the plates heaped in the sink.

—What for, Mama! Why leave it tidy?

She resumes quietly until she has rinsed the last plate. Then she opens the fridge, takes out our tomcat's promised meal from the freezer.

—What kills me is that we'll never get to know the baby . . . she finally spits out, then, stumbling over her lie, scurries out of the kitchen.

I follow her upstairs, intent on finding out the truth. It is now or never. Tomorrow, it will no longer matter to me. Tomorrow, mother's passion, or friendship, or love, or jealousy will recede into the past, like grandfather, who will recede further still into the past perfect. Mother has locked herself in the toilet. I listen hard, expecting sobs or sniffles, yet the only sound I make out is that of water gushing from the tap. I peep through the keyhole. She is on the toilet seat— tiny, pallid, like some miniature porcelain figurine, reaching for the sanitary towel package from the shelf.

I stomp to my room, grab Teddy-Pasha, hurl him into the waste paper. To hell with straw, with stone, with our entire past. I eat up the last segments of the tangerine, spitting the pips over Pasha without removing from the floor those that miss.

They ring twice, shortly past midnight. Father leads the three visitors into the guest room. Shuli rushes in with the paraffin stove. Father remains standing, not even trying to hide his perplexity. Nothing is wrong, the elderly woman reassures him. She has just given the smuggler last minute instructions to start the journey from our place. For the sake of precaution—father surely understands—for the Kurd's vehicle stood in front of their house twice this week.

Father understands.

—She could have notified us, mother grumbles, pouring tea in the kitchen. My fridge is empty. I've no cake, not even biscuits to offer.

She hands me the tea tray, reminds me who to serve first. First the old lady, then the old man, then Wedad, the younger woman. She follows me, with plates filled with pistachios, peanuts, pumpkin seeds, hazel nuts. They protest vehemently. She is embarrassing them. They had no intention of troubling her. She objects with equal vehemence. It is our pleasure, our honour too, to receive them in our house. She only hopes they will forgive us the sparseness of our hospitality.

When the exchange of proprieties is over, Wedad's mother groans,

—Curse on it! This rheumatism won't relent before it cuts me to pieces. There's no single day I'm allowed to forget my pain. Yet, *alhamdellah*, God is merciful. He does not close us in from all directions. Look how it worked out with you, in spite of our short notice! By my life, it was easier to find a smuggler than a decent family in whose hands I could entrust my daughter.

Father mumbles his thanks for the good words, meant for him. Wedad's mother goes on talking, summing up her maladies, her offspring, her world views, her life. No, neither she nor her husband wish to emigrate. Too frail for such undertakings, too weary for new starts, they would rather spend their last years in their native land. Since no regime lasts long in Iraq, this government too will fall, sooner or later. Soon enough for them to see it, she hopes. Yet Wedad, the very last of their six, must go! She must find her own *nesib*, lot, elsewhere. No matter how it tears their hearts, they would not hold on to her, God is their witness.

—May God help you, nothing's more precious than one's own children, mother puts in. Blood never turns into water.

Father is tapping his thigh restlessly, like someone marking the seconds. He is uncomfortable with this talk verging on intimacy with people he hardly knows. Moreover, the smuggler is late. Thirty minutes only, yet punctuality is for him the measure of reliability.

Wedad pulls out her watch for the third time. More than ten years older than Shuli, her shoulder-length frizzled hair hides the sides of her face. Her opaque grey eyes give no hint of her thoughts or feelings. Two incisive folds have settled on the sides of her mouth, yet her thin lips remain sealed, unwilling to talk or smile —not even to her father, who is quietly puffing his pipe, without taking his gaze off her. If it were up to him, he would extend this hour until infinity.

Our preparations turn into reality the moment he rings, twenty minutes later. Shuli hurries to the gate, mother to the kitchen. Wedad' s mother squeezes her husband's hand. Shuli returns with the middle-aged man, one hand's-span taller than he. His stout figure, stately gait, turbaned head, thick well-trimmed moustache match my fantasy of the fearless Pesh Mergah, the Kurdish guerilla fighters. Father stands up to greet him. Wedad's mother introduces Kaka J.—*kaka* the Kurdish for mister. The newcomer shakes hands with the men. Once he has received his tea, father leads him, together with Wedad's mother, to the living room.

Wedad's father sits up, suddenly talkative,

—He wanted to charge us 300 *dinars* a head, but my wife brought him down to 215, and she's determined to hand him not more than half the amount tonight. She'll have it her way, you'll see! He'll receive the rest only when he's back from the north with a coded message from Wedad saying you've all crossed safely.

The mixture of his white hair with the ebony moustache gives him the expression of some soft, old man. He smiles. Wedad holds on to her reticence. I pretend, out of politeness, not to notice the scene, wondering whether it fits into the latest gossip. That Wedad's parents had strongly opposed her wish to emigrate. That she had refused to speak to them the entire summer. That only her eventual hunger strike had forced her father to give her permission to leave.

The negotiations end sooner than expected. Wedad's mother winks to her husband, rubbing her left thigh while resuming her seat. Wedad leaps to pull the stove nearer to her mother's legs. Father looks relaxed. Kaka J. must have won his trust. Wasting no time, our man replaces the empty *stikan* on the table, then picks up our two suitcases. Wedad's parents recognise the signal. Reluctantly, the three stand up, hug each other so tight that they seem to merge into one flesh. Wedad's tough façade shatters. She is sobbing, rebuking herself, kissing whatever parental hand she may seize, pleading for forgiveness. Mother gestures us to leave the room, out of regard for the family's last moment of intimacy.

From my window I watch Wedad's parents step out of our house, their heads lowered like two orphans. Kaka J. is loading our woollen quilts into the trunk of his vehicle. He stops to exchange some words with them, then pats the father on the shoulder.

Wedad' s mother starts the engine. I join the others in the living room.

Shuli has gone out to make sure that the night watch is not passing, that no neighbour is parting from late guests. We put out the lights, except for the one in the living room, to suggest our presence. For the same purpose, father turns the radio on, trying out the optimal volume—loud enough to simulate movement, yet low enough to remain indistinct.

—Fortunately, tomorrow is Saturday, so the schoolbus won't be honking who knows how long for Lina, mother says.

If tomorrow is Saturday...

—The rubbish! They'll ring for the rubbish tomorrow morning. Shall I take it out, father?

—By no means! The empty bin will roll around for days in front of our gate and draw much more attention than its absence on one morning would.

Shuli returns, gasping,

—The street's fast asleep, let's go!

We put on our overcoats, walk quietly out of the house with our totebags. Our tomcat is sprawling on the gatepost, watching nightlife in the street. Five houses from here, Lawy junior is sleeping in peaceful ignorance. We load the rest of our luggage into the trunk. It surprises me to find no other suitcases next to ours. What of Wedad's luggage, I wonder, yet keep the query to myself, lest it triggers further tears. On the number plate stands Suleimaniyah, the Kurdish province where Kaka J. lives. We hop in to the vehicle, men in the front, women in the rear. Except for the glittering eyes of our satisfied pet, nobody seems to notice us pull out, pierce the night with our yellow headlights.

—Mama will be back in a few minutes to pour water on your threshhold, Wedad says.

No joke, no ironical remark. Not even Shuli minds the old ritual. Let Wedad's mother wash the traces of our wheels, let her foil the evil eye. Whoever needs so much luck may well end up flirting with superstition. While Wedad peers out of the window, hoping for one last glimpse of her mother's yellow Opel, the wish to have somebody to part from sweeps over me. Nobody in particular, just some schoolmate or Jewish neighour who would happen to see us, wave hello. Only later, when the news of our escape reached him, would he recall the encounter, realise that while he was waving hello, we were waving goodbye. Yet no single pedestrian is on the road. No vehicles either, except for one or two taxis. The metropolis has run out of night tales to tell. It has nothing to say to me either. I feel hollow myself, with neither glee nor sorrow in the face of this point of no return. Too superstitious to think "goodbye" too soon, I just whisper "goodnight," unable to imagine the long night into which my hometown is sinking.

Gradually, the neighbourhoods lose their familiarity. Even mother fails to recognise the old quarters north of Waziriyah. Shortly past the outskirts, we get to the first military post. Kaka J. stops, shows his licence. While the sentry is going through the papers, three military lorries loom up opposite us. Kaka J.'s papers still in his hand, the sentry struts over to them, then, wasting no words, motions them on.

—They're transporting their dead. They don't dare do it in daylight, Kaka J. sneers.

The sentry now storms towards the hut, pelting insults, until one unshod soldier leaps out. He is instantly slapped on the face with Kaka J.'s licence. Flinching from the headlights, the young man pretends to examine the papers. Sleepily, he returns them to Kaka J., lifts the roadblock, waves us through.

Kaka J. takes off, whistling—some Kurdish tune perhaps.

—There's no landscape outside Kurdistan, he soon grumbles. There's nothing here but empty desert.

Except for the occasional wailing of the jackals, which reminds me of the time when father took us for night rides in the wasteland to run in his new Ford. I used to lie on the rear seat, listening to the jackals half in fear, half in wonder. Tentatively, I lay my head on mother's shoulder. No rebuff. I hope she has forgiven me my meanness in the kitchen. She, too, seems less nervous, more secure with every mile we travel further from home.

THE GREY VOLKSWAGEN

I wake up to the voice of the muezzin summoning the faithful to sunrise prayer. Not only is the melody identical to the one in the metropolis, the voice too sounds familiar! Profound, musical, meditative with tinges of passion. Kaka J. parks the motorcar in some sidestreet. Good morning, Suleimaniyah, I yawn, stretching myself out, savouring the security the Kurdish province is giving out. From the subsequent silence round me I gather that security is not the prevailing feeling in the vehicle. Wedad's lids have swollen overnight. Mother's wry smile tells me I was the only one who had the heart to nap through the journey.

I jump out, keen to stroll through the neighbourhood with the sun rising. Icy wind whips my face. Fastening my overcoat, I walk up the narrow street. Is father hailing me? I pretend not to hear. The second time, I turn round. He is gesturing me to return. I obey. He pushes our woollen quilts into my hands, motions me to Kaka J.'s house. Once in the frontyard, he passes on our smuggler's instructions: we should keep strictly to our quarters, the neighbours ought not to know of our presence. The neighbours? I thought they were Kurdish, unconditionally on our side! I must have rejoiced too soon. Sightseeing is off the programme. Reading my frustration father softens his tone,

—It's only for one or two more days, and then we'll never have to hide again.

—Kaka J. leads us to the spacious, unfurnished room near the staircase. Warm, however, thanks to the oil stove in the middle. One large indigo kilim is laid out over the tiled floor, while mattresses, mats, pillows in various shades lie scattered throughout the room. We unload our luggage. Wedad inspects the six rolls of Persian rugs lined up next to the four trunks under the window. She strokes the rugs to verify whether they have got wet, removes the mud stuck on the fringes, proceeds to test the locks of the trunks. My parents watch the scene with irritation.

—Kaka J. picked them up last time he was at our place, Wedad points out, revealing the least interesting part of the story.

Some old woman serves us hot tea, lays loops of orange peels on the stove, then leaves the room, giving our luggage one long inquisitive look.

—The crossing's due for tonight. Rest as much as you can, a long night's in front of you, our smuggler imparts on his way out.

Mother spreads out sheets of newspaper on the kilim, on which she lays the milk products, the olives, the fried vegetables, the salad, honey, marmalade. Wedad surprises us with keymar, milk fat.

—The table is set! mother says with untypical joviality.

Unaccustomed to sitting on the floor, father tries out several positions—folding his legs, or tucking them up under him, squeezing pillows wherever possible. Finally, he huddles himself up, leans on the wall, supporting his plate with his knees.

—I'm just not made for the circus, he says jokingly.

Yet our meal is far from festive. Mother's jaws move so painfully slowly, you would think she has just had her wisdom tooth pulled out. Shuli is worn out, like someone who

has walked the whole night. Wedad's tears well up, then
mysteriously vanish. Father flicks on the transistor radio,
tunes it to the news from London. I have the impression he
is not listening. He is just relieved to have someone talk to
whom he is not obliged to reply.

I seem the only one in high spirits in this gathering.

When it is time to give out the name of the station, father
lowers the volume. Not unaware of the gesture, he wonders
if he will outgrow this habit, learn to listen uncaringly to the
radio in the future.

Nobody is in the mood to reflect on the future of father's
habits.

When the newscaster launches into the football results,
Wedad voices her own thoughts.

—Now that we've left Baghdad, we've got nothing to fear
any more. Kaka J. has very good connections with the border
police. The money we paid will be distributed among the
guards at the checkpoints. You'll see. The man was highly
recommended by . . . reliable sources.

—And who are your reliable sources, if I may ask? mother
inquires.

—No, you may not! Wedad gruffly retorts. Such sources
should remain secret. It's safer for everybody.

—Oh, I beg your pardon! snarls mother with stinging
irony.

The face she makes tells me she has taken offence. What
right has this girl, years younger than her, to reproach her
with indiscretion? What manners! No wonder she has found
no husband so far, in spite of her sumptuous rugs. Instead of
safety, they should try honesty perhaps. Instead of puffing
herself up with self-importance, Wedad might well tell us
why she is travelling in luxury, smuggling out her trousseau,
while we have to go virtually naked. Haven't we paid the
same price? Or had her precious mother thought we owned
nothing more than the two suitcases?

—And to whom can we pass on the secret sources—now that we're here? mother snaps.

Wedad says nothing. Mother starts packing the food, signalling the meal is over. Wedad pours herself one more glass of tea, retreats to sit next to her luggage—keeping out of mother's way. Nonetheless, mother's hard feelings seem to magnify with whatever movement Wedad makes. The tinkling of her spoon, stirring the sugar. The fashion magazine she takes out of her handbag. Her occasional sips of tea. Seething, mother noisily piles up the used plates, seals the glass jars, gathers the sheets of newspaper. Wedad reads on, undisturbed. Unable to pierce the young woman's tranquil facade, mother picks on me.

—Lina, get up, go and wash the dishes. Don't just sit there and wait to be served like a *khatoun*!

Unprepared for this outburst, I turn to father, seeking his support. His gaze is weary, imploring rest. Shuli picks up the stack of plates, hands it to me, winking his own request for peace. It's not fair, I would have hollered on some other occasion, yet, overwhelmed with sudden fatigue myself, I grab the plates, then go off fuming to the front yard.

I hardly recognise it, hung from side to side with lines of washing. I plunge my way through wet towels, skirts, trousers, in search of the tap. Men's underwear sways insouciantly in the wind, next to the women's, their hems overlapping, the way their owners would never touch in public.

The sink is set in the middle of the yard, made from the same yellow mountain stone with which the ground is paved. I put the plates inside, turn on the tap. In less than thirty seconds, the stout old woman who served us tea shows up, her hands full of wooden pegs. She greets me with lavish friendliness.

—Did you enjoy your breakfast? Aren't you going out to have a look around? Yes, rest, rest, but not the whole day! What do you mean you don't know? Where are you from?

Allahu akbar, Baghdad's hot and dusty, and full of thieves and beggars. No, I've never been there. Don't you go to school, girl? *Rissmas* holidays?

I turn off the water, politely tending to her questions, yet remain squatting, hoping she makes it short.

—Tell me, she goes on, which one is your mother and which one is your sister? But why did Kaka J. put you all in one room? It's not comfortable. The house is large, we can find you a second room. How long are you staying with us? Don't you need sheets, blankets, we've got plenty of them. Come with me...

—Thank you, it's not necessary. I...I don't think we're staying here overnight...I falter, immediately regretting my slip, questioning for the first time her familial relationship to Kaka J.

—You're not staying here? So where are you heading for, my girl?

I have spoken too much, I think. I must leave her this very moment. Say I have forgotten some unwashed tea glasses, or run to the toilet, feigning stomach pains. The woman repeats her question: "Tell me what you're up to, my girl!" The white sheet is lifted. Kaka J. is glaring indignantly. The torrent of Kurdish words he pelts her with sounds very much like rebuke. The old woman scurries out of sight. How handsome Kaka J. looks now that he is wearing the traditional Kurdish *sherwal*, with sash round the waist. He reaches for his Rafidain packet, viewing me from his six-foot height, softly, or maybe only possessively—his jealously guarded secret. His pupils glow with vitality, not in the least red or sleepy. Suddenly, our physical proximity in the middle of the wet white sheets unsettles me. I turn on the tap, splashing water on his trousers, unsure whether I want him to stay or to go, unwilling to let him forget my face too soon. His soiled shoes, inches from me, stay firm in their place. I start rinsing the plates, splashing more water.

—You should be resting! he finally lashes out, then vanishes through the white sheet.

The gate jangles twice. I whisk the plates off to our room, keen to share my insight with father: Kaka J. is keeping us secret from his own family.

Wrapped in his overcoat, leafing through yesterday's newspaper, father raises his forefinger to his lips, requesting quietness. The radio, too, is silent. The scent of orange peel has soothed the tempers. Scattered through the room, mother, Shuli, Wedad, lie nestled in their woollen quilts, their faces to the wall.

Kaka J. turns up in the evening, together with Faris, his nephew, or so he introduces him. Hardly over twenty, his shining hair parted in the middle, Faris, in his woollen jacket, looks like some university student. It is time to go, Kaka J. says. We pack the food, fold the quilts, put on our overcoats. Kaka J. hands us torches.

—In case you're asked, your names from now on are: Hamdi and Omar. You may keep your name, Wedad, it's Arabic enough. You'll be Zehra, and your daughter, Asmahan.

She was one of the most renowned singers in the Levant until the mid-'40s, when some misfortune on the highway terminated her life. The rumour was that she had involved herself in spying for the French in the Second World War, which led some local Nazi gang to liquidate her.

—I bet the name appeals to you, Shuli teases me. Is it the star or the spy you're infatuated with?

Kaka J. lifts up two of Wedad's trunks, returning us to practical matters. Faris follows suit. You're not touching her things, mother whispers to Shuli, referring to Wedad's heavy Persian rugs. I warm my hands over the stove for the last time, then start to lug the stack of woollen quilts. Trailing the two men through the faintly lit front yard, I stagger to the Land Rover parked outside. While Kaka J. is loading our luggage, one scarablike grey Volkswagen trundles past, then reduces speed. Kaka J. pushes me inside the yard, instantly putting out the lights. He speaks to Faris in Kurdish, his voice trembling.

—Lina, where are you? I can't see a thing in the dark! mother grumbles. Watch out, Shuli, you've just bumped into me. What's going on for God's sake?

When they have gathered near the gate, I recount the incident.

—A grey Beetle? Here, in the north? Plague on us!

—But that doesn't have to mean anything.

—It could be just as likely in the north as in Baghdad.

—Hurry up! Kaka J. interrupts. Abu Shuli, your son and Wedad will go with Faris. I'm taking the rest of you in the Land Rover.

—No way! We're not splitting up, father firmly replies.

—It's safer . . . just do as I say, please, we've got no time to argue. Wedad?

—I said we're not splitting up! father repeats, his voice slightly rising.

Wedad makes no response.

—Look, I can't explain everything right now. Believe me, I know what I'm doing.

—I bet you do, Kaka, our lives depend on it! Still, I'm the one in charge of this girl here, and I'm not sending her, nor my son, anywhere with a boy, and definitely not with one I've never seen before.

—But it's Faris, my nephew, my own flesh and blood! Hell, we've got no time to argue. *Yallah*, get into the Land Rover, all of you, quick! Wedad, you sit at my side. Faris, listen . . .

Wedad takes the passenger seat. The four of us huddle in the rear. The two men rapidly transfer our luggage to Kaka J.'s vehicle. Wedad views the hustle with uneasiness. She throws father questioning glances, yet he is more preoccupied with the resumption of our journey than with the luggage. Our smuggler hops in the Land Rover.

—Women, put on your *abayas*, there's a checkpoint at the outskirts. Wedad, I'll say you're my wife. Let's hope they won't ask for any identification!

He only hopes? What if they wanted to see our papers? What is the use of our fake names if we have to prove our identities? Unlike his smooth ride out of the metropolis yesterday, Kaka J. is now streaking through the winding unlit streets of Suleimaniyah. The grey Volkswagen has scared him out of his wits. Perhaps it is, in fact, the security police's standard vehicle. Wedad suddenly yells. I pitch forwards, striking the front seat. Had Kaka J. not promptly stopped, we would have rammed into some stray mongrels. Fiercely they pounce upon the Land Rover, while our smuggler scorches onwards, unimpeded by the hoarse howls pursuing us through the streets.

Nearing the outskirts of Suleimaniyah, he warns:

—Don't forget your fake names. If they ask, you're my guests from Baghdad and we're paying a visit to relatives down in Halabja.

—*What a sophisticated cover story. I thought he had made arrangements with the soldiers at these checkpoints*, father grumbles in his favourite language.

Wedad spins round, throws father one long pleading look.

The sentry gestures us to halt. Kaka J. lowers the window. The soldier interrogates him in Kurdish. Kaka J. quickly switches on the light inside the Land Rover to let him glimpse our faces. Following further instructions, Kaka J. hops out to unlock the trunk, which holds nothing more than our hand luggage.

The soldier waves us through. Wedad sits upright, proud of her fictitious husband.

—Seems the Beetle hasn't been here after all, Shuli remarks.

—What about our things? Wedad inquires.

—With Faris. We're meeting him in Penjwin. It proved to be the right decision to send them separately, Kaka J. replies, hoping for gratitude.

—Is that Faris behind? Shuli says, indicating the pair of gleaming headlights.

Kaka J. glances in the mirror.

—No! My car has yellow headlights. Those are white.

—Would Volkswagens have white ones?

My question is ignored the way tactless jokes pass unacknowledged. Kaka J. speeds up, heading for the mountains. The two white lights follow us steadily, neither gaining on us nor receding. Shuli keeps turning round to report the precise location of our pursuers.

—They've left the foothill . . . they're moving towards the ridge . . . they've just disappeared round the shoulder . . . have they tumbled off the mountain . . . *inshallah*? No, here they are again, the bastards . . . climbing up the slope . . . but, how come four lights, out of nowhere? Goodness, two cars are chasing us now . . . No, it was just an illusion . . . sorry. I didn't mean to alarm you . . . there's only one car behind . . .

—Shut up Shuli, for God's sake! Not every car behind us is necessarily chasing us, snaps mother.

—And not every grey Beetle is driven by the security police! Wedad says.

Kaka J. races on, regardless of the steep mountain slopes, jolting too frequently over rocks or potholes.

—*We've put ourselves in the hands of an amateur,* father groans hiding his face in his hands. *It's all improvisation. No wonder he's panic-stricken, he didn't plan anything.*

Grey Volkswagen scarabs keep scuttling through the folds of my memory, linking oppressive recollections with their malevolent patrols. The two security men who picked up Shuli in 1967. The men who kept watch on Hai's *saba'a* last year. The rowdies who roughed up the handful of Jewish traders in the *suq* last month. The officials who plundered the houses of Jews several weeks following their flight. Whenever some grey scarab pulled up in front of the grocer-informer in our neighbourhood, the latter would hasten out of his store with *sitkans* on his tea tray matching the number of the men inside. This vehicle has nine lives, Zeki used to say in praise of his white Volkswagen scarab. The security police must have shared his view, otherwise they would not have purchased who knows how many thousands of this model, scattered them in the metropolis, in the hearts of important towns, on the highways from the mountains in the north to the marshes in the south.

—The headlights have gone. We've lost them!

For some reason, Kaka J. sharply reduces speed. The Land Rover screeches, starts spinning, its headlights illuminating sections of the landscape in rotation like police lights. In spite of the pains he is taking with the steering wheel, Kaka J. has lost grip of his vehicle. Mother seizes my wrist. Her hand is icy. She is unusually quiet, neither screaming like on the Ferris wheel nor resorting to God. They say in your last moments, fleeting scenes of your life unfold in front of you. If nothing of the sort is happening to me, maybe it is not over with us yet. Just when Kaka J. seems to have regained mastery of the Land Rover, it shudders, skids forwards, jolts over some rock, then stops. I feel suspended, yet not in the least light.

I wonder if we have reached heaven.

—Don't move, Kaka J. pleads. The front wheels are in the air! Keep still, especially you in the back.

We mumble our understanding, quietly, lest our voices upset the fragile stability.

—Is everyone all right? Kaka J. remembers to inquire.

We reassure him.

—Good. I'm getting out first. Just keep still, no matter what happens, otherwise we'll all fall over the precipice. Do you hear me? I'm opening the door.

The hinge squeaks. The vehicle rocks faintly. Kaka J.'s left leg steals out, in slow motion, or so I imagine, since my vision is restricted to his swathed head projecting over the front seat. The turban glides towards the opening with surprising smoothness for his robust figure.

The next moment he has slipped outside. How remote he suddenly looks, like in outer space. Instead of rejoicing over his rebirth, however, the man slaps his head, lumbers round the Land Rover, inspecting the tires, fretting over the position of the vehicle—fortunately in Kurdish. For no matter with what horror he may regard our situation, the fact is that his feet trod straight from the front seat onto the ground—meaning that two-thirds of the vehicle is on firm land.

Our two-thirds probability of survival.

He lights one of his filter-tipped Rafidains, then squats on rocks—waiting for what? For fate to tumble his Land Rover over the precipice? For the hand of God to flip it on to the road? Or for the security men to show up, play heads or tails with our lives? His gaze is fixed on the headlights—wastefully illuminating the valley. He is still talking to himself, gesturing like someone who is unable to figure out what has happened, or how.

—Kaka, where are you? My door won't open. Come and help me out! Wedad shouts.

Forced to return to our reality, he pulls himself together, gets up, goes over to Wedad's side. The hinge squeaks once more. Wind gushes in from one opening, surges out from the other. The seat under me gently springs. Wedad merges into the night.

—*Alhamdellah*, thank God, father whispers.

Now that the weight of two passengers is off the front seats, the peril of falling over is significantly reduced. Instead of relaxing, mother has only tightened her hold.

—Your turn, son, father says.

Shuli swallows hard, while his left leg sneaks slowly out. Pressed to the rear, his trunk remains still, his right limbs motionless, unrelated to the left. Kaka J. pulls on his Rafidain. His left foot on the ground, Shuli skilfully pulls out his right half, smiling, for he has lived to tell the story.

The familiar sound of father's stiff joints tells me he is stepping out. When I turn to wish him luck, his hips have left the seat. He sets himself upright, loops his muffler round his neck, peering inside the Land Rover, uneasy that his own rescue had to precede ours.

—Asmahan, you now! Kaka J. says,

It takes me some moments to remember my new name, the only name with which he will, or will not, remember me. Though mother must have heard Kaka's instructions too, her grip has not loosened.

—Mama, you go first if you want to.

She voices no reply. No intention. No wish.

—Mama, none of us will make it if you hold on to me. You have to let go of my hand!

It's like talking to the wall. The wind is lashing her, yet she seems not to mind, like someone who has switched off her sensations. The pressure of her grip verges on pain. Is she requesting help in some impossible way, or is she resolved to take me with her to the grave? Panic seizes me, once I realise I no longer trust her sense of judgment. With utmost force, I pull her index finger from my wrist. Though rigid, it hardly resists. Keeping it out of the way with the heel of my hand, I work on the rest of her fingers until I have pried them from my wrist—sore, flushing red.

Her hand lies palm up on my lap, the four fingers stiff, like fork tines. Wasn't she the one who taught me their names, years past, gently folding, gently uncurling them? I take her hand, rub warmth into her palm, kiss it, then replace it on her lap, like some unwanted packet returned to sender. Mother shows no interest in my leavetaking. I open my legs wide, make one long stretch to the opposite side. Shuli keeps pestering me with instructions. No sooner has my left foot poked out, than he grabs my hand, yanks me outside. I trip on my robe, fall on the icy ground.

—I'm terribly sorry, Lina. I got anxious, he says, helping me up.

—Go to Mama, for God's sake. She wouldn't move! She's petrified!

—What!

They rush over to her, while I rise slowly to my feet. The sight of the slanting vehicle on the verge of suicide makes me feel queasy. Father has squatted on his knees to speak to her, reassuring, reasoning, urging, imploring. She stares forwards, straight into the rear-view mirror, yet surely not to study her reflection. When father has used up his repertoire of persuasion, he stops talking, reaches out to her.

Mother wastes no glance on him.

—No use, he sighs, standing up. It happened once before, during the pogrom of '41. She was in a stupor for two days, hiding in the cellar while rioters swarmed in and out, looting their house. She can't handle physical danger. I'm afraid she won't budge, not of her own will.

—Let her stay inside. The five of us will push the Land Rover back to the road, Kaka J. suggests. Her weight in the back won't make much of a difference.

He positions us near the four openings, signalling me to team up with him next to the steering wheel. When he shouts *yallah*, I shove hard with my shoulder. The motor, still on, gives me the illusion it has joined forces with us. Harder, he urges. In front of us, Wedad is moaning under the strain. The steel is on the point of penetrating my flesh. Kaka J.'s stomach is pressing on my waist, while my head is swimming in the smell of his fresh sweat. The vehicle gives no hint of retreat.

—Stay with me, one more push, it's on its way. Just hold on. One more try, and we'll . . .

The front wheels slip up on to the rocky mountain slope, resettle on the ground. Hooray! We whistle. We laugh. We tell mother we have made it. She remains inert, unconcerned, like some passive toddler in its pram. When we have pushed the Land Rover on to the road, Kaka J. hops inside, steers it on to the right lane.

—Let's get going. We've lost enough time already.

Having regained our seats, father holds mother's hand, reassures her that she is safe, that our journey is resuming. Mother pays no heed to his offer of rapprochement. Too tired to persist, he soon gives up, sinking into the general lassitude.

One hour later, father suddenly shatters the silence.

—*I don't believe it! This fellow can't even drive!* he says shrieking with ugly laughter.

—*Why, what's the matter with you!* mother protests. *Nothing's wrong with his driving. Why are you picking on him?*

She similarly fails to understand why five faces instantly turn to her, first gaping, then overwhelming her with meaningless questions. How is she feeling? What happened? Was she in panic? In shock? Was she really unaware of the goings on round her? Mother has not the slightest notion of what we mean. I pull up my sleeve to revive her memory, yet the marks of her fingers have faded.

—What happened when we lost the grey Volkswagen? I insist.

—Nothing in particular. We went on driving.

—Don't you remember the Land Rover skidding?

—No, she replies, innocently, like someone who has simply not seen the film.

—Never mind now, father says. Main thing is that she's back, safe and sound.

Reverting to our schedule, Wedad questions Kaka J. regarding the rest of the journey. He tells us of his plans. He

is taking us to Penjwin, the last town until the frontier. Faris
will meet us there with our luggage. From Penjwin onwards,
we will have to proceed on mules. No, the Land Rover will
not make it through that strip of land, now that it is snowed
over. Yet the path is so short, the ride will not last longer than
twenty to thirty minutes. He or Faris will guide us to the
frontier. The moment we get to the Iranian side, we must
surrender to the soldiers who have orders from the Shah to
let Jewish fugitives in.

Kaka J. lowers the window to throw out his used Rafidain
pack. Icy wind steals inside. Mother, her old self once more,
voices inquietude.

—What if it starts snowing again tonight?

—Don't worry, Sister, Kaka J. replies. If there's snow in the
air, I'd sense it.

Father shakes his head with misgivings. He no longer
trusts Kaka J.'s senses, not just on the weather.

Kaka J. pulls up in the middle of the white valley.

—The asphalt road ends here. Over there's Penjwin, he
says, pointing to the faint lights fifty yards to our right.

Further on is no paved road, no order, no law.

We stagger out. My shoes sink into the virgin snow. My
first snow, shining under the starlight. Snow White occurs to
me, palpable for the first time. I plunge my fingers into the
ground, wondering where the white goes when the snow has
melted. The sight of ten or twelve mules, several yards from
the Land Rover, interrupts my flight of fancy.

The three riders walk towards us, their galoshes stomping
on the snow. Their gait is light, unmistakably youthful.
Gradually I make out their knitted khaki hats, their *sherwals*,
the *kaffiyahs* wrapped round their necks, raised up to their
noses. Kaka J. shakes their hand with his usual reserve, offering his Rafidain packet, speaking Kurdish.

—Faris hasn't shown up yet, he says, putting us in the picture. We'll have to wait for him. He should be here any minute.

—Wait! Now that we're so close to the border! Shuli objects.

—Of course we'll wait! Wedad hastens to say.

Father purses his lips in uncertainty. Mother pleads with him.

—We can't do without our suitcases. We have to change. We need underwear, she stresses, mouthing the last word silently.

—All right, but I'm going inside. It's too cold for me out here, he replies wearily.

The low temperature soon sends the rest of us into the Land Rover, save Kaka J., who stays on with the young smugglers. Shuli fetches our night snack from the trunk. Mother hands out roast meat sandwiches, passes the jar of pickles, the figs, fills the glasses with hot tea from the thermos flask. Like Shuli, I feel uneasy with the hold-up. Waiting summons fatigue, stirs up latent fears. When Kaka J. takes his seat, he immediately switches on the radio, sweeps through foreign news, scratchy stations, pop music, local music. He is shunning us, I suppose, reckoning it would result in tedious questions if not reproaches. Politely, he refuses mother's sandwich. Paying no heed to his mood, she refills her glass, nudges me to pass it to him. Her poke shakes the glass, spills tea over my skirt.

—I'm sorry Lina! Take a handkerchief from my bag and try to soak it up. Quickly. You shouldn't stay with a damp skirt in this cold.

Scrabbling through the handbag for the Kleenex, I find her keys—tucked in the unzipped side pocket. Something is odd, I sense, unable to make out what or why. Mother frequently left the house without her keys. If nobody was home on her return, she would pace the yard waiting for one of us to show up, too shamefaced to go to the neighbours. In vain she would think out new methods to prevent herself forgetting them. Why, now that she no longer needs them, has she remembered then!

—Forever misplaced! I tease her, fishing out the keys.

—Mama, doesn't your sentimentality know any limits! Shuli jumps on her. What is it you want to retain? The one thousand two hundred and ninety-three days of hell we went through?

—Shut up, Shuli, you're not one to judge me. You're just a youngster, what do you know about loss or regret? What do you know about Baghdad before the *taskit*?

—Yesterday night, I secretly dropped my keys into Abu Khaled's garden to enable our landlord to get into our house, if he chooses to, before informing the police, father says. But now that we're talking about it, I guess I was also telling myself that no matter what happens, there is no going back. There is no way back to Baghdad.

Indifferent to Shuli's mockery or to father's pragmatism, mother rattles her keys like some naughty girl.

—Shall I tell you which is which? This is the key to our front door. This flat one unlocks the back door in the kitchen. This is the key to the roof, this, to my wardrobe, and this small one is for my empty jewellery box.

—The key for an empty box! Mama, now you're really overdoing it! Shuli sneers.

—Frankly I don't understand what's wrong with her grief! Wedad suddenly wheels round in the passenger seat.

—The timing is wrong, father replies. You're free to make yourself miserable over irreversible facts. But to indulge in regret at a moment like this can only confuse you.

—Don't you have any soft spot yourselves? Wedad insists. Haven't you ever indulged in anything sentimental?

Shuli sits up.

—Indulged, yes, sentimental, no. Yesterday evening, I put my last turd under my pillow. I've been conceiving this farewell since the summer. I owe it to them. How I'd love to see their faces when they search my room this time!

—Shuli, how could you! It's disgusting, it's unacceptable, it's . . . father stammers indignantly.

Wedad is shaking with laughter.

—You're the only person who understands me! Shuli says, throwing her one long meaningful glance, which mother fails to miss.

Showing no interest in our squabble, Kaka J. switches off the radio, gets out. To smoke one more Rafidain with the young men, he says. To relax with workmates, I suppose. Yet he looks no less tense with them, nodding his head mechanically, pretending to listen, while his gaze repeatedly returns to the mountains.

Having smoked who knows how many Rafidains, Kaka J. joins us, rubbing his hands.

—I'm afraid we can't wait any longer. They want to start off. They've got to be back before dawn.

—It's still two in the morning, Wedad replies. Where are we and where is dawn?

—They've got other things to arrange after they drop you. Besides, the poor boys are shivering from the cold.

—Who told them to wait outside? Let them come in here. We're not crossing without our luggage, Kaka! That was our deal.

—The luggage is the easiest thing to handle. I'll have it sent to you in no time. Tomorrow or after tomorrow, as soon as possible.

—But we need our blankets for the crossing! mother protests. My husband can't possibly withstand this cold.

—He can have my own blanket. It's very warm—made from camel hair, Kaka J. replies, pulling the ochre fabric from under his seat, passing it to father, glad to have settled this problem.

One of the smugglers taps on the side of the Land Rover. Kaka J. lowers the window. The young man sounds nervous.

—He says they can't wait any longer, Kaka J. translates. A border patrol might pass by and interrogate us.

—I thought you were on familiar terms with the border police! Isn't that what you bragged about in our sitting room last week?

—Not with every single guard and soldier. Wedad, for God's sake, come to your senses!

—Guards can be bribed, I wasn't born yesterday! Listen to me carefully, Kaka: I've left my elderly parents to die alone. I've forfeited our house and all our land back in Baghdad. Those bundles are the last things I possess and . . .

—Spare me your wailing, woman. No sacrifice's too high when you're heading to your *watan*!

—What *watan*, whose *watan*, you Kurds are obsessed with your *watan*! I've got no homeland, I'm just fleeing. Did you hear me, I'm fleeing for my one and only life!

—I agree with the Kaka. We can't afford further delay, father puts in with such finality that it stops the row, sets the party in motion.

Wedad gets out last, stifling her tears. Now that the totality of our losses has levelled us, mother hugs her, placating her with hollow words. Shuli picks up our hand luggage from the trunk. Kaka J. pays the young smugglers their fee—ten Iraqi pounds per person. Two men will set off with us, while the third will return the mules to the stable. The rest seems settled.

Our man nods gallantly to Wedad, his tone now placatory.

—Don't forget to give the boys the coded message in Iran. Wedad sulks.

—What do you mean "give the boys"? Aren't you coming with us? says father shocked.

—I've got to find Faris. I hope he didn't get into trouble. Don't worry, Brother, you're in good hands. Nobody knows this stretch of land better than they. *Yallah*, may God be with you!

—But they don't even speak Arabic!

Kaka J. is in too much hurry to reply. He leaps into the Land Rover, makes the fastest U-turn I have seen in my life, then streaks off towards the mountains.

The mules set out in one line. I find myself riding last. The smuggler who had helped me mount is leading my mule with the halter. He is smoking, no longer muffled. His straggly goatee tells me he is in his teens, hardly older than I. Shuli, some paces from us, is having trouble managing his mule. It trots, strays, or turns on its heels. Whenever it goes too fast, Shuli's silhouette fuses into the night.

The stars have scattered themselves to the four winds. I spot Ursa Major straightaway, then the Milky Way. Shuli might have located the Goat, had he had the sky map with him. The map, where had I seen it last? Wasn't it spread out on the roof, held firm under three slabs? How thoughtless of Shuli to have forgotten it out there! If the rain has not soaked it, the wind must have torn it to pieces. Then it hits me, that it no longer makes sense to refer to our possessions in terms of neglect, that we have no obligation to them from now on. Neither map nor picture nor window nor mirror. Nor the washing line hanging on the roof—which is no longer our roof, nor the hose rolled up in the garden—which is no longer our garden, with or without mother's keys.

The recognition is far from shattering. In fact, I feel relieved, free from longings, ties, roots. Roots, some metaphor! It is trees which should long to have feet, have the privilege to walk, to move on, to seek the future far away from the past.

Has he just touched my foot? The lady killer, I'll show him! Next time I will scream. Scream to summon father to twist his neck, or louder still, until I wake up the soldiers on the two sides of the frontier.

His fingers land on my foot for the second time. I open my mouth to warn him, yet no sound slips out. My voice has run out on me. My throat feels stuffed with sand. He fondles the toes, massages the instep, nestles the heel in the hollow of his hand, rubbing, squeezing. He repeats the sequence without interrupting the pace of his walking, without much fuss, just stealing samples of illegal goods.

Shuli! Where is Shuli? Why is father so far off? Why have they left me in the rear?

Shuli turns round. Telepathy? No, just waving some flask, father's vodka. The smuggler lets go of the halter, lunges towards him. I urge the mule to hurry up. If only I were to make it to Shuli, nothing would prevent me from staying next to him for the rest of the journey. Yet the mule is reluctant to speed up. I kick its flank, slap its thigh. In vain. My mule obeys only its master. The smuggler has snatched the vodka, is flaunting it rapturously.

—What's your name? he inquires jovially.

So he speaks our language too.

—'smahan . . . I reply, swallowing the first letter.

He hands me the vodka in return. The smell of mother's lipstick on the mouth of the flask somewhat reassures me. If out of sight, mother is not totally out of reach. I wonder if it is possible for people to send messages through smells. Warnings of fire or of slippery rocks for instance, or SOS signals, saying please get rid of this man, he is harassing me. The Lawy son never thought of that. Toasting Lawy Junior's stupefaction upon hearing the news of our flight, I take my first sip of vodka. Worse than volcano lava! Spluttering, I pass the flask to the smuggler, who helps himself to one long swig, wipes his mouth with his sleeve, then runs with the vodka to Shuli.

Was he playing the gentleman, offering me the flask first?

My toes have stiffened. My insides have frozen. I hope father will withstand the weather. One glimpse of his white head, held upright, would quell my worries. Though father is reasonably healthy, we have no guarantee that his strength will hold out under prolonged strain. It was he who raised the subject yesterday when we were having our last supper in the house,

—No matter what happens to any of us, the rest must continue. You have no other choice. There is no way back to Baghdad.

He let slip "you" instead of "we"—have no option. Father immediately tried to put it right, jokingly said that he would have preferred the plane, that migration was on the whole not recommended to people over sixty.

—Asmahan, he gasps, repeating the sequence of fondling with obsessive precision.

Some misty figure looms up from nowhere, trudging through the snow, leading two overloaded mules. The smuggler raises his hand. The stranger returns the greeting. The nearer he gets, the more perceptible his Kurdish outfit grows. The smuggler pulls the halter. We stop. The two men shake hands with obvious familiarity. I scan the jute sacks piled up on the mules. They look too puffy to hold rugs or weapons. Narcotics? The thought makes me shiver. Suddenly I notice the stranger observing me. His gaze is mistrustful. Worse, hostile. I must have shown too much interest in his wares. Shuli is out of sight. It would take him hours to miss us. If, within ten seconds, this man has not taken his stare off me, I will jump off the mule, run for my life. Ten, nine, nine, seven, six . . . He is nodding to my smuggler understandingly. Have I heard the word Israel? He looks less threatening now that he is stroking his mule's mane, listening to who-knows-what tale my smuggler is recounting.

Finally, they slap shoulders, go their separate ways.

In incomprehensible words, the smuggler orders the mule to gallop, himself sprinting next to us. Having no stirrup or saddle to hold on to, I lean forwards, grasp the neck of the mule, nearly strangling the poor thing. No matter how still I try to stay, however, the trotting keeps shaking me up, scaring the life out of me.

When Shuli's silhouette finally reappears, we revert to our walking pace. The smuggler is recovering. I wipe the sweat off my forehead—twice relieved, for I have realised that he has no intention of straying with me from the rest of the group.

My watch indicates we have ridden for more than one hour. Had Kaka J. not said the journey would last twenty to thirty minutes? Though the path has wound round once, perhaps twice, the landscape has remained virtually unchanged: ranges of white mountains unfold to the horizon—indifferent to our rendezvous with sunrise on the Iranian side of the frontier.

—Asmahan!

He hands me the vodka. I stretch out my hand. He withraws his. Heavens, what is it he wants this time! He showers the mouth of the flask with wild noisy kisses. Has that previous swig of vodka intoxicated him? His tongue now snakes out, licking the glass mouth greedily like soft ice. Then he offers me the flask, so gravely you would think it was love potion. Not on your life, I shake my head. He pushes it into my hand. I shut it tight. He stops walking. The mule follows suit. The two stand still, on strike, waiting for me to give in. The moment Shuli steps out of sight, I grab the flask. Its mouth reeks of his saliva. The idea of putting it to my lips makes my stomach turn. I wipe it thoroughly with my glove, tell myself that mule plus master have resumed their walking, that the trip will not last long, that it is my last ordeal, that one sip will not kill me. My indignation finally soothed, I spit inside the flask, repeatedly, gratified to see his shock.

He takes the flask with his fingertips, with repugance, like some used sanitary towel, hastens to pass it on to Shuli.

The latter gulps unsuspectingly. The smuggler saunters over to my side, smirking with triumph. I find it hard not to snicker myself. It serves Shuli right for leaving me in the lurch, letting me handle this mad Romeo on my own.

—Asmahan!

The flat of his palm falls heavily on my foot. His fingers mount my shin, stroke my knee, momentarily nestle in the hollow underneath. His hunger is growing, I fear. It is time we reached our goal. The tapping of the hooves treading on frozen snow irks me. Our pace sounds hopelessly slow.

—How long is there still to go? I inquire.

—Don't know. Half an hour perhaps . . .

—That's impossible! Kaka J. said the whole journey would last less than thirty minutes!

He shrugs his shoulders.

—When will we reach Iran?

—This is Iran, he replies listlessly, his finger pointing to the ground.

—Since when?

—Since the stream.

—Which stream? When?

—The small white stream we crossed a while ago.

There was no white stream. Was it frozen or hidden under the snow? He shrugs. I want to see the line of the frontier, I insist. It has haunted me for years, the red winding line on the map. He snickers. His frontier line is sober, hard labour. If only life had not mocked me. Without prior notice, it has shifted the high point of our journey from the future to the past, kept the frontier line intangible though we have physically trodden over it.

He is not listening.

The gates of our school will open in the morning. The smell of the scouring material is wafting from the mopped hallways. On the first floor, in the fifth form, the poster of the Periodic Table is hanging on the wall. Teachers will not lose their temper with my stammering today, the way they have recently. The time it took me to reply to their questions was gradually increasing—owing to the growing number of words I had to renounce. My faltering would then trigger some fellow student to utter the forbidden word in my place, or offer this or that synonym—out of pity or just for the sake of the joke. Today, it is my vacant seat which is unsettling the lesson. Is it rumour, is it news—they whisper. Those who live in our neighbourhood might pedal past our house tonight. Not totally unlit, nor quite silent, they will have to figure out for themselves whether it is inhabited or forsaken. Tomorrow, Selma will take my seat, gloss over my flight with her own reluctant presence.

—Asmahan, he summons, shaking my foot.

—What now?

He looks up in surprise. It is the first time I have verbally responded to my fake name. Without forethought, I switch on Kaka J.'s flashlight, point it straight into his irises. Yelping, he withdraws his hand from my leg to shield his face, snatches my torch with the other hand.

—But why!

—My torch, give me my torch or I'll . . .

He hurls it forwards, nearly hitting Shuli's shoulder. The latter swings round, reins up his mule, waits for me to ride near.

—What's the matter? Anything wrong?

—No, just the torch, it's no good.

—With your black *abaya*, you fit perfectly into the black and white landscape, you know that?

—Shuli, we're in Iran, you know that?

—What!

—You were stargazing, weren't you? Show me the stars you've found, I say, using no matter what pretext to stay next to him.

—Oh no, I wasn't in the stars at all. I was brooding over

earthly matters, like my relationship with Baba and all the quarrels we've had lately. For example, our argument last week, when an ambulance screeched through the streets and I said good news, they're one man less, and Baba scowled and warned me against contaminating myself with hatred, and I stood my ground and said they deserved it, and he said but I didn't deserve it, and I said he who can't hit back must content himself with hatred, 'cause they've left us no other choice but to hate them, and then Baba got really upset and told me that I alone was responsible for my feelings—a statement I couldn't deny—but I challenged him again and said I hadn't harmed or killed anybody with my feelings, only rejoiced at counting their dead, and added that hate was nothing more than a spoonful of whipped cream to which I treated myself at teatime and that would slide out of my bowels the next morning, so what was all the fuss about?—and Baba replied that it wasn't worth the fuss if, in fact, it ended in my bowels but he feared it was rising into my head and, sooner or later, would narrow my mind and blur my distinction between right and wrong, which was an insult to my intelligence so I struck back saying that I didn't understand how he, who had been unemployed for over three years, could just sit in the living room and rot in dignity.

—Well?

—Well, I think I owe him an apology, at least for the last sentence.

The smuggler walks quietly next to me, keeping his hand strictly to himself. I wonder if in the new world, too, girls need men to get rid of other men. Now that our journey is nearly over, the white landscape finally relaxes me, like one huge silk Persian rug spread over the mountains.

Good morning, Iran!

The mules halt in succession. We get off. The impact with the ground painfully stirs my frozen feet out of their numbness. The two young men have tightened their *kaffiyahs* up to their noses. One of them points out the hill in front of us, indicating the location of the Iranian frontier post. His muffled voice sounds unfamiliar. I study their outlines, unable to identify "my" smuggler.

—And the coded message?

—You won't have it, Wedad firmly replies. Not before I get my trunks and carpets back.

—Your parents, Wedad! They won't know what to think, mother says.

—I'll wire them from Teheran. It's a matter of two or three days. They'll survive. Kaka J. should in no way get the rest of his fee unless he retrieves our luggage!

The smuggler gives his partner the signal to withdraw. They will pass Wedad's terms to Kaka J., he says. Father tips them one Iraqi pound per person. They leap on to their mules, gallop out of sight, the three other mules on their heels. We squelch up the hill, our feet plunging in the mud, gradually recovering their sensation. Two unarmed soldiers spot us from the top. They run towards us, shouting in Persian.

—*Yahoud*, Jews, father says, with utmost precision. *Yahoud*.

The word works like "Open Sesame" on this side of the frontier. Without interrupting their torrent of loud speech, the soldiers motion us to follow them up the hill. They lead us into the spacious hut, gesture us to stay, then go off.

—The door's open! Shuli says, turning the handle. They didn't lock us in.

Father, wrapped in Kaka J.'s quilt, relaxes on the floor. In spite of his strain, he looks in good shape. Mother huddles herself up next to him. She removes her shoes, rubs her feet, grumbles over the filthy floor, the smashed window. Father fishes out the Vick's inhaler from his pocket, pokes it in his nostril. It occurs to me that the Vick's is one of the few things father still owns.

—Look, it's snowing outside, mother says. Thank God we've been spared the storm.

Her head resting on the wall, Wedad wipes her tears. Shuli squats next to her, offers her vodka thinned with my saliva. Too tired to feel, I remove my robe, spread it out on the tiled floor. Once I sprawl on it, my lids fall. I reopen them, searching for the Persian sign I have just glimpsed on the wall. I read the sentence, understand nothing. The floor is freezing, yet my heart is laughing. Foreigners! We have made it! We have finally fled to freedom. Flight. Freedom. For years we have reduced our lives to these two wishes. Now that we have realised the one, reached the other, I fail to grasp their meaning or understand their implications.

Flight. Freedom.

It is still night outside. Sleep will soon overcome me. Flight. Freedom. The two words repeat themselves, in the same order, until they freeze in my mind, together, the latter reliant on the former.

Flight–freedom.

It will take me twenty-five years to separate them.